ICE AGE

ICE AGE

Brian Freemantle

severn
House

This first world edition published in Great Britain 2002 by
SEVERN HOUSE PUBLISHERS LTD of
9–15 High Street, Sutton, Surrey SM1 1DF.
This first world edition published in the USA 2002 by
SEVERN HOUSE PUBLISHERS INC of
595 Madison Avenue, New York, N.Y. 10022.

British Library Cataloguing in Publication Data

Freemantle, Brian, 1936-
    Ice age
    1.   Virus diseases - Antarctica - Fiction
    I.   Title
    823.9'14 [F]

    ISBN 0-7278-5828-9

Typeset by Palimpsest Book Production Ltd.,
Polmont, Stirlingshire, Scotland.
Printed and bound in Great Britain by
MPG Books Ltd., Bodmin, Cornwall.

WITHDRAWN

*Indications are that it is too late
to prevent global warming.*
Dr Klaus Topfer, head of the
UN Environmental Programme.
London, 15.9.99

Acknowledgement

I wish to offer my very sincere and grateful thanks to Professor Martin Bobrow, CBE, DSc, FRCP, FRCPath, FMedSci, head of Medical Genetics at the Cambridge Institute for Medical Research, not only for his patience in trying to guide me through the labyrinth of DNA technology, but for afterwards reading the manuscript of *Ice Age* to correct my layman's misunderstandings and ignorance. My thanks also go to Professor John Shearer, MBCHB, PHD, MRCS, for his equally patient responses to my many orthopaedic questions. And to Lachlan Mackinnon, who knew the word.

Author's Note

Ice Age is a work of fiction. It is not intended to be a polemic on global warming. The disease around which the plot revolves does not occur in adults, although forms of it are rare conditions affecting children.

Much of the book is, however, factual.

The ice caps of the Arctic, Antarctic and Greenland are melting at an unprecedented rate. The American Geophysical Union estimates that in four decades the Arctic ice sheet has become 40 per cent thinner and Russia's Perma-Frost Institute at Yakutsk predicts that in less than fifty years Siberian cities will sink to destruction into the melting ground. In 1999 the body of a perfectly preserved 23,000-year-old woolly mammoth was exposed by global warming near the town of Khatanga. Scientists are seriously discussing cloning a living creature from the DNA still existing in the animal. Microbes and viruses, unknown to modern science or medicine, are being released into world oceans after being trapped for millions of years. In a core sample sunk in Greenland, scientists discovered a 140,000-year-old virus still capable of infecting plants. A scientific team from the University of Montana found a 500,000-year-old microbe linked to proteobacteria and actinomycetes 11,000 feet beneath the East Antarctic ice sheet near the glacier-covered Lake Vostok.

Science, the journal of the American Association for the Advancement of Science, in 1999 recounted several instances of marine mammals and sea life either dying from inexplicable causes or from cross-species infections. Birds transmitted influenza – a species-jumping disease that in a 1918 pandemic killed at least forty million – that resulted in the deaths of hundreds of seals and whales. An unknown virus decimated the oyster beds of Chesapeake Bay, Maryland. Viruses carried by porpoise and dolphin killed incalculable numbers of Mediterranean monk seals off the coast of Mauritania. The same infection killed grey seals in Britain's North Sea. Sea urchins, a key herbivore in the Caribbean food chain, were virtually wiped out by a mystery disease. An epidemic of a herpes-like virus destroyed hundreds of blue-fin tuna off South Australia and the unique fresh water seals of Siberia's fresh water Lake Baikal died from dog-like distemper. Lake Baikal is a geophysical phenomena, provably dating from the Paleocene and Lower Neocene era. It has the greatest depth of any water in the world. Its twenty-five million-year-old virus and microbe-active sediment bed is estimated to be more than a mile thick. Only indigenous sea creatures and plants can survive in its waters. Any outside living thing dies and its remains – including bones and clothing in the case of humans – is untraceably devoured by a connate species of minute crab. So unique is the lake that a special scientific institute has been permanently established at Listvyanka to study it.

Nearing completion, worldwide, is the Human Genome Project. On June 26, 2000, in a satellite-linked joint press conference, US President Bill Clinton and British prime minister Tony Blair – supported by genetic scientists – announced the mapping of 90 per cent of the genetic 'Book of Man'. It will be fully sequenced by 2003. The American president described it as 'learning the language in which God created life'. The book is DNA, a huge coiled molecule over three feet long packed inside every human cell in twenty-three chromosomes. The chromosomes contain genes that control the behaviour and health of every human cell. Already some of these chromosomes – 5, 16 and 19 – have been partially decoded. Chromosome 22 – the smallest in the human body – has been completely read.

The plant-attacking virus was discovered in the Greenland ice by a joint scientific team from Syracuse University,

New York, and the State University of New York. Their virologists, as well as those from the universities of Montana and Oregon, readily speculate about the risk of long-frozen, unknown viruses and bacteria causing worldwide pandemics against which there are no vaccines or antibiotics.

Ice Age is such a speculation.

Winchester, 2002

One

Patricia said: 'Oh dear God! What is it?'

No one else spoke: was initially able to speak. They instinctively, protectively, pressed back against the insulating door of the out-station, repelled because they were scientists who worked by and to formulae – so far understood rules and so far unarguable equations – and there was no formula, no rational explanation, for what they were looking at.

Jack Stoddart, the project director and at that numbing moment leader of an intended rescue mission, knew he should say something but couldn't. He felt as frozen as the razor-winded wastes outside, sharpened by the briefly interrupted blizzard that had prevented their arrival until now but, from the increasing battering sounds outside, was blowing up again.

'Oh dear God,' said Patricia again.

All four of the field team were dead.

Harry Armstrong, the team leader who'd tried to raise the alarm, was slumped at the table in front of the powerless radio, his arthritically twisted hand beneath the useless tuning dial from which it had finally fallen. His white hair – as white as the packed snow beyond the station – was so long it merged with the white beard spread like a sheet in front of him. What skin that could be seen, on his face and hands, was shrivelled and pocked with liver spots. They could see Jane Horrocks on her bunk, through the open door of the adjoining sleeping quarters. She, too, was hugely white-haired, a disordered, uncut and uncombed straggle, but she had lost a lot on the crown of her head, the baldness showing through. Her face and hands were wizened, the untrimmed nails like claws, and

1

she lay as she would have stood in fading life, almost foetally, her back hunched by osteoporosis. George Bedall, who appeared to have fallen trying to move between the two linked rooms, had begun to lose his hair when he was twenty-one. Now he was totally bald, his skull deeply furrowed above a more tightly, fissure-riven face. Both outstretched, entreating arms had snapped, where he'd collapsed, and spread out distortedly, like a child's discarded puppet. Buckland Jessup, whom they'd called Bucky because he'd come from Texas and claimed to ride in rodeos, was the closest and the figure from whom they most obviously seemed to be withdrawing. He couldn't have been intentionally praying – more likely reaching out, desperate to escape through the door at which they stood – but he'd crumpled oddly, rigored in a kneeling position, his hands clasped before him in supplication. Like all but Bedall, he was enveloped in a profusion of ancient hair, his face dalmationed with liver spots. The eyes were what horrified the most. They bulged, with panicked terror, although they were whitely opaque from geriatric blindness.

It was Patricia Jefferies who spoke yet again, although only a dry-voiced whisper. 'Old . . . they're all so old! Eighty . . . ninety . . .'

Stoddart said: 'Harry was the oldest. Forty-two. Muriel gave him a birthday party just before he came out here, three months ago.'

The carcase of the minke whale was hauled slowly, trailing blood, up the lowered rear ramp of the ice-speckled factory ship towards the waiting, waterproofed fishermen, their chain-sawed cutters churning in readiness.

It had been a good beginning to the illegal, Convention-ignoring season in the Antarctic. There were four whales already roughly dissected in the refrigerated holds, their unwanted entrails and bones discarded for the scavengers that shoaled anxiously in the ship's wake.

There wasn't room for any more whales after this one was cut up. The support ships had a record catch of tuna, too.

It was time to go home.

Two

It was Stoddart who moved at last, the leader he was supposed to be, forcing himself further into the newly constructed building that was technically part of the South Pole's Amundsen-Scott Station, itself an outer field base of America's Antarctic programme headquartered seven hundred miles south at McMurdo. It was from McMurdo that Stoddart had launched the rescue, able at last to skirt the early winter blizzard that had closed in nearer the Amundsen base for the past three weeks. It was precisely twenty-two days since Armstrong's first static-broken plea for help over the just installed short-wave radio.

The station was an ice tomb, numbingly sub-zero, because the generator – the generator that should have taken over powering the radio after the outside aerial had blown down – had failed. Stoddart was beside the blindly praying Bedall, unthinkingly reaching out to touch the solidly frozen body, before he became conscious that the others in the team were still huddled in the doorway, unable – certainly unwilling – to shift.

Stoddart said: 'Let's move it! I want all their data, everything . . .' He looked more fully at Chip Burke. 'We able to fly them all out at the same time?' McMurdo's normal, US Navy bulk-carrying LC-130 was grounded with a rear ramp hydraulic malfunction and they'd come up in a little used English-built DHC-8.

The pilot, on his first Antarctic tour, frowned. 'Four people, dead weight. We'll be pushing it.'

The new and strengthening blizzard smashed and tore at the protective sheath of the stilted field shelter, snow hitting the outer fabric like bullets from a gun and with what sounded like the same velocity.

Stoddart said: 'You think you could make two runs?'

'I'm not sure we'll get out from this one,' said Burke. He shivered, not at the cold but at the thought of being trapped with four grotesquely aged corpses.

As if prompted by the thought, Patricia said: 'It's the dead weight of four very wasted old people. None of them can be more than a hundred pounds.' The two women had been friends – Patricia a virologist, Jane a geologist – inducted into the US Science Foundation programme at the same time. Patricia had been Jane's bridesmaid, eighteen months before.

No one had moved from the tight cluster directly inside the door. 'If we're going to get out at all it's got to be right now!' said Stoddart.

Patricia was the first, going past Stoddart and the statued Jessup to where her friend lay in the adjoining room, curled in her bunk.

Stoddart called: 'Bring everything you can from there: diaries, notebooks, anything that might help. Tapes, too. They might have dictated something.' He had to get everything right the first time: no second chance. He looked back to the door, where the other two men – Morris Neilson, McMurdo's winter resident medical doctor and James Olsen, a glaciologist – still remained behind the pilot. 'Jim, for Christ's sake! Morris!'

There was a final stir. Neilson came to where Stoddart stood, reaching out to touch the kneeling figure. The doctor said: 'He's frozen virtually solid. There's nothing I can do . . . could have done . . .'

'Was that how he died, frozen to death?'

Neilson shook his head. 'I don't know. We'll need autopsies.'

From the radio bench Olsen said: 'Jesus!' and turned immediately to Stoddart's look. Then, 'I've found the log.'

'What!' demanded Stoddart.

'The writing, it's normal, firm, three weeks ago. At the end it's an old man's. I can't make out the last three days . . . he's talking of growing old . . . all the time getting older . . . getting weaker . . .'

'We haven't time—' Stoddart started, but stopped at Patricia's sudden appearance at the connecting door.

'Jack! I'm not thinking . . . *we're* not thinking . . . it's got to be viral. Or bacterial. We're not protected . . . !'

'Oh fuck!' said Olsen.

For the briefest moment Stoddart thought his stomach was going to open, the sensation strong enough for him to clench, holding himself. He'd failed: failed them and himself. Failed Patricia, whom he was newly beginning to love. It wasn't his science but it didn't need to be. It had been obvious – too glaringly fucking obvious from the moment of their entering – and he'd let them stay there exposed for . . . for how long? And to what? He didn't know. Too long. Long enough for . . . 'Oxygen!' he blurted. There were no mountains or ice plateaux high enough to need oxygen support in the event of a forced landing, but it was a regulation that all McMurdo air transport carry breathing apparatus.

'I'll go!' declared Burke at once, anxious to get out of the station. 'I need to check the plane's de-icing. Need to be there instead of here . . .'

Everyone remained as rigid as the frozen bodies among which they stood, as if not moving would lessen their chances of infection. His voice fraying with the beginning of panic, Olsen said: 'We're dead: we're going to die, like they did . . .'

'No, we're not!' refused Stoddart, intentionally loud. 'It's a sensible precaution, that's all.' He looked at Patricia, whose expertise was the study of viruses. She stared back tight-faced but expressionless.

'We should salvage their rubbish,' decided Neilson, quite controlled, contributing to the need for calm. 'It'll be important to know what they ate. If it's something they all ingested it'll be all right . . . for us it will be all right . . .'

'Yes,' agreed Patricia from the doorway, although doubtfully. 'If they were poisoned . . .' She trailed off, unable scientifically to support the reassurance.

Olsen said: 'If we're blizzarded in we shouldn't keep the bodies inside with us.'

'They'd be covered, lost, if we put them outside in the snow,' said Neilson.

'It would be best, to bury them here,' said the other man.

5

'There needs to be autopsies, to find out what happened. What it is,' insisted Patricia. She paused, talking directly to Stoddart. 'I don't want to leave Jane here.'

'We won't,' promised Stoddart. Where the hell was Burke with the oxygen sets!

'They could be contagious!' argued Olsen.

'I've got ranking authority,' reminded Stoddart. 'Go on collecting everything there is.'

'That authority doesn't apply any longer,' dismissed Olsen. 'This isn't the fucking army.'

Stoddart exaggerated his dismissal by walking towards the radio table; at his approach Olsen flinched away, as if frightened of any physical contact. Still ignoring the glaciologist, Stoddart reached out to start assembling strewn-around paperwork, but before he could, the double doors opened behind him. Chip Burke was already wearing an oxygen set, only just visible through a head-to-foot covering of snow. More confidently – believing himself now safe – the pilot went to each of them, distributing masks and backpacks.

Before putting on his mask, Stoddart said: 'Can we still get off?'

Burke retreated as far as possible from the dead bodies before lifting his own face covering. 'The de-icing is only just managing and the batteries are being strained keeping the engine idling. And there's a lot of drifting. I'd say another thirty minutes . . . as it is the skis are freezing to the strip . . . we could get out now. Come back for the bodies when it lifts. Nothing's going to happen to them . . .'

'That makes sense,' seized Olsen at once. 'They're frozen . . . preserved . . . there's nothing we can do to help them . . .'

'We have to find out why! What it is,' insisted Stoddart. 'What if it's not confined to here? There's two hundred and fifty Americans at McMurdo. Thirty at Amundsen.'

'What good are we going to be, dead?' demanded Olsen, his voice rising.

'We're taking them,' determined Stoddart, flatly.

'They *are* frozen,' said Neilson, still trying to help. 'I don't think any contagion would have survived in this temperature.'

6

He gestured to the ice formed on the inside of the hut, at the joins between ceiling and wall.

'We don't have body bags,' protested Burke. 'How are we going to carry them?'

'Sleeping bags,' decided Stoddart. 'Morris and I will handle the bodies. Jim, you and Patricia get everything else together . . .' He looked back to the pilot. 'We need their garbage. It'll be in plastic bags. Sealed. Load it aboard. Try to raise McMurdo on your radio. Say it's a major emergency: that we have fatalities but they're to wait until they speak to me for details.'

Enclosing the bodies was a problem. All had to be contained in the way in which they'd frozen, which made the kneeling Buckland Jessup the biggest difficulty, almost too squat to encompass in a sleeping sack. They had to leave the top unzipped. George Bedall's disjointedly broken arms wouldn't fit until Neilson abruptly and professionally snapped them again to be dropped alongside the body. Armstrong wasn't in a convenient shape, either, and again they had to leave the bag partially unzipped. Patricia Jefferies had finished collecting her share of all the logs, experimental data and records before they got to Jane Horrocks and came to help the two men lift the dead woman from the bunk. She'd physically diminished so much they were able to completely enclose her in the bag in which she'd partially been laying.

'I'll carry her,' announced Patricia, muffle-voiced, and was able to, without any help. Stoddart, Olsen and Neilson were just as easily able to carry one body apiece.

The blizzard hit them like a solid blow as they emerged, making Olsen stagger, but it wasn't yet the white-out that Stoddart had feared although the drifts were heavy, knee-deep in places. Neilsen stumbled and fell, dropping the corpse of Harry Armstrong which actually sank several inches into the soft snow. The ski-plane was quite visible, twenty yards away, despite the permanent near darkness of Antarctic winter. The engine was idling uncertainly, seeming to miss sometimes. Burke kept jerking up the power. As they stowed the corpses at the rear he said: 'Too much magnetic interference to reach McMurdo.'

'Can we get off?' demanded the mind-blocked Olsen.

7

'If we leave right now.'

'We've got to get the data and records,' said Stoddart.

'And burn the station,' announced Patricia, quietly.

Everyone looked at her. Again there was silence. She said: 'We have to burn it: that's my professional opinion.'

'You saying we're infected?' demanded Olsen, jagged-voiced.

'No,' refuted the woman. 'I'm saying that if there are bacilli there that can resist a sub-zero temperature it should be destroyed by fire. It's not automatic that we'd become infected by being exposed to it . . . that there even *are* bacilli.'

'What if I can't get off?' demanded Burke. 'We couldn't survive in this plane if you burn the station down . . .' He looked further back into the aircraft. 'And they're here . . .'

'You've killed us.' Olsen accused Stoddart, hysteria bubbling up. 'You've killed us, whatever we do . . .'

'No one's killed anyone,' said Neilson, sternly. To Stoddart he said: 'We're lessening our chances, every minute we stay here talking.'

'I'll get the rest of the stuff,' said Stoddart.

He wasn't aware of Patricia stumbling along with him until he was some way from the plane, leaning forward against a wind-blasted white wall. It was impossible to speak but he reached out, curling his arm around her to help her on and by so doing was pulled down when she sank into a drift. They groped around, needing each other. Once back inside the station they both, momentarily, had to go on clinging to each other, needing the mutual support to recover.

Patricia said: 'We do have to burn it, Jack.'

'What if we can't take off? We'll be destroying our own protection.'

'The plane's still our best chance, until the weather lifts.'

'So we are infected?'

'God knows.'

'What are the odds?'

'To gamble I go to Vegas.'

'I daren't risk any more by destroying the best protection we've got.'

8

'The plane's safer,' she insisted. 'There'll be a tracked vehicle somewhere. Maybe a Snowcat. Move it out to be ready when the storm lifts and we can get to Amundsen overland.'

There was a fresh, bullet-hammering blast against the outside wall. Stoddart said: 'We don't have time.'

'I'll stop them taking off.' Patricia grabbed the satcheled documents and shouldered her way out of the door, leading him back into the storm.

Stoddart found the storage shed to the right, almost buried under a drift too deep properly to open the door. He pushed it back as far as he could. There was a tracked transporter, but no Snowcat. The motor whirred but didn't fire, the battery almost at once beginning to fade. It sounded virtually on the point of collapse before it caught and Stoddart revved it desperately, to keep it alive. He drove the transporter hard into the door, bulldozing it open, knowing the wood would be splintering but not able to hear it above the combined noise of the engine and the blizzard. At the point of emerging, the vehicle suddenly rose and tilted dangerously to the left and for a moment Stoddart thought it would topple, so he tensed to throw himself clear but it dropped back to right itself. He drove about ten yards from the main building, seeking the radio mast for a marker. It had been snapped off about two metres from its top aerial, leaving a tangle of cable, but the guy wires were still intact to keep its lower part upright and above the snow. He parked as close to it as he could and struggled back towards the shed. He found the can of special carbon-thickened lubricating oil just beyond the now shattered door, needing to wrap both arms around it to carry it back into the station. He upended it from the table at which Armstrong had died, leaving it to gush rhythmically across the floor while he emptied into the stream bundles of unused paper and log books from the storage cupboard at the end of the desk. He kept the Zippo alight to fire the floating paper as he backed towards the door, wishing it burned more strongly.

The wind suddenly, absurdly, dropped as he emerged, although it still snowed. In the abrupt silence he heard the

9

revved engine of the plane obviously taxiing, moving away from him, and blundered forward, actually shouting for it to stop before realizing he was still masked. He tore the set away from his face, letting the cylinder drop behind him and stumbled forward through the thick, cloying drifts, waving his arms and shouting. The plane was disappearing, going further away from him into the thickening, perpetual darkness. Stoddart hesitated, knowing they wouldn't hear or see him and actually thought, calmly and rationally, of turning back in time to stop the fire before it properly caught: to save something at least to provide shelter.

Like a tap being turned off, the snow stopped and he saw the DHC-8 stationary. He blundered on, snow snatching at his feet and legs, needing to lift high for each step, like an artificial ceremonial march. At first he thought he imagined it, but then saw an open door and Patricia seemingly half in and half out. At last she saw him and shouted but he couldn't hear the words. But the plane didn't move. It was difficult to breathe, the frozen air burning into his lungs, and he wished he still had the oxygen. His entire body ached, with the constant effort. Twice he fell. The second time he was actually seized, insanely, with the thought of lying there and letting them go without him, but then he did hear Patricia, just calling his name again and again.

It was Morris Neilson who got out of the plane to get him, virtually carrying him to where Patricia waited, arms outstretched, finally to drag him into the aircraft. Stoddart remained for a long time lying where he fell, on the fuselage floor, the breath groaning into him, all his strength gone.

He was only vaguely aware of Burke finally gunning the engine and of the plane appearing to slide sideways, not continuing in a straight take-off line. The feeling of the ground, of something solid, beneath the skis went and the aircraft lifted and there was Burke's hysteria-tinged voice.

'We're off! We're OK . . . we're going to be OK.'

Then Stoddart heard Patricia speak. She said: 'Bastard sons of bitches.'

*   *   *

10

The storm did die, so immediate that the next voice Stoddart heard was Neilson's saying: 'Look at the smoke! It's burning, totally,' and with Patricia's help he managed to push himself up, first against a seat and then into it just in time to look out and see the dramatic black smear marked out like a sign – a warning sign? a death sign? – on the shrouded whiteness below.

Stoddart felt a physical pain dive through his tired eyes. He had to close and then open them carefully, to refocus and even then was not sure he could see everything. What awaited outside could easily have been choreographed on a Hollywood – or maybe Fellini – directed set. Everything was glaringly whitened by fierce lights. The waiting vehicles were lined up – in reverse and with their back doors open – so tightly together it looked like a solid barrier against an escape. They were all white. So were the protective, head-dressed uniforms of the people he could see.

Beside him Patricia said: 'Jesus!' although more in disbelief than in despair.

A disembodied, metallically amplified voice said: 'Please remain seated, as you have been told.'

The repeated instruction seemed to be the cue. Four-man teams, each with collapsible gurneys, reacted simultaneously, but in prepared order, forming a line which came up the ramp running between the webbed-off area and the plane, each assigned a body to lift on to the ambulance trolleys. From the way the bags sagged when lifted, Stoddart guessed the bodies had thawed during the flight. The procession back down the ramp was as meticulously precise as the ascent. One man, quite apart from the ambulance attendants, carried the satchels.

The voice said: 'You are being taken to the microbiological research establishment at Fort Detrick, where there are the necessary isolation facilities. They're on standby for every medical examination and test. Everything else will be explained to you on your arrival.'

Stoddart suddenly felt a burst of irritation. As he stood he

11

said: 'Who's in charge here? My name is Stoddart: I headed the rescue attempt.'

'We're responsible for your transportation, sir,' echoed the voice. 'Everything else will be explained in detail at Detrick. Please, sir, sit down. You'll be escorted from the aircraft one by one, once your protective clothing has been checked.'

Neilson said: 'I want to talk to my wife.'

'Please wait until you reach Detrick,' came the refusal.

There was a fresh surge of white ant figures from the bottom of the ramp. Again there was an allocation of escorts, three to each person. Before they were encouraged to move, one man checked the security of each protective suit fastening and then gestured for them to stand legs apart, arms outstretched, to be sprayed from head to foot. Through his bemusement Stoddart noted that the decontamination device was pump driven, not activated by an aerosol that would have released ozone-depleting chlorofluocarbons.

Patricia said: 'We're being taken prisoner!'

The man siphoning his spray up and down her body said: 'Ma'am, everything's being done for your safety and protection.'

'That's a comforting thought.' Patricia's intended cynicism was lost in the distortion of the sound system.

'That's what it's meant to be, ma'am,' said the man, finishing his hosing-down. 'There's no living microbe – nothing – that can survive what I've just covered you in: you're the most germ free thing on the planet.'

'Let's hope you're right,' said Patricia, no longer sarcastic.

A stronger feeling of unreality engulfed Stoddart as he began to be moved and he at once needed the physical support of his assigned attendants, groping sideways for their out-stretched arms. He felt one of his own arms being shaken, for attention, and realized he was being addressed, asked his name for the already prepared and chained identification tags, and that he couldn't remember it. Then he did, blurting it anxiously. Robot-like he allowed himself to be led out of the concentrated light, not aware he was being helped into

12

a helicopter – unable to remember climbing in – until one of his escorts began fastening a seat belt. To the second identically McMurdo-suited figure sitting directly opposite, he said: 'Patricia?'

A man beside him said: 'She's in another machine. She's being looked after.'

Dull voiced, Neilson recited: 'I want to talk to my wife.'

Stoddart lost consciousness as the helicopter lifted, not able to feel the pressure of the seat belt as he sagged against it or of the men either side closing up, to hold him steady. He didn't detect the almost immediate landing or know he was actually walking until he found himself doing so, held up between them. His first half-conscious appreciation was that the other four were in a room ahead of him, seated in a row, and when he slumped alongside them he saw they were facing what appeared to be a long window.

At once, from the other side of the observation gallery a voice, no longer distorted, said: 'My name's Walter Pelham. I'm the director here. Our concern is whether or not you have been infected by whatever it was that occurred in the Antarctic. You are to be quarantined, separately, for examination and investigation . . .'

It was a superhuman effort for Stoddart to hold on, to force himself to concentrate with any sort of lucidity, but he did. 'I led the rescue party . . . Stoddart . . . station's burned . . .'

'. . . We're not going to attempt a debrief now . . . you need to rest . . . we've got other things . . .'

'. . . two to three days,' said Stoddart, knowing his voice was switchbacking, unevenly, in his anxiety to be heard. 'That's the symptoms cycle . . . the beginning . . .'

'You've read the logs?' demanded Pelham. 'What . . . ?'

'Not analysed . . .' withdrew Stoddart, needing to stop as the window behind which the unseen man sat or stood misted before him. Nothing about warming, he told himself: had to avoid that. '. . . read them, in parts. Jane . . . Jane Horrocks . . . she was pregnant.'

There was a pause. 'Thank you for telling us that.'

13

'The onset's very quick . . . two, three days . . . we've been . . .' tried Stoddart again.

'We've already calculated your period of exposure since you found them,' stopped Pelham. 'That's why you're here . . .'

'Well?' demanded Paul Spencer. It had been five hours since the obediently shambling figures had been led unprotestingly away from the observation theatre, finally to be stripped of all protective, personal and inner clothing and to be swabbed and skin-scoured before, even more finally, to be bathed in water later to be filtered, and then laid then to sleep – linked to heart, lung and respiratory monitors – in the individually partitioned quarters where they would remain, in solitary confinement, until they were diagnosed free of any disease or infection.

During those intervening five hours Spencer, the tall, fat, balding aide from the Chief of Staff's office, David Hoolihan, the director of the polar programme at the US National Science Foundation, and Pelham read all the salvaged field base documentation, studied yet again the amateurishly taken McMurdo Polaroid prints of the dead scientists and even more intently – over several replays – watched the multi-cameraed video footage of Stoddart's group, from the moment of the ramp lowering through to their being settled in bedrooms in which there were permanently running and noise-activated video and sound recorders, so sensitive they already knew that James Olsen suffered a flatulence or constipation difficulty, either of which could contribute to a diagnosis, if it hadn't been a prior problem.

Pelham said: 'Autopsies as necessarily detailed as these will take days . . . weeks. There's all sorts of things that have to be eliminated. There are ageing illnesses, genetically caused. But they affect children. Progeria. Werner's Syndrome. Shock can send a person white-haired overnight. So can Shy-Drager Syndrome, as well as making them blind . . .'

'What about the condition of the living?' persisted Spencer. There'd been just the slightest risk he'd knee-jerked his reaction to Hoolihan's Antarctic photographs, but after seeing

14

the bodies through the mortuary observation window, as well as witnessing the automaton-bodied group that had travelled back with them, he knew now he hadn't.

'I'm not going to pre-judge anything,' refused the director, a thin man pedantic in everything he said and did. 'They've every reason – and cause – to look the way they do after what they've been through and the time it took them to get here.'

'Stoddart was the shakiest of them all,' suggested Spencer.

'He was able to say more than any of the others,' Pelham pointed out.

'You know his reputation?' asked Hoolihan.

'Yes,' said the director.

'What do you think about the log notes reporting that it had been unusually warm around the new station?'

'I think, scientifically, it would be interesting – but at this stage no more than that – to know if that was confined to that location or whether there's a record of it extending to Amundsen-Scott or McMurdo.' Pelham was a man who needed corroborative scientific proof for every opinion.

'We have to consider the families,' said Spencer, more a reflection than a statement.

The quality and abundance of the catch had justified a crew bonus and the captain had delayed his intended sailing until the morning to allow the celebration, but he was anxious to leave Misaki, in Kanagawa prefecture, to get back to the Antarctic fishing grounds. Shoals, like they'd just found, could disappear as quickly as they built up and if the minke whale mating season was going to be this heavy he wanted to get back to take every advantage of it.

He waited impatiently, an hour longer than he intended, and when the two crewmen failed to arrive he sailed without them. There would be more bonus money to go around among a smaller crew if they did as well this time as they'd done last.

He'd kept enough *toro*, tuna belly, to provide the *sashimi*, for which he'd bought beefsteak plant leaves and chives. And it was a celebration. So he'd have some of the raw whale tongue he'd kept back, for his own personal enjoyment.

15

Three

Some large men are extremely nimble and Paul Spencer was very fast on his feet indeed, mentally as well as physically. He was convinced now of the personal career advantages of the situation and saw the early morning White House meeting as essential in establishing his intended role as the always visible, ever necessary mover and shaker at the epicentre of things, the co-ordinator and conduit between the worker drones in the foothills and the oracles on the mountain top. It was a strategy he had successfully pursued since the earliest days of the current presidency – his getting into the inner sanctum of the Chief of Staff as planned as everything else – but the determination was far more than opportunism. That began, and ended, with his entering such a core office. Once there, he was ruthlessly efficient. Setbacks were obstacles for the hard driven drones to surmount, rare failure the professional problem of others, never that of Paul Spencer. His respected and untarnished reputation was that of the man who got things done, which was why he'd risen to be the Chief of Staff's deputy and why he'd known the chief himself, Richard Morgan, would unquestioningly agree to the short notice meeting, which he did. Morgan was unsettled, like the leader of a herd becomes fidgety at the first scent of a predator.

The meeting, of course, had to be at the White House, his and Morgan's workplace, but the impressiveness fitted into Spencer's scheme of things, even though the necessary space with projection facilities – for the video and still pictures – meant that the workplace was, in fact, in the windowless basement. David Hoolihan was visibly awed,

16

which Spencer had known the Science Foundation executive director would be. Walter Pelham wasn't, outwardly. The agenda was Spencer's, so the encounter began with the videos and photographs after which Morgan was stiff faced, which he always became when confronted by a potential crisis. Spencer had anticipated that, too.

Morgan, a man almost as big as his deputy and given to college football profanity, said: 'What in the name of Christ is it?'

'A disease – or infection or virus or bacillus or maybe none of those things – that we've never encountered before and know nothing about,' said Pelham, a declaration so helpfully dramatic that Spencer could have scripted it.

'They're completely isolated now?' asked Morgan, eager to catch up.

'The living and the dead,' assured Spencer. Too theatrical, he criticized himself, objectively.

'That's how they've got to stay, until we discover what the hell's going on,' decided Morgan, believing he could identify Spencer's manoeuvring. 'Total black-out, absolute security . . .' He looked at his deputy. 'Your job, Paul. Personal control, hands on all the time . . .' He extended his attention to the other two men. 'We're locking this up, totally out of sight, until we've got answers . . .'

'We might have a problem there,' encouraged Spencer, seeing the trap. 'There's a burned-out field base . . . everyone at McMurdo and Amundsen-Scott know something happened, if not precisely what. And satellite telephones that usually work as clear as a bell, as well as instant internet contact . . .'

Morgan rose to his feet, to walk as he talked, another crisis indicator. 'You've surely warned them?' he demanded of Hoolihan.

'Absolutely!' said Hoolihan.

'But I don't think we can guarantee it,' said Spencer. 'We're talking scientists, academics. Government employees, notionally, but not people as bound by regulations as the military who brought everyone out.'

17

'What are you saying?' asked Morgan, wishing he would be able to completely trust whatever answer he got.

'I think we need some control down there, actually on the ground,' said Spencer. 'Some military restrictions, certainly on outside communication.'

'I don't believe scientists need to be put under quasi house arrest to guarantee the secrecy of something like this,' said a professionally-offended Pelham, defensively.

'I want you to get on to McMurdo again. Amundsen-Scott direct, if you think it's necessary,' Morgan told Hoolihan. 'Tell them the level of the order. And that we're sending down some military support . . .'

'I'll talk to the Pentagon,' anticipated Spencer. He'd hooked Morgan into being a part of the cover-up, which was important.

'What about the group who came back alive?' said Pelham.

The Chief of Staff appeared surprised. 'It's your installation. You should know more about your security than me!'

'The McMurdo doctor, Neilson, keeps asking to speak to his wife,' reminded Pelham.

'He can't: none of them are speaking to anyone outside the base,' ordered Morgan.

'Haven't we got a civil liberties – a constitutional – problem here?' persisted the Fort Detrick director. 'And there are the relatives of the victims. What are they to be told?'

The man *was* a politically-minded survivor, admired Spencer. Pelham was even covering his ass for the medically necessary quarantine separations he'd already imposed. And at the same time, concluded a more than satisfied Spencer, covering his ass as well.

Morgan said: 'You want me to spell out the legislation – quote the Congressional statute numbers – covering emergency measures ascribed to the Executive Office to ensure national security and the prevention of civil unrest, sir?' The final word – sir – came like a punch.

'I don't want there to be any misunderstandings,' said Pelham, unbruised.

'You won't be allowed any, as of now!' declared Morgan. 'Tell me, in detail, what you are doing at Fort Detrick?'

'Autopsies have already begun upon the dead. The woman, Jane Horrocks, was pregnant. The foetus will be removed from her body. Its organs, as well as those of the adults, will need to be subjected to a lot of tests –' he looked to Spencer, '– as I've already warned Paul, it'll take some time.'

'What about those still alive?'

'From the apparent speed of the ageing, there'll be an indication within the next twenty-four hours if any of them have contracted it—'

'What indications?' interrupted Spencer, needing to get back into the conversation.

Pelham frowned. 'Externally, that which is most obvious *in* old age: in the pictures you've seen. Loss of skin elasticity: heavy wrinkling, liver spots. Hair seems to be greatly affected, from the condition of the dead. So is colour loss. Hair loss itself. As it progresses, degeneration of bone strength. Memory loss . . . Alzheimer's . . .'

'They've been at Detrick for twelve hours!' challenged Morgan. 'Nothing external yet?'

'Nine and a half,' qualified Pelham, looking pointedly at his watch. 'Before which they'd gone through the severe trauma of discovery, brought out the bodies, and flown non-stop, apart for refuelling, what must have been about fifteen thousand miles in two days in aircraft with canvas seats. To have attempted anything more than the most perfunctory medical examination last night would have been counter-productive, positively misleading.'

The time had come to appear to support the Chief of Staff, who certainly needed to be extracted from what was becoming too much of a confrontation, Spencer decided. Quickly he said: 'We need to do a lot more than send a military detachment to Antarctica.'

Hoolihan shifted uncomfortably. 'What?' he asked, inadequately.

19

'It's not just us Americans, down there is it?'

'No,' agreed Hoolihan, relieved at having the answer. 'There's an international agreement, the Antarctic Treaty, signed as long ago as 1959. Over forty countries have signed it now, prohibiting nuclear explosions and radioactive waste . . .'

'So other countries have stations there?' cut off Spencer, refusing a tourists' lecture. Spencer, who'd practised law before entering politics, still followed the lawyers' creed of never asking a question to which he didn't know the answer, as he did now because he'd read the Foundation's web-site fact sheet before their arrival that morning.

'Yes,' agreed Hoolihan again. 'British. Russian. Some joint projects.'

'We heard of a similar outbreak from anywhere else down there?'

'No.'

'So we can ensure the secrecy?' demanded Morgan.

'I think so,' said Hoolihan, hopefully.

'Here's what I want you to do,' Spencer told the Foundation official, way ahead of his superior. 'I want you – your people – to run a computer check, worldwide, on any unusual or unexplained phenomena. Don't restrict it to scientific papers: let's look at newspapers, magazines, stuff like that . . .' He hesitated, deciding to allow himself the entendre, to show he was unfazed by the responsibility Morgan imagined he'd just sidestepped. 'It's the Net. Let's spread it wide.

'That's a pretty big undertaking,' protested Hoolihan.

'It won't be confined just to you,' promised Morgan.

'Who else is to be included?' demanded Spencer. The Fort Detrick director and Hoolihan had been escorted to the White House service gate and Spencer and Morgan had moved to the Chief of Staff's more comfortable permanent office. They'd had coffee and Danish delivered from the cafeteria. In ancient Rome, reflected Spencer, he would have waited for Morgan to eat and drink before taking anything himself.

'The Agency,' suggested Morgan. 'They've got facilities, people, everywhere in the world. Most of the stuff they provide for presidential briefings comes straight out of local newspapers. National Security people spend all their time listening to other people's telephone conversations: they might have heard something coming out of McMurdo already!'

'They have to be told *why*?' pressed Spencer. There was a risk of his being elbowed out – losing control completely – if the CIA and NSA got too much of the pie. Or of Morgan gaining too many allies.

Morgan shook his head, thinking for several minutes. Speaking as the excuse appeared to formulate, he said: 'Tell them it's a personal presidential request, so they don't lay down on it . . . something he intends putting into a major address, State of the Union even . . . we think it's something to do with the health programme but we're not sure yet . . .'

Spencer frowned, unhappy at the generalities. 'You think they'll go for something as vague as that?'

'It's got to be as vague as that,' insisted the other man. 'And they don't have a choice of going for it or not.'

'The CIA director has direct access to the President,' reminded Spencer, alert for the reply.

'I control access to the President!' Morgan pointed out.

'Everything they get is to be channelled through me to you?' established Spencer.

'It's your assignment, Paul,' confirmed Morgan. The smile was the showing of teeth that a victim sees when a shark twists for the unexpected strike.

'Pelham had a point about relatives of the dead.' Spencer hoped to be able to locate the direction from which the attack might come from the man's reply: from the body language or innuendo at least.

'You unhappy about the national security provisions?' asked Morgan, who was also a qualified lawyer.

'I think there could be a constitutional argument. And there's quite a few hungry lawyers who'd be willing to make a high profile case.' Spencer wished it was a warning that could have been placed on record.

21

'You got an alternative?'

'No,' admitted Spencer. Perhaps having a record wouldn't have been such a good idea after all. Constitutional infringement – an impeachable offence for a president – was clearly the factor worrying Morgan. 'How long before we tell the President?'

Morgan thought before replying. 'There could be a legal problem,' he allowed, reluctantly. 'There's got to be plausible deniability.'

The CIA had long ago added that avoidance phrase to the Washington political lexicon, Spencer remembered. Along with another of its former director's, identifying the agency – or The Company, as it enjoyed to be known for some reason he'd never understood – as 'the President's bag of tricks'. Spencer suddenly had the unsettling feeling that he was going to need a lot of boxes, containing a lot more tricks. There was nothing that could come out of any box – *anywhere* – he couldn't handle. 'Always,' he agreed at once. Just as quickly – maintaining the pressure – he qualified: 'That's one of the daily decisions we've got to make, you and I . . .' The pause was intentional. 'You've got to make. Just how long we keep this from him.'

Morgan's head came sharply up, at the caveat. 'You're totally right, Paul. *My* decision.

Fuck, thought Spencer. A bad mistake. The first – the only – for a long time. He steadied himself. Morgan was *really* worried, overcompensating with bravado. Back away, pretend-not-to-notice time. 'I think we've covered it all.'

'I think so too, Paul. Don't lose sight of the ball, will you? When I do tell the President, it's you he'll be depending on.'

'I know,' accepted Spencer. The president would know, too.

Jack Stoddart knew he was dead. He couldn't move. So his body had gone. Useless. Everything was white, Fellini-like again. He'd read, sneered at, point-of-death people always talking of blinding whiteness from which they'd retreated.

22

Come back to be given a second – or reintroduced – existence. Maybe he wasn't quite dead. Maybe he was still on
the unsignposted road. Had another – that reintroducing –
chance.

'Hello!'

'How you feeling?'

There were hands on him, more firmly holding him
down, even though his initial instinct hadn't been to move.
'Where . . . ? he started and stopped, knowing. Everything
avalanched in, overwhelmingly. Now he did try to move,
pulling up against the hands, whatever, that were holding him.

'Easy now! Take it easy.' A female voice, matter-of-fact.
'You've got a lot of monitors – catheters too – connected
here. Let's not have any jerky movements, OK?'

'OK,' said Stoddart. He could remember – thought he could
remember – it all but he needed time to think, to be sure. The
figure beside him was totally enclosed in a protective suit.
He couldn't focus a face behind the vizor.

'Don't those fucking outfits come in any other colour?'

'That's good,' said the filtered voice.

'What?'

'That reaction. That's very good.'

'You a doctor?'

'I applied for the garbage collector's job but failed the
practical.'

'That's not good at all.'

'It is, Jack. You might not appreciate it now but so far
you're doing very well indeed. So, how do you feel?'

'Trapped. Held down.'

'Good again! Now tell me what you know I wanted
to hear.'

'Tired, still. Ache like hell. I'm thirsty.

'Ache anywhere particular?'

Stoddart thought. 'Back, maybe. Kinda general.'

'You see my fingers?'

'Yes.'

'How many am I holding up?

23

'Four.'

'Now?'

'One. You're giving me the stiff middle finger.'

'I'd never give you the stiff middle finger after what happened.'

Stoddart didn't know what to say, so he said nothing.

'So?'

'What?'

'What happened?'

Again Stoddart didn't reply.

'Jack?'

'Yes?'

'I asked you what happened.'

'I heard you.'

'Can you remember?'

Stoddart snorted a laugh. 'You think I can't remember?'

'I might, until I hear you tell me.'

'What about the others?'

'What others.'

'The people I came back with.'

'What people you came back with?'

'I get it,' he said, at last. He was alive!

'Get what?'

'What we're doing?'

'What are we doing, John?'

'Jack,' Stoddart corrected, at once. 'My mind's OK.'

'You didn't tell me what happened.' She let him talk for a full two minutes before saying: 'OK.'

'No!' he denied her, at once. '*You* didn't answer *me*! What about Patricia . . . ?' Quickly he added: 'And the others . . . ?'

'They're being looked after every bit as good as you are.'

'That wasn't what I asked you . . . what I meant. Which you know . . . You want to tell me your name . . . ?'

'I'm not allowed to do that.'

'OK, lady, if that's what I've got to call you. Don't fuck

24

with me, lady. I want to know how the people are who came out with me . . . particularly Patricia Jefferies. She all right? The rest of them all right?'

'We've been talking an hour.'

'That's not an answer!'

'It *is* the answer. I don't know if any of the others have even woken up yet! Said anything. *What* they've said.'

'I'm sorry.'

'You don't have to be.'

'You a medical doctor or a psychiatrist? Or psychologist? What?'

'Two out of three: medical *and* psychologist. You're getting two for the price of one.'

'So how am I?'

'You know I can't make a diagnosis that quickly!'

'What can you say?'

'Mentally you're sounding fine.'

'That's all?'

'Let's go on finding out. Let's get you disconnected, shall we . . . ? Strapped you down because we didn't want you pulling out any plugs . . .'

Stoddart felt the restraining straps come off and then the cuffs and bands of the monitoring machines. When she gently pulled out the catheter he got an instant erection. 'I'm sorry . . .'

'Don't be. That's the sort of response I wanted. Can you sit up by yourself?'

He did so, wedging an arm beneath himself as a lever. He was naked, under the covering. He was glad the erection had collapsed. He was sore.

'How did that feel?'

'OK.'

'Still ache?'

'Yes. Not too bad, though.' He looked at the Band Aid in the crook of his left arm.

'Helped ourselves to some blood. You want to get out of bed?'

'I guess . . .' He looked around and saw underwear, mules

25

and what looked like a surgeon's operating tunic, green, neatly folded on a bedside chair.

She said: 'All your stuff's been taken for forensic examination. Can you manage by yourself?'

Stoddart swung his legs off the bed and reached for the clothes, unhappy at the feeling of weakness. He tried not to show it as he dressed.

'Not so good?' she asked, perceptively.

'A little weak. Like you feel after being in bed a long time.' He sat back, on the cot edge. She remained standing. He supposed it was more comfortable to stand: the suit looked stiff and made crackling sounds when she moved.

'You ever been in bed a long time, like in hospital?'

'No.'

'What's the scar on your lower abdomen?'

She'd been very thorough, he thought. 'Appendectomy.'

'When?'

'When I was a kid. Eighteen, I guess.'

'How long were you in hospital then?'

'A day or two, I guess. I can't . . .' He stopped himself saying he couldn't remember because what he did remember was the purpose of every question. 'I was in the Henry Sexton Memorial Hospital in Butte, Montana, for five days. And it was when I was eighteen.'

'No other illnesses?'

'No.'

'What about long term: asthma, anything like that?'

'No.'

'Allergies?'

'No.'

'Ever suffered a venereal infection of any sort?'

'No.'

'You on any medication?'

'No.'

'You smoke?'

'Stopped, ten years ago.

'Smoker's cough?'

'No.'

'Your personnel file says you were married?'

'Jennifer,' sighed Stoddart, understanding the routine. 'College romance in Butte. She got a position as an intern at George Washington, in DC, when we moved east, fifteen years ago. That's where she met Harry. He's a doctor there, too. Never knew there was an affair until she told me she wanted a divorce. That was nine years ago.'

'You in any relationship?'

Stoddart hesitated. Did the three months he'd been with Patricia – hardly 'been with' at McMurdo, furtively slipping into each other's rooms like high school kids discovering sex – qualify as a relationship? Hardly. 'Not really.'

'What's "not really" mean?'

'It means I've just started seeing someone.'

'Patricia Jefferies? You made the concern obvious.'

A psychologist, he remembered. 'I'd like to know how she is. See her.'

'You're in quarantine, remember?'

'How long for?'

'Until we're sure.'

'How long's that going to take?' he persisted.

'Until we're sure,' she repeated, just as persistent.

'You're not taking notes. Everything being recorded?'

She nodded. 'How about a tour of your new home?' She gestured Stoddart ahead of her, to judge how he walked. 'That's the bedroom,' she said, as they left it. 'Here's the bathroom. Shower, shaving gear in the cabinet . . . two toilets, clearly marked. Pee in the left, crap in the right . . .'

'There's no flush.' Everything was polished metal.

'Don't want to adulterate the specimens. You go, leave it. There's a mechanically revolving chute arrangement activated when you close the lid. It just disappears to those who want it –' she gestured again for him to precede her – 'and here's what passes for your living room . . .'

It was mostly metal again, the walls and even the table, against which there were two upright chairs. The only normal furniture were two leather armchairs in front of a wooden, closed-door television. On a table alongside were four glasses and a bottle of mineral water, in a cooler. She motioned to it. 'Go ahead. You said you were thirsty. That's all it's going to be, I'm afraid. Water. No booze, obviously. Or coffee or tea . . .' She picked up a sheet from a bureau close to an expansive internal window. 'Menu,' she identified. 'When did you last eat?'

He drained a full glass and refilled it before answering. 'There was a packed meal in Auckland . . . Chicken, like it always is on planes . . .'

'Tick off what you want and post it through that letter box there . . .' She pointed to a slit to the left of the window, beneath which there was a handled, square door about the size of those on a rubbish chute. 'It's air locked. Whatever you order will be delivered, at the time you asked for it. Not up to the Four Seasons but it's edible.' She picked up a pad from the bureau. 'We want you to do something very important. We want you to write everything – and we mean everything, the tiniest detail – from the moment you entered the field station and found them. Write what you thought – felt – as well. Don't hurry. Take all the time you want. Break off, sleep if you want to, then come back to it. Can you do that?'

'I guess.'

'And will you sign this for me,' said the woman, producing a third paper. 'It's an authorization for us to have access to your medical records. You still have the doctor at Fairfax, listed on your file?'

'Yes,' he said. His signature was shaky, not like he usually wrote it. He said: 'I should have sat down.'

'Maybe you should,' she agreed.

Stoddart saw that the small clock set into the bureau showed two twenty. 'That a.m. or p.m.?'

'Daytime.'

'It's been four days.'

'And three hours.'

'Something should be registering by now, if I'm infected.'

'We can't go by the apparent schedule in the victims' logs.'

28

'That an observation window?'

'I need to come in: wear the moon suit. It's easier for people to see you and talk to you from the other side of the glass.'

'I'm locked in?'

'That's how it's got to be, obviously. Until we're sure.'

'How do I speak to anybody outside?'

She nodded to the telephone on the bureau.

'I don't see an extension list,' he said.

'There's twenty-four hour switchboard.'

'This suite . . . others too, I guess . . . already existed. What were people suffering from, to need to be put into isolation here?'

'Things we don't know how to handle.'

There had been good fishing in the northern hemisphere, too. The factory ship and all the accompanying trawlers themselves were full when the fleet docked at Provideniya, on Siberia's Chukotsky Poluostrov peninsular. It was mostly cod but there were tuna and one minke whale.

Four

Paul Spencer acknowledged the initial mistake of concentrating too much on what had already happened and not sufficiently upon the wider view of the future. The forward thinking had to cover – or appear to cover – the safety, not the security risk, of about two hundred and fifty scientists and support staff at McMurdo and around thirty at Amundsen-Scott, who were far closer – and therefore, logically, at far greater risk – to whatever had overwhelmed the field station.

The military mission to Antarctica shouldn't – and wouldn't – therefore be described or mounted as a security operation against an information leak. In each of his written, Eyes-Only classified communications to the Pentagon it would be set out as anticipated rescue planning, to evacuate endangered Americans. Which, neatly rounding the circle, countered any suggestion that anyone's constitutional rights or freedoms were violated.

During his conversation with the Science Foundation director the emphasis was entirely upon a possible McMurdo and Amundsen-Scott evacuation, if it were judged necessary, that morning's discussion referred to as having already been agreed between Hoolihan and the Chief of Staff, without any detail. Hoolihan promised to be at his terminal, personally to receive the email which Spencer personally sent, from his end. As instructed, Hoolihan telephoned immediately to guarantee no one apart from himself had seen the message.

Spencer spoke by telephone to the operational directors of both the CIA at Langley and the National Security Agency before sending the email requests. Intentionally to avoid any

30

attention-attracting impression of urgency – which he didn't consider there was in terms of hours with this general enquiry – Spencer avoided further email, using instead the second of the twice-daily inter-governmental courier deliveries.

By the time the two Pentagon officers, an army and air force colonel, were shown into his office, Spencer had completed the documentation they would need. Sheldon Hartley, the soldier, was black and clearly shaved what little hair remained, so appeared completely bald. William Dexter was bespectacled and uncaring about his thickening waist. Both wore Desert Storm service ribbons among the decoration technicolour on their immaculate chests. Spencer thought Hartley's collection also included a Vietnam citation but wasn't sure. Neither showed any outward reaction to being in the same building as the president of the United States but Spencer knew it would be there. Without any preliminary discussion, Spencer escorted both back to the larger projection room and ran the video and still photographs. Neither officer allowed any facial or verbal reaction to that, either. Or interrupted Spencer's account.

'We don't know what it is – what causes it – but provision has obviously got to be made for a mass evacuation,' Spencer concluded. 'We obviously don't want a total upheaval if it can be avoided but we've got to be instantly ready. We think there should be a support force, to prevent panic . . . and of course a restriction on outside communication, until a decision is reached. The preparations should be as if your men were flying into a germ warfare situation: all necessary clothing and medical protection, with sufficient to equip all the scientists and other personnel already there.'

'How many's that likely to be?' asked Hartley.

'It's winter there. Basic staffing,' replied Spencer. 'Allow for four hundred, in addition to whatever force you consider necessary. That should include doctors and field isolation units. The whole operation – here and there – naturally needs the highest security classification. I am your only liaison here at the White House. No open fascimile communication: use email. Everything written will come to you hand delivered

31

under presidential seal and from you must be by Pentagon messenger, under seal. My telephone is secure. Yours must be, at all times, too. And there'll need to be secure communication facilities from McMurdo.'

'That's all pretty clear,' said Dexter.

'How long before you can be underway?' demanded Spencer.

'An advance party will be airborne within twenty-four hours,' undertook Dexter.

'With a full support group twenty-four hours after that,' endorsed the bald-headed man.

'There's written orders . . . authority . . . for this?'

Spencer offered the anticipated and prepared briefing, in its sealed envelope. 'I want constant liaison.'

'We understand,' said Hartley.

'This is a monster . . . horrifying . . . isn't it?' said Dexter at last, although still expressionless and with no shocked intonation.

'Horrifying,' agreed Spencer. He supposed he found it as difficult to be moved – believe it, even – as they did. He'd have to remember to show some emotion when it was publicly necessary to do so.

Jack Stoddart ordered steak and a jacket potato but when it was delivered decided he wasn't hungry so he stopped eating after a few mouthfuls. As he returned it virtually uneaten through the pull-down hatch, he guessed his lack of appetite would be noted, as part of the intense examination. Along with the fact that he'd already drunk the two full bottles of mineral water and was halfway through the third, which he'd ordered with the meal. He didn't think thirst – dehydration – was an indication of age. Or remember any reference to it in what he'd read among their logs or data.

He sat at the bureau with the paper and pens arranged in readiness but didn't immediately write, distracted – unsettled – by the empty observation window. It really *was* like being under a microscope. His written account would be another test, he supposed, a comparison against the recollection of the others, maybe for a composite version to be compiled. Would the others – Patricia in particular – have woken up, seen their doctors, ahead of him? Be writing a few yards away? He put down the pen with the page still blank, reaching out for the telephone.

'What can I help you with, Dr Stoddart?' enquired a voice at once.

'Put me through to Dr Jefferies, will you?'

'I need authority for that, sir.'

'Get it for me, please.'

'I mean I need to be told that everyone in isolation can receive calls. I haven't had that advice, yet.'

'Have there been any outgoing calls from Dr Jefferies's suite?'

'No, sir.'

'Anyone else's?'

'No, sir.

Patricia would have obviously called him, as he was trying to call her. Maybe the others would, too, although remembering their attitude on the plane he doubted it. Would he put their intended abandonment in his unwritten report? Not something that needed an immediate decision. He was letting his mind drift. Didn't normally happen. Usually better able to focus. Patricia, he thought again. Patricia would have called him. Unless . . . ? Stoddart refused the thought. 'Will you make a note that I'm awake? That I can take calls?'

'Yes, sir.'

Stoddart picked up the pen and at once put it down again, his eyes drawn to the window. He abruptly thrust himself up – conscious of the remaining ache in his back and arms – and went into the bathroom. Self-consciously and with some difficulty in moving between the two, he used both toilets and felt embarrassed at not being able to dispose of his own waste, although accepting its need as part of his medical examination. Everything he did and said – thought even – a test. With how he looked being the first. So how did he look? He was surprised that the question – *the* essential, overriding question that he could answer himself! – hadn't occurred before.

The bathroom mirror was large, giving him a stand-back reflection that went from his head to below his waist, practically to his knees. But he didn't stand back. He went closer, so close the basin edge was tight against his thighs, and strained even further forward to put his face so near to the glass he almost lost focus, needing to pull back. He'd had his hair cut very short, closer than a crew cut, expecting to spend the winter in the Antarctic, but there was enough regrowth – and contrast – with the overall deep blackness to show the grey at the sides. But that's all it was, grey. Not white. And no more, he was positive, than there had been before. Four days, he reminded himself, as he had unnecessarily reminded the examining doctor. Despite her reservations Stoddart was convinced there'd be more obvious signs than any he could see in his face at that moment. There weren't, in fact, any positive signs at all. His eyes were as deeply blue as he believed they'd always been (why hadn't he looked more closely at himself: known for sure!) without the blind milkiness of the kneeling George Bedall. He'd always, oddly in these bizarre scrutinizing circumstances, been remarkably clear skinned for someone of thirty-nine and there wasn't any change now: what lines there were around his eyes he was causing himself, right now, squinting to look at himself! And there was colour, although that was scarcely a fitting contrast because all the dead had been frozen into a death-mask greyness. There were no liver spots, either. Not on his face or hands or arms. He moved back, finally, opening the tunic top and pushing the elastic banded trousers unashamedly down, having to straddle his legs apart to prevent them falling completely. No tell-tale brown marks, anywhere. No wrinkling, either. Actually tight-bellied, from the jogging he'd been concerned about missing during the winter months' inactivity at the South Pole.

Stoddart pulled his trousers up and refastened the tunic front. He was all right! Had to be all right, no matter what caveat the unidentified doctor felt she had to invoke. He felt the briefest surge of light-headedness, although quite different from the sensation he'd experienced before. All right! All right! All right! echoed in his head, like a chant. A cheer.

Strangely, the ache didn't seem so bad as he hurried – walked positively, not scuffed in the mules as he'd scuffed in the protective suit – back into the observation-windowed room, not bothering to look at it on his way to the bureau. He lifted the telephone, still standing.

'Dr Stoddart?' enquired the same voice.

'I'd like to be put through to Dr Jefferies.'

'I'm sorry, sir. I still haven't been authorized to connect you.'

'Authorized?' challenged Stoddart. 'Earlier you were waiting to be advised.'

'I still haven't been advised.'

'The others?'

'I haven't been advised that they can take calls, either.'

'Put me through to . . .' Stoddart had to pause, for recollection, '. . . the director, Pelham.'

'I'll see if he's available.'

'Tell him I want to speak to him!'

The line went dead but only for a few moments before the voice that Stoddart didn't immediately recognize from the previous night said: 'Pelham.'

'Why can't I speak to the other people I was brought here with?'

'I explained last night. Everyone's quarantined, for the obviously necessary examinations. Which you're undergoing.'

'Talking on a telephone isn't breaking any quarantine.'

'You can't interrupt medical examinations. You surely accept that?'

'I don't accept that at this precise moment I can't speak to at least one out of four people.'

'Our priority – the medical, diagnostic priority – is at the moment greater than yours, Dr Stoddart.'

'Are they all infected?'

'I have not told you that anyone is infected.'

'But they are, aren't they?'

'I have told you that the four people with whom you came out of Antarctica are currently undergoing medical examinations and tests.'

'Will you authorize your switchboard to connect me when those medical examinations and tests have been completed today?'

'I'll follow the guidance of the specialists conducting them.'

'When are we going to have a sensible conversation?'

'Soon, I hope.'

'I'll keep calling, every thirty minutes, until we do.' The threat sounded as empty as it was. His total, locked-away impotence burned through Stoddart.

All Paul Spencer's security clearances had been established the previous day and he'd telephoned ahead to warn of his arrival at Fort Detrick, so there was no delay and Walter Pelham was waiting in his office.

'What's it look like?' demanded Spencer, too glibly.

'Like the worst nightmare we never wanted to happen,' said the other man.

Five

It was Paul Spencer's moment to be horrified, which he genuinely was, and couldn't remember being before, not like this. Not *beyond* emotion. The video and still photographs that had shocked others, had for him been of already dead, atrophied people more like statues than anything or anyone that had once been human. If he'd had a feeling about them at all it had been of uninvolved curiosity.

Patricia Jefferies wasn't a lifeless statue. She was someone he'd seen just thirty-six hours before, through a glass screen like the one separating them now, exhausted, confused but still obviously attractive – beautiful even – lustrously auburn-haired, smooth-skinned, interestingly firm-bodied.

Just thirty-six hours ago. She wasn't now.

Now the hair wasn't any longer lustrous or auburn. It was grey and so thin he could in places see her shined pink scalp and her face was already faintly filigreed by lines, as was the skin on her arms and hands, which were blackly corded with veins. She appeared smaller, shrunken, her knobbled spine visible through the fabric of her tunic. She didn't hear them enter the observation room – Pelham had warned him of the deafness – and she didn't look up from the paper over which she was bent low, laboriously writing, squinting at the words she was finding it so hard to fashion.

'Dr Jefferies . . . Patricia . . . ?' said Pelham, beside him.

She looked up, at last, and Spencer realized she couldn't see them behind the glass. 'I want to get this done while I can.'

'I know . . . Thank you . . . How do you feel . . . ?' said Pelham, gently.

'Tired. But I'm not going to stop . . . Jack? How's Jack? Can I see Jack?'

'The tests aren't finished yet,' avoided Pelham. 'As soon as they are . . .'

'Is he all right?' the woman demanded. There was meant to be indignation, irritation, but it was too much of an effort.

Pelham turned questioningly sideways. *I waited for you*, Spencer remembered. *That's what you wanted, wasn't it? White House decisions, if it came to this.* Blame-weaving bastard. Spencer nodded.

Looking back to the window, Pelham said: 'We think he's OK.'

Patricia's sigh of relief was an effort, too. 'That's good. Very good. Can I speak to him, at least?'

Another sideways look. Spencer nodded again, swallowing. There was acid in his throat, vomit, burning him.

'I think so,' promised Pelham.

'Soon? I'd like it to be soon.'

'I know. Of course.'

Patricia turned back to her composition, as if the strain of looking up towards the glass was too much. 'It's almost all written down now . . . everything I can remember . . . everything that happened.'

'Thank you,' said Pelham again, emptily.

Patricia made a vague gesture over her own body. 'Have you found anything? . . . what . . . ?'

'Not yet. Too soon . . .' said Pelham, finally not bothering to seek approval.

'I don't want to hurt.'

'No.'

'I'll do everything . . . all the tests . . . but I'm not good with pain . . .'

'There won't be any pain, I promise.'

'Thank you.' Patricia was wheezing at having to speak so much.

Spencer began to retreat, repelled and despising himself – which he never had before – for feeling repelled. He had not once taken his eyes off the bent old woman in front of him who had to use both hands to pick up and arrange the pen that had fallen from her fingers in order to write again.

'I'll go and see about Jack,' promised Pelham, following the other man. Patricia Jefferies didn't look up, not hearing him. The pen pushed slowly up and down.

Spencer needed the support of the corridor wall, leaning his shoulders back against it, uncaring about the theatricality. 'Jesus Christ!'

'I warned you.'

'Not enough. How long?'

'She's thirty-two. There's clearly more internal than external deterioration; going through the menopause as she clearly has would have literally been a hormonal explosion. Who knows how long? Who knows anything! We've found nothing so far in blood, urine or faeces. Nothing to indicate poisoning.'

'Stoddart is OK?'

'We think so. It could be the gestation period is longer in some people than in others.'

'What about those others?'

'See for yourself,' invited the installation director, almost impatiently, leading the way further along the viewing gallery corridor.

James Olsen was also at the table, writing far more quickly than Patricia Jefferies. His head jerked up the moment he heard them. 'He's not my lawyer!' the glaciologist said the moment he heard Spencer's voice. 'I said I wanted my lawyer, Jacobson. Who's this?'

Pelham didn't respond, leaving the reply to Spencer, who hesitated. Hysterically angry, Pelham had warned. Not so far advanced as the woman. Litigious, with a paper and pen before him. Spencer said: 'Government.'

'What's your name?' demanded the scientist, pen poised. What hair remained had kept its brownness, but it was only a narrow hedge around a completely shining bald pate. He seemed as shrunken as Patricia Jefferies but the arthritis was very advanced, lumping not just his hands but his wrists and even his left elbow, and Spencer was surprised the man

39

appeared able to write as quickly as he had been doing when they'd entered. Olsen's skin was very wrinkled and brown spotted where it was visible on his face, arms and throat, and he was turkey necked, a positive wattle flapping in his anger from chin to throat. Veins stood out blackly, like welts.

'We're doing all we can to help you,' Spencer tried to avoid.

'You're going to help me!' said the man. 'I've got a wife, just 35, who's going to be a widow. A daughter who hasn't gone through high school yet. So, here's how you're going to help me. You're going to get the lawyer I asked for, Jacobson . . .' The accusing finger came up again, towards the window. 'He's got the number. I want Jacobson here, now, while I'm still able to set the case out that I'm going to bring against you, the government . . .' Olsen had to stop, to recover himself. '. . . And Stoddart. Going to sue that son of a bitch. Wouldn't leave them, like I told him. His fault – the government's fault – that we travelled with those bodies back to McMurdo not even properly sealed against infection . . . then all the way here . . . infected me. I've been killed . . . murdered . . . you're going to pay . . . pay millions . . . going to expose it all . . .' He had to stop again.

Legally there was probably an indefensible case, Spencer acknowledged professionally: minimal mitigation, whatever the terms and conditions of the glaciologist's federal employment contract. The pages already torn from the pad upon which the man was writing were stacked almost as high as those that remained empty in front of him. Would the federal contract be covered by national emergency regulations? It hardly mattered that Olsen didn't have his name. He *was* the government – representing the Executive – and his was the only name, the instantly recoverable, instantly identifiable name, on the visitors' and security logs. Hopelessly – sure he could physically feel the contempt from Pelham next to him – Spencer said: 'Everything's being done to reverse this . . . stop it and reverse it . . .'

Instead of a renewed tirade, which Spencer expected, the

40

man beyond the window said: 'And I want Harriet. Not in here. Don't want her to catch it . . . Out there . . . I want to talk to my wife . . . say . . . say goodbye . . . Want that soon. Very soon . . . before –' he waved his misshapen hands over his body similarly to how Patricia had, as if he was afraid to touch it – 'before this gets any worse . . .'

Spencer knew there wasn't any legislation, covered by any statute book, that could be hidden behind. To deny this man – this justifiably outraged, pitiful, dying man – everything he asked was blatantly, constitutionally and morally illegal. Recognizing his cowardice, Spencer said: 'We're going now . . . going to talk to people . . .'

'Not people!' Olsen forced himself to shout after them. 'Jacobson . . . Pelham's got the number . . . Harriet . . .'

In the outside corridor again Spencer was not at once able to talk, not leaning against the wall this time but with his hand outstretched towards it, head bowed, dragging the breath into himself like someone suddenly released after being held too long under water. 'I don't know . . .' he started but then straggled to a halt.

'None of us do,' said Pelham, having had more time to adapt. Relentlessly he said: 'There's the pilot. And the doctor.'

Chip Burke was in one of the easy chairs in front of the television, which was on, showing an old black and white movie. Spencer identified Bette Davis but wasn't sure if the other actress was Joan Crawford. Pelham called the pilot's name but Burke gave no response and initially Spencer thought the man was deaf, like Patricia, until he saw the way his head was slumped and realized Burke was asleep. The man came awake with a snuffled start when Pelham raised his voice, jerking his head around in frightened confusion until Pelham said: 'It's OK, Chip. You're OK. It's me, Walt. Remember we spoke a while ago?'

Burke turned towards the sound of the voice, blinking, unfocused and only managed to get up from the chair on the third attempt. 'Guess I do . . . help me again a little. Walt, you say . . . ? What can I do for you, Walt?'

Spencer had been warned about the dementia – severe Alzheimer's, Pelham had diagnosed – but was as unprepared as he had been with the other two. Burke hadn't lost any hair, but it was as white as that on the bodies found at the field station. He was whitely unshaven, too, and there was a dark stain on the front of his tunic trousers, where he'd wet himself. His face was more lined than either of the other two, etched like a collapsing balloon the day after a party.

'You managed to write anything for me, Chip?'

The man sniggered but didn't reply.

'You remember I asked you to write down for me what happened?'

'What happened?' It was a question, not a rhetorical answer.

'You don't remember, Chip?'

'Can't say I can call it to mind. Like to help though, if I could. Tell me again what it is you want.'

'You remember a few days ago? Flying a plane in Antarctica? Something happening there . . . ?'

The man's already creased face creased further. 'Cold. Cold as hell.'

'That's it,' encouraged Pelham. 'You call anything else to mind?'

Burke's face remained grimaced with effort. 'Maybe in a little while . . . maybe a little while to think . . .'

'You do that, Chip,' soothed Pelham. 'You sit back again. Think for a while . . .' In the outside linking corridor the man said: 'At least he doesn't know. Won't know.'

'I don't need to see . . .' began Spencer, but stopped at the expression on Pelham's face.

Morris Neilson's room was not immediately adjacent to the rest. The doctor was in what was obviously an infirmary section further along in a single medical isolation ward. The man was white-haired, white-faced, eyes closed and tethered to tubes and monitors that snaked above and below the bed coverings, green indicator lights struggling unevenly across black screens.

42

Pelham said: 'He was the oldest of the rescue party, forty-one. He'll be the first to die.'

Spencer shook his head, with nothing to say.

Pelham said: 'The last words he uttered were to ask to speak to his wife.'

Spencer had nothing to say to that, either. Instead he said: 'Can you help any of them?' He felt lost, inadequate, another rare sensation.

'No,' said the director, brutally. 'They're all going to die and there's nothing we can do to stop it . . . to save them . . .'

'I need to talk to the White House.'

'What about Olsen? The lawyer? And Olsen's wife?' persisted the director.

'Wait until I've spoken to people in Washington.'

'Patricia?'

'You say there was a personal relationship?'

'Apparently.'

'You think Stoddart's up to seeing her like that?'

'He'll probably prefer it while she's alive to when she's dead.'

Spencer winced at the new brutality. 'Let him see her.'

Stoddart wasn't any better prepared than Spencer had been, although Walter Pelham spent far more time trying to warn him, actually – by the end – showing him one of the freeze frames of Patricia from the monitoring camera and offering to come with him into the observation deck. Stoddart's gasp came out as a whimper, too soft for her to hear, and his eyes fogged. He said: 'Patricia,' but his voice was too weak, broken, and he coughed and called her name again, louder.

She squinted up and said: 'Jack? Is that you?' and leaned forward and smiled. There was a gap, to the left of her mouth, where she'd lost at least two teeth.

'It's me,' he said, needing to cough again.

'Will you just look at me?' she said. 'Not a pretty sight, eh?'

She was trying to make a joke of it: trying to make it

easy for him! What could he say? Do? He said: 'How you feeling?' and loathed the emptiness.

'Pretty shitty. Beats flu every time.'

'I'm coming in!' Stoddart declared.

'No! You can't . . .'

'One of their suits . . .' said Stoddart, already backing out of the room. Pelham was directly outside. 'I want . . .'

'I heard. I don't think it's a good idea.'

'I'll wear the sort of thing the doctor wore. There won't be any risk. I'm not talking to her as if she's in some sort of goldfish bowl, an exhibit. It's not up for discussion.'

'It won't be much better . . .'

'I said it wasn't up for discussion.' Hadn't he told Olsen that, surrounded by dead bodies in the field station?

'I'll need something . . . a medical disclaimer . . .'

'We're being recorded, right?'

'Yes.'

'I am demanding to go into the isolation chamber occupied by Patricia Jefferies,' said Stoddart, at dictation speed. 'I do so at my own risk, having been warned against it by Dr Pelham and exonerate Fort Detrick from any legal liability. There! Satisfied?'

Pelham shrugged and turned to lead the way out of the corridor and down a flight of stairs, taking them to the level of the isolation suites. At one end of the new connecting corridor there was a hi-tech, medical replica of a sports stadium locker room, except here everything was sterilizable steel and there was the constant loud hum of extractor fans. Each locker held the sort of vizored protective all-in-ones the woman doctor had worn to examine him. There were individual oxygen packs to fit inside each outfit. Pelham showed Stoddart the sterilizing shower cubicles outside Patricia's suite he was to use, still suited, as soon as he left and the incinerator chute down which to put the protection – using long-handled grips to avoid touching the outside of the fabric even though it would supposedly be decontaminated – immediately afterwards. There was a row of shower stalls at the far end of the locker room he was to use at once after disposing of the suit, making sure he washed every part of his body with the disinfecting liquid each stall contained.

'It'll sting,' the man warned. 'You know the rooms are wired. You get into any trouble – sometimes people who aren't used to these suits get claustrophobic panic attacks – just call and we'll come in and get you out. Whatever you do, don't try to take off your suit, OK?'

'Sure,' said Stoddart impatiently, reaching into a locker.

'I haven't finished,' stopped the director. 'The entry is double-doored, with an air lock sterilization chamber in-between. The asepsisitication won't operate without both doors being secured. It works automatically. There are stop-go indicators set in both doors. They're pressure locked on red, open at green.'

Stoddart realized his hands were shaking when he fitted the oxygen pack into his suit and didn't care if the intently watching Pelham saw it too. It was very cold through the thin cotton of the hospital-type tunic he still wore and he shivered when the outer covering came into contact with his skin. There was no claustrophobia although there was only limited sideways vision through the face mask. The locking devices on the air-sealed doors operated as Pelham had said they would. Patricia was standing directly beyond the inner door, waiting. From outside Patricia's hospital tunic hadn't been noticeably too big. Standing as she was before him now it swamped her: she looked like a child wearing grown-ups' clothing except she'd gone beyond being grown-up. Grown old, he corrected himself.

Patricia half held out her arms, to be embraced, then let them fall. 'I guess we can't.'

'You sure?' She looked so frail and shrunken! He went forward and put his enclosed arms totally around her. Even through the thickness of his protection he could feel how thin she was. Her backbone was ridged, bowed near her shoulders.

'Yes,' she said. 'I'm sure. It won't work.'

Stoddart stood back, not knowing what to do or say. She was still trying to joke, keep everything light.

'We'd better –' she made another half gesture, looking around the sterile room – 'sit down. I need to sit down.'

She did so, in one of the easy chairs. Stoddart lowered himself awkwardly into the one facing her, feeling encumbered for the first time. Whatever the suit was made of felt rough, unfinished inside, against his skin. 'Is it just tiredness? Or do you hurt . . . ?' Why was he testing her? He wasn't a doctor!

She looked towards the table, where the sheets of paper were spread out. He saw there were more on the bureau. She said: 'I've been trying to get it all down, while I can . . . working quite hard.'

'I'm doing the same,' he told her. Eight pages, he remembered. From the look of it she had written three times as much.

'I've told Professor Pelham to use me. For whatever they want to do . . . experiment with. Just as long as there's no pain.'

'You're very brave.' Momentarily his eyes misted, and his chest heaved where he suppressed a sob.

She saw the judder and said: 'You all right? What's the matter!'

'Nothing! I'm OK!' he said hurriedly, not wanting the panicked arrival of a rescue team.

'I don't feel brave. It seemed the obvious thing to do. It might be important, to have someone who's dying from whatever it is.'

'You don't know . . .'

'Stop it, Jack! Thanks for trying but I *do* know . . . accept it . . .'

'You're not dead yet!' he insisted, swallowing against the tremble in his voice.

'I can only just hear the fat lady singing,' she said, still trying for his benefit. Her smile showed the gap of the missing teeth. 'I'm glad you're OK.' She looked briefly back to her written account. 'I've put in how we sat on the plane coming back. Out of our suits, unprotected. That might be important . . . give a clue about transmission . . .

immunity. Pelham talked to you about checking out your immunity system? Comparing it to mine . . . ?'

He'd forgotten she was a virologist. He hadn't referred to how they'd flown home in what he'd so far written. He would, he decided. He'd do the whole thing all over again: try to be as detailed – as scientifically accurate – as she'd obviously been. 'He hasn't mentioned it.'

'What about the others?'

He hadn't checked with Pelham whether he should tell her or not. He couldn't see any reason why he shouldn't. 'They've all got it.'

'Shit! They managing OK?'

'Not as well as you.'

'I probably won't be so good at the end.'

'We haven't got there yet.'

She lapsed into silence, her head lowered, and Stoddart wondered if she'd fallen asleep. Pelham had cautioned that talking tired her and she'd dominated the conversation because of his inadequacy. As the thought came to him she looked up, giving another gap-toothed smile. 'You think we would have made it, you and I? Fallen in love?'

'I thought we had.'

'Thanks, for making the effort. I don't think I had, with you. But it was looking good. Hopeful.'

'I wasn't making the effort. I'm telling you the truth.' It didn't matter, whether he was or not. He didn't *know* whether he was or not.

'That would be nice to think.'

'Think it.'

'This is how I'd have looked when I got old.'

Stoddart swallowed again. 'We could have done it together,' he said, wincing behind the cover of his vizor at the meaninglessness.

'Will you do something for me?'

'You know the answer to that.'

'Be with me, at the end. I'll need help at the end. I'd like it to be you.'

'It will be.'

47

'You really mean it? About thinking you love me?'

'Yes.'

'That makes me feel good. Maybe there's still time for me to fall in love with you.'

'I hope so.'

'I hope so, too. I'm getting very frightened, Jack. About how much time there's going to be.'

'There can't be any mistake?'

'Dick, for Christ's sake!' protested Spencer. 'I've seen them. It's . . . it's terrible.'

There was a pause on the line. 'Then I guess we need to tell the President.'

'I'll stay over, here. Bring some stuff back he should see.'

'We've got a lot to do . . . to think about now,' said Morgan.

Wait until you find out what I've already done, which you will at the same time as the President, thought Spencer.

Six

Henry Partington intended his place in presidential history to be that of an honest politician, although within strictly self-imposed and followed guidelines, welcoming the comparison with Harry Truman, whom he vaguely physically resembled. Partington recognized his ambition required a firm handle as well as a very tight lid on the accommodations and arrangements that had been necessary since his governorship of Illinois, a state famous for inventing the political science of accommodation and arrangement as well as for spawning the country's most notorious Mafia figures. If some contributions to his various campaign funds had been in cash upon which no tax had been paid, Henry Partington did not provably know of them, nor had he ever condoned any special way of expressing his gratitude. He didn't write – and certainly didn't sign – letters to people of whose backgrounds he was unfamiliar and was extremely careful with whom he was photographed. Throughout a long and successful political career, Partington had dealt ruthlessly and at once with any suggestion of corruption or illegality within his varied administrations, particularly if any ordinary member of the public was the sufferer. He was just as fulsome and quick to reward staff loyalty: people who closely surrounded Henry Partington thought as he thought, often so instinctively that it was scarcely necessary to express an attitude in words. This was really a verbal extension of not casually signing letters or enquiring too deeply about campaign contributions.

Richard Morgan and Paul Spencer were the two members of his staff most fluent in the very personal patois in which Partington spoke. Particularly in the Oval Office, equipped as it was with the automatic recording system which probably still caused Richard Nixon to turn in his grave.

Taking his turn – prompting at the same time – Spencer said 'It's a contained crisis, sir. Everyone's isolated here. Evacuation is planned in Antarctica.' Which translated as: *Everything's safely under wraps, for which I'd like to be acknowledged.*

Partington said: 'You handled everything exactly as it should have been handled, Paul. You and Dick both. Now we've got to think forward.' *There's your reward. You were ahead of Morgan with the evacuation planning so go on smart-assing against each other.*

Morgan said: 'There needs to be an early decision about McMurdo and Amundsen-Scott. And the requests from those still alive at Fort Detrick.' *Using your authority, Paul Spencer has imprisoned 400 people at the South Pole and has refused a dying man his constitutional rights in a government installation in Maryland.*

Spencer said: 'The need is to do everything we can to find out why four people and an unborn child died in the Antarctic and why four of their rescue team are going to die. Everything *is* being done to protect everybody still in Antarctica. The concentration has got to be here, at Fort Detrick. That must be our immediate concern.' *There's your lead, Mr President.*

'The concentration does need to be at Fort Detrick,' seized Morgan. 'There's a decision that has to be reached quickly.' *Is James Olsen going to be allowed or denied the lawyer and the wife he's demanded to see?*

Spencer, with the advantage of having faced Olsen's tirade through the observation gallery glass, was prepared. He was also disappointed Partington hadn't isolated what he thought he'd made obvious. 'We're medically advised that the four infected people there have to be kept in strict and absolute isolation . . . unfortunately there does already appear to be some mental deterioration . . .' *I can't spell it out any clearer than that, Mr President.*

'We're entirely dependent upon medical advice,' picked up Partington. 'Is there any indication when there might

50

be a diagnosis?' *How long before Olsen becomes too ill to continue being a problem?*

'None,' replied Spencer, confident he was ahead. 'They're undergoing every conceivable test but it'll take time. They're co-operating totally, of course . . . Dr Jefferies particularly . . . it's been five days since they were at McMurdo.' *And in what I gave you to read before you saw the photographs, ten days was suggested as the maximum survival period.*

'Is there anything more, medically, that can possibly be done . . . anything at all?' demanded Partington. *If this ever becomes public, here's the proper presidential concern.*

'I don't think so,' said Morgan. 'Everyone at Fort Detrick is a leader in their field.' *I'm joining in that concern but leaving it open ended in case there's something more we overlooked.*

'Get counsel to see what sort of employment contracts they've got . . . those who've already died and the four being treated at Detrick. We've got to see their families are properly provided for . . . kids got enough to go through college. If necessary I'll go to Congress for special funding,' said the diminutive president. *After the proper concern, the compassion and forethought.*

'Already in hand,' assured Morgan. *Clever thinking and now I'm on record as being part of it.*

'Shouldn't a specialist group be formed, to concentrate full time on it?' suggested Spencer. *This is an out and out bastard, so let's give ourselves a fall guy – better still a group of fall guys – if the shit hits the fan.*

'You suggesting a constant monitoring group?' asked Partington. *You're stacking up the brownie points, Paul. I'm impressed.*

Morgan muscled in to take over, before Spencer could answer. The Chief of Staff said: 'This qualifies as scientific, I'd say. Amanda O'Connell is responsible in Cabinet for science but I think we need to maintain liaison. Paul's been involved from the beginning. I think he should continue to be part of it, so that we're represented.' *See what happens when you try to outmanoeuvre me, smart ass!*

Partington hesitated. 'Yes, I think that's necessary. I'll brief

51

Amanda. Maybe Stoddart should be part of the group, too.' *Sorry, Paul. But you made the first move.*

'You'll expect to be briefed first-hand yourself, of course, Mr President?' anticipated Spencer. *You're not going to be able to filter or claim credit for anything, you son of a bitch.*

'Absolutely, Paul. Until this is sorted out the door's always going to be open.' *Fight among yourselves, guys. Just don't involve me.*

Jack Stoddart had already been transferred from the strict isolation wing by the time he emerged from Patricia's suite and had spent most of the previous evening – not even bothering to order food – in new, although he suspected still segregated, living room, bedroom and bathroom quarters where the nighttime doctor – male, black and intense – was waiting to extract what seemed a vampire's feast of blood, as well as taking hair and skin samples.

As he did so the doctor, anonymous again, said: 'That was a good idea of her's, immunology dysfunction. Need to keep on top of that.'

Stoddart said: 'What else you got?'

Patricia had been moved, too. It wasn't a room-divided suite any more. There was a bureau and telephone – and a separate, adjoining bathroom – but it was really a hospital room and Patricia couldn't have got to the bureau or the bathroom. There were two intravenous drips and she was connected to a heart monitor tracing irregular mountain chains on its screen. Three other tubes disappeared beneath the bed coverings, which were canopied from what would have been her chest to her knees by some frame-like support. Despite the headband registering her brain's electric impulses, Stoddart could see she'd lost a great deal more hair, making her practically bald. She didn't focus on his entering the room until he spoke and when she smiled he saw she'd lost more teeth. Her gums looked raw.

She said: 'It's good I finished what I had to write. I'm too tired now.' Her voice was slurred, the sibilants hissing.

Stoddart said: 'I finished mine, too.' He was holding her hand but couldn't feel it, through the protection.

'What's it like outside?'

'Warm. The blossom's out.' The weather forecast that morning had been from The Mall. People who looked as if they needed to, had been jogging.

'I always liked Washington when the blossom came. Funny how you never pay enough attention to things until it's too late. Don't do that, will you? Look at things. Make sure you enjoy them. Promise?'

'I promise.'

'You don't know about me, do you?'

'Enough.'

'No!' Patricia said, in weak indignation. 'It'll be on my personnel file. My parents are dead but I've got a kid brother, John. In Sán Antonio. Tell him . . .' She had to stop, to rest. The heart monitor mountains were peaking more sharply. 'Just speak to him . . .' Her unfocused eyes closed and her breathing became more regular. The mountains plateaued.

Stoddart was abruptly seized by an enormous anger, a need to physically hurt – punish – whoever or whatever had caused this to happen to this close-to-mummified person whose body he'd held and kissed and enjoyed and made love to just . . . just when? Nine days, eight days ago? No longer than that. No longer than that ago she'd been a voluptuous, uninhibited, exciting lover. Awakened him, in every way, from the boredom that his ostracized, criticized life had imploded into. He could have loved her, Stoddart decided. Given the time, the chance, he was sure he could have grown to love her enough to have asked her to marry him.

Patricia jerked awake and he felt the snatch of her hand through the glove. 'I thought you'd gone.'

'No.'

'You know what I'm sorry about?'

'What?'

'On the plane coming back . . . when we were all right and not bothering with the suits . . . ? We didn't kiss goodbye . . .'

'I'm sorry, too.'

'But if we had you might have caught it, darling. So it's best we didn't.'

When Paul Spencer got back to his office there were two messages from David Hoolihan, both marked to be returned urgently on his private line at Arlington.

Hoolihan said: 'There's been an emergency rescue call from another of our stations, at Noatak. It's the same thing.'

'Where's Noatak?' demanded Spencer.

'Northern Alaska, close to the Arctic. So it's spread to both Poles. And the Noatak station's a shared project: English as well as French. A Frenchman is one of the people sick. How we going to handle it now?'

'As an international incident,' replied Spencer. With me right at the very centre of it, he thought again, contentedly.

Seven

A nother of Henry Partington's posterity intentions was to be remembered as an international statesman and he instantly identified the potential of Alaska. By the time he placed his first overseas call – to London – Partington, whose relaxation was chess, had every move and countermove firmly established in his mind. A specially equipped relief plane was already on its way, he told the British prime minister. Logistically as well as medically, it made every sense for the afflicted British personnel to be treated in America: there were already American sufferers, from Antarctica, under intensive care and examination in a special isolation unit. There was room there for British scientists to form part of the already created US medical investigation team. He was in the process of establishing a Cabinet-level crisis committee and would obviously welcome – indeed, expect – British participation at a similarly high level. Partington phrased the need for any public awareness to be suppressed as if the suggestion came from London, not him. His second conversation, with Paris, was in several places a verbatim repeat of that with the British premier, particularly about the necessity for secrecy.

As he replaced the receiver, Partington said: 'Neither knew anything about it until I told them. They're grateful how far we are ahead. They've accepted our help offer and are getting back to me first thing tomorrow.'

Morgan said: 'State have to be involved now.'

'Already are. Secretary's due in thirty minutes. Amanda O'Connell, too,' said the president, gesturing towards the summoning Spencer. Before either of the other two men could speak, Partington got briskly to his feet. 'It's a warm evening. Let's walk in the rose garden until they get here: clear our minds.' *And not have to worry ourselves about those damned Oval Office tapes.*

The small, clerk-like man waited until he was some way from the building, dwarfed by Morgan and Spencer on either side, before saying: 'We've got a very changed picture now.'

'Very much so,' agreed Morgan, which was more a reflection upon Paul Spencer's manoeuvrings than it was about either Alaska or the Amundsen-Scott field station. There was every practical and pragmatic reason to let Spencer have his day. As many days as he wanted. The longer Spencer went on ducking and diving the more inevitable his forgetting to duck or dive in time.

'But we're still totally in control of it,' suggested Spencer. They were almost at the end of the orderly garden layout. Beyond the immaculate lawns, the traffic was fire-flying along South Street and even farther away, along Constitution Avenue, creating a ribbon of lights. The Washington Monument was thrust up blackly against a sky yellowed and oranged by the just finishing day. The sun would have set permanently for the winter at McMurdo, Spencer knew. How brilliantly would it be shining upon the ageing, dying men at the other frozen extreme of the world where the northern summer had just begun?

'There's no way we can keep this under wraps forever,' decided Partington, realistically. 'We need insurance, whichever way the ball bounces. It's got to be our people who come out with a cure or a prevention of whatever the hell it is, to stop this happening to people. And if it becomes public *before* there's a cure, then we went along reluctantly with the suppression, at the urging of the Europeans whose affected scientists had to come to American facilities for American expertize to try to save their lives . . .' Because of their size, he had to look up in discomfort to each man in turn. 'How's that sound?'

Both Morgan and Spencer appreciated the political realism.

Hoping to continue it Morgan said: 'We might have a problem claiming the credit if the breakthrough is provably made by someone from France or England.'

'You heard me invite their investigative scientists or doctors to be part of a team: *our* already created and already hard at work team,' reminded Partington, patiently. 'If one of our people find the answer, it's ours, absolutely. If it's English or French, their having had to come to America and use American facilities, it's a jointly shared discovery. What other reason, in the public mind, could there be for their having to come here to us in the first place?'

'Sounds good to me,' said Spencer, dutifully. 'It's false starts and claims we have to be most careful about.'

'Which puts the burden on you, Paul,' snatched Morgan, seeing the opportunity. 'Looks to me as if your liaison role has grown a lot, between the investigating doctors and a political oversight group.'

'Dick's right,' agreed the president, at once. 'You're more than ever the eyes and ears now, Paul.'

'Yes, sir,' accepted Spencer. It wasn't anything he didn't already know, wasn't prepared for.

They were approaching the covered verandah on the garden side of the White House. Partington said: 'Quite obviously Paul's got a twenty-five hour a day job. It's going to put a lot of extra pressure on you, Dick.'

'I understand that,' said Morgan, seeing another unsettling opportunity. 'Paul takes a lot off my shoulders. Maybe it'll be necessary to bring somebody else in . . . on a temporary basis, of course.'

Cheap shot, asshole, thought Spencer, as an idea completely formed in his mind. He actually smiled. 'Nice to know I'm indispensable, Dick. But I think we've got to think it through carefully. If I just disappear from the office . . . but am around as much as ever, which I'm going to need to be, to keep you fully up to speed, Mr President . . . there'll be the sort of rumours we're trying to avoid . . .' He let in the pause, which Partington predictably filled.

'What you got in mind?'

'A positive reassignment, in title at least,' declared Spencer.

Partington stopped walking along the verandah, bringing the other two men to a halt with him. Standing as they were, Morgan and Spencer were facing each other literally over the President's head. Morgan was stone-faced, expressionless. Partington said: 'Reassignment as what?'

'Special advisor,' announced Spencer. 'Covers everything without saying anything. And prevents any gossip before gossip or rumour is allowed to start.'

'That's good. You think it's good, Dick?'

'Yes, sir,' said Morgan, with no alternative.

'Congratulations,' laughed Partington. 'People are going to think you got a promotion.'

And I'm the first of them, thought Spencer.

Fulfilling it at once, it was Spencer who gave the background to the Antarctic discovery and what was taking place at Fort Detrick after the initial speechless response of the Cabinet newcomers to the photographic evidence. Partington only took over when they returned from the projection room to the Oval Office, recounting the apparent second outbreak in Alaska, the already en route American rescue operation and his conversations with the British and French premiers.

'We don't know what it is, where it'll break out next or how to stop it,' declared Partington. 'All we do know is that we're looking at a medical or biological horror . . . a potential catastrophe . . .'

'Do the British and the French properly know that, too?' at once questioned Robin Turner, the Secretary of State. Turner was an urbane, white-haired, white-moustached man who'd been the Ivy League infusion into Georgetown University, where he'd been the acclaimed professor of international affairs and from which he'd been plucked by Partington to achieve the president's intention to be equally acclaimed, by carefully following the man's academic advice. So far in the presidency, Turner had not been tested to produce anything more than suggest what would have occurred to Partington

58

anyway, but on television and at press conferences Turner looked and sounded impressive.

'They will, when you show their ambassadors here what you've just seen on film. And after that taken them to Fort Detrick, to see their own nationals,' said Partington.

'You really think we stand a chance of concealing this?' demanded Turner, doubtfully shaking his head in advance of the answer.

'I think for all the obvious reasons we've got to try, for as long as possible.'

'There's a risk of a huge public backlash,' warned the political theorist.

'Against the risk of a huger – now worldwide – public panic,' countered Partington, pleased with the discussion going on record. 'That's the fear of Paris and London. Mine, too.'

Partington brought Amanda O'Connell into the discussion by announcing that she would be the chairperson of the governmental crisis committee that would now include British and French, just as the scientific group at Fort Detrick would be headed by an American. Paul Spencer was introduced as the liaising conduit between the two groups.

Amanda O'Connell had waited patiently for her specific participation to be set out, because Amanda O'Connell was a person who always waited, although rarely patiently, before intruding or committing herself, preferring always to assess the intrusion or commitments of others. She was aware, because Amanda was professionally a very astutely aware woman, that her inherent, second-look reserve had, in the early months of Henry Partington's presidency, led to her being considered – openly described even – as nothing more than a politically correct totem to feminism. Which, in those early months, she had accepted herself to be in theory, although not in practice. From her staff-starved, bowel-basement quarters which even Amanda referred to as the roaches' rest room, she'd not once, so far, failed to advise or warn the man high above in this office, in which she was now sitting for the first time, of any scientific or environmental development of which he should have been informed, which is how she'd finally earned herself her place in Cabinet.

The totem disparagement, which she'd learned to turn against her critics, was very much in her mind as she dissected with the biologist's skill befitting her Master's degree, the contents of the previous hour's conversation, grateful to Partington for dominating it because it had given her analysis time. From the photographic evidence, which was the only proper, available evidence upon which she had to make a judgement, this was scientifically and medically a plague-like illness that – because its transmission was for the moment unknown – could be even worse than AIDS. So much, so far, for science and medicine: not her priority. America – and Partington – had been landed with it because the first outbreak had occurred in a US base in Antarctica. But not landed for long. Amanda, whose university exchange year in Sienna had given her a surface knowledge of European political history to go with that of her own country and who found it easier to compare Partington to the small-statured Machiavelli than Truman, was unsettled by the president's demeanour. She thought the serious-faced, sonorous-voiced gravitas was just slightly off-key. If there was a hidden agenda, then the newly elevated Paul Spencer, to whom she hadn't before existed but whose eyes at that moment moved from appraising her tits to meet hers, would be the ledger clerk.

Responding to the president's introduction, Spencer smiled and said: 'I'm sure we're going to work together just great.'

'I'm sure we are,' said Amanda, although looking at Partington. 'Where, exactly, is the political group to work *from*? It obviously can't be from here. Or, I wouldn't think, from Fort Detrick.'

'Blair House,' announced Partington, at once.

'I want to go to Maryland, though. Tomorrow, before anyone arrives from Europe,' decided Amanda. In a question that was more loaded than it appeared, she went on: 'I wonder if it'll be practical for the two groups, when we're properly set up, to work so far apart?'

'Here's where any political group should be,' said Partington. 'I'll want you as close as possible and the British and French will want to be next to their embassies.'

Exploring still she said: 'Whoever comes from London and Paris will presumably be from their science ministries, possibly with support staff.'

Partington looked at her blankly. 'What's your point?'

'This *is* an unknown. Whatever, whenever the outcome, there'll need to be the fullest scientific research papers publicly available. Proper records.'

From the briefest spasm that crossed Spencer's face Amanda knew it hadn't occurred to anyone. Spencer said hurriedly: 'The medical research is being carried out at Fort Detrick. Pelham will know the needs well enough.'

'I hope he will,' said Amanda, mildly. 'I think it's something about which we should be politically aware. I'll remember to raise it at our first meeting: ensure it's minuted . . .' She inserted the pause. 'Which brings us to another point. If we're going to be the host country, I'm going to need a secretariat.' Was it possible – conceivable – that she could get her own properly designated, properly recognized department? There was no reason why she shouldn't allow herself the thought, improbable though it might be. At least achieve sufficient recognition to lift herself out of the roaches' rest room.

Turner said: 'There'll certainly need to be a full publishable account when everything becomes public: diplomatically as well as scientifically.'

His official record – his place – in the whole affair, Partington realized furiously. Something that should have been anticipated – already have been organized – by Morgan or Spencer instead of circling around each other, sniffing their asses like dogs on heat.

Quicker to read the president's body language than his former deputy, Morgan said: 'You've surely got that in hand, haven't you, Paul?'

'Now that I know it'll be Blair House everything will be set up, ready, by tomorrow,' assured Spencer.

It was Amanda who in turn read the body language between

61

the two men and mentally filed the antagonism away, along with everything else. To Spencer she said: 'I'll take my own staff from here. And let you know what extra people and facilities I want, as the situation becomes clearer.'

'And that can't be soon enough,' said the Secretary of State.

Patricia hadn't spoken for a long time, although her face quite frequently twisted as if she were in pain. Stoddart sat, encumbered and uncomfortable, as close to her bed as possible, her hand enclosed in both of his although still not really able to feel her fingers. It was difficult to keep the sleeves and gloves from snagging some of the leads to which she was attached. They were as much to keep her alive as to monitor every bodily function: it had to be close to two days since she'd become unable to eat or drink normally. Very little hair remained and the skin on her face and arms was crumpled and wizened.

There was a fresh grimace and her eyes opened. In immediate alarm she tried to twist her head to where she knew he would be sitting, but the brain scan band stopped her turning completely.

'I'm here,' said Stoddart.

She relaxed, moving her hand slightly between the gloves. 'I can't see you, not very well . . . just a kind of fuzzy outline.' Her voice was thick, the words clogging. 'Am I very ugly?'

'No.'

'I am if I'm anything like Jane and the others, at the station.'

'You're not,' he lied. If anything, her appearance was worse.

'They found out anything yet? About it?'

'I don't think so.'

'I was hoping . . .' she began, then stopped.

'There's still time . . . a lot of time . . .'

Patricia didn't speak for several moments, breathing quickly. 'Remember what I told you, about being scared at the end.'

'That's not something to talk about now.'

'Yes it is,' said Patricia, insistently. 'I'm frightened now, Jack. Very frightened.'

'We're going to be all right,' said Stoddart, desperately. 'They're working on something here . . . any minute now . . .'

'Keep safe, Jack.'

'Yes.' His throat blocked.

'I want . . .' she managed, but had to stop. She slightly raised her head, moving her mouth to form the words.

'Don't . . . just rest . . .' he said, and she went back against the pillow and the alarm bells went off on two machines as the brain and heart monitors stretched out in straight, even lines.

The three suited figures did not hurry into the suite or attempt any resuscitation. Two began gently disconnecting the tubes and leads. The third – the woman doctor who'd examined him – said to Stoddart: 'She's dead. I'm sorry.'

'I know,' said Stoddart.

'They're all dead now.'

Eight

A manda O'Connell, who'd been the innocent party to the divorce, wasn't involved in any relationship and was comfortable looking after herself. She had expected to go to Fort Detrick alone but the newly appointed presidential aide had demanded to take her, insisting as the White House meeting broke up the previous night ('we really do need to get to know each other') that the journey to Maryland gave them time to talk. Amanda had accepted at once, although by the time he called for her at her Georgetown apartment – clearly expecting to be invited up for breakfast coffee, which he wasn't – she'd read all the salvaged material from the Antarctic field station and what little there was so far from Fort Detrick itself. Amanda's introduction to the jungle law of Washington mating had begun as a college graduate intern at the White House and she wasn't surprised at Paul Spencer's renewed sexual appraisal as she got into his car, although from his eagerness she guessed he'd be a prematurely ejaculating failure which she had neither wish nor intention of finding out. What she did intend discovering, observing her own far more practical Washington jungle law, was if there really was a second agenda and to achieve that she was quite prepared to give Spencer as much false hope as was necessary.

Amanda was encouraged by how anxious Spencer appeared to be to impress her, talking in sound bites of horrors and catastrophes and time limits for cures and preventions, and it was when he was unnecessarily stressing that urgency ('it can't become a plague') as they were climbing the memorial parkways towards the Beltway that Amanda isolated a phrase that had more meaning than much of what he'd so far said.

'*American* medical breakthrough?' she queried. 'According to what I've read and what was said last night, Detrick haven't got anywhere yet.'

Spencer looked quickly across the car. 'Just a way of talking. We're heading everything up, after all.' She was very smart as well as having legs that went on for ever.

'Heading up what's intended to be a joint medical investigation, surely?'

'I hope that's what it'll turn out to be but something like this could easily become xenophobic. I think you should be careful about that, among whatever political grouping is set up.'

'*You* think?' qualified Amanda, heavily again. 'What's the President think?' There was definitely a message here: one not being particularly well delivered, if indeed the man had been deputed the messenger. She turned fully to look across the car at Spencer now, even though the movement rode her skirt up slightly higher.

'Having been with him from the beginning I'm pretty good at tuning in to the President's thinking,' Spencer said, smiling confidentially.

The faithful servant, ensuring his master's hands remained clean, judged Amanda. Maybe it was time Paul Spencer really did get to know her better: to know, from the outset, that she got out of the subterranean roaches' rest room often enough to see things very clearly in the Washington political daylight. 'What other telepathic conversations have you had with Henry Partington about this?'

Spencer looked sharply across the car this time. 'Just sharing a few thoughts . . . impressions . . . that's all . . .' This wasn't going as he'd intended. She was treating him like an office boy!

'Let's go on doing just that,' said Amanda, deciding to get things as she wanted between them from the beginning. 'We *have* got a terrible situation here. One we can't estimate . . . guess or know what to do about . . . We get it wrong, politically, we're as dead as the poor bastards who've caught it. So here's how I want you and I to work. I don't want telepathy or clairvoyance or innuendo. You got something to tell me the President doesn't think he can tell me himself, I want it straight. That way we don't get any misunderstanding because we can't afford misunderstandings . . . you with me so far?'

What the fuck rules did this woman imagine she was playing by? Spencer was abruptly, totally, disoriented. Thank God – whoever He was – there were only two of them, no proof of anything said or suggested. 'I think maybe we're getting off on the wrong foot here,' he tried, anxiously.

'No!' Amanda rejected. 'We're getting off on the *right* foot. Just so you know how right, let *me* tell *you* where we're at. If I – politically – head up whatever group is being established, I don't need to be velvet-gloved into knowing how important it is that we, America, come out in front. That *I* come out in front. Which is where I am always going to be –' she finally tugged down her skirt '– with or without you. I'd rather it be with you – with us both on the same side, because there are going to be too many other sides – and if it's going to be with you, then I want to know all the backdoor, smoke-filled-room shit. That way we both stand a chance of surviving. Try the bullshit you tried a little while back and one of us isn't going to make it. And I'm definitely going to make it. There's no risk of your misunderstanding that, is there?'

Spencer drove for several moments without replying, half thoughts swirling around his mind like leaves in a wind. If the merest suggestion of this conversation – this little-boy ultimatum lecture – ever reached Morgan, became as much as a vague rumour, Amanda O'Connell would be right: he'd be a dead man. Resurrection, knee-bending survival time. 'I'm glad we've cleared the air.'

Let him back in with a little face-saving grace, decided Amanda: he wouldn't need to be told, either, that there was no future ogling her legs and tits. 'I'm glad, too. Anything else I need to know before we get there?'

She had him by the balls in quite a different way from that

which Spencer had intended and he didn't like it. 'Stoddart is to head the medical investigation.'

'That doesn't make any sense,' she protested at once. 'He isn't a clinician. It should be Pelham.'

'It's not hands-on. It's an administrative function. Stoddart is the only survivor of what was supposed to be a rescue but wasn't . . .'

'. . . So it'll play well later, in the media?' she anticipated. 'Deflect the heat, even . . . ?'

'And I heard before we left Washington that his girlfriend was the last victim to die . . . during the night,' completed Spencer, matching the cynicism.

'Even better,' agreed Amanda. 'What's Pelham's problem?'

Spencer hesitated, recognizing the irony before responding. 'Too forthright. A personality clash.'

'Always a need for timing and judgment,' said Amanda, relaxing in her seat as Spencer swung off the I-395

Both of which, Spencer acknowledged objectively, this morning he'd got seriously wrong. 'You heard of Stoddart?'

'Oh, yes,' said Amanda. 'I know all about Stoddart.'

Amanda's impression of Walter Pelham was that he'd been a forgotten experiment that had dried out at the bottom of a test tube. Even the handshake was dry and cold. The emotionless, desiccated man listened expressionlessly as Spencer elaborated upon the impending arrival of the Alaska airlift he'd already been warned to expect, occasionally nodding in private agreement with himself.

'All our isolation facilities are now free,' he said. Heavily, looking directly at the president's aide, Pelham added: 'Jim Olsen's was the first.'

'And sufficient room for the British and French scientific people?' Spencer pressed on. The bastard had guessed why they'd held off the scientist's demand for his wife and a lawyer. The pause was brief. 'We thought we might move a few more military in, too. Logistics, administration, security, stuff like that.'

67

Amanda matched Pelham's quick, frowned concentration, although she remained silent. So did the facility director until Spencer became discomfited. Finally Pelham said: 'This is a military scientific research compound with the highest security classification. Our security arrangements are fine, like our logistics and administration.'

'It's precisely *because* Detrick is the sort of place it is that the President thinks it's necessary,' said Spencer. 'We don't want people wandering into divisions and departments they've no right to be in, do we?'

Smoothly handled, conceded Amanda: the bastard should still have warned her. Pelham said: 'So everyone's to be restricted?'

'We've got a major priority, Walt! Are all your involved experts taking time off for barbecues and happy hour?'

Pelham looked at Amanda. 'You'd better get ready for the protests.'

Amanda, in turn looking at Spencer, said: 'I suppose I had.' Going back to the scientist she said: 'What about the necessary division, between everything these new arrivals will entail and the sort of research you normally carry out?'

'The isolation wings are just that, isolated,' said Pelham. 'So there's no security difficulty. But there's obviously limitations . . .' He went back to Spencer. 'And once you have to start putting your old people anywhere outside of here – or somewhere like here – you're compounding your public awareness problem.'

Neither of these men liked each other, gauged Amanda. Which wasn't a working necessity – she didn't *like* Paul Spencer – but there seemed to be an animosity, which she hoped wouldn't develop. The leadership of the scientific investigation group, she remembered. Quickly she said: 'There's been some thought in Washington about your position here and the incoming people, from Paris and London . . . obviously your doctors already involved – and you, yourself – have to work with whoever arrives but we thought it might be diplomatically better if you, as the installation director, didn't appear automatically to head

68

the oversight group. Which might have been the assumption. We want, if possible, to avoid compromising you . . .'

Pelham said: 'I'm not quite sure I follow the reasoning . . .'

'Detrick's got precisely the facilities that are needed but it's known to be the country's micro-biological research establishment,' continued Amanda, easily. 'The President wants a measure of independence from that . . .'

'If that's the political thinking,' he shrugged. 'Who . . . ?'

'Jack Stoddart,' announced Amanda, surprised the scientist wasn't putting up more of an objection. 'It's a liaison function, like Paul's will be between what's going on here and us in Washington. Stoddart's been involved from the beginning. And it in no way affects your authority here, internally . . .'

Pelham was smiling now. So too, faintly, was Spencer.

Amanda said: 'How is he, after the woman's death?'

'It only happened during the night. I haven't seen him yet.'

'Let's see him together,' suggested Amanda. She paused. 'I'd hoped to be able to see – talk to, if that had been possible – some of the victims.'

'All there are now are bodies,' said Pelham.

'Yes,' said Amanda, after a further hesitation. 'I suppose I need to see the bodies.'

As he'd plodded heavily back over Lambeth Bridge in the pissing rain that morning, freezingly burdened by the sodden and intentionally worn supermarket tracksuit, without there having been a single photographer to record his agonizing commitment to health, science, youth or whatever other bollocks the spin doctors wanted to attach as a label, Peter Reynell determined that the publicity value of jogging was well past its sell-by date and that it was time for an already promised doctor's verdict ('a serious risk of permanent damage to the Achilles; this man who's been an example to all should not risk at his young age being permanently in a wheelchair') to get him off the hook. He could install an exercise bike or a rowing machine or something in Lord

North Street and pose on it for carefully chosen and vetted friendly cameramen and give himself at least an extra hour in bed, whoever's bed that might be.

The previous night it had been his own, alone, because the private dining room gathering at the Carlton Club had been disappointing. Not one of those carefully chosen from the 1922 Committee had turned up and if he hadn't been as careful as he had – using the by-election celebration of the most newly elected Member to test his own popularity – it would have been disastrous. As it was, Reynell was still nervous of the subterfuge being realized and ground out by the Westminster gossip mill. All in all, it had been a pretty shitty twenty-four hours.

Reynell left the tracksuit where it fell and continued shivering for what seemed to be a long time despite running the shower as hot as he could bear. With the inferred – although tantalizingly still only dangled – support of Lord Ranleigh, the backroom manipulating party grandee who was conveniently his father-in-law, he'd worked hard cultivating what he believed to be a solid backing over the previous twelve months, seeding the rumours of a leadership challenge so that he could deny them, pledging unfaltering loyalty to the current but increasingly inadequacy-exposed prime minister, and had been sure his troops had been there, simply awaiting their call to arms. There was an obvious explanation. Simon fucking Buxton had anticipated him: read the runes – maybe even had a spy – and had a pre-emptive word in too many receptive ears. For the next few days – or weeks or months – he needed to tread very carefully indeed. No more rumour denials or tracksuited photo opportunities or television debate programmes. No more relying on inferred endorsement from a man who'd taken the abolition of hereditary peerages as a personal insult. A tactical retreat: in fact, regroup, replan and be a bloody sight more careful next time. If he could survive for a next time.

Reynell was towelling himself dry, warm at last, when he heard his private phone – his parliamentary phone – in the adjoining bedroom, its tone quite intentionally different from

70

Henrietta's. He actually ran to snatch it up on only the third ring, wondering who it was – what it was – from last night.

'Sorry to call you so early, Peter. Hope I didn't wake you.'

'I was already up, Prime Minister,' replied Reynell, hollow-stomached the moment he recognized the voice.

'I forgot. You exercise, of course,' said Buxton, in apparent recollection. 'We need to talk. Urgently. Could you come over?'

Dismissal, thought Reynell at once. His campaign *had* been infiltrated and last night had been his Last Supper, betrayed by a Judas to be sacrificed. The resignation letters would be exchanged by lunchtime (Dear Prime Minister, it is with the greatest regret . . . my continued and fullest support . . . Dear Peter, it is with the greatest regret . . . your enormous commitment and contribution . . .) and by tonight . . . By tonight what? A rare dinner with Lady Henrietta, perhaps? A familiar recital of the three hundred years of Ranleigh family service to Crown and country and the disappointment the still infuriatedly disenfranchised Lord Ranleigh of Henslow would feel at not at least having a son-in-law in a junior ministerial position? Reynell said: 'What time would you like to see me?'

'Now,' said Buxton peremptorily. 'Fifteen minutes. You can get here easily in fifteen minutes, can't you?'

'Easily,' agreed Reynell.

He made it in ten, on foot, and by the time he got to Downing Street he'd determined on complete denial, although acknowledging it wouldn't save him. Buxton couldn't have any factual, written proof of his mounting a leadership challenge because there wasn't any – his inner caucus would damn themselves by admitting anything unless one of them was the spy – and it was even conceivable that he could turn his dismissal into an advantage by getting the stories circulating that it was the desperate act of a desperate party leader deservedly about to be overthrown. Which might just be enough to start a groundswell.

Simon Buxton was a man who had virtually been manu-factured by the group of similarly disenfranchised grandees and party activists in opposition to Lord Ranleigh, a skeleton – Reynell preferred coat rack – upon which a performing figure had been moulded. Buxton was a large, artificially avuncular man whose ancestry rivalled that of the Ranleigh family but without any inherited intellectual or even common-sense ability, a shortcoming the insecure and inadequate man tried to disguise by attempting to anticipate, usually wrongly, whatever point or argument was being advanced. So frequently had Buxton's shoot-from-the-lip propensities been used by the Opposition to lure the man into misinterpreted interruptions and interventions during Prime Minister's Question Time that the deputy leader was now always restrainingly at his side.

None of which, Reynell reflected as he entered Buxton's private office overlooking the rear garden and Horseguards, was of any immediate benefit to him now. Befitting Reynell's belief in the reason for his summons, the other man was solemnly grave-faced. Without any explanation, Buxton offered a sheaf of photographs, which Reynell accepted and took his time going through because he needed time, in his total bewilderment. Whatever this was it had nothing to do with last night's dinner or any coup attempt! Listen, don't talk, he told himself.

Looking up at last he said: 'Who are they?'

'Americans,' replied Buxton. 'The oldest was forty-one. That's from the Antarctic but some of our people have caught it on an American station in Alaska.'

Reynell looked down again at the photographs. 'What are we going to do?'

'You're the science minister,' Buxton pointed out. 'You're going to Washington, to be part of a crisis group that's being set up. I'm making you personally responsible, Peter.'

Exiled! thought Reynell, at once. 'I'll do my best, Prime Minister.'

'I'm sure you will, as you always do,' smiled Buxton.

Amanda O'Connell's reaction to seeing the aged bodies, even from beyond the glassed protection of the mortuary's viewing gallery, was as numbingly chilled as Spencer's had earlier been. The man had made an excuse to avoid accompanying her, saying there was no purpose, and Amanda conceded there hadn't been for her, either. It was voyeurism: shaming. She actually did feel ashamed, disgusted with herself, hurrying from the gallery and the ghastly sight regimented for her benefit, covering her embarrassment by talking animatedly with Pelham about the medical investigations so far conducted, which began emptily but from which a small, justifying point emerged.

She was still disconcerted when she re-entered the director's office, so much so that she was startled to find Jack Stoddart already waiting there with Spencer, even though that had been Spencer's excuse for remaining behind. Amanda was sure it hadn't been obvious to any of them, most of all not to Stoddart, who responded with self-enclosed disinterest to their introduction. Stoddart was the unpredictable factor, one she didn't think she could assess or compartment and most certainly the last person with whom she wanted to start out at any disadvantage. She was at once further embarrassed by that attitude, remembering the early morning death of the woman – the woman whose age-withered corpse she'd just looked down upon – with whom he had been personally involved.

It was her first face-to-face encounter with Jack Stoddart, although she'd watched him on television and film more times that she could recall and read even more of his articles and all his books, but her initial perception was yet another surprise. He was physically much smaller than she'd expected, in both height and build, but what was more marked was the total absence of the electric-current vibrancy she'd been so conscious of in every screen appearance. For every good reason, Amanda reminded herself, after what he'd been through. Her embarrassment began to go, replaced by an even more unsettling irritation. Instead of the psychological posturing of judging everyone else's act, perhaps she should analyse her own, confronted as she was by the biggest and best career chance she was ever likely to get. She wasn't thinking right, reacting right, *being* right.

Thank Christ she'd realized it. She said: 'You must be exhausted.'

Stoddart shrugged slumped shoulders. 'I haven't thought about it.' He didn't feel tired. He'd actually managed to sleep, after Patricia's death. So what did he feel? Anger, at his impotence to have done anything. Say the right words. And guilt. Most of all guilt, a huge, hollowing self-blame at causing the deaths of four people, one of them Patricia Jefferies. Because he *had* killed them, as surely as pressing a trigger or depressing a plunger: not evacuating them from the field hut the moment he'd seen the condition of the bodies inside and, even worse, insisting upon carrying them, inadequately sealed, back to McMurdo and finally here, to America. Was that what they were here for, this woman whose name he'd already forgotten and the man who'd said something about the White House: here to talk about culpable negligence and liability, maybe caution him about legal representation? Was there a criminal charge, as well as a civil claim? It didn't matter. He'd plead to both. Or either. There wasn't any defence. Mitigation maybe, but only just. That scarcely mattered either.

She needed to remain in charge, Amanda decided. As she had been at the end of the earlier meeting: in charge, calling the shots – the right shots – and cracking the self-pitying shell Stoddart was creating around himself before it had time to harden. She leaned forward, forcing him to focus upon her, to disclose the Alaska outbreak, repeating it when at first it didn't appear to register.

'The northern hemisphere!' Stoddart groped. 'It's travelled . . . happening there . . . Oh Jesus! How, so far apart? What was the cause? The conduit?'

Having got him, Amanda refused to let him go, realizing as she talked of international co-operating groups and combined research, that she was talking in Spencer-like sound bites to keep Stoddart's attention. By the time she finished he'd straightened and was leaning towards her, intent not to miss anything. There was, however, still doubt in his attitude.

'What about my bringing the bodies back . . . the others who died?' he said.

Amanda picked up the point, way ahead of the other two men. She said: 'That's what you had to do. The right thing. For the research to start . . .'

'The others . . . ?'

'That couldn't have been prevented. You didn't know. None of us knows yet.'

Stoddart's mind wouldn't hold a consistent thought and he decided that perhaps he was exhausted, although he didn't feel anything like he had when he'd landed at Andrews Air Force base. 'This investigation . . . ? Am I to be part of it?'

'You're to head it,' declared Amanda.

Stoddart's doubt returned. He looked directly at Pelham and said: 'Surely that's—'

'I'm going to be practically involved,' cut off the director, ahead of any longer explanation.

'Yes,' said Stoddart, to himself more than to anyone else. 'I need to know what it is. What caused it and how to stop it. I must do that.'

It was Amanda's decision – still unsettled by what she'd seen in the mortuary and insisting medical examinations had the obvious priority – that they shouldn't remain for the C-130 arrival from Alaska, still at least three hours away. There wasn't any further sexual appraisal as she settled in the passenger seat. As they made their way through the security checks, Amanda said: 'I thought we reached an agreement.'

'So did I.'

'Don't smart-ass, Paul. You didn't warn me about any extra military presence.'

'I'm sorry.'

'I don't want to be sorry about anything, certainly not you keeping something from me. I thought I made that clear.'

It was stupid and he shouldn't have done it, Spencer conceded. But he didn't like the way he was being relegated. Despite which, trying to ingratiate himself, he said: 'You handled Pelham brilliantly.'

Amanda shook her head, refusing the flattery. 'He didn't want to head the group. Why not?'

Spencer shook his head in return. 'Maybe he doesn't think they're going to find out what it is or how to stop it. And doesn't want to carry the can.'

Amanda was silent for several minutes, until the direction signs to the Beltway began to come up. Then she said: 'What was the point Pelham was making to you, about James Olsen?'

Didn't she miss a fucking thing? thought Spencer. 'I didn't think he was making any point. If he did, I don't know why.'

The bastard was lying, at least partially, Amanda decided. He'd only have himself to blame: she'd warned him clearly enough.

At the National Security Agency the deputy analysis director read the translation for a second time and decided it was precisely what the White House wanted. In fact, according to regulations, he should have immediately started to ring alarm bells, particularly with the CIA. When there was no reply from Spencer's telephone he sent an email alert and decided he could afford to wait a couple of hours, three at the outside. But no longer than that. This was something he should move on. The NSA is at Fort Meade, in the same state of Maryland as Fort Detrick, and at that moment Spencer was, ironically, only twenty miles away but driving in the opposite direction.

Nine

The transcript was absolute, even to the pauses and inter-jections, but they scarcely needed to follow the trans-lation to understand the interception. Or, from the babbled, whimpering collapse of everyone towards the end, to pic-ture the bizarre scene – hysteria muted to whispers by age and infirmity – there would have been inside the Siberian research station.

There were three dated and timed tapes, the first four weeks earlier, the initial relevant remark precisely at 12.20 p.m. The beginning almost casual, filling in a scheduled contact:

How are things generally?

We're all feeling tired.

You've been working hard, getting ready for the summer season. What do you expect?

I suppose you're right. I didn't imagine us all to be feeling the same, though . . . not like this.

You worried about it?'

It's not right.

You talked to Andrei Ivanovich about it?

He said he expected it but much later. Months away. He wanted to bring some stay-awake medication . . . vitamins, things like that, but there weren't any.

Life was better for scientists under the old regime. Then you could have anything you wanted.

Life was better for a lot of people under the old regime, not just scientists.

Maybe you wouldn't be so tired if you stopped screwing the natives up there.

You seen what the natives up here look like!

The next applicable transmission was 6 p.m. three days later:

This is Andrei Ivanovich. I have three people ill with symptoms I can't diagnose. I have taken blood, urine and faeces samples which I need analysed. Can you send a helicopter from Anadyr and then arrange the transfer to you, in Moscow?

I will make enquiry, doctor.

There seems to be a malaise throughout the station. I am affected myself for no proper reason: I haven't been working as physically hard as everyone else setting up their experiments. I think this is urgent. Will you please make that clear, that I consider it urgent?

The Moscow response came three hours later:

I am sorry. The Institute has been told by the Ministry that there is no emergency transportation available. That you will have to wait for the next regular supply visit, for the collection.

The next scheduled supply drop is two months away. I can't wait that long. The station cannot properly operate with the people here in the condition that they are. Have you told them it's urgent?

Yes. The supply visit was the message I got back.

You go back to them again . . . are these conversations being recorded?

Yes.

Take them the recording. Make them listen. I will demand an enquiry into whether you've done this . . .

I want it done.

The next transmission was on the second tape, two days later, timed at 9 a.m.:

78

This is Andrei Ivanovich. Why hasn't there been any response? Conditions here are worsening. There is hair discolouration I cannot account for. I have found evidence of Yuri Sergeevich developing a left eye cataract for which there is no medical record before we left Moscow less than a month ago, which is medically impossible. And two more, Valentina Valerivich and Oleg Vasilevich, are now confined to bed. I want personally to speak to someone from the Institute. Arrange that for me? Urgently. We are in an emergency situation here!

The voice was breaking, becoming cracked, a different person on the next communication, at 4 p.m. the same day. This was fainter, unidentified:

Andrei Ivanovich has fallen, outside the station . . . he thinks it's his pelvis that is broken . . . we're trying to lift him on to a sled but it's difficult, with only three of us still strong enough . . . not strong enough . . . who's there from the Institute . . . ? I can relay messages . . . help . . . you must help . . . please help . . .

There is no one here from the Institute. Where's Gennardi Varlomovich? We need to speak to the team leader. Bring Gennardi Varlomovich to the radio

Gennardi Varlomovich is unconscious . . . he's still breathing but can't be roused . . . get someone here, quickly . . . we're dying . . .

There was a gap of three days between the next dated and timed exchange and it was disjointed and discordant, like a recording device accidentally left on at a gathering – a meeting or a party – that the participants didn't know about. There was no call sign or identification. The demands to know if the connection was to Moscow were faint and uncertain, people shouting from a distance. Or closer but weak-voiced, forcing themselves hopefully to make themselves heard.

. . . Moscow . . . ? Is that Moscow . . . ? One voice, no name.

. . . help us . . . please help us . . . A woman's voice, no name.

. . . they're dead . . . Viktor [indecipherable] *. . .* A shot [indecipherable]. A third voice, male.

This is Moscow. You are talking with Moscow. The Ministry have promised a helicopter but we have no time . . . no day . . . there will be people coming . . . leave your receiver channel on . . .

Two hours later the woman's voice, sounding fainter than before: *Moscow . . . where's Moscow . . . where's the helicopter . . . ?*

No notification yet.

The following day there was no discernible exchange, just demands from Moscow: *Research Station Eight? Research Station Eight? There will be a rescue team in three days . . . we need contact. Research Station Eight . . . ?*

Movement, shuffling, once a cry – maybe a woman's voice – but no words.

Every hour – reducing after three to thirty minutes, then quickly to fifteen – came the Moscow demand for contact with the promise of rescue although still not for three days. 'Research Station Eight, Research Station Eight' became an unanswered litany. There was only one final exchange on the third tape, dated the day – within an hour – of the initial alarm from the American station at Noatak:

Moscow . . . ? Moscow . . . ? This is Viktor Porfirevich . . . there are only three of us left . . . we have . . . There was a very long, wheezed pause, with indecipherable talk in the background. *. . . We've managed to get the tender on to the snowtrack, for Valentina Valerivich . . . unwell . . . very unwell. Petr Viktorovich is blind. The weather . . .* Another long break, an actual scream of either pain or frustration, then a male shout *. . . the disease . . . have to get away from the disease . . . Polyarnik . . . we're trying for Polyarnik . . . send rescue there . . . can't wait . . .*

Viktor Porfirevich! Don't leave the station! The helicopter

80

is on its way. Just wait . . . don't leave the station . . .

. . . Can't wait . . . too late . . . A sudden background noise, the woman's cry again *. . . waited too long . . . Polyarnik . . .*

Paul Spencer turned the machine off with a positive snap. There was the immediate silence that seemed the inevitable response to every new development. Spencer, who'd seized the opportunity to operate the playback to regain the centre stage he'd lost earlier in the day, said: 'That's it. All of it.'

'Where's the Russian station?' demanded Partington.

'A place called Iultin. It's in the Chukotsky Khrebet region of Siberia, inside the Arctic Circle,' replied Spencer.

'How were we listening?' persisted the President.

Spencer hesitated. 'Noatak.'

'How far, in terms of miles, is Noatak from Iultin?' came in Amanda.

Spencer shrugged. 'A thousand miles. Maybe less, in fact I think it could be less. Say seven hundred fifty.'

'You think they monitored us, from Iultin?' asked Amanda.

'It's possible,' admitted Spencer.

'If they did, they'll know our people were infected, too,' picked up Robin Turner. 'You think it could be the same source of infection?'

Amanda said: 'It certainly sounds like the same *cause*. It's a question for Stoddart's team.' Events were moving too fast for the sort of detailed consideration she intended – she'd only had the car ride back from Fort Detrick to reflect upon it – but the encounter with Jack Stoddart had unsettled her. Even taking into account the personal effect of Patricia Jefferies's death, he'd been unnaturally subdued compared to the combative, coherent person she'd seen on TV confront – and usually out-argue – industry and political figures who tried to dismiss ozone depletion as unimportant. She hoped the obvious self-recrimination was quickly recoverable. With every passing day – every passing minute, it seemed – the chances of maintaining the insisted upon secrecy diminished.

Stoddart had in the past been an insufferable political pain in the ass. He had cost scientific research in general, and

81

in particular the environmental lobby of which he was the appointed messiah, a lot of withheld or withdrawn finance. But Amanda didn't regard that as her current problem, despite carrying the administration's scientific portfolio. Her current and possibly ongoing problem was going to be weathering the storm – a scale ten hurricane at least – that was going to break around them when everything became public. And when that happened the publicly known, publicly respected and usually publicly eloquent Jack Stoddart was going to be a very necessary publicly waving standard-bearer. Which, judging from that morning's performance, he was far short of being. It was something that had to be corrected.

'Left them there to die?' demanded Partington, nodding to the tape player. 'Moscow abandoned them, didn't they? Nothing since then?'

There was an awkward silence which Richard Morgan didn't hurry to fill, as he would normally have done, leaving Spencer to stumble the reminder of what Partington had clearly forgotten. 'Noatak was destroyed . . . burned . . . like the Antarctic. To prevent any spread, if the station was in some way the source, had caused, the outbreak.'

If Partington was discomfited he didn't show it. 'Don't we have any other way of hearing what's going on there?'

'Not ground source,' said Spencer. 'We could reposition a satellite.'

'What Institute were they talking about?'

'Their Scientific Institute,' responded Amanda, at once. 'Part of their Science Ministry.'

Still addressing Spencer, the President said: 'Can we hear what's going on there?'

Spencer said: 'It's one of the Moscow satellites we'll have to move over Siberia but there are others, in geostationary orbit. I can use the time and dates on the tapes we've already got for references to run a transmission check on anything from the Institute.'

'Do it. What about that background stuff we couldn't properly hear?'

'Already being enhanced, from the master tapes,' promised

82

Spencer. 'We've already voice-printed. There were seven, in total. We're going back, through everything recorded before, to pick up what identities we can.'

'This elevates a problem that didn't need to get any bigger,' said the Secretary of State. 'There's no way we can open any dialogue with the Russians without their knowing we're still spying on them.'

'They know that anyway, just as we know they're still spying on us,' said Partington impatiently. 'What's the big deal?'

'And Moscow will know we've evidence of the abandonment,' said Spencer.

'We can't go on referring to all this without a code name,' announced Partington. He snapped his fingers in feigned recollection. 'What was that place – that valley or something like that – where it was perfect and people always stayed young, as long as they didn't leave it?'

'Shangri-La,' provided Spencer obediently.

'That's what we'll call it!' declared Partington, thinking in future headlines. 'The Shangri-La Strain.'

'That's good, Mr President,' praised Morgan hurriedly. 'That's very good indeed.'

Jesus! thought Amanda, although she smiled and nodded in matching praise.

The arrival from Alaska was another recreation of a sci-fi film set – Stoddart and Pelham in protective moon suits, like everyone else – except for the familiarity of the four sagging body bags. The three suited survivors were able to walk unaided into the isolation building, although each was flanked by attentive escorts. Stoddart couldn't remember making the same journey. He stripped off in the director's area, in which he'd been allocated an office, and followed Pelham along the viewing gallery corridor. The arrival room was at the very end, the three men already seated, still suited. Stoddart only had the vaguest recollection of having been in the same room himself, four – or was it five, six maybe? – days earlier. On the ledge in front of the observation window the identities – with their sciences and nationalities – were allocated against the numbered seats in which the three sat, which Stoddart found vaguely offensive, making them numerical experiments. The one American, Darryl Matthews, was a paleobotanist. Harold Norris, the Englishman, and Henri Lebrun, who was French, were both recorded as climatologists.

'You're in charge,' prompted Pelham.

'I . . .' started Stoddart, but stopped, swept by his inadequacy. 'I need your help . . . need to know what you want, medically . . . what to tell them . . .'

The men on the other side of the glass straightened at Pelham's voice, their heads coming up towards the window. Stoddart thought Lebrun's reaction was slower than the other two. Pelham talked of their being quarantined for immediate medical examination and investigation for which they would be isolated each from the other. That would take at least twenty-four hours, after which they would be asked for their personal recollections which were needed in the most precise and intimate detail.

'Please think about it, during the examinations. Talk to the doctors when things come to you . . . everything will be recorded automatically. We don't care how much repetition there is. The importance is that nothing is missed.'

'You don't know what it is?' challenged Matthews, at once. Even through the distortion of the headset his voice was strong.

Pelham hesitated. 'Not yet.'

'So there's no treatment?' said Norris. His voice was weaker but Stoddart decided more from uncertainty that from affliction.

'There will be antibiotics,' said the installation director.

The various cocktails that were experimented with upon Patricia, remembered Stoddart. He was recovering, annoyed at his difficulty a few minutes earlier.

'Right away?' pressed Norris.

'There'll need to be the preliminary examination . . .'

Pelham hesitated again. 'Do any of you think you're infected?'

There were cowled head movements between the three. In scarcely accented English Lebrun said simply: 'My hair is changing colour. And I'm losing it. That happened to the others. It means I'm dying.'

'Antibiotics could halt it, until we make a positive diagnosis,' said Pelham.

Sure he was not visible through the separating glass, Stoddart looked sharply at the other man, who didn't return the look. Wanting now to get into the exchange – sure that at least two of the men were physically capable of answering – Stoddart quickly identified himself but before he could ask his question Norris said: '*The* Jack Stoddart? You think warming's to do with this?'

'We haven't even begun the assessment yet,' said Stoddart. 'But what about your data? Has it all been brought back?'

'I think so,' said Norris. 'Bill Perkins was the team leader: died two days ago. I know he began assembling things but I don't know what happened to it. It was panic in the end.'

'What about your readings over the last month?' pressed Stoddart, remembering Jane Horrocks's notes of unexpected ice softness but not wanting to lead the other man. 'Anything that surprised you?'

'The warmth,' said Norris, at once.

'Did you bring your personal data back with you?' asked Stoddart.

'Some notebooks, maybe,' said the man. 'Most of the stuff was among what Perkins was assembling.'

'Henri?' coaxed Stoddart.

The Frenchman's head was slow coming up again. 'What?'

'Any of your experiments in the last month produce something you didn't expect?'

There was no immediate reply. Then Lebrun said: 'It was the beginning of summer—'

'Predictable temperatures, in your opinion?' Stoddart interrupted, abandoning the determination not to lead and wanting to concentrate the Frenchman's wandering mind.

'At least three degrees warmer than it should have been, for the time of the season.'

'Have you brought back your personal research with you? Or was it part of the main archive?'

'Some. Not all. Some in the main archive . . .'

Pelham made a positive move beside Stoddart and said, softly: 'We need to get them into examination.' To Stoddart's nod of acceptance the scientist said more loudly: 'Let's get you into treatment now,' and on cue overalled medics came in to lead the three away.

As they made their way back along the corridor, Stoddart said: 'There's something obscene about that . . . like going to mental asylums a hundred years ago to look at the afflicted.'

'It's not the same,' rejected Pelham, almost irritably. 'It's practical. Necessary.'

'"Get you into treatment"?' quoted Stoddard, questioningly. '"Antibiotics could halt it, until we make a positive diagnosis"?'

'People who give up in the expectation of dying die quicker than those who believe they've got a chance,' said Pelham. 'I'm not expecting an overnight cure but there just might be something we could identify and block.'

He'd been presumptious, Stoddart decided. 'I think it would be a good idea if I was brought fully up to date with what medical findings there have been.'

'Wouldn't it be better to wait until the British and French contingent arrive, for everyone to hear at the same time . . . ?' The man allowed one of his predictable pauses. 'Setting out what we've found so far won't take long.'

Within thirty minutes of settling into his assigned office, Jack Stoddart realized he would have been overwhelmed trying to assimilate medical evidence in addition to what else there already was to absorb.

He picked up the logs from the Antarctic field station and started to leaf through them. The only thing that appeared out of the ordinary – and to which he was refusing to attach too much significance because he would appear once more to be

86

mounting his favourite, ridden-to-exhaustion hobby horse – were the early references to the unexpected mildness at the beginning of the South Pole's winter.

Harry Armstrong's team had been the first to occupy the newly built and now destroyed field station, forty miles east of the Amundsen-Scott base, and the initial indication, six weeks earlier, was predictably in the official log of Armstrong himself, like Stoddart a climatologist. It was, in fact, on the second day of their arrival, before any of the scientists had properly set up their experiments.

Bikini weather Armstrong had noted, light heartedly. Then, more seriously, two days after that: *Thawing, despite the onset of darkness, instead of freezing.* The next mention, one day later, was in Jane Horrocks's notebook. As the geologist in the party her job had been to take deep core bores, hopefully to retrieve samples dating from the Oligocene period from the permanent Antarctic ice sheet, and she'd already recorded surface softness far more extensive than she'd experienced anywhere around Amundsen-Scott or McMurdo. *Making the job easier*, she'd logged. *Maybe possible to sink deeper than intended.* There was, however, no record of her having done so. Her data log ended with her bore penetrating less than two metres, little more than a start.

That was on the fifth day after their arrival: the day of the first mention of whatever it was that attacked them. Again it was in the log of Armstrong, the team leader. *Bucky complaining of extreme tiredness. George too.* Then: *Have decided not to bother assembling satellite dish until the fatigue passes. Feeling it myself.* The entry was followed, with fateful irony, by: *Jane says we're all getting old.* There was another weather reference the day after: *Literally the lull before the storm. Heavier than normal snows. Need to get the dish operating as soon as possible. Need help. Urgently need help.*

Jane unwell, like the rest of us, read the next entry. *Weather closing in. Need to talk to Neilson at McMurdo.*

Which he had, Stoddart remembered. The first disjointedly relayed symptoms had been that day, baffling the resident physician. Armstrong wrote of lassitude and of forgetting the necessary field station routine and of arguments with George Bedall, the astrophysicist. The first mention of hair change was in the diary of the already balding Bedall: *Everyone's hair changing. Mine gone. This is ridiculous.*

All the handwriting was changing by now, scrawling and unsteady. Jessup wrote: *We're becoming old. Visibly. I'm having problems seeing. Harry can't properly raise McMurdo. No one knows why it's happening. Very frightened.*

On the day that Bedall had written of his growing blindness, Jane's entry read: *Too tired to eat. Do anything. Please let the weather lift: please God. There's the baby. What about the baby?*

The reason for Jane Horrocks's request to shorten her McMurdo tour, Stoddart guessed. Brownlow, the director of McMurdo and their boss, couldn't have known: he wouldn't have approved of Jane going on an arduous field mission if he had. And she clearly hadn't told Patricia. What about her husband, Peter? Stoddart remembered. An air traffic controller, at Reagan airport. Would he have been told – would all the families have been told – as the result of Brownlow's message to Washington?

For the next thirty minutes Stoddart did little more than sit and stare at the stacked dossiers, including those that had just been delivered from Alaska, unsure in what order to begin a master file for the scientists on their way to Fort Detrick as well as for Amanda O'Connell's political group in Washington. Chronologically, he determined finally, at least totally to prepare himself. The master file could provide an abbreviated account, annotated for longer references from the mass of disordered material in front of him.

He separated the already scanned, but incompletely remembered logs of the Antarctic field station and further subdivided them against the names of those who'd manned it, beginning with that of Harry Armstrong, its leader. It was a predictable recitation of the initial, early days' occupation of a field station: allocation of living quarters and space within the building between the scientists for their individual working areas and the outside setting-up of equipment and testing facilities. The only thing that Stoddart did not expect was the failure, within those early days, to assemble and erect the satellite dish, which contravened established procedure. And the bikini weather reference, so quickly followed by the more seriously recorded fact that it should have been colder with the onset of winter. Eager to find more, Stoddart jumped pages for an outside temperature reading, which he couldn't remember having seen as he picked through, and which was the most basic of operational requirements. Which hadn't been completed. The listing stopped on the day panic began to grip the station, although it was neatly recorded for the days of the bikini and thawing references. They *were* higher than the seasonal norm, fluctuating between 24° to 27°F. Stoddart acknowledged that he obviously needed an empirical comparison – and that the limited statistics in front of him didn't scientifically comprise it – but from memory he knew the temperature figures were showing it to have been at least five degrees warmer that the early seasonal norm.

Stoddart searched just as anxiously for the necessary wind speed and strength, to equate the wind chill factor, expecting to find it low. Which it wasn't. It was, if anything, slightly stronger – higher – than he expected, which made the thaw even more inexplicable. And for that reason it needed highlighting, not just as an unaccountable anomaly but as a suggestion for how the infection could have been transmitted, and not necessarily from the proximity of the affected station itself. Nowhere in Harry Armstrong's notes was there any positive, professional climatic observation, which Stoddart conceded to be hardly surprising, so quickly did they fall victim to the senility strain; the man hadn't had time properly to *start* working professionally.

Determined upon absolute scientific objectivity, Stoddart moved on to what records had been established by Bucky Jessup, almost at once knowing a sweep of disappointment, although what the meteorologist had noted was more precise, more properly scientific, than Armstrong's log. The very precision was the problem. Jessup had minutely recorded the installation of his wind speed and direction monitors, as well as the cloud, precipitation and moon duration sensors but nowhere was there any analysis, which again Stoddart conceded was probably impossible over so short a period, but which still might have helped.

From the experimental agenda in the preparation of which he had participated at McMurdo, Stoddart knew Jane Horrocks and George Bedall had been expected to work jointly on their overlapping research. Jane's principal geological project had been to sink ice cores as deeply as possible to retrieve oxygen isotopes for age comparison with similar core sinks in Greenland. During the McMurdo planning, they'd speculated the possibility of a 'gold lode' discovery of an interglacial volcanic ash layer that could have been chemically dated even to the last of the tectonic shifts when the Antarctic was just separating from the temperate land mass known as Gondwanaland, made up of what was now South America, Africa, India, Australia and New Zealand. Stoddart had personally doubted a field station bore capable of penetrating the ice sheet that deeply, but hadn't argued against the inclusion of a palaeobotanist. George Bedall's remit had been to isolate any nothofagus fossils that would have been further proof of Antarctica's land link with New Zealand – where the bushy nothofagus was still indigenous – during the Pliocene era.

There was no record in either of their logs of a single core being sunk, but rereading Jane Horrocks' notes, Stoddart appreciated for the first time that Jane had used technically improper but possibly vitally important words to describe the ice softness. More than once she'd called it frazil, which was a slush of ice crystals in the first stages of forming sea ice, when the water surface cooled to 28.8°F. And she'd twice referred to it being grease ice, thin plates of crystals that slip easily over each other in the early formation of pack ice. Both applied to comparatively warmer sea conditions, not the minus temperatures of the inland South Pole.

Stoddart pushed away the raw data from the Antarctic

station and the master file notes he'd made, letting his impression form. Lax routine from Harry Armstrong, which had prevented more accurate and complete medical questioning, although they could still not have been rescued any earlier than they had been. Insufficient science – insufficient time to provide more – from anyone. Which left only the inexplicable – but still insufficient – references to unseasonal climatic conditions. Which certainly hadn't existed by the time they'd managed to get in from McMurdo. But from the viewing gallery conversation with the two trained climatologists from Alaska, appeared to have been mirrored in the Arctic Circle.

It was automatic for Stoddart to move on to the recollections of those who'd flown in with him, although having retrieved them from the waiting pile he stopped, unwilling to go on.

That's what you had to do. The right thing. For the research to start. Who'd said that? For a moment Stoddart's mind blanked. Amanda O'Connell, he remembered. Easy, glib reassurances, empty politician's reassurances saying he couldn't have known and that the deaths couldn't have been prevented either. Patricia hadn't blamed him, though. Not once, not even when she'd been dying. Or had she? Had she written what she couldn't bring herself to say?

Stoddart sorted the dossiers, finding hers. The writing was hurried from the beginning in her urgency to get everything down, the pen often not lifted from the page so that the words were looped together. But everything – on the initial pages at least – was legible. And she'd written as the scientist – the virologist – that she was. She'd suggested that the senility was caused by an unknown virus trapped within the ice but somehow released by an experiment or even by the sinking of the piles upon which the station had been built to lift it free of its ice foundation A wild hypothesis, though Stoddart, but then what else was there, apart from wild hypotheses! Patricia's account, the writing beginning to fade from precision into unevenness, nevertheless led seamlessly into the scene upon their arrival at the field

91

station. Her observations remained scientifically precise – each of the South Pole victims described in as much detail as Patricia had felt able to note for a medical opinion – and it was not until the seventh page of her account that Patricia reached the decision to bring the bodies out with them. Which she recorded as being her insistence. Had she really believed that, in her dying days? It wasn't his recollection. Stoddart's memory was of her supporting his demands that the bodies be evacuated, not of her initiating the decision as she'd recorded here. *It was essential that autopsies be conducted as soon as possible to isolate the cause of the infection, which I repeat, I believe to be viral.* His near abandonment followed chronologically – dispassionately – in the narrative. *Before team leader Stoddart returned with the station data, James Olsen demanded take-off, insisting he had seen Stoddart fall and remain lying just outside the station, an obvious victim of the infection. Olsen was supported by everyone else. My objection was ignored. Olsen stated 'He's dead. Dying. If we stay we'll all die.' The pilot reported the aircraft in danger of being stranded, through icing, and commenced take-off. I made it clear I would demand an enquiry upon return to McMurdo. Dr Neilson, who until now had remained silent, supported me, claiming to be able to see team leader Stoddart. The plane turned for take-off. I claimed to be able to see team leader Stoddart too, which I could not, initially, because of the severity of the blizzard which unexpectedly lifted. The pilot, Burke, said he could see Stoddart, too, and stopped the aircraft. Stoddart, in an advanced state of collapse, was brought aboard, with the documentation he had retrieved. I consider an enquiry should still be held and wish this statement to be included as a deposition if it is not possible for me to record a separate account, under oath.* So close, thought Stoddart: so hair's breadth close to his being left to die made all the more overwhelming – if that were possible – by the paradox of his being the only one to survive.

Patricia's handwriting, already uneven – the looped joins becoming more prevalent – began to degenerate almost immediately afterwards. She'd begun omitting conjunctions and prepositions, too, so that before it became virtually unreadable it was just primary word notes, although still comprehensible. Nowhere was there any recrimination or accusation of his having caused her death.

Nor was there in the much shorter and more quickly illegible statement of Dr Morris Neilson. Like Patricia, Neilson had attempted to keep his declaration as unemotionally – and medically – factual as possible, in which he'd only partially succeeded. The emotion came towards the end, in what amounted to a farewell letter to his wife, Barbara, which Stoddart stopped reading, embarrassed. *I want to speak to my wife,* Stoddart recalled. What about all the relatives? He'd promised Patricia he'd speak to her brother, John. In San Antonio. The fuller address would be in her personnel file. He jotted a reminder on his master file pad and separated the doctor's letter from the man's Antarctica account. It needed to go to the man's wife. The American address would also be in Neilson's file.

James Olsen had made no attempt to write a coherent statement. It was entirely a personal accusation – a diatribe – against Stoddart personally for insisting on removing the bodies. Twice Olsen used the word murderer and had attempted quasi-legal phrases insisting his wife instruct a lawyer named Jacobson to sue Stoddart, by name, as well as the US government, which he accused of imprisonment and refusal to allow him his constitutional rights.

Stoddart was shocked, needing to read twice what Olsen had recorded to fully absorb it, all his guilt and self-doubt flooding back. Although not necessarily coherent, the argument about whether or not to leave the bodies was factual enough, even to him invoking his authority as group leader. It *had* been his decision, conceded Stoddart. It didn't matter that Patricia and to a lesser extent the doctor had supported him. He was responsible and if he was responsible then he supposed that legally he was liable. For what, he asked himself. Millions, probably. He doubted his government contract to work at McMurdo carried any sort of personal liability insurance and he certainly didn't have any policies to cover the situation. Financially – as well as professionally, perhaps – he would be wiped out. Destroyed, with no defence.

Olsen had been kept in isolation, here at Fort Detrick. The man might verbally have made the accusations, leaving them on the automatically registering tapes, but there was the possibility that the four pages at which he was now staring down were the only formal complaint. And that hadn't been witnessed or notorized by anyone. There was the Antarctic data he'd already read and now that from Alaska. And the survivors from there would be asked to write their recollections. By the time the senility disease was identified there would be a mountain – several mountains – of paperwork. It would be very easy to lose these four pages: remove them from the record. It had been the right – the proper – decision to bring the bodies back and destroy the station, particularly now that the disease had spread to the other Pole. Had he not done what he did, it could have infected Amundsen-Scott and even McMurdo, killed dozens more. Hundreds, thousands. Which it still might – could – having broken out virtually 13,000 miles from its first appearance. Every justification – *unarguable* justification – for bringing the victims out, enabling the medical and scientific investigation to begin, even though from what Pelham had just told him it didn't appear so far to have resulted in any findings. Pelham would swear to that: Walter Pelham, director of the Fort Detrick microbiological research establishment, the man who would be named – accused – in any imprisonment litigation. So easy, Stoddart thought again: so absurdly, justifiably, arguably easy to erase the problem.

James Olsen had a wife to whom he'd issued his dying orders, so anxiously that there had been no words of love or affection, as there had been in what Neilson had written. But did Olsen have children? Did Neilson? Or the pilot, Chip Burke, whose Alzheimer's had been so bad and so quickly developing that nothing he had written made any contribution?

Stoddart was engulfed, almost literally, by a tidal wave of embarrassment and near guilt. What the fuck was he thinking about? Contemplating? Men – husbands and maybe fathers – had died, children, possibly, orphaned. Carefully, particularly, Stoddart neatly re-established James Olsen's complete, accusational dossier, finding it difficult to believe that he could ever have allowed himself to dispose of it. The only separation Stoddart allowed himself was that between what he considered personal and should go to the families and what he believed contributed to the investigation, which had been the purpose of the accounts in the first place.

Stoddart was reaching out for the first of the Alaska station details when his telephone rang, startling him because it seemed a lifetime ago since he'd heard the sound of a ringing telephone.

Amanda O'Connell said: 'We've got intelligence that it's affected a Russian research station in Siberia.'

In Misaki two men – one aged twenty-two, the other thirty – whose hair had turned inexplicably white, both of whose skin had begun to wither and one of whom had begun to go blind, were admitted to hospital by baffled primary care doctors. So were four members of their individual families, including a father and grandmother who died within twenty-four hours. The two men had been seamen on the recently successful Japanese fishing fleet, the factory ship captain of which, deep again in Antarctic waters, was confined to his cabin with what seemed to be influenza that he'd already passed on to three other crewmen. He'd become ill within hours of treating himself to the raw whale's tongue delicacy of his previous voyage. The Misaki families had also eaten whale meat.

Ten

There had initially been a lot to hear – as well as to see – although there had been very little conversation within the starkly functional State Department conference room at Foggy Bottom. Virtually nothing more, in fact, beyond what Paul Spencer needed to identify the remarkably similar satellite and aerial footage of the fire-destroyed stations in Antarctica, Alaska and Siberia, the configuration of what had been the outbuildings at Noatak and Iultin forming an ironically appropriately shaped black question mark on the snow bleached Arctic landscape.

There were equally large question marks, for an even larger number of uncertainties, in the minds of everyone present, none of which was outwardly obvious because this was a serious gathering of politicians and diplomats for whom expressing either sincere emotion or binding opinion was unthinkable.

Central to each, after the Russian disclosure, was that it was absurd to believe they could for much longer prevent this ever-escalating situation becoming public. From that acceptance stemmed the individual attitudes, which despite very slight variations came down to personal survival at the expense of everyone else. Completing the cynicism was the fact that everyone knew, or thought they knew, what everyone else intended and were prepared for the figurative arm-wrestling that was to come.

Having surveyed those assembled around him, Peter Reynell, who never suffered self-doubt, was quite confident he was strong enough. American Secretary of State, Robin Turner wasn't, recognizing what the president wanted him to achieve to be too blatant.

'Has there been any discussion with Moscow?' opened Reynell, carefully skirting the awkwardness of how the Russian outbreak had been discovered, intent on getting as much protection as possible with the benefit of having British ambassador Sir Alistair Dowding – and the records of the limited and strictly vetted secretariat – as a witness against London back-stabbing.

'We thought there should be this meeting first, to get everyone's input,' said Robin Turner.

The Secretary of State's personal decision or something agreed between him and Henry Partington? wondered Amanda O'Connell.

To give the impression in Moscow that it had been British or French eavesdropping, not American, Reynell instantly recognized. 'America had the advantage of the information before today: of having had time to consider it. How do you think it should be handled?'

Turner shifted uncomfortably and Amanda decided that behind the stripe-suited, club-tied languid elegance of the Englishman was a professional strongarm not to be underestimated, a mistake Turner was coming ever closer to making.

Gerard Buchemin entered the contest before Turner could reply. The French science minister said: 'There's obviously little sense in working independently.'

'That goes a long way towards our thinking about the Shangri-La Strain,' seized Turner, spared a direct reply.

'The *what*!' exclaimed Reynell, disbelievingly.

'The President's choice,' said Amanda quickly.

Reynell kept any further reaction from his face, turning briefly to the record clerks and their apparatus. Determined against letting the Secretary of State escape he said: 'So you have already decided to talk to Moscow?'

'After allowing you both the opportunity to consult with your respective governments,' Turner tried again.

Betraying – and admitting – his Achilles elbow far too easily, judged Reynell. 'I don't consider it's at all necessary for me to talk to London. We're quite willing for you to deal with Moscow.'

'So is France,' quickly came in Buchemin, alert to Reynell's manoeuvre. 'You are, after all, hosting the investigation: giving us the benefit of what you've already learned and done.'

Barely bothering with spy-gathering ambiguity, Reynell lifted and let drop the Russian translation and what had been enhanced from it before saying: 'What else do you expect to get from sources like this or from how you obtained the photographs of the Iultin station?'

'Very little,' conceded Turner. He acknowledged how badly he'd done with an impossible remit and wanted to end the encounter as quickly as possible.

'There was no trace of the three who apparently fled the station?' asked Buchemin.

'None that we were able to detect.'

'Do your photo-analysts think you would have done, if they'd still been out in the open?' persisted Reynell.

'They think so,' said Turner, looking openly towards Amanda for help.

'So it's fair to assume they were picked up: rescued?'

'I think so.'

'It's possible, of course, that the Russians will know of this disease,' lured Reynell, refusing to use the preposterous presidential title. 'Have a treatment or a cure.'

'It doesn't sound like it, from the transcript,' said Amanda, responding to her superior's plea.

'If they haven't, are you going to invite the Russians here, as well as their scientists?' asked the saturnine, sleek-featured Buchemin, beginning another arm-wrestling bout.

Turner said: 'That would depend upon Moscow's reaction.'

There *had* been Oval Office discussion between the Secretary of State and Partington, Amanda decided. So, she was the chosen one to fall, in the event of failure or disaster. But she'd already accepted that, so she had no reason to feel surprised or disappointed. Just to be tip-toe careful. But she'd already accepted the need for that, too.

The Frenchman tapped his copy of the Russian material and

98

said: 'It might make easier your conversation with Moscow if they knew Paris has been brought in to share the problem: that we're aware of it.'

Why not, thought Reynell. 'And London, too.'

'They were slow responding to an emergency,' Amanda pointed out, wanting them to know she understood the inference of their gesture.

'Remarkably so,' smiled Reynell. He hadn't expected a woman to be part of the team: certainly not a full busted, long-legged thirtysomething blonde whose fittingly glacial, distant-eyed aloofness it might be diverting to thaw. He wondered if she'd be more difficult to manipulate than her Secretary of State. Still smiling at her he said: 'How do you see us operating?'

Amanda chose not to regard the question as a *double entendre*. Succinctly, announcing them as arrangements already in place rather than suggestions for them to agree, she outlined their working use of the presidential guest quarters at Blair House, provision for a matching scientific group at Fort Detrick and Paul Spencer's role as liaison between the two.

'At what stage – and how – do you envisage our going public?' Reynell asked the Secretary of State.

Christ, this man was an operator! thought Amanda, in reluctant admiration. Turner – America – was likely to be damned by whatever answer the man gave. On the basis of this discussion she doubted if Turner would risk another appearance. It began as a cynical reflection but hardened into a positive thought: if Turner was frightened off she'd have to be included in – or at least be told of – the inner thinking from the Oval Office.

'We'd welcome your thoughts on that,' invited Turner, following another presidential instruction. Ineptly he added: 'I assume there was some discussion before your leaving London?'

'Not at Cabinet level,' avoided Reynell easily and for once honestly. 'At this stage my being here hasn't gone beyond it being a fact-finding mission, any more than that of my chief scientific advisor assigned to Fort Detrick.' Had Buxton's insistence that he leave London at once on Concorde, leaving Geraldine Rothman to follow later, been another move against him? Probably.

'Which fairly accurately sums up my position,' said Buchemin, content yet again to follow the Englishman's lead.

'Premature disclosure could result in unnecessary public alarm,' recited Turner.

'Yes?' coaxed Reynell, questioningly.

'Which should therefore be avoided,' continued the American.

'Until when?' asked the Frenchman.

'Until a cure or treatment is found,' said Turner.

Amanda wasn't sure if she'd prevented the wince. She hoped she had.

'What if one isn't found?' demanded Reynell, slamming the American's arm once more flat against the imaginary table. 'There hasn't been, for AIDS . . . not even for the common cold. There's surely got to be proper contingency planning?'

Turner smiled at last. 'Which is precisely the reason you have been invited here, to work with Amanda. *You're* our contingency planners.'

Good try but not good enough, dismissed Reynell. 'I was looking beyond, to the time and place when the President and our respective premiers have to make such a declaration . . .' The pause was to metronome timing. '. . . Any announcement of this magnitude will surely have to be a joint one, at their level of authority?' For once – briefly – he felt a blip of uncertainty, willing the man towards the right response.

'I would expect so. Of course,' conceded the flustered Secretary of State.

The euphoria exploded through Reynell. This was better than any back-door campaign of whispered, nudged innuendo. He had, on record – in front of the witnessing British ambassador – established that Simon Buxton couldn't avoid being one of the harbingers of doom disclosing a worse-than-modern equivalent of the Black Death. While he, Peter Reynell, could

100

emerge as a man who'd so tirelessly battled behind the scenes to defeat it. It needed finessing but he could make it work.

It had all been too quick, too confusing, for Geraldine Rothman to encompass properly. There had been a bewildering, near offensive insistence that she re-sign the Official Secrets Act she'd already sworn and an even more bewildering drive to London airport with an anonymous Cabinet Office mandarin who'd smelled of tobacco and talked with arm waving, frustrating vagueness of epidemics. So, on the flight to Washington she'd only been able to think of the running-away escape so suddenly thrust upon her from the mismanaged wreckage of her personal life over the last two years. After the third gin, none of which she should have drunk with the medication she was still taking after the operation which like everything else had gone wrong, she'd mumbled aloud 'Goodbye, Michael' uncaring at the curious look from the man sitting beside her. She hadn't expected to be met by another anonymous figure – this time an urgent, polished-faced embassy official – at Dulles, but expected at least some guidance during the drive to Fort Detrick. But again the man had said he didn't know, as quickly as he'd denied any knowledge of Fort Detrick's function. She wished she hadn't had the wine and brandy with the meal, after the gins. But most of all that Peter Reynell hadn't been such a pompous asshole and gone ahead, leaving her virtually without the slightest idea why she'd been despatched in the panic that she had.

Geraldine had been to the British microbiological research establishment at Porton Down, in Wiltshire, and recognized the similarity between the largely single-storeyed, segregated blocks of Fort Detrick. As she walked towards a fenced-off area to the right of the gatehouse, where a carphone-alerted Jack Stoddart had been waiting to get her through the security checks, Geraldine said: 'We got some disaster from an experiment that's gone badly wrong?'

Stoddart said: 'A disaster, but not from here.'

101

Eleven

Jack Stoddart thought the awkward introductions and exchange of justifying academic qualifications was like seeing who could piss the highest up a lavatory wall, even though Geraldine Rothman, who won with a degree in forensic pathology in addition to those in genetics and epidemiology, was a woman, which might have made it physically difficult although not totally impossible. The French scientific advisor, Guy Dupuy, virtually tied in comparable masters and doctorates with Walter Pelham. An already prepared Stoddart acknowledged he was so lacking in any medical discipline that it was hardly worthwhile unzipping his fly.

Geraldine wished she hadn't drunk so much and hadn't forgotten about jetlag or tried to sleep while she'd waited for Dupuy to arrive, because she hadn't properly – only dozed – and had awakened with an aching head full of cotton wool. She hoped the coffee she was eagerly consuming would help although, unaware of Stoddart's comparison, she knew if she kept on drinking it she'd be up peeing all night or day or whenever it would be when she properly went to bed.

Stoddart actually felt a flicker of unease at consciously withholding the Iultin news from Pelham until now, to establish himself as the man in charge. Geraldine Rothman and Guy Dupuy still had so much to catch up with that the significance initially scarcely seemed to register.

Pelham, in whose office they were gathered, spread his hands in exasperation at the news and said: 'So what now!'

'Now we go straight on with what we've got to do; try to do,' said Stoddart, prepared for that question, too. 'Russia is, at the moment, a political consideration.'

Pelham let the decision settle. 'But our knowing it's affecting Russia hugely adds to the . . .' The director stumbled to a halt, groping for a large enough word. Unable to do so, he said, in disbelieving awareness: 'It's becoming a pandemic, isn't it? Growing, spreading, worldwide . . . ?'

'Unless we find a way to stop it . . . treat it,' said Stoddart.

'We haven't, not yet,' said Pelham, flatly.

'What have you got?' demanded Dupuy. 'Give us a starting point.'

For a moment Pelham hesitated, staring down at the preliminary autopsy reports and the pathology test results that made up the research dossier already given to each of them during the introductions. Coming up to them he said: 'If you want a name, it's classic Progeria afflicting adults. Which wasn't, until now, believed to be medically possible. It had not, however, visibly affected the foetus in Jane Horrocks's womb. In children, Progeria restricts body growth and stature—' he shuffled the papers in front of him, seeking something. 'We obviously had the full and very complete medical and physical records of everyone who died in Antarctica and those in the rescue party who contracted it. In each case there was the minimum of a two-inch height loss and every body measurement – chest, waist, biceps – diminished by almost an inch in circumference.' He made another pause. 'And from the time scale, which we also have, it occurred over a period of about twenty days.'

Geraldine said: 'I don't think we should restrict ourselves by labelling it Progeria. There are other conditions: Werner's Syndrome and a genetic mutation, Dyskeratosis Congenita. And physical shrinkage is normal in old age, through osteoporosis.'

Pelham nodded. 'Their size loss actually worsened the skin affect – in the end their body casings were literally too big for what they contained – but there was additionally substantial reduction of skin elasticity. Everyone, without exception, lost hair colouring and in most cases hair itself, sometimes resulting in extensive baldness . . .' He hesitated, to make a point. '. . . When those age conditions afflict they prevent

103

the growth of facial or pubic hair. Each adult victim so far has lost all body and pubic hair.'

'What arterial and vessel degeneration was there?' asked Dupuy. He was a fat, dishevelled man with over-long, ringletted hair, whose suit, clearly buttoned throughout the entire Atlantic flight, was concertinaed around him.

Pelham nodded again, acknowledging the symptom awareness. 'Atherosclerosis in three of the Antarctic victims and in two of those from the Noatak station. In the fourth Antarctic victim, George Bedall, it had developed into full blown arteriosclerosis, with heavy cholesterol in both atheromas and lipomas.'

'What about the women?' demanded Geraldine. Her head was clearing and the pain was going. She still needed to feel a lot better before going through the American findings in detail but this discussion was a useful beginning.

Pelham smiled, noting her symptom recognition as well and glad of the early indications of both their professional abilities. 'The body of the woman in Antartica, Jane Horrocks, was solidly frozen. It's possible she froze to death rather than ultimately died from old age, which would have halted the degeneration sufficiently to mislead us—' he hesitated, looking at Stoddart. 'That wasn't the case with Patricia Jefferies, one of the rescuers who fell victim and died here. We were able to keep her under the most intense observation for five days. Knowing the anti-ageing effect of progesterone it was one of the earliest treatments we attempted. Her final degeneration, like that of the other woman, was less pronounced than in any of the male victims.'

'So there is some slowing effect by administering the hormone?' persisted Geraldine.

Stoddart came forward in his chair, no longer embarrassed at withholding the Russian outbreak from the installation director, who hadn't told him this. 'Could that be a treatment? Something as simple as the female sex hormone?'

'It's a possible research path to follow,' allowed Pelham, doubtfully.

104

'Dependent upon the amount that's needed to be administered,' warned Geraldine, at once. 'A comparatively modest dosage can – and has – produced female characteristics in males. The development of breasts being the most obvious. A man could face the choice between dying or becoming hermaphrodite.'

It wasn't in any way intended to be amusing. No one smiled.

'The aetiology of Progeria isn't known,' reminded Dupuy, simply.

'Until now?' suggested Stoddart, remembering what Patricia had written. 'It's got to be an infection – a virus or bacteria – which for some reason is suddenly manifesting itself, becoming virulent in close to sub-zero conditions.'

Pelham helped himself to what little of the coffee Geraldine had left. 'That was our first investigation. We've subjected the organs, faeces, urine and tissue of every victim to every toxicological examination that is known to us here at this establishment. Which *is* every toxicological examination that's scientifically known and recorded. We failed to locate one single virus or bacteria we couldn't identify . . .'

'It's an unknown condition,' Dupuy said. 'Logically it could be caused by a bacterium or virus you couldn't recognize. If we don't know it, how can we identify it?'

'There would need to be some commonality,' argued Pelham. 'We isolated every schizomycete—' he looked at Stoddart. 'There was nothing rotting . . . putrefying . . . at the station?'

'Absolutely not. Everything was frozen solid.'

Indicating Stoddart again, Pelham said: 'Fortunately Jack thought to bring back their garbage. Again, no putrefaction in which bacteria could have grown.'

'I know it was the Antarctic . . . and the Arctic . . .' qualified Geraldine, before asking her question. 'But what about saprophytes?'

Again Pelham looked enquiringly at Stoddart who considered the question, glad he understood it. Slowly he said: 'There was no decaying plant matter, upon which any bacterium could have fed . . . no plants grow in the Antarctic . . .'

105

'But . . . ?' pressed Geraldine, aware of Stoddart's doubt.

'George Bedall was a palaeobotanist. His experiment was to work closely with Jane Horrocks, who was to sink ice bores as deeply as she could to retrieve oxygen isotopes, for period dating. George was looking for any nothofagus fossils – evidence of plant life during the Pliocene period. There might have been if Jane had sunk low enough . . .' He paused. 'The only anomaly I've discovered in the logs – not just from the Antarctic but from Alaska as well – is that temperatures at both places were higher than normal when the outbreaks occurred . . .' He stopped again, conscious of the abrupt concentration from the others in the room. '. . . Jane herself records that because of the ice softness she might be able to go deeper than she'd expected.'

'What about Bedall?' broke in Dupuy. 'Is there anything about plant fossils . . . plants even . . . in the core samples . . . ?'

Stoddart shook his head. 'No. There's nothing to suggest they even sunk one, before they became affected.'

'No samples . . . experiments . . . obvious at the station?' asked the Frenchman.

He couldn't remember, Stoddart realized, his stomach hollowing. No, he decided, just as quickly. They *had* collected all the data: he and Patricia and Olsen, and if Bedall had started collecting, making slides, there would have been a reference in his personal log and there wasn't. 'No.'

'You're sure?'

'Yes.'

'What about Alaska?' demanded Geraldine.

'I'm not through with everything from there. But one of the survivors, Darryl Matthews, is a palaeobotanist, too. He must have been there to carry out some plant research and he's here for us to ask.'

'This is good!' said Geraldine, excited despite her tiredness. 'We've potentially got something here!'

'It's a definite line of enquiry,' allowed Pelham, more soberly.

106

'We haven't considered parasitic bacteria,' said the Frenchman, also refusing any overreaction.

'No internal parasites were discovered by the autopsies in the faeces, urine or resident in the gut,' reported Pelham.

'What about external: fleas, mites, body lice . . . something you hadn't seen before?' said the Frenchman.

In the briefest of pauses that followed from the installation director, Stoddart wondered if such a search or test had been made. Then Pelham said: 'Nothing.'

The doubt had clearly occurred to Dupuy. He said: 'Nothing on the bodies or nothing on – or in – the clothing?'

'The bodies,' admitted Pelham. 'The clothing is still being examined. It's already been done visually and microscopically. Now it's being dissembled, for fibre tests under fluorescope lighting. After that there will be chemical analysis extending beyond parasitic search, to include microbes.'

The reply was too detailed for Pelham or his appropriate team not to be genuinely conducting the experiment, conceded Stoddart. 'So something might emerge from that source?'

'I would have expected to have found an indication by now,' cautioned Pelham.

'Which brings us to viruses,' said Dupuy.

'Hostile environment,' said Geraldine flatly.

'Some resistant or unaffected pathogens existed there. And in Alaska and in Siberia,' out-argued Dupuy. 'Anyone ever heard of anything that can survive in those conditions?'

'Yes,' replied Stoddart simply, glad to be able to make a contribution. 'In 1999 scientists from Montana University found proteobacteria and actionomycetes, microbes commonly associated with soil, embedded in ice in Lake Vostok, which is one of the ten deepest lakes in the world, almost 12,000 feet below the surface of the East Antarctic ice sheet. The estimate is that the microbes, which were still active, could be 500,000 years old: maybe even older than that.'

'And there's a famous experiment with scorpions, the oldest known prehistoric arachnida species,' reminded Geraldine. 'A number were frozen, until the ice blocks became solid; just as, according to what I've understood today, the victims' bodies were frozen in Antarctica. The scorpions were entombed in ice for varying periods: some for as long as a year. They went beyond hibernation – which they're not capable of achieving – into suspended animation. Within minutes of being released from the ice they were unaffected: their poison was actually more toxic than the scorpions that had been left unfrozen as part of the controlled study.'

'And if you're looking for viruses, what about the common cold? And influenza?' added Pelham.

'There's reference in the Antarctic logs to cold symptoms,' remembered Stoddart. 'The team leader, Armstrong, believed at first he was going down with flu—' Stoddart looked at Pelham. 'Did anyone who came back with me get a cold or flu?'

'Neilson and Burke had respiratory difficulties but nothing developed,' said Pelham.

'From the log dates, the last person died in the Antarctic station three days before we got there,' said Stoddart. 'By then it was way below freezing yet whatever it is was still virulent enough to infect four people.'

Pelham said: 'That's a pointer I've already flagged up in the preliminary medical assessments: it's in your dossiers. If it is a virus it's more likely to be transmitted through respiratory exhalation – coughing or sneezing or quite simply by breathing out – than through bodily function expulsion, after internal incubation. Any virus exiting the mouth would initially, very briefly, be wet but just as quickly it would dry, into an infectious droplet nuclei. It could survive – and travel – for a surprisingly long time: viruses are destroyed far more effectively by sunlight than by wet or cold.'

'What about a long *way*?' interrupted Stoddart. 'I haven't checked the wind speeds in Alaska yet but we know for a fact, because it stopped us getting there, that there was a blizzard around the Antarctic station for over a week. And there is log reference to strong winds even before the blizzard. How far could a gale blow droplets nuclei?'

'Answer your own question,' said Geraldine, which sounded

sharper than she'd intended. 'Ground winds can get into upper atmosphere wind flows, right?'

'Right,' agreed Stoddart.

'And upper atmosphere wind can be gale force?'

'Yes,' the climatologist agreed again.

'So there's your answer,' smiled Geraldine. 'If the virus got into the upper atmosphere it could be blown thousands of miles.' The smile went. 'Are there regular air currents, from Pole to Pole, like there are permanent sea currents in the oceans?'

'Yes,' said Stoddart. 'And I see where you're coming from. Two problems. Sun kills viruses, according to Walt. And it would be subjected to continuous sunlight – radiation – for most of an upper atmosphere transmission. Secondly, surely an airborne virus wouldn't stay in the upper atmosphere all the way from the south to the north pole, without some dropping and infecting people en route?'

'There's no logic in that,' supported Dupuy, to Pelham's nodded agreement.

Unabashed, Geraldine said: 'Let's agree that if it is a wind-borne virus there's the potential for it to be carried to the populated areas of the world?'

There was a moment's silence. 'Certainly something else – a risk – to be flagged up,' accepted Stoddart. 'Which brings us back full circle to where we began. And the point at which to establish a working understanding. What about your support staff?'

The question appeared to surprise both scientific advisors. Briefly lifting her fact file in front of her, Geraldine said: 'Yours is the research. Ours – as far as I can see at the moment – is the interpretation of your already assembled and tested data, which –' she swept her hand generally, to encompass the installation – 'we accept as empirical . . .'

Dupuy took up her pause. '. . . which is how I see it, too.'

The above-politics, internationally accepted dissemination and analysis of scientific information? Or a pathology-blaming escape hatch? wondered Stoddart. He was at once irritated by his own cynicism. That was Washington thinking, not for here.

After enough buck passing and paper shuffling at Langley to have defeated a Las Vegas casino pit boss, Paul Spencer's intentionally limited White House briefing became the burden of the CIA's directorate of science and technology and of Robert Stanswell, a twenty-five-year-old advertisement-responding Berkeley graduate who fortunately kept – and played – the hand he'd been dealt.

His initial curiosity was at influenza being given as the common cause of death for a shoal of minke whales washed up at Kochi, on Japan's southern Honshu island, and five others – two humpbacks and three bowheads – far to the north, at Oamori. When he carried out a computer search cross-referencing whales and influenza, he discovered similarly caused deaths in minke, fin, sei and humpback whales on Macquarie Island, the Australian protectorate deep in the southern Pacific, at Vishakhaptnam and Madras on India's Bay of Bengal, further south at Batticaloa on the east coast of Sri Lanka, and Concepción in Chile and Arica on the Chilean-Peruvian border. Astonishingly, until Stanswell ran a specific check through the CIA stations at the US embassies in Canberra, New Delhi, Colombo, Santiago and Lima, no connection had been made between the whale deaths and those so far caused by the outbreak of human influenza in the same locations. Most of the 1,200 fatalities were elderly. Fifteen of them – in Vishakhaptnam and Arica – were aged far beyond their years, the oldest being fifty, but in such places their premature ageing went unregistered.

A pedantic crossword fanatic to whom lateral thinking came naturally, Stanswell created programs to surf the net for newly manifesting, non-marine diseases in sea mammals. Within a week he had a file on the deaths from a dog-like distemper, on a near epidemic scale, of harp seals from Greenland and grey seals in England's North Sea.

Coincidentally the Science Foundation's David Hoolihan,

110

responding to the same remit, discovered that marine biologists were describing as an epidemic the wholesale death
of blue-fin tuna off South Australia from a herpes-type virus,
and when Hoolihan added marine biology as a reference term
to his web search, he found that whatever was destroying
the oyster beds of Chesapeake Bay, Maryland, was so new
it didn't have a name in any marine biology lexicon. A
bleaching disease devastating coral reefs in the Indian Ocean
was recorded as having reached the Caribbean in less than a
month. By the same coincidence, Hoolihan's account landed
on Paul Spencer's desk at the same time as that from the CIA
headquarters at Langley.

Twelve

H enry Partington had spent his entire political life trying – and usually succeeding – to avoid coming off the back foot, the inferior position he objectively realized he now found himself to be in. The inference of Moscow's abandonment of its Siberian station – and inference was all it could ever be – didn't, upon longer consideration, equate or mitigate American spying, despite every which way he'd tried to rehearse his approach. Which by itself was more than enough to be thoroughly pissed off about. But it wasn't by itself. In front of him was the word-for-word account of Robin Turner's meeting with the British and French science ministers, both of whom had handled Turner like the amateur he'd shown himself to be. He regretted now planning the telephone conversation as a witnessed exchange with the Russian president. He certainly wouldn't have agreed to the inclusion of Amanda O'Connell if he'd read the Turner debacle earlier. If he'd been able to – if there hadn't already been the necessary preliminaries of alerting Moscow to the intended call and delegating interpreters through whom the conversation would be conducted – Partington would have aborted the whole idea.

The Secretary of State and Amanda, escorted by Richard Morgan, arrived promptly on time, as instructed half an hour before the scheduled telephone link-up. For Turner's benefit – or rather the man's unsettling awareness – Partington very obviously lifted and tapped into order, with the title page facing outwards, the transcript of the previous day's meeting and just as obviously relegated the folder to a side table.

As he did so, only half looking at Turner, he said disparagingly: 'Anything emerged since that – or from that – to make what I've got to do any easier?' Would it be too blatant, even now, delegating Turner to make the call? Too late for that. Moscow had already been told it would be him, president to president: it would be a protocol offence substituting Turner. And from what he'd just read, Turner couldn't be risked to handle it anyway.

Turner said: 'I'm afraid not, Mr President.'

Amanda settled comfortably in her chair, conscious of the tension. Take your time, she told herself. That was essential, timing everything. The closer it got to the Moscow connection, the more effective she was going to be. From the man's alertness, she guessed Morgan detected the atmosphere, too.

Partington said: 'I'm going in bare-assed and I don't like it. Nothing from Fort Detrick?'

Turner, relieved, looked to Amanda. She said: 'Nothing that would help the conversation with Moscow.' Or improve Partington's temper, she thought.

Openly accusing, Partington said to his Secretary of State: 'I'd hoped for more from your initial meeting.'

'They both came with prepared agendas,' tried the academic.

'I thought we had one, too?' persisted Partington, relentlessly.

Fifteen minutes to go, timed Amanda. Morgan sat, withdrawn protectively inside his shell.

'Which I'm sure Amanda will be able to establish,' said Turner. 'It would have been a great mistake to have attempted to rush things on the basis of just one meeting.'

Bastard! thought the woman irritably. She didn't feel any sympathy for the man, after his trying to switch the onus on to her. Ten minutes to go, she estimated. Time for Robin 'Failure' Turner to witness some long overdue professionalism. She said 'I'm sure I'll be able to get things back on course.'

All three men looked sharply at her. Partington said: 'That's good to hear.'

113

'I've also been thinking of the difficulty of your approach to Moscow, Mr President,' she continued.

Partington's concentration came around fully upon her. 'And?'

'The North Pole has a strong magnetic field. And there is a lot of unpredictable electrical activity, particularly in the ionosphere. It quite often creates freak radio conditions: interference, interruptions . . . sometimes even interceptions . . .' Amanda had everyone's absolute attention now and liked it.

Partington, who rarely needed signposts, was beginning to smile. 'Go on!'

'I talked about it with some people at NSA last night. There's a lot of instances of airliners picking up outside communication . . .' She answered the president's expanding smile. 'All American carriers use the polar route, to and from Europe, when there's a stopover at Anchorage, Alaska. Some, in fact, virtually fly over Iultin. I checked that out last night, too . . .' Amanda had been unsure whether to disclose how far she'd taken her idea but from Partington's attitude decided she could. '. . . I'm told it would be possible, in fact, to splice some of the Noatak intercepts into an American pilot's exchange with Anchorage, just after take-off, and make a master tape from which it would technically be impossible to detect that it wasn't one original, freakish transmission. I told the NSA people that I found that difficult to believe and they said they could prove it so I told them to go ahead . . . just as an experiment, of course.'

'Of course,' accepted the beaming president. 'They say how long it would take them?'

'Midday today,' said Amanda. She steadfastly refused to answer the looks from either Robin Turner or Richard Morgan.

Partington said: 'You are one hell of an impressive girl, Amanda O'Connell.'

'Thank you, Mr President.'

'Thank *you*,' said Partington. He picked up the secure telephone on its second ring to be told Moscow was on the line. 'I'm ready,' he said, lounging back comfortably in his chair.

*　　*　　*

114

Henri Lebrun, who was thirty-two, was obviously – too obviously – dying. He was bowed by osteroporosis and his almost bald head was patched with isolated tufts of hair. He squinted heavily, near blind, towards the observation window when they announced their presence behind the glass. Softly, in French, Dupuy said: 'That's incredible!' More loudly, still in French, he identified himself and the climatologist tried to straighten at the desk at which he'd been laboriously writing.

Lebrun said: 'Can you help me? I've caught it, haven't I?' He was wheezing and blew his nose heavily.

'We're trying,' said the French scientific advisor.

'Quickly,' said Lebrun. 'It's got to be quick. This is how the others went . . .' He disturbed the paper before him. 'I've written it all down, here . . .'

Dupuy turned to Pelham, who shrugged. Quietly again Dupuy said: 'Progesterone?'

'Being administered,' said the American.

'Give him more,' insisted Dupuy. 'On my authority. We'll worry about side effects later. Just slow it down.' Louder he said: 'We're going to give you something, a hormone.'

'Quickly!' repeated the man. He began to cry. 'I don't want to die. Stop it happening. Please stop it happening . . .'

Now it was Dupuy who shrugged helplessly. 'We'll do all we can . . . are doing all we can. Everything . . . we'll talk later . . .' He was sweating, red-faced.

'Don't go! I don't want to be left.'

'I have to go, if we're going to find out what it is . . . we'll talk again. I'll come back . . .' The Frenchman hurried out into the linking corridor, not bothering to conceal the impression of his running away. Outside the observation gallery he stopped, breathing heavily. 'Is that how they all are . . . how they go . . . ?'

'Yes,' said Stoddart. How quickly – easily – he seemed personally to have adjusted.

Dupuy shook his bowed head. More controlled Geraldine said: 'I didn't expect it to be like that . . . I should have

115

done, I suppose, but I didn't . . .' She shook her head, too.

'The other two seem to have been luckier,' said Pelham, leading the way into the next observation chamber.

Stripped from his protective suit and now in a sterile tunic, Darryl Matthews became a short, slim bodied man appearing much younger than his thirty-eight years . . . The most startling feature – and comparison to the Frenchman they'd just left – was a thick shock of deeply black, disordered hair. Like the Frenchman, Matthews was at the desk, writing, but came up sharply when Stoddart spoke.

'I feel OK,' said Matthews, without being asked. The accent was clipped New England.

'You look it, too,' said Stoddart.

'How are the others?'

'Lebrun's not well.'

'Shit! How about Hank?'

'Seems all right. We haven't spoken to him yet.'

'You know what it is?'

'Not yet. That's why we need your help.'

'I'm writing, like I was asked . . .'

'. . . We need some specific answers, right away,' broke off Stoddart. 'You feel up to it?'

'Go ahead.'

'You'd been at Noatak five weeks; time enough to set up?'

'We were set up. Working.'

Stoddart breathed in, deeply, hopefully. 'I've been through all the stuff that was brought back. There isn't any experiment data . . . slides, anything like that . . .'

'Shit!' said Matthews again, more vehemently this time.

'So we're down to memory: your memory,' said Stoddart. 'Had you collected plant samples?'

'Yes.'

Stoddart was aware of the stir around him. 'What?'

'Usual stuff. Lichen, fox moss, boreal fossils—'

'Stop!' ordered Stoddart. 'Boreal fossils might not be usual. We want this nice and slow, Darryl. Did you bring

116

up anything, on any bore, that *wasn't* usual: a plant, fossil, anything at all, that you hadn't seen before? Anything that excited you?'

Matthews gave the question time. 'Not right off.'

'Did you analyse everything you collected?' asked Geraldine. Seeing the surprise through the glass, she added: 'There are a few of us here. Geraldine, Geraldine Rothman, from England.'

Matthews shook his head. 'We hit lucky, like I think we said when we got here. Summer came all at once and I decided to take advantage of it: get as much up as I could in case the weather went against us.'

'We'll come to the weather in detail later,' promised Stoddart. 'But the ice *was* softer than you expected . . . ?'

'And the permafrost.'

'You went into permafrost? Soil?' Stoddart's demand was a split second ahead of Geraldine's, so that they were talking over each other at the end. Stoddart repeated: 'You sunk a bore into soil?'

'A good six inches. That's what I mean. I didn't think I was going to get a chance like that again, so I went for it like a kid in a candy store.'

Geraldine looked sideways to Stoddart. 'We got any permafrost soil samples?'

Stoddart shook his head, tight-lipped. William Perkins, the Noatak station head, had fucked up big time leaving so much behind to be destroyed.

'Let's slow things down again,' urged Geraldine, talking to the man in the isolation room. 'Are you absolutely *sure* there wasn't a permafrost sample or specimen you hadn't seen before?'

Matthews shook his head. 'I already told you I didn't put anything under the microscope; just got it up, labelled it with a site number, date and time and stored it for later.'

Geraldine cupped her face in her hands, eyes tight with frustration. 'Stored how?'

'Refrigerated at the temperature at which it was extracted!'

117

said the man, indignantly. 'I do know how to maintain samples!'

'I'm glad you do, Darryl,' said the woman, encouragingly. 'So you'll know the answer to my next question. How many of those permafrost temperatures were *above* freezing, where whatever was in the bore might have thawed? There were some, weren't there?'

'Yes,' said the paleobotanist, cautiously. 'I don't remember how many, exactly – it'll be in my log, of course – but there were definitely some.'

'Give us an estimate?' asked Dupuy, coming into the exchange.

Matthews hesitated at the new voice. 'Four or five. Not more than that.'

'So they weren't refrigerated?' pressed Stoddart.

'Of course not!' said Matthews, indignant again. 'They wouldn't have given a true reading if they had been, would they?'

Instead of answering, Stoddart said: 'So how were they stored?'

'I had five specimen cases in which I could maintain a fixed temperature.'

'So although they weren't refrigerated they were enclosed?' said Geraldine.

'Yes.'

'No outside ventilation at all?' pressed Stoddart, with the advantage of having worked on a polar station.

'Those above freezing had been exposed to outside air temperature: that's what softened the permafrost. So that's how they were maintained.'

'What about filtration?' asked Dupuy.

Instead of answering, Matthews said: 'You think this is where it came from? Something unlocked from the ground, by a thaw?'

'We don't know,' admitted Stoddart. 'It could be. So what's the answer about filtration?'

'No. There wouldn't have been any point in cleansing the air, would there?'

It might, conceivably, have saved a few lives, thought Stoddart. 'Freak weather?'

'I already told you that.'

Stoddart didn't like the belligerence. 'You troubled much by bugs?'

Matthews sniggered. 'Funny you should ask. People got bitten to hell.'

'Billington!' remembered Stoddart, from what he'd read. 'Joe Billington was the entomologist with you at Noatak. He say anything about the bugs being unusual? Any he hadn't seen before?'

Again the man didn't answer directly. 'Joe was the first to get ill. And to die.'

There was another stir in the observation chamber. 'Was he working with specimens . . . dissecting them, perhaps?' asked Dupuy.

Matthews shrugged. 'I don't know.'

There was a collective sigh of disappointment.

'Let's get back to the question,' said Stoddart. 'Billington say anything to you about the bugs?'

'Not that I can remember.'

'What about from your permafrost samples?' said Geraldine. 'Did he find any fossils . . . atrophied insects . . . that he thought were unusual?'

'I told you I hadn't begun work on the soil samples. If I'd found any insects I'd have passed them over then. He wouldn't have touched my stuff first, ahead of me.'

'The live plants you collected?' said Dupuy. 'Any rot, degrading, in any of them?'

'You want to help me with the point of that question?' asked Matthews.

'Bacteria or virus gestation,' said Geraldine flatly.

Stoddart detected the edge in her voice and found it easy to understand her irritation. He hoped Matthews didn't pick it up. It wouldn't help.

'Definitely not,' insisted the paleobotanist. 'Everything I collected was undamaged.'

'Surface stuff,' prodded Stoddart gently. 'But anything

119

held in a bore – in a soil sample – wouldn't have been undamaged, would it? It would have been crushed, distorted, under sedimentary pressure.'

Matthews gave an embarrassed half shrug. 'Core samples, sure. That goes without saying.'

'Nothing can go without saying, with what we're trying to do,' said Stoddart firmly. 'Let's get this absolutely straight, Darryl. You brought up unfrozen samples which you stored in specimen boxes with unfiltered ventilation? And there was a lot of bug infestation?'

'Yes,' said the American.

'But you didn't get the chance to fix your samples . . . decide if there was anything unusual or let Billington look at any bugs that might have been trapped?'

'That's about it,' agreed the now subdued man.

'What about dating?' persisted Stoddart. 'Were there any oxygen isotope readings, to give us a guide what age you were boring into . . . getting samples from . . . ?'

'There would have been, obviously,' said Matthews. 'I don't know what they were . . . what happened to them . . .'

They didn't have a data base, Stoddart decided. Not from Antarctica or from Noatak. Which was completely understandable to someone like himself, who'd worked research stations and knew that things were never established by the rules and how those rules were bent – ignored – to fit local circumstances, like gathering in everything you could in a freak break in the weather. But no one outside would understand it: conceive how scientists supposedly working within strict scientific rules could have failed to be able to provide a single answer to however many questions were going to need to be answered.

Doggedly Geraldine said: 'You absolutely *sure* that Billington, your entomologist, didn't find any insect he wasn't expecting?'

'We weren't close; not friends!' said the patient, exasperated. 'He probably wouldn't have mentioned it, even if he'd found anything.'

Protectively Pelham said: 'We've had this guy on the rack

120

for quite a while. I think it's time we gave him a break. There's still the Englishman.'

Harold Norris wasn't at the table, although handwritten papers were, neatly stacked, awaiting collection. He was in one of the easy chairs, his head back against the rest, eyes closed. The pose stretched his face and neck backwards, straightening out any lines there might have been although there were no traces that Stoddart could see. The man's hair was blond, which made it difficult to isolate any discolouration, but it was still very full. There appeared no obvious height or weight loss, either: even seated, bodily relaxed, Harold Norris was very obviously the big, heavy man of his medical records, well over six feet and easily the 196 pounds he'd been weighed at, before going to Alaska.

He came awake as soon as Stoddart spoke, with no momentary, unaccustomed surprise at his surroundings and there was immediate recognition of Stoddart's name.

At once the man said: 'I know I haven't got it, but Henri has, hasn't he?'

'Yes,' admitted Stoddart.

'You think you can save him?'

'We don't know.'

The English climatologist was so prepared that Stoddart quickly became convinced the man had used the already completed written account as a rehearsal: every response was succinct and factual, an opinion only offered when asked for. Although all his recorded data had been left behind and destroyed, Norris appeared to have perfect recall of the majority of his readings – specifically isolating those he couldn't to avoid any misunderstanding or confusion – and insisted that with the exception of just two of the thirty-eight days they had been at Noatak, the temperatures, unaffected by any wind chill factor, had been between eight to ten degrees higher than any early seasonal average he could remember. 'I even imagined I was going to get a paper published in *Nature* or *Science*; actually thought of trying to reach you personally on email, to talk it through with you.' He'd measured the calcification of permafrost and

121

tundra five degrees higher than any he could previously recall and believed the unexpected warmth had given them the infestation problem. 'Flying things everywhere,' he said in answer to a question from Dupuy, 'but nothing, as far as I know, that hadn't been seen before: mosquito, midges, things like that.' Despite the warmth, Norris was sure nothing had been allowed to rot or degrade around the Noatak station to provide a breeding ground for bacteria. Again in answer to a question from Dupuy, the man was also sure no one had an infected injury or wound which might have produced bacteria.

'I don't know if it'll help, but I'm diabetic: maybe insulin's a preventative.'

'Something that needs to be recorded,' agreed Pelham. His pager sounded as he spoke. Looking up from its window he said: 'The science ministers are here.'

Stoddart was curious that Amanda O'Connell hadn't travelled down from Washington but supposed there was no practical reason, after her previous visit, just as there was no point in his immediately returning to the isolation wing with the ministers and their scientific advisors: this *was* political, a duty presence, and he certainly had no need to be part of it. He'd expected Paul Spencer to go with them but quickly recognized the opportunity when the White House liaison aide made no move to follow the newly arrived group.

At once Spencer said: 'Anything I need to be told as we're by ourselves?'

Stoddart frowned. 'We've only just started. I've been through the stuff the rescue group wrote, separating personal stuff to the families that doesn't fit here.'

'Needs to be done, I guess.' Spencer's decision not to see the Alaskan survivors was more a personal protest for his own self-satisfaction than a reluctance to confront a possible horror he didn't want or need to look at again. The way he'd planned it, he was always going to be at the very centre of things, Mr Indispensable, not Mr Hey-You who worked the photo-slide machine and prepared the papers and acted as a tour guide to foreign ministers with delusions of grandeur who looked right through him most of the time and who appeared affronted at his temerity in expecting to talk to them as equals on the way to Fort Detrick. Which was very much Amanda O'Connell's attitude, too. Snooty bitch, making it seem an afterthought, which it probably had been, telling him dismissively she was staying behind ('the place I need to be') for the president's conversation with Moscow. Which was where he should be as well, Spencer knew; needed to be as much as her. In the Oval Office, listening to what was being said, being planned. That's where Richard Morgan would be, hearing it all, knowing it all.

'What's new from your end?'

'The Russian situation makes it a whole new ball game.'

'What's happening there?'

'The President's making some sort of approach today.'

'You tell Amanda I'd like to hear from her as soon as there's anything, OK?'

'OK,' said Spencer, tightly.

'I also need to talk to her about this personal stuff.'

'What sort of stuff?' demanded Spencer alertly.

'Farewell messages, mostly.' He paused. 'James Olsen left some legal instructions.'

'Guess you'd better let me have it all; I can show Amanda.'

'What are you going to do about relatives?'

'It's a security problem.'

'The relatives have a right to know, for Christ's sake,' insisted Stoddart. 'I've got to talk to Patricia Jefferies's brother; should have done it already . . .'

'Take pause here, Jack. I hear what you're saying but we don't want any scare stories leaking out, half-cocked—'

'Half-cocked scare stories! Are you serious?'

'Jack! There's been a decision made.'

'Decision made by whom?' seized Stoddart.

'I'm giving you the White House thinking. That's what I'm supposed to do, remember? The lid's to be kept on, until we decide otherwise.'

'Do me a favour,' said Stoddart. 'Tell Amanda I need to

talk to her about this. That I want to do it today, before calling Patricia's kid brother.'

'The Americans say it was a freak interception, picked up by one of their civilian aircraft; they're making a tape available to the ambassador in Washington,' said the Russian president. 'It's a lie, of course.'

'What about the illness?' asked Gregori Lyalin, the Russian science minister.

'They don't know what it is,' said Ilya Savich. 'But international groups are already assembled: political and scientific. We need to be part of it. It's important and I don't mean medically.'

'How?'

'We need American support for our IMF and World Bank application,' disclosed Savich. 'We'll co-operate totally on this. Make sure you choose the best and most appropriate scientist. Politically I'm putting every reliance on you.'

Thirteen

Gregori Lyalin knew he only had one choice although he privately wished there had been an alternative. Raisa Ivanova Orlov was not simply his principal advisor at the Institute. She was an actively working research scientist so internationally respected for her work in virology that the previous year she had been confidently expected – predominantly by herself – to win the Nobel prize for medicine for which she'd been nominated. Had she done so at the age of thirty-nine she would have been its youngest ever recipient. That it had been awarded instead to a black American, whose discovery and sequencing of three genes responsible for prostate cancer had been derided by her advocates and personally denounced by Raisa, was proof not just of American pharmacological domination, but of pandering to Western ethnic political correctness. It hadn't helped the Russian protests that the American treatment had proved to be ninety-three per cent successful.

In addition to all of which was the fact that she'd also, for the past ten days, headed the team investigating the senility disease that killed everyone at Iultin.

Raisa, a tall and therefore physically imposing woman, listened thrust forward in her chair, head bent, to the supposed airliner-intercepted radio exchanges from Siberia. When it finished she said, in self-absorbed disgust: 'America got it – however they got it – but we didn't even have a recording!'

'Is it of any use?'

Raisa gave a dismissive flick of her hand. 'Frightened people, panicking. What do you expect me to learn from that!'

Lyalin, an idealist whose embrace of the Russian reforms extended to a personal determination to be as uncompromisingly honest, as far as he was able, in his professional dealings as he was in his contentedly married private life, said: 'There might have been something!' Why had he expected – hoped – that this encounter would be any different or better than others in the past?

'There wasn't,' the woman said, with another hand flick. 'What do we know?'

Lyalin made a gesture of his own, towards the now silent tape. 'That was personally handed to our Washington ambassador by the Secretary of State, after the conversation between the presidents. With the repeated invitation to join their investigation teams, which of course we intend to do.'

'How soon after?' demanded the blond, statuesque woman.

Lyalin didn't know. He said: 'Two hours.'

Raisa nodded, as if getting a confirmation. 'What, precisely, does the ambassador say?'

'That there's been an outbreak in an American base in Antarctica, as well as Alaska. And deaths.' He wasn't going to enjoy any prolonged period with this autocratically demanding woman. He never did. Which wasn't a consideration, simply a weary recognition.

'How many?'

'I don't know.'

There was an impatient, pained sigh. 'What about survivors?'

'I don't know that, either. If there are any, even.'

'I'd like a survivor: need a survivor,' said the woman, more in conversation with herself than Lyalin.

She wasn't thinking in terms of a human, living person, the man thought, just of something upon which she could experiment. 'Neither the French nor the British have sent entire teams: just political and scientific observers . . .'

'Does that mean we *can't*?' she broke in.

'I've decided it's only going to be the two of us, initially.'

'*You've* decided!' challenged the woman, at once.

'Until we discover what the full situation is.'

126

'It will mean I'm dependent upon American pathology . . . upon precisely what's made available to me.'

'We're not there yet, don't know what we can expect.'

'I know what to expect from America!' She came forward again, head bent in contemplation. 'They haven't got anything. That's why they've approached us. For help.'

Lyalin shifted, uncomfortable at the confused cynicism. 'Aren't we just as desperate?'

The woman shook her bowed head, refusing an answer. 'I don't want them told everyone – even those who tried to run – died at Iultin. They'll be readier to share whatever they've got if they think we're managing to keep some alive.'

There was, supposed Lyalin, some negotiating logic, but it offended him. 'What *have* you discovered from our victims?'

The woman's head came up sharply, suspicious of an accusation. 'We're close.'

She was lying, Lyalin decided at once. 'To what?'

'A diagnosis.'

'Which is?'

'It's a virus we haven't encountered before.'

'What sort of virus? Caused by what?'

'That's what we're still running tests to establish.'

'It will be useful to let them know that,' said Lyalin, to prompt a response.

Raisa did not immediately reply. Then, smiling, she said: 'Yes, it might.'

She'd out-bluffed him, conceded Lyalin. And wanted him to try to bluff those already in Washington in the hope that they'd concede something instead of withholding. He said: 'There's been an outbreak of a horrifying disease which we need to be able to control but at the moment don't. I want you to follow the principle of scientific knowledge and progress being achieved by freely open exchange; everyone being totally honest with everyone else.'

Raisa's lip visibly curled in contempt. 'You concern yourself with politics. I'll deal with science.'

Reminded, Lyalin said: 'For every obvious reason nothing is being made public.'

127

The renewed suspicion came at once. 'Washington's decision?'

'There are three countries involved, apart from us,' said Lyalin.

'We're going *to* them. We're dependent on *their* pathology. And *they* decide when – and if – there's to be any public awareness.'

She'd already decided it was a contest. Them and us, them and us, thought Lyalin: out-dated, out-of-touch attitudes. 'You're prejudging a great many things; forming a lot of conclusions on very little factual evidence.'

'I've already told you, I'm a realist.'

It was probably pointless at this stage – at any stage – but he had to make some effort to curb this arrogance. 'Then let me remind you of a much more necessary reality. As your science minister, taking you into a very uncertain and difficult situation, I want you at least to remain scientifically open minded. I don't know, yet, how we are going to work and until we do – even *after* we do – I want you at all times to acknowledge and observe my authority. If I decide the Americans and the British and the French are totally co-operating with us, then I – and you – will in turn totally co-operate with them. The race is to find a cause and a cure, not to pass a winning post first.'

Raisa was too affronted for any immediate response. When she did she said: 'Has it occurred to you that we've been invited because of my reputation in my particular science?'

Now a reply was Lyalin's difficulty, his breath almost literally taken away by the conceit. 'No,' he said, soft-voiced in his vehemence. 'It hasn't occurred to me. Neither do I think it's true: even remotely possible. We've been invited because the Americans know we've been affected, as they have, and they want the maximum input. *I've* chosen you – no one else – because of your proven expertise and because you've headed the Iultin medical investigation. The Americans didn't ask for you, by name: have no idea, yet, that you're the person coming with me . . .'

Raisa Orlov's tight-together lips weren't any longer curled.

They made a thin line bisecting a face bright red with rage and her hands were clenched into white fists in her lap.

'. . . So,' concluded Lyalin. 'Are you quite clear how I intend we should work and conduct ourselves in Washington?'

'Yes.' The answer was begrudging, like everything else about the woman.

'That's good. I don't want – won't have – any misunderstandings between us.' He'd confirmed an enemy, Lyalin accepted: one, he guessed, who'd even undermine him if she got the opportunity. It was a distracting awareness he could have done without, as he could have done without the woman herself. But Raisa Ivanova Orlov was *the* Russian scientific leader in her field. It was, of course, unthinkable to tell her the financial reason for being completely open with America. As she'd rightly said, his was the political responsibility.

They got together – in Stoddart's temporary office this time – variously disorientated by the delaying intrusion of the politicians, Geraldine and Dupuy with more immediate personal reason to be unsettled than Stoddart, who was simply irritated by the confrontation with Paul Spencer. Stoddart was glad he'd taken the precaution he had with what he'd judged to be personal to the relatives of the dead rescue group.

Taking the lead, no longer with any hesitation, Stoddart said: 'OK, let's talk through where we are: what we might think we've already got to help us here—' Leaders lead, others follow, he thought. 'For my part, for my science, a common denominator between the two Poles certainly seems to be the higher than average warming. And if it was warmer at Noatak, I think we can assume the same applied at Iultin.'

'So this could be your vindication,' declared Pelham, at once. Seeing Geraldine's frown the scientist said: 'Jack's our foremost global warming guru; upsets a lot of people with warnings of a climatic apocalypse.'

Geraldine, who in her scientific past had met professional carping, recognized the underlying ridicule. 'They're going to be even more upset if he *is* right. I'm not suggesting it's the direct cause of what we're looking for here, but

129

genetically the sun's ultraviolet does bring about oxidization. And oxidization can trigger the ageing process.'

'What positive, empirical evidence is there of warming?' demanded the Frenchman, so anxious to get everything – even the most unarguable – recorded, that he wasn't disturbed by the incredulous looks from Stoddart and the woman.

'It's established,' declared Stoddart flatly. 'There's British research that 1999 was their hottest year since their records began, globally it's likely to be one of the four hottest. The prediction is that by 2100 global temperatures will increase by as much as four degrees. One of several effects, causing flooding sufficient to wipe out coastal cities like New York and Tokyo – all coastal cities in fact – would be substantial thawing of the Antarctic. As it is, studies at the University of Washington have found from analysing nuclear submarine radar data that Arctic and Greenland sea ice has, in the past forty years, melted by as much as forty per cent.' He paused. 'I'm not proposing we overstress it.'

'I wasn't arguing we shouldn't,' retreated Pelham, over-whelmed. 'Something we should also note is that Lebrun's blindness, which is now almost total, is ADM – macular degeneration – and not glaucoma. ADM's an old people's disease, a build-up of dead cells within the eye. Ultraviolet light is again suggested the most likely cause for its onset.' He spoke directly at Dupuy. 'I've given him as much progesterone as I safely can. It doesn't seem to be having any slowing effect. He's got two days, maybe less . . .'

'What about insulin?' demanded Dupuy.

'He's not diabetic. Insulin would kill him even quicker. We can't save him: we don't know how to.'

Dupuy visibly winced. Geraldine was surprised at the man's apparent inability to remain clinically uninvolved, as she had been surprised by his initial reaction at seeing the dying climatologist. Briskly she said: 'Let's talk more about this warming. There also seems to be a commonality with bug infestation. What's the thinking about an emergence – a mutation maybe – of an infection-carrying insect or parasite?' She made a general, sweeping motion with her hand. 'The

130

trypanosoma gambiense, for instance, which is endemic to Africa and causes encephalitis lethargica, sleeping sickness. My understanding is that both the North and South Poles were once sub-tropical. Our victims talk of extreme tiredness. Could something have survived in the frozen tundra and been released by the warming?'

Stoddart said: 'Let's not forget the Vostok discovery. Or the survivability of scorpions. I don't see why not –' he looked at Dupuy – 'with so much empircal evidence it's not impossible to imagine that something from the Antarctic's tropical past could simply be in suspended animation.'

'I would have expected to find a spore of something like sleeping sickness in the victims' blood,' cautioned Pelham. 'We haven't found anything to account for the respiratory problems, either.'

'Haven't we already agreed you wouldn't know what you're looking for in a mutation?' reminded Dupuy.

'It's something to take on board,' accepted the installation director, although too obviously without any conviction.

Stoddart sat trying to assess what was, in fact, their first proper, impression-exchanging session. He wished there had been more upon which to base any one, single impression, rather than so many generalities.

'What about physical evidence of insect or lice infestation?' pressed the Frenchman. 'The sleeping sickness parasite is mostly carried by the tsetse fly.'

'We still haven't found anything,' insisted Pelham. 'The chemical fibre tests aren't completed yet. And the tsetse is as big as a house fly: we'd have certainly found that – or anything like it – on the first, visual examination.'

'I'd like to have tissue samples from those who've died to compare genetically with those who've lived,' announced Geraldine. She smiled at Stoddart. 'You think you could spare a hair or two?'

Stoddart smiled back. 'I guess. What are you looking for?'

'Mutants,' said Geraldine, simply. 'In 1999 the European Institute of Oncology in Milan found that mice lacking the gene for protein p66shc had a forty per cent increase in lifespan

131

expectation. The mutation made them more resistant to the oxidization I mentioned earlier; in simple terms it removed any obstruction to natural, body immunology cell repair or replacement.'

'Is it possible to create that mutation artificially?' demanded Stoddart quickly.

Geraldine smiled again, although sadly. 'Medical science is brilliant at creating the fittest mice in the history of the world. As far as I remember, Milan didn't discover what caused the mutation. Genetically the problem is transforming and transferring the technology from animals to humans. Britain's contribution to the Human Genome Project is coming from the Sanger Centre at Cambridge. That's where we entirely decoded human chromosome 22 and where I want molecular biologists to see if they can find any gene differences between the victims and survivors. And check as well to see what progress there's been in Milan. Problem with that is we know it happens, but not why.'

'How difficult is that, technically?' pressed Stoddart.

Geraldine wished she could meet the obvious expectation. Instead she said: 'Think of it this way. Tear each page out of a dozen copies of the Encyclopaedia Britannica. Then rip each page up into little bits and put them all in a bran tub and mix them up, like a tombola. And after that, invite someone who doesn't read or speak English to stick all the pieces back together, in the proper, readable order.'

'Is that supposed to make sense?' protested Stoddart.

'It wouldn't – couldn't – without automated gene-sequencing computers running twenty-four hours a day, seven days a week,' accepted Geraldine. 'There's twenty-three different chromosomes in the double helix, between them comprising three billion DNA bases. Apart from chromosome 22, we don't know in which proper order those three billion bases should be – although we're learning all the time – but which isn't helped by there being far more junk, non-functioning DNAs – deoxyribucleic acids – than there are those that have a purpose. But which can affect those that do. And which therefore we need to identify and put in their sequential order

132

to understand their function and the illness and afflictions they can cause or affect.'

'It's not viable even to attempt,' dismissed Dupuy.

Geraldine looked at the Frenchman in renewed open astonishment. 'If I didn't think it was viable I wouldn't suggest it. And if you've got a better, quicker idea I'd like to hear it. I've been talking general genetic research –' she nodded towards Stoddart – 'which I thought was the guidance I'd been asked to give. All the discoveries I've mentioned give us a starting point. It's an *obvious* route for us to go, not an impossible one!'

Dupuy flushed. 'If you recommend it then of course I support it.'

'I do recommend it.'

Pelham's question – 'What about leaks?' – was too obviously an attempted buffer between the two of them and Stoddard acknowledged it should have been him who made it, having allowed the irritation to grow.

'Independent scientific tests, examination, have got to be conducted!' said Geraldine, impatient again. 'The risk of any genetic leaks is surely more a question for America – and your scientists who want to patent their gene research for commercial benefit – than for the United Kingdom which has accepted the principles of the Genome Project to make every discovery freely available on the internet!' Pull back, Geraldine told herself.

If Pelham was offended by her outspokenness he gave no outward indication. He said: 'I've been thinking about the burning of both our stations: particularly in Alaska where the ice was so thin they were bringing up tundra in which this infection might have been held. If that's where it did come from, torching it will have melted, conceivably releasing, even more. Why don't we send people back – properly suited this time – to extract more samples and specimens that can be properly, scientifically examined?'

'I think that's a brilliant idea,' said Geraldine, at once and meaning it.

'So do I,' said Stoddart, just as sincerely. 'And I think we

133

need to leave static climate monitoring, particularly temperature equipment, at both sites.'

'I hope I didn't upset anyone,' said Geraldine. She was the only one left with Stoddart. The Frenchman had gone back to talk to the dying Henri Lebrun and Pelham to organize tissue specimens.

'No one seemed to be.' Stoddart would have been surprised if they weren't. He thought he might have been if she'd come back at him as she had to the other two men. It shouldn't be a question, he corrected himself. They were supposed to be a professional, dispassionate group among whom irritable spats had to be expected. He supposed, as its nominal, so far unchallenged chairman, he should be the placating mediator.

'Seems to be a problem I have.' Her impatience had been one of Michael's several criticisms. Along with quite a few others. Difficult, now, to believe she'd stuck it so long: tolerated him so long. Hindsight, she reminded herself. The conviction that she'd been in love and that he'd learn to accept her as she was: love her for what she was. Hindsight again. She had been in love with him; stayed in love for too long, even after realizing it was a one-way exchange and that he didn't have the slightest intention – even when she became pregnant – of divorcing Jill to marry her, his usual before-fuck promise so quickly forgotten afterwards. His fiercest, tearing-apart criticism of all had been that she'd purposely become pregnant to force him to choose between her and Jill. Which he had, although not as she'd hoped, instead stuffing the pitifully few possessions he'd kept permanently at her flat (why hadn't that been sufficient warning?) to hurry back to his wife. Geraldine was glad to be out of it. Out of the dead end, for him sex-without-payment relationship. Out of England. And into this totally absorbing, totally time-consuming, time-occupying situation. 'On the subject of problems I have, I hope I didn't offend you, either?'

'How?' frowned Stoddart.

'Not knowing your Friends of the Earth credentials.'

'I'm not part of – or interested in – any pressure group

and I don't wear T-shirts with slogans. I'm an environmental scientist wanting people – governments – to recognize the obvious.'

'If you weren't offended before, you are now.' She was abruptly caught by a sideways thought. She hadn't told anyone where she was going; her answering machine would still promise she'd call back as soon as she could. Surely Michael wouldn't think she'd harmed herself – killed herself even – if she failed to make contact. If he did, he didn't properly know her. But then he never had. And he was arrogant enough to imagine she might kill herself, devastated by his abandonment.

'Nothing to apologize for.'

'Just anxious not to create a problem.'

'Our problem's not having enough to work on; work from.'

Physically straightening in her chair she said: 'Pelham's was a good idea, to go back to source.'

'So was yours. You want to take your personal specimen now?'

Attuned, as she believed herself to be, to sexual nuance, Geraldine felt not the slightest vibration from the man. Any more than she had from Walter Pelham or Guy Dupuy. How it should be; how she wanted it to be: emotionally uncluttered equality. 'As we've got so little to work on, you're entitled to tear out your own hair.'

Stoddart jerked out some hair, saying 'ouch!' as he did so because he didn't expect it to hurt like it did. He felt stupid sitting there with the few strands in his hand. 'You need to do something to keep them sterile?'

She got up, took the hairs from him and folded them in a sheet she tore off from his yellow, legal notepad. 'I'll properly label them as a specimen with all the other stuff. Sterility doesn't matter with a hair sample.'

'What causes a mutation: a change or distortion?' demanded Stoddart.

'We're not totally sure,' admitted Geraldine. 'Infection – bacterial or viral – can make it happen. Sometimes we think

– think but don't actually know – that it can be an interaction between the genes themselves. Chemicals and ultraviolet light can be implicated . . .' Seeing Stoddart's obvious scepticism she said: 'I never told you it was easy.'

'I'd like at least a passing straw to clutch, instead of those few hairs.'

'Maybe it'll come from Moscow.'

Stoddart said: 'You think it's a good idea to call it the Shangri-La Strain?'

Geraldine, who had been told of the presidential naming during the politicians' visit, said: 'Not particularly.'

'Neither do I,' said Stoddart. 'Let's not.'

If Paul Spencer had believed in a god he would have thanked him, but as he didn't he thanked his good luck instead. Although luck didn't have much to do with it, either. Enjoying the analogy – wishing he could share it with someone who would understand the ironic significance – Spencer reminded himself that he had spread the net, merely leaving the CIA to pull in the trawl. He enjoyed being able to summon the supercilious sons of bitches – and Amanda O'Connell – to a meeting they hadn't expected, which he'd planned anyway after the encounter with Jack Stoddart, even before receiving the email from the climatologist, which further added to what he was going to dump on them. It would be his test, Spencer decided, to see how well they did their job; he was, after all, the President's eyes and ears. Did Amanda properly appreciate that? Before the day was out, she'd certainly know he wasn't someone prepared to be an unsuspecting scapegoat. It would be interesting to see how she avoided being one.

Spencer was intentionally late crossing Pennsylvania Avenue to Blair House, wanting them to be waiting for him, which they were. As soon as he entered the conference-converted dining room Amanda said: 'So much for such importance that you couldn't keep to your own schedule!'

'The difficulty is knowing exactly where to begin,' said Spencer, who had the presentation perfectly ordered in his mind. 'I'm afraid I haven't even had time to make copies, although I will, of course . . . I suppose I should start with all the other things that don't make sense . . .' Spencer made a pretence of shuffling through his already arranged papers to extract the CIA print-out, which he recounted with long pauses between each separate marine discovery, followed by what David Hoolihan had supplied. There was no interruption or ready reaction when he finished, and before there could be he announced the Russian participation, pleased it was Reynell who moved to speak. Before he could, Spencer very obviously talked over the other man with the details – and decisions – of the Fort Detrick scientific group.

'Where's the connection – your reason – for introducing this?' Reynell finally managed.

'Inexplicable illnesses,' answered Spencer, at once. 'It's for Fort Detrick to decide if there's any connection. Our job, surely, is to provide them with anything and everything that might be linked.'

'I'm glad you did. There might not be any link but I agree the scientific group should judge,' said Amanda. It would be a mistake to become irritated by Spencer's too obvious need for recognition, or by his equally obvious ambition. They were attitudes to be used, not derided. Since Robin Turner's debacle, she'd allowed herself similar reflections of higher office. There was, after all, a precedent for a woman to be Secretary of State.

Gerard Buchemin said: 'I know the Russian minister, Lyalin. A forward-thinking man. I don't know the woman.'

'Well respected, scientifically,' supplied Spencer, who'd run a biographical check before leaving the White House. 'An unsuccessful Nobel nominee, for virus research.'

'So Moscow's sending its best person,' mused Reynell. 'Fort Detrick should be told that, too. Shows the direction of the Russian investigating and proves they haven't yet got a cure either . . .'

'What's the feeling here about gene experiments and what the Fort Detrick group want to do at the sites in Alaska and Antarctica?' pressed Spencer. They were talking about and deciding the easy, obvious things. It was time for the politically contentious judgments, which was what they'd been brought together to make.

'Sounds to me exactly what they've got to do. They don't need our approval for that,' said Reynell, poised for the discussion. It was a relief to know that Geraldine Rothman was doing exactly what he'd told her during his Fort Detrick visit, channelling things to achieve a British success. That morning in Maryland he'd got the impression she was one of those openly exchanging pure scientists who hadn't properly understood – or accepted – what he'd told her was expected of her.

Amanda said: 'It *was* a good idea, getting the CIA and Hoolihan to monitor all those other strange marine outbreaks. I think Stoddart's group should see them right away. Get it all down to him, will you?'

'Sure,' said Spencer. 'I'll arrange—'

'I mean now,' cut off Amanda. She looked to Reynell. 'With the security involved I think Paul should do it personally, don't you?'

There *was* an attitude, decided Reynell. Responding as he knew he was intended to, he said: 'I think that would be best.'

'But before you do, can you get back to your guy at the Agency – and Hoolihan – to tell them to keep the tightest handle on what they've already picked up. And at the same time extend and intensify the monitor.'

'There's something for the two of us to talk about before I go,' he told her and fifteen minutes later enjoyed the obvious uncertainty when she finished reading James Olsen's diatribe.

Jack Stoddart looked up in surprise when a flushed Geraldine Rothman barged into his office without knocking, and said: 'I've just been told by the guards on the gate that I can't leave the base! And I've got a carload of specimen and samples to get in tonight's diplomatic bag from the embassy. What the hell's happening?'

'Mistakes,' said Stoddart. 'Not yours. Other people's.'

Fourteen

A manda hoped Paul Spencer would learn from the way things were working out, which appeared to be far more to her advantage than she'd originally imagined, but if he went on being an asshole after this he'd have to be even more directly put back in line. She wouldn't need any more than the five minutes Richard Morgan insisted was all that was available in the President's diary, herself restricted to a tight, self-imposed schedule. She was curious what dinner with Peter Reynell would be like: she hoped it would be amusing as well as predictable. And it would be useful meeting Jack Stoddart.

She arrived at the White House early, but Morgan was already waiting at the West Wing entrance. Without any greeting he demanded: 'We got a problem?'

Don't fire all the bullets too soon, Amanda warned herself, intrigued at the Chief of Staff's eagerness; in fact don't fire any at all. 'No,' she avoided easily, forcing their pace along the working corridor. 'Just some adjustments I thought the President should be made personally aware of.'

'Like what?' demanded the man, openly.

'The changed situation with the arrival of the Russians,' avoided Amanda again.

'You could have told me, on the telephone.'

'Unsafe line.'

'Paul then?'

'He's busy doing something else. You heard when the Russians are getting here?'

'Tomorrow,' said Morgan impatiently. 'I thought we'd talked everything through?'

Almost at the Oval Office, Amanda saw, knowing her surroundings. 'Talked, maybe. But I don't think we'd properly *thought* things through.' Not as properly as I have, during the last two hours, she thought.

'What did you say Paul was doing?'

An interesting persistence, Amanda decided. 'I didn't. But by now he should have got to Fort Detrick. I'll explain inside.' She nodded ahead, to where she saw the appointments secretary's brief intercom exchange with Henry Partington to advise their arrival.

They were only halfway across the Oval Office when the president echoed the Chief of Staff's gatehouse demand.

'No problem, Mr President,' she said, seating herself. 'But there could far too easily have been one, so I made some on-the-spot decisions.' Just the right pitch, she decided: confident but not overly so. Someone in charge of the situation.

'Like what?' said the diminutive man.

Conscious of her time limit, Amanda quickly recounted Geraldine Rothman's protest – and the reason for it – and said: 'It was an unworkable idea to confine the people at Fort Detrick. And would have gone badly wrong if it hadn't been corrected before the Russian arrival. Can you imagine Moscow's reaction at finding their scientific advisor was virtually imprisoned?' From the look between the two men Amanda was sure neither had, until that moment. But were very actively imagining it now and not liking the picture they were seeing.

Partington said: 'That was good thinking.'

Quickly Morgan said: 'The restriction was Paul's idea, wasn't it?'

Instead of replying, Partington said: 'Turner should have anticipated it as soon as he knew of the Russians' participation, for Christ's sake!'

Her turn, judged Amanda. 'I'm trying to extend my function as widely as I can: to think as I believe State might think, to avoid awkwardness.' Should she feel shitty? She didn't have any reason to. Perhaps not Robin Turner, who shouldn't have been in the job in the first place, but Paul

140

Spencer had already shown himself quite prepared – eager even – to shaft her. All she was doing was playing by the same rules: do unto others as they do unto you, but do it first if you can.

'That's exactly what I want you to do.' Partington snapped on his own intercom. 'Hold my next meeting.'

The man really was concerned, Amanda recognized. From his back and forth body language Morgan clearly recognized it, too. It was the Chief of Staff who said: 'Tell us, exactly, what you told the British woman?'

'I dealt with Stoddart. I'm having him drive her up, incidentally, so that he and I can have a meeting while she's at the British embassy. I've told Stoddart to explain it was a misunderstanding: that the extra security was because of the Russians being allowed into Fort Detrick but that it wasn't a restriction upon her or any other scientific advisor . . .' Possible thin ice time, thought Amanda, hesitating. Then she said: 'The guard commander wanted to know my authority for standing down what he understood to be his instructions. I said the White House.'

Morgan went to speak but stopped, waiting for Partington. The president said: 'Which it is – and was – one hundred per cent.'

Morgan said: 'They making any progress down there?'

Amanda looked at the man quizzically. 'I'll get a better steer on that from Jack, later. But from what I understand at the moment it's just generalities. Sending people back to the sites is positive . . .' Another staged pause. 'I approved that, too.'

'Quite right,' endorsed Partington again, enthusiastically.

'I also told Jack that informing relatives of the dead was a decision for Washington, not for them . . . not even those of someone to whom he apparently made a promise.'

'He accept that?' demanded Morgan.

'He said it was something we needed to talk about. Which was another reason for bringing him back.'

'Tell him there's going to be special funding: compensation,' said Partington.

141

'He talked a lot about integrity,' said Amanda.

'Tell him to invoke a lot of it himself in his own thinking,' insisted the president. 'To think of the repercussions if news of the Shangri-La Strain leaked out a moment earlier than we can possibly prevent it, before his group's got it cracked.'

She wasn't restricted to five minutes any more, remembered Amanda. 'He might already be showing integrity. Incredibly so. Olsen, one of the rescue people who died, left instructions to his family that Jack Stoddart should be sued, as well as the government.'

The reaction wasn't what Amanda expected. There were renewed looks between the two men but both were smiling. Partington more so than Morgan. It was the Chief of Staff who spoke. Lapsing into the double-speak in which Amanda was not initiated, Morgan said: 'These instructions were written?' *I'll start, Mr President. Show me the way you want to go.*

'Yes,' said Amanda.

'Where are they?'

'At Blair House.'

'We've got them, up here?' *We've got the smoking gun.*

'Yes.'

'What about copies, distributed to the others at Detrick?'

'We've got everything that Olsen wrote.'

'Stoddart's high profile?' said the president, in what Amanda thought to be rhetoric but which Morgan took as an answer. 'A recognizable media figure? And from what you've told us he might even be proved right about global warming . . . ?'

'I'm surprised he's prepared to risk that.' *Which could be a pain in the ass because the United States topped the list of industrialized countries reneging on the carbon monoxide emission limits agreed at the Kyoto conference,* translated Morgan.

'We were talking integrity,' reminded Amanda, aware of an undertone but not knowing what it was.

142

'I tell you what I want you to do, Dick. I want you to look at the contract Jack had, to work at McMurdo.'

To make sure the son of a bitch doesn't have any insurance cover, which it was almost inevitable that he wouldn't, read Morgan. 'I understand what you're saying, Mr President.'

'And I want you, Amanda, to tell Jack what we're doing,' urged Partington. 'You can tell him, if you like, that the Olsens will be more than generously compensated; that the families of every American who's suffered will be cared for. I don't want Jack, whom I've admired before I knew him but respect and admire even more now for what he's done and is doing, to risk not only his possibly vindicated professional reputation but his entire financial future without making sure he can afford to do so.'

Not even Amanda needed a translation to understand the double meaning of that. She said: 'I'll certainly make that clear to him, Mr President.'

'Don't forget to tell him how much I admire him.'

'I won't, sir.'

'And I think this meeting has been useful . . . maybe something we should do again, with the Russians arriving. That definitely puts a whole new uncertainty into the mix. All you've got to do is call Dick, if Paul's busy elsewhere.'

Paul Spencer is dispensable, interpreted Morgan.

Amanda's understanding was close. 'I'll do that.'

Morgan only accompanied the woman to the outer office on her departure. When the Chief of Staff re-entered the presidential quarters Partington said: 'Well?'

I'm impressed, gauged Morgan. 'I think Amanda O'Connell is someone we've been underestimating.'

'That's what I'm thinking,' confirmed the president. 'Let's keep a close eye, when it's time for changes.'

And see how she does in the meantime. 'It's a good idea, Mr President.'

'How's it all going?'

'Good, I think.'

Amanda shook her head to Stoddart's gestured invitation to

another drink. She'd chosen club soda, as he had. Something she'd have to do all over again, later. So, she supposed, would Stoddart. She said: 'No difficulties working together?'

'I'll tell you after the latest arrivals get here but at the moment, no.' They'd met in the Old Ebbitt Grill, opposite the Treasury Building, for convenience but had to wait half an hour at the bar for a table Amanda judged sufficiently isolated.

He was showing the proper caution, which was good. 'We don't want any panic from premature disclosures.'

Lecture time: there'd had to be a reason for the cocktail drink invitation. 'I don't accept that, conducted properly, telling people who need to be told would inevitably lead to that.'

'Others do.'

'I know all the arguments.' Stoddart was adjusting to the bedlam, enjoying it. It wasn't until he'd started the drive from Fort Detrick – being in a car, on an open road, with ordinary people all around him in ordinary cars doing ordinary things – that he'd fully appreciated how unnatural, how totally unreal, his life had become.

'You thought about personal effects?' Amanda was caught by how easy it was to be direct, speaking so indirectly.

'Yes.' Was Amanda O'Connell what was known as a Washington Witch, a woman who'd subjugated everything – sex, family, any personal life – to political ambition?

'You quite sure about that?' Why, she wondered, was he looking around the bar and the restaurant as if it was his first time in such a place?

'Yes.' He hoped he was.

'You a rich man, Jack?'

'No.' Why, back in this real world in which he so gratefully found himself, was this conversation so *un*real? Because it wasn't, he answered himself at once. This was don't-fuck-with-the-fairies, don't-believe-in-Santa bedrock Washington reality.

'You know what you're doing?' Amanda was curious, like someone encountering a new biological or animal species,

144

which was perhaps yet again – too often – appropriate to the current situation but didn't fit their immediate conversation.

'Maybe not. It's what I feel it's right to do.'

'I'll take that second drink now,' abruptly announced Amanda. 'Scotch and branch water: Macallan if they have it.' An off-balancing ploy, further to off-balance a man open to persuasion.

Stoddart looked away, searching for their waiter. He stayed with club soda. Feeling a need to fill the silence he said: 'So there it is: how I feel.'

Amanda was sure no one could overhear them but she still leaned forward, reducing the possibility, and lowered her voice, too, the closeness adding to the seriousness of what she intended to say. 'You didn't kill them, Jack. They were dead – all of you were potentially dead – from the moment you went into that outstation. You got lucky, the others didn't.' She was getting very good at this, Amanda congratulated herself. 'You've no idea what it is, where it came from, how it's transmitted, have you?'

Stoddart glanced hurriedly around them.

'Just you and I, Jack. No one's listening. *Can* listen.' There couldn't, upon reflection, have been a better place to have met.

'OK.'

'So answer the question!'

'No,' admitted Stoddart. 'We don't know any of those things.'

'So bringing the bodies back – Olsen's accusation – is only a possibility.'

'A sufficient possibility.'

Amanda clinked her whisky against Stoddart's soda glass, her very private celebration. 'Is it?'

Stoddart frowned, as she'd expected. 'I don't understand?'

Pedantically Amanda recited: 'You've no idea what it is, where it came from, how it's transmitted.'

'I still don't understand.'

'You're heading an investigation to answer all those questions. And at the same time proposing to risk the disclosure that would cause public hysteria. And by the same inevitability destroy yourself and every argument you've ever scientifically advanced, as well as getting yourself taken off the investigation. All that and total financial wipe-out. And all for nothing, if in the end you find that Olsen's death – the deaths of everyone who went in with you on the rescue mission – had nothing whatsoever to do with your bringing the bodies back. Which, from every scientific and medical judgment, you should without question have done. That seems a very wasteful suicide to me.'

A Washington Witch weaving spells, thought Stoddart. Except that spells were fantasy and what this icy woman (witch of the north? witch of the south?) had just enunciated with crystal clarity was the sort of return to real life he'd so very recently appreciated.

Amanda ached to go on but knew that at that precise moment another word would be too much.

'I just . . . it doesn't sit right,' groped Stoddart. 'And I made someone a promise.'

'Which I'm not suggesting you shouldn't keep, at the right and proper time. That's all I'm saying, wait until the right and proper time. You get forced by public reaction into a resignation and the practical, working part of this investigation get's fucked, for God knows how long. You think this person you made a promise to would want you to do that?'

'No,' Stoddart admitted at once, not needing to reflect what Patricia's attitude would have been. He gestured to the waiter again and ordered himself Scotch this time, without the branch water.

'It's been useful to talk it through; reach the same conclusion between ourselves.'

'Is it between ourselves?' demanded Stoddart, wanting the woman to know his awareness that there were more Washington warlocks than witches.

'It's a political decision. When it has to be made, it'll be made from here. And you have my word that you'll be told in advance so that you can fulfil any personal promise.' Had

146

he genuinely loved Patricia Jefferies or was he motivated by a guilt-driven sense of duty? None of her concern. 'Anyone resent your being in charge?'

Stoddart shrugged. 'The question hasn't really arisen. Not until Geraldine was stopped from leaving the base and came to me, so I suppose that's her acknowledging the fact.'

'But now we've got the new arrivals,' reminded Amanda, using Stoddart's own phrase. 'We'll get over any problem by making it clear that the Russian is the deputy.'

Stoddart exaggerated the eye-widening at the matter-of-fact announcement. 'What if she won't accept being the deputy?'

'She'll be told from here by her minister. She'll have to accept it. I'm just putting you in the picture.' Which she hadn't yet done with either Reynell or Buchemin.

Seemingly sharing the thought, Stoddart said: 'Guy going to be told from here, too?'

'Yes.' She leaned forward again to outline the CIA discoveries that Spencer was delivering to Fort Detrick and at the end said: 'Could there be any significance?'

Stoddart pursed his lips reflectively. 'Could be, in certain circumstances. I'm anxious that because there is so little to follow we don't clutch at everything and make too much out of nothing. That's a blind alley approach. But it's certainly worth putting on the table precisely because we do have so little.' He looked at her curiously. 'Why have Paul go all the way back to Fort Detrick? You could have given it to me, tonight. Saved him the journey.'

'He was already on his way before you and I arranged to meet,' lied Amanda easily. She swept her hand around the beehive humming bar. 'And maybe documents marked White House Eyes Only and stamped with the Agency's crest might have caught somebody's attention.' She saw the awkwardness with which he reached for his glass, to look at his watch. 'What time you meeting her?'

'Fifteen minutes.' He jerked his head in the direction of the next block. 'Thought we'd do the tourist bit and have

147

a drink at the open penthouse bar of the Washington Hotel. Then Georgetown.'

'This gene thing anything to get excited about?'

He shook his head. 'Beginning at the beginning. Pelham hadn't got to genetics.'

Amanda said: 'Could be that you're going to be proved right about warming?'

Stoddart made another doubtful head movement. 'Still only a possibility. And if I am, it's sure as hell not the way I wanted it proved.'

They got a table at the verandah edge, with an uninterrupted view of the Washington Monument and the planes landing at faraway Reagan airport to their left. Almost as soon as they sat, there was scurried movement on the roof of the Treasury Building directly opposite as the guards took up their routine positions and then the roar of a helicopter taking off from the White House lawn beyond. At once the machine lifted into view clear of the buildings and wheeled away over the park.

Geraldine said: 'That the President?'

'I had him do it just for you.'

She smiled, politely. 'Wonder where he's going?'

'It's never announced in advance, for obvious reasons. There are stories that he goes out to dinner that way if the host has a place big enough to land. Must make a hell of an entrance.' Stoddart was swept again by the pleasure of doing something ordinary. He ordered Scotch for himself, chardonnay for her.

'How'd your meeting go?' This was nice, Geraldine decided. A perfect setting on a warm night, with no undertone between them. She shouldn't forget the last of her antibiotics. There was no pain at all – hadn't been for several days before leaving England – or discharge, either, and she was sure the infection had completely gone. She'd asked the embassy doctor to arrange an appointment with a gynaecologist to ensure there was no permanent damage.

Stoddart looked around, assuring himself again there was

no risk of their being overheard. 'CIA have picked up some odd marine outbreaks worldwide, infections not normally suffered by sea mammals.'

'But fish illnesses?' she qualified.

'Whales dying from what seems to be influenza. Some instances of the same disease in humans.'

'Confirmed?'

'Not as far as I'm aware.

'So there's no strain identification?'

'No.'

'No reason for it to have anything to do with us?' she suggested.

'None at all,' he agreed. 'At the moment it's nothing more than an interesting coincidence. Useful to know about, though.'

Geraldine asked for water with her next glass of wine and took her antibiotic as soon as it was served.

Stoddart said: 'You all right?'

'Headache. Aspirin will shift it. Still jetlagged, I guess.'

Stoddart wouldn't have expected aspirin to be in what was clearly a prescription bottle. 'Everything go OK at the embassy?'

Geraldine decided there was nothing hidden in the question. 'My minister is curious how things will work out with the Russians.'

'So's Amanda.' It was the obvious opportunity, Stoddart recognized. 'You have any problems with my being chairperson?'

Geraldine looked at him half smiling, as if expecting a joke. 'Hadn't really occurred to me that you were, but no.'

He smiled back. 'The political group think it might be a difficulty for the Russians: want their woman to be deputy.'

Now Geraldine laughed, openly. 'For Christ's sake! Aren't we supposed to be engaged on something a little more important than titles?'

'We are. I guess they're not.' She was refreshing, after the meeting he'd just had with Amanda.

'Quite frankly, I couldn't give a shit. My only problem is

149

with nonsense like that – any nonsense, for that matter – getting in the way, my way, your way, anybody else's way.'

'Thanks.' Stoddard didn't think the deep drink she took was irritation at him, personally.

'I read what you wrote, about what it was like when you got to the outstation. I'd like to hear it again.'

Stoddart looked at her quizzically. 'A second time?'

'You wrote it intending it to be read,' she said. 'Thought about the words. You might describe it differently when you just talk.'

'Could it be important?'

'I won't know until I hear it. I'm thinking forensic pathology now.'

Stoddart looked around him again. 'Not here.'

'I thought you promised me dinner?'

Stoddart wished he'd made a reservation because they got refused at the French restaurant opposite the Four Seasons, but they got into a Mexican cafe just off the turn from M Street, on Wisconsin. She insisted he order for her ('Your neighbouring culture, not mine') but suggested tequila ('that much I do know'). After the lime and salt ritual she only sipped. 'From the moment you found them as they were,' she urged.

Talking *was* different. Stoddart began stiltedly – actually trying to remember what he'd written – but very quickly lost the way and then let it become a conversation between them because several times Geraldine guided him back, wanting details greater than he had given – certainly than what he had written – earlier.

'Patricia was getting close but she didn't realize it,' said Geraldine, distantly, when Stoddart finally finished.

'Close to what?' He'd read everything, knew everything Patricia had written.

Geraldine made no immediate effort to reply, a taco suspended briefly before her. Eventually she said: 'Buckland Jessup was actually kneeling, arms lifted. "As if he was praying," Patricia said?'

'Yes.'

150

'George Bedall was between the rooms, both arms broken from where he'd fallen, reaching out . . . ?'

'Yes.'

'No!' refused Geraldine, positively.

Stoddart waited, while automatically she used the taco as a spoon for the guacamole. Eventually she said: 'People don't die like that. I know that's how it appeared to have happened. That's what Patricia Jefferies wrote. Morris Neilson, too, although not so definitely. Now you've told me the same. But it's not possible.'

Stoddart only just stopped the impatience becoming loud. 'That's how it *was*!'

'A person can't die, arms outstretched, kneeling like Jessup was kneeling. Arms don't snap cleanly, like a dried stick, as Bedall's arms snapped.'

'They did!'

'I know – accept – that's how it was. How you found them. But if Jessup had died kneeling, arms in front of him, he would have collapsed: fallen sideways or forwards. Not remained upright, like a statue. And Bedall's arms wouldn't have *snapped* as the autopsy showed they were, quite separately from how they had to be broken again, to carry the body . . .' She stopped again, talking more to herself than to him. 'I need to look at those breaks, see the differences . . . look at the Alaska bodies, too. And talk to Matthews and Norris . . .'

'If we're going to go on exchanging thoughts you've got to help me!' pleaded Stoddart.

'I *can't*,' said Geraldine, still more to herself than to him. 'I don't know what I'm trying to say: what's wrong with what you clearly found. Just that it shouldn't – couldn't – have been like that.'

Believing he understood something of what she was saying, Stoddart said: 'Bucky was *frozen* as he was, kneeling with his arms out in front of him.'

Geraldine shook her head again, positively. 'I need to go back through all the autopsies, maybe carry out some again. It's a mistake! Sub-zero as it was the bodies wouldn't have frozen like that . . .' She snapped her fingers. 'And rigor would only have set in – despite it being below freezing – *after* Jessup had toppled frontwards or sideways, not quickly enough to have kept him upright.'

'So what have we got?' demanded Stoddart.

Geraldine finished her tequila in one gulp, forgetting the lime and salt. 'What we always had. A total bloody mystery that I've just further confused myself about.'

The reservation was at Paul Young's, on Connecticut Avenue, one of the three must-go, socially-to-be-seen Washington restaurants that Amanda had guessed Peter Reynell would choose and she wished she could have bet on it, to win the cab fare home. As they arrived, to Krug already in the cooler, their seats at the bar as well in the restaurant reserved, she made herself the second bet that Reynell would expect to share the taxi and a lot more besides. She waited for him to invite approval – a reference to the '62 wine vintage, perhaps – but he didn't and Amanda, objectively aware of her rocket-like escalation from the cockroaches rest room, sat back to enjoy it, making more bets. She lost at once, expecting him patronisingly to insist upon ordering for her, although he didn't ask her preference for wine, choosing without consulting the list a Puligny Montrachet and a Pomerol. Reynell started with oysters, which she'd never ever been able to try, and seeing her look he offered her one. She declined, waiting for him to make the obvious aphrodisiac remark, but he didn't do that, either, and Amanda decided it was time she stopped making bets, even to herself. If money had been involved she would by now already be losing heavily. It wasn't, of course, a wasted indulgence; rather a necessary one. She'd been testing herself – her expectations – against the man and so far he was ahead, despite her initial, first-guess success.

Reynell said: 'Pity Gerard couldn't make it.'

'It was nice of you to ask him.' Was this going to be the first pass?

Reynell hadn't invited the French minister but knew she

152

wouldn't ask the man, whose turn on Reynell's divide-and-spin carousel was planned within the next two nights, depending upon the assessment of Gregori Lyalin. 'If he had been able to come – instead of needing to go to the embassy to talk to Paris – we perhaps could have rehearsed ourselves, without the intrusion of official records.'

'Rehearsed ourselves?' This wasn't at all what she'd expected.

'I like how it is – already – between the three of us.'

Amanda only just avoided the sigh of grateful recognition. 'So do I.'

'It would be unfortunate if the Russians upset it all.'

'We don't yet know they will,' said Amanda, in mental step with the man. He always had to know she understood; was running in step with him. What he didn't have to know – suspect – was when she'd sprint ahead.

'I'm just covering eventualities.'

They stopped talking for the presentation and the carving of the chateaubriand. After it was served, Amanda said: 'Which are?'

'Is. Just one. That the co-operation won't be as complete as it was obviously going to be.' Reynell had rehearsed the insinuation with Sir Alistair Dowding, before the ambassador composed his account to London, but avoided mentioning it to Downing Street during his conversation with Simon Buxton three hours earlier. That very day, the prime minister had inferred, personally answering a House of Commons scientific question – planted, Reynell was sure – that Reynell was absent from the chamber on personal, instead of unspecified government business.

Predictable, gauged Amanda: maybe too predictable. 'What are you saying?'

'That I don't want any division – any stupid, unnecessary nationalism – to come between us.'

Amanda, who had been uncertain, began to relax again. 'I don't want that either.'

Reynell smiled a sculpted smile. 'So we understand each other. That's good.'

'I won't engage in any separate arrangements,' pledged Amanda, sincerely insincere.

'Neither will I,' matched Reynell. 'If I am approached, to come to any understandings, I'll tell you. You have my word on that.'

It was, Amanda supposed, the opening. 'We need to be aware of Russian sensitivity. I talked about it earlier to Jack.'

Let it run, Reynell decided. 'Talked about what, precisely?'

'Raisa Orlov being the deputy of the scientific group.'

Which Geraldine Rothman had already outmanoeuvred, thought Reynell. 'Deputy to whom?'

'No one, in point of fact. Their coming here infers Stoddart will chair their scientific sessions, although from what he said tonight everything's as open there as it is here: everyone working together, not worried about a structure.'

'It would be a gesture, wouldn't it?' Reynell agreed. It made good – but most of all protective – sense; each and every mistake or problem could be explained away as the inherent distrust between Washington and Moscow.

'You don't object?'

'Not at all.'

The meal was excellent and the wine possibly the best Amanda had ever tasted. Reynell made her laugh genuinely, with brilliantly recounted stories of political scandals and intrigues in London, but never once turned anything into what could have been construed as a sexual approach. He ordered two taxis while they were still on their coffee, helping her into the first without any physical contact. As she drove away, Amanda acknowledged that the evening had been completely different from what she'd expected and resolved against any more personal bets. There still appeared quite a lot for her to discover about Peter Reynell. She was, in fact, sure about only one thing so far. He'd been lying through his teeth in promising to let her know about any side approaches from the other ministers, just as she had been making the same empty promises to him.

There was a reassurance in knowing that she was dealing with another political professional.

The round journey to and from Fort Detrick took Paul Spencer four hours, time enough for the anger to run its full gamut from unreasoning, revenge-promising fury, through half-formed schemes to undermine Amanda O'Connell in Henry Partington's mind with insinuation and innuendo, to calm, clear-headed objectivity. He only had himself to blame. He'd miscalculated – underestimated her – and she'd taught him a lesson. From which he had to learn. The acceptance didn't affect the promise to himself to get even. It reinforced it. As far as she would be aware, he'd dutifully continue fulfilling to the letter his liaison role between the two groups and the White House, all the time alert for the opportunity that would surely come, and when it did he'd explore and refine it so completely, that when he pressed the button Amanda O'Connell would be politically blown into oblivion. The satisfaction was going to be in letting her know, just before it happened, that in the end it was she who'd underestimated him.

Fifteen

Jack Stoddart got an abrupt feeling of being a referee between two contestants – at their echelon it would have to be gladiators, he supposed – and just as quickly hoped he wouldn't need to become one. Certainly, from the moment-of-meeting exchanges between Geraldine Rothman and Raisa Ivanova Orlov, Stoddart decided physically they would have been ill-matched. The wise money would have been on the heavyweight Russian.

Raisa was gladiatorially big in every way, maybe a foot taller than Geraldine and broader, too, but her size was in proportion to her height: she was a commanding rather than an overpowering figure. The grey wool suit was professionally businesslike but loose and her blonde hair hung free, almost to her shoulders, curtaining a prominently featured, angular face. Her eyes were very dark, black almost, and adding to the authoritive presence was the unwavering, almost unblinking attention she'd earlier directed intently upon him and which she was now imposing, with equal intensity, upon Geraldine.

Geraldine most definitely didn't appear intimidated by the Russian. But then, Stoddart acknowledged, there was no reason why Geraldine – or anyone else – should have been. Raisa Orlov was smiling, openly friendly, offering her hand ahead of waiting for the contact to be offered to her, the English seemingly easy although quite heavily accented. He was, accepted Stoddart, allowing a long outdated, black hats versus white hats attitude to influence his thinking. Worse even: to influence his judgment.

The black hat, white hat comparison wasn't confined to him, Stoddart acknowledged. Amanda O'Connell had only just stopped openly using the expression during the totally

156

unexpected call from Washington, before he'd even showered that morning.

With the greetings over, Stoddart realized, further surprised, that Raisa expected to start. She was looking enquiringly at the conference table that had indeed been installed to accommodate the Russian expansion to one side of his makeshift and now overcrowded office. He said: 'I thought you might like to settle in first; rest after the flight, maybe? We've got a lot to exchange and read, to bring ourselves up to date.'

'I've seen my quarters here,' announced Raisa. 'They'll do. I'd like to talk about what there is.' It was important to establish her position from the start. She was sure that she could detect the uncertainty towards her, particularly from the American who seemed to consider himself in charge.

Stoddart was aware of Geraldine's uneasy shift, knowing from their previous night's conversation that she'd planned to start her pathology re-examination, maybe even to repeat some autopsies. He hoped she'd control any impatience at the delay.

Pelham said: 'It'll be great if you've got something to help us with right away.'

They were all nervous of her, Raisa decided. Which was an attitude that had to be built upon: strengthened. She'd let pass being relegated to a secondary position because that could be equally useful, giving her every access – and every right to demand it – but leaving America ultimately responsible for the errors and wrong decisions. 'What have you discovered?' Her voice was deep, almost masculine.

'Very little,' admitted Stoddart. 'The only commonality – and we're putting no more importance to it than it being a denominator – is a higher-than-average temperature at the scene of both our outbreaks—'

'Climate is your science,' Raisa cut in, wanting Stoddart to know her preparation; she didn't intend being secondary in any discussion.

'We expect the positive analysis of our autopsies today,' offered Pelham.

'What were the climate readings at Iultin?' demanded Stoddart.

Raisa didn't know. She couldn't remember, even, if any were recorded in the Iultin logs, only a sample, four of which she'd brought with her, but hadn't read during the flight.

'Your science, not mine,' she repeated, sure her uncertainty wasn't showing, refusing even the thought of uncertainty, although accepting – just – being off balance from the start. At every other scientific conference she'd attended in the West, she was the acknowledged and unquestioned authority, the person to whom everyone else deferred. She hefted her bulging briefcase on to the table. 'I'm afraid there wasn't time to get any of it translated . . .'

There were various movements around the table, the most obvious irritation from Geraldine. Making no effort to hide it she disbelievingly said: 'There's nothing we can read – compare – right now?'

'Not immediately, no.' She'd made a mistake insisting upon a discussion before studying what material they had, Raisa accepted; a stupid, self-ridiculing mistake.

'But you obviously know what's there,' persisted Geraldine. 'What's it say about temperature!'

This was an inquisition, as if she were on trial or being tested! 'I've concentrated upon the medical examinations . . . I left climate research to others . . .'

'But it's there, somewhere?' persisted Geraldine. Where the fuck did this Amazonian think she was coming from! From the other side of the opposing line, she answered herself. Surely the bloody woman didn't expect to work – not work, this wasn't working, this was being obstructive – to *behave* like this, she corrected herself.

Raisa was inwardly squirming. They wouldn't know she'd headed the medical investigation in Moscow, she realized, in brief relief. 'I haven't had time to study everything. It was only delivered to me, in full, at the airport.'

'And you didn't read what was new to you during the flight?' demanded Geraldine. She was hardly the person to criticize international travel!

It *was* becoming a contest, Stoddart decided. Geraldine's annoyance was justified, if this was to be the best the Russian

158

could – or would – provide. Judged on this basis he needed a much more detailed conversation with Amanda. Trying to diffuse the growing tension he said: 'So let's talk medically. What have you found?'

Raisa tried to answer the question with a question. 'Don't you think it's viral?'

'It's a possibility, along with several others,' replied Pelham, as annoyed – and disappointed – as Geraldine. 'Have you positively isolated what could be a virus from your victims?'

'We believe it to be the most likely cause,' said Raisa, desperately. Jack Stoddart was the only one of the group upon whom there'd been any biographical information from the Washington embassy. She was glad Lyalin wasn't here, to witness the fiasco.

Guy Dupuy said: 'If that's your belief you've clearly isolated the pathogen and its chemical composition . . . ?'

'. . . Which will give us a DNA!' picked up Geraldine, instantly ready to change her opinion of the other woman. 'We'll have something from which we can genetically create an interferon; a vaccine even!'

Raisa was seized by panic, a feeling so unusual she didn't at first understand it and when she did, wished she hadn't. 'It hasn't been positively isolated *as* a virus,' she backtracked. 'All I was told – a message just before I left Moscow, with no time to explore it in any detail – was that there's a pathology indication of something that *could* be viral . . .' Bringing her exaggeration back to fact, Raisa went on, 'It's far too early even to think of chemical composition: it's no more than a haemolytical indicator. Most definitely not – at this stage – something from which we've been able to culture a reagent.'

'So there's no diagnosis – no reason whatsoever – to claim the outbreak is viral?' demanded Geraldine, openly disdainful.

'We're getting blood analysis we don't understand,' admitted Raisa, truthfully but reluctantly.

'For which there could be a dozen different explanations, none of which helps us,' persisted Geraldine. This was a total waste of time! She was seized by the thought of walking out –

actually moving again in her chair – but sat back at Stoddart's curious look.

Whether he wanted it or not – whether the two women realized it or not – it was becoming a contest, although hardly gladiatorial. Stoddart thought that on a scientific level – on every level – Geraldine was proving herself the stronger.

Dupuy said: 'Is there *any* analysis? Anything at all we could exchange with haemotologists here – or in London or Paris – to examine?'

Raisa acknowledged she couldn't have appeared worse – more amateurish or more ill-prepared – if she'd set out to try! 'I didn't bring anything with me . . .' Evading again she added: 'I can go back through the embassy. Get it. That's what I always intended to do, of course, not having enough time to explore it further before I left . . .' Striving to recover, she said: 'But what about your victims? Any unusual blood findings among any of them?'

'None,' said Pelham, shortly.

He had to close this down, Stoddart decided. They *were* supposed to be a cohesive, co-ordinating team, which didn't allow for Raisa Ivanova Orlov to be humiliated, even by her own incomprehensible invitation. He gestured to the stack of dossiers beside his desk. 'Everything we've got – all that's been done so far – is there. It looks a lot but doesn't amount to any practical progress . . . things that could be inconsistent but which might have an understandable explanation . . .'

'And it's all been translated into Russian,' finished Geraldine. Pointedly she looked at her watch. She really would leave if this went on much longer.

Raisa said: 'I'd like everything in the original.'

There were renewed shifts around the table at the obvious distrust. Stoddart decided it was hardly surprising, in view of the Russian's performance, that everyone else in the room would be making the black hat, white hat comparison, which didn't after all seem to be outdated. He said: 'No problem.'

'None of us speak Russian so the translation will delay the interchange we all hoped there'd be,' said Geraldine, trowelling on the sarcasm.

He was going to have to referee, Stoddart accepted. 'Save us time,' he urged. 'Apart from any climate irregularity and this blood thing, about neither of which you can help us, is there anything that might possibly take us forward?'

She was being made to look stupid at every turn, Raisa realized, hoping the inner, burning fury wasn't reaching her face. 'No.'

'Any of your victims still alive?' asked Dupuy.

Raisa hesitated, rethinking the deception she'd impressed upon Lyalin in Moscow, anxious not to be caught out. 'Two were when I left . . .' She looked as pointedly at her watch as Geraldine, moments earlier. 'Which was almost two full days ago now. I need to check.'

'If you still have people living now they're exceeding our survival average,' said Pelham. 'That could be important.'

'I said I'll check,' repeated Raisa.

'We're wasting time,' declared Geraldine, finally. 'I've got practical things to do.'

It was a superhuman effort, spurred by her eagerness to get out of the room and this humiliation, for Raisa to avoid asking what such practical things were. Instead she sat mute, virtually dismissed; she couldn't ever remember enduring such a demeaning experience.

'I think you should bring yourself completely up to date with what we've provided,' said Stoddart, waving his hand again to the stacked files. 'While we get translated and read what you've brought.'

'That will give you time to get the blood samples shipped over. And find out about your survivors,' said Geraldine. 'Perhaps then we can start working – behaving – properly.'

The disaster hadn't been entirely of her own making, Raisa at once tried to assure herself. Perhaps her biggest mistake had been failing to anticipate the inherent animosity she'd face as a Russian, particularly from the other woman. A geneticist, she remembered, a geneticist like the man who'd robbed her of the Nobel award. She could recover. Had to recover. More than just that; come to dominate – control – the group. It might require her liaising more closely than she'd imagined with

161

Gregori Lyalin, to benefit as much as possible – as much as now might be necessary – from the political attitudes and manoeuvrings among the Washington committee. As the awareness settled, Raisa decided there was every reason to reach Lyalin at once, to get her account in before exaggerated rumours and stories spread down from Fort Detrick.

She remained for several minutes, with growing frustration, while Lyalin's embassy-allocated number rang out unanswered, deciding against going through the general switchboard to leave a message for him to contact her.

From the solitude of his own office, Stoddart had been more successful in contacting Amanda O'Connell at Blair House and agreed with her that what had just happened with Raisa Orlov was a worrying beginning which he hoped wasn't worsened by Amanda's impending meeting with the Russian science minister.

'It doesn't sound good,' agreed Gerard Buchemin, when Amanda relayed the account.

Peter Reynell was almost too preoccupied to contribute, although being as adept as he was, he managed to suggest it was a situation they had to confront and rectify at once if Lyalin mirrored the attitudes of his scientific expert. The rest of Reynell's concentration was upon what Paul Spencer had told them, before Stoddart's hurried telephone warning.

Like most good ideas, it had come complete in Reynell's mind. He acknowledged that there were risks but Reynell believed he was a sufficiently accomplished manipulator.

Unlike Stoddart at Fort Detrick or the rest waiting expectantly at Blair House, Peter Reynell did not consider the Russians' arrival in terms of a contest. Had it occurred to him, Reynell wouldn't have entered the arena. Reynell's philosophy was that shoulder-against-shoulder slugging, from which no one emerged unbloodied or unbruised, was for others, never for him. Reynell was a scavenger, a guerrilla fighter who picked over the bones and defeats of others stupid enough in the first place to get into direct conflict. Which is what he regarded the ever-eager-to-prove-himself Simon Buxton as having done –

162

openly issuing a challenge by sending him into Washington exile – which Reynell now planned to reverse completely in his absolute favour.

Gregori Lyalin made what even the cynical Reynell conceded to be a dramatically impressive entrance, although there was a tempering hesitancy which made it appear it was not intended to be that way at all. The effect was achieved by a grey-flecked, unrestrained waterfall of a beard, which the plump Russian had defiantly worn as the recognized badge in Russia of orthodox religious conviction long before the end of atheistic communism. It plunged in disordered contradiction to the blue, clerk-like suit and subdued and collared shirt, both of which were largely lost under the overflow.

Amanda thought the man looked like Santa Claus on his way back to the office the day after Christmas. The handshake was very firm, although the hands were soft. The concentration, upon every introduction, was intense, as if he were burning the names along with the facial images into his mind.

Lyalin waited politely to be accorded his place at the table and the moment he seated himself, in advance of any further preliminaries, said: 'I want to make it clear to everyone here, every government represented here, that we – Moscow – welcome this co-operation. And to give you my personal pledge of our total commitment.'

The announcement was so totally unexpected, as well as being so quick, after what they had just been relayed from Stoddart, that momentarily there was silence.

From that declaration, Amanda decided it wasn't premature – rather, it was what they'd already hurriedly decided – to put a little stiffening into the diplomatic marshmallow. She said: 'Let me return that commitment, on behalf of the rest of us . . .' She indicated the assembling secretariat, which now included a Slavic-featured man from the Russian embassy. 'Our proof of that commitment is having already had translated everything we have . . . we'd hoped for the same, at least with any medical or scientific material from you . . .'

Both Amanda and Reynell continued to be surprised,

Reynell wondering if he was the only one to detect the faint flush beneath the beard. Unaware until that moment of Raisa's failure to get their material put into English and French, Lyalin said: 'There should of course have been a translation. I will arrange for it to be done at once . . .'

The scavenging Reynell pecked at once. If Gregori Lyalin, the science minister, had been working as he should have been with Raisa Orlov, his chief scientific advisor, he'd have known there wasn't an interpretation. An interesting bone to chew upon, he decided. But not too soon: Amanda was doing perfectly well without his intervention.

Nodding towards Paul Spencer, Amanda said: 'Arrangements have already been made to have it done by our State Department people. It's important that the rest of the scientific group read what there is from you as soon as possible.' She believed the Russian's apology, Amanda decided, further surprised. Or could it be a trick, a far better performance than the other Russian up in Maryland? Careful, she warned herself; she'd dizzy herself trying to revolve in ever decreasing circles: It was disconcerting having to run the meeting, preventing her from adopting her usual sit, watch and assess role. The Russians – here and at Fort Detrick – weren't her only personal concern. She still wasn't sure about Paul Spencer, which meant it was very important to get into the record everything he'd provided that morning, to avoid the accusation of her not responding to everything as quickly as she should. It might have been his thinking that she'd delay, until they'd had time to consider what Lyalin had to contribute. 'We'll all of us have a lot to catch up with,' she said briskly. 'What about anything additional to the Iultin outbreak?'

Good, judged Reynell at once. Almost time for his entry

Lyalin looked blankly around the people confronting him. 'I don't understand that question. There's been no other outbreak apart from Iultin, if that's what you mean?'

Spencer was ready with what had come in overnight from the CIA and Science Foundation monitor, but observing his new self-imposed restraint he held back from responding uninvited and was glad because Amanda began to talk without any reference to him. Spencer listened, hoping she'd forget something that he'd be able to prompt her upon – which she didn't – but so intently was he mentally rehearsing a discreet correction that when Amanda did defer to him, for that day's update, he almost missed the invitation. Hurriedly he said: 'There are human influenza outbreaks, in all the coastal regions where whales have been reported dying from the same illness: India, Japan, some Pacific islands and in Chile. And some places where it hasn't yet appeared to affect sea life: Norway, Germany and France, with sea coasts in the north, and Australia and New Zealand in the south. And it's no longer coastal. There have been isolated reports of respiratory illness in four British cities – Manchester, Bristol, Newcastle and London – and in Budapest and Vienna in continental Europe, and Amman in Jordan. In India again there are cases in Nagpur and Bangalore, which are hundreds of miles inland . . .'

'How many?' asked Buchemin, to establish a fact there hadn't been time to find earlier.

'Under seven thousand in total,' responded the prepared presidential aide. 'That's why it hasn't yet been picked up by world health monitoring. Still wouldn't have been without us establishing our own far more detailed checks. But added together, from so many places, it's significant.'

'I still don't follow what this has got to do with what we're trying to deal with,' protested Lyalin.

It did seem an abrupt – and disassociated – intrusion, thought Reynell, worriedly. It was difficult to hold back, to guide it as he wanted it guided.

'We're waiting for the opinion of the scientific advisors,' said Amanda. 'At the moment a strain of influenza that appears to be able to jump species, from whales to humans – and all the other maritime occurrences I've outlined – remains inexplicable, as whatever it is that aged all our victims is inexplicable. That's the *only* significance we're offering. If our scientific advisors tell us there's no possible cause to include it in our thinking then we'll dismiss it. I've mentioned it today, this early in our discussion, to explain why it forms part of what you've still got to study.'

165

'North Sea grey seals are dying from distemper, a domestic dog disease?' queried Lyalin slowly, echoing Amanda's earlier explanation.

'That's one of the confirmed reports,' said Amanda.

'Are you familiar with Lake Baikal?' asked the Russian minister.

'Siberia,' identified Gerard Buchemin.

'What's happened there?' demanded Reynell, hurriedly, moving at last to take over. Could it be any better than he'd imagined, from what Paul Spencer had recounted?

'There's a species of freshwater seal, the *nerpa*, that isn't found anywhere else. For the past three months there have been reports of a disease decimating them. Just before I left Moscow there was confirmation that it was the same sort of distemper that affects domestic dogs,' disclosed the Russian.

'Another cross-species jump,' remarked Buchemin, solemnly.

'But not involving humans,' Amanda pointed out. 'Nothing we should allow ourselves to be deflected by, until we hear the opinion from Fort Detrick.'

'I don't agree,' declared Reynell, smiling towards her to take any offence from the contradiction. He wondered how long it would take her to completely follow his lead. 'OK, we're none of us health ministers but holding the portfolios we do we're certainly involved in the health of our countries. And we've just learned of an outbreak of one of the most feared and closely monitored diseases in medicine. No one knows how many people died in the influenza pandemic of 1918. Estimates range from forty to a hundred million. I'm fairly sure, from memory, that it was a cross-species infection. In late 1997 there was a human outbreak of influenza – fortunately limited – in Hong Kong that originated in chickens – a medically and scientifically proven species jump . . . whatever the opinion of Fort Detrick, we certainly can't ignore something that could become a cross-species pandemic on the scale of 1918. Something that, even on the small scale that our discoveries so far suggest, already appears to have spread far more extensively throughout the world than the Hong Kong incident of 1997.'

'You're right, of course,' came in Amanda, quickly. 'I didn't mean it should be forgotten . . . I meant in connection with what we are doing—'

'And I wasn't for a moment suggesting you were,' said Reynell, just as hurriedly, wanting Amanda as an ally – albeit an unwitting one – not someone resentful. He looked quickly towards the secretariat, where the record of what he needed to say would be made. Made, but not published, he told himself; not until it was too late to affect everything he wanted to achieve. 'And we must be extremely careful that we don't allow the connection to become blurred. We're all agreed on the need to keep the ageing illness from becoming public knowledge for as long as possible?'

'Yes,' said Lyalin, although doubtfully.

'But that there will more than likely be a public outcry when it is disclosed?'

'Yes,' agreed Lyalin, still cautious.

Reynell switched his attention to Spencer. 'We've got to thank Paul for creating the monitor that means, at this moment, we're the only people to have pulled together all these isolated, inexplicable things . . .'

Spencer smiled openly at the recognition. Amanda's face began to clear.

'A possible species transmission of influenza, a fatal disease, from mammal to humans is horrifying . . .' continued Reynell.

'. . . Undeniably so,' encouraged Amanda, not wanting to commit herself until she was sure.

'The sort of Frankenstein thing that will occupy the undivided attention of a lot of people,' suggested Reynell.

Like starting a brushfire war to divert the voting public from domestic difficulties, acknowledged Amanda. Did Reynell want the credit or was he offering it to her? When the man didn't continue she said: 'The influenza should be brought to the attention of world health authorities . . . and to the general public . . .'

'*The* World Health Organization,' insisted Reynell. 'Through our respective governments, to avoid directly drawing attention to ourselves of how and why we discovered the instances.' It was almost as if they were performing to a script, or rather a prologue to an even more complete script that he had already learnt virtually word for word for his equally well planned conversation with Simon Buxton. Was there any more to achieve today? Not here, Reynell decided. And he was sure there was a lot more mileage he hadn't yet worked out. But would, before very long. Maybe, even, on the flight back to London he decided at that moment to make.

'That would be the responsible thing to do,' agreed the French minister, joining the political quadrille.

Gregori Lyalin let the dance swirl around him, strangely – wrongly, he at once and realistically accepted – saddened by it. There was every political justification for what they were deciding – and with which he'd go along, for the same reason as they were agreeing it – but he wished the first concentration had been upon the unarguable medical need to alert the medical authorities and not upon minimizing any personal or political backlash, which it was easy enough to recognize. Did he have the right to such mental pretension? Lyalin asked himself, refusing the hypocrisy. He *would* go along with it. Which, in practical political terms, wasn't even dishonest. It was necessary expediency; the sort of thinking that was going to have to come as naturally to him as it automatically appeared to come to those with whom he had to establish himself. He said: 'It's definitely something that should be passed on, quite irrespective of whether it affects our remit or not.'

'I'm pleased that we're obviously going to work so well together,' said Amanda.

Nowhere near as pleased as I am, thought Reynell.

Geraldine Rothman changed her mind about immediately conducting secondary autopsies as she strode angrily from Stoddart's office, halted by what she half-heard of the conversation between Pelham and the Frenchman.

168

'Lebrun's got twelve hours,' confirmed Pelham, answering her question. 'Maybe not even that long.'

'Then I need to see him now,' she announced.

'We can both see him,' frowned Dupuy. 'That's what I'm on my way to do – to be as supportive as I can.'

'I mean *in* his room. I want to examine him myself . . .' She hesitated, as Dupuy's expression deepened. 'As a forensic pathologist.'

'No!' refused Dupuy at once, unthinking.

'It'll be no different from any examination he's undergone from any other doctor. I'll cause him no discomfort. I don't want to argue, but I don't think you can stop me. And of course you can watch all the time, from the observation gallery.'

'What do you want to do?'

'Examine someone who can hopefully answer questions; help me towards things I don't understand.' She hadn't repeated to any of them the doubts she'd raised with Stoddart the previous night, unwilling to create more mysteries she might be able to answer from her own, specifically directed examination.

'I'm not comfortable with one of our own group doing it,' said Dupuy.

Geraldine clenched her hands at her sides in renewed frustration. When the fuck was this man – were any of them – going to start thinking dispassionately, behaving dispassionately, like the medical specialists they were supposed to be! 'You know my professional qualifications.'

'I'm not arguing your capabilities.'

'Then what the hell are you arguing about? I've had some thoughts – valid, medical questions I want to answer – and I need to examine Henri Lebrun while he's still alive. *Please*, stop getting in my way!'

Dupuy nodded, capitulating under her outrage. 'I'll watch, from the gallery.'

'I'd like you to.' She switched to Pelham. 'You, too. I'd welcome input.'

The protective clothing was very different from that with which Geraldine was familiar – had actually been part of

169

approving – for British post mortems upon AIDS sufferers: thicker skinned and therefore more difficult to move in, the gloves most awkward of all, as thick as the rest of the uniform but seamed, which medical gloves were not. It would make it difficult to handle instruments with any sort of damage-restricting skill. She was glad it hadn't yet got to a dissecting blade operation with Henri Lebrun. Which was nothing more than a postponement, in the case of the Frenchman and any of the others upon whom she decided it was necessary to perform secondary examinations. Literally an operational bridge to cross when she reached it, not before.

Lebrun was awake, although tethered to his various catheters and drip feeds, his head moving at once although slowly to the soft sigh of the time-released lock of the inner sterilization chamber. At once, fragile-voiced, he demanded: 'What do you want?'

The watching Dupuy would have warned the man while she changed, Geraldine guessed. 'To talk. Check some things out.'

'You know it all.' The man's nose was running.

'I wish we did,' said Geraldine.

'You're not going to be able to save me, are you?' The Frenchman was emaciated, wasted, milky eyes not actually focused upon her but in the direction in which he knew the door to be.

'No.'

The man went to speak but his voice caught, like a hiccup. Then he said: 'Why did the others say they could help?'

'We hoped we could.'

'Fucking bastards!'

'Yes.' Geraldine thought she could hear movement on the relay microphones from the observation gallery but it equally might have been from her own movement, inside the suit. It *was* emaciation – wasting – despite his being able to eat protein and carbohydrate supplemented solids until a day and a half ago and having been on even more enhanced drips since then.

'You shouldn't have said that!' Guy Dupuy's metallically distorted protest echoed into her headset.

Geraldine ignored the man, reaching out for Lebrun's unprotesting, flacid hand. The bloody gloves were too thick to feel anything adequately! For the briefest, thwarted moment she considered tearing them off.

'Leave me alone!'

'You heard what he said,' came Dupuy's voice.

Again Geraldine ignored the unseen man, fumbling with her other hand for Lebrun's pulse which she couldn't effectively feel although she was conscious of the body heat, permeating the glove fabric. She squinted through the vizor for the heartbeat monitor, frowning at the reading, a fluctuation between 150 and 165, mostly the higher. She'd told the man he was dying, she accepted. So an increase was understandable. But not an increase – what appeared to be a consistent increase – of fifty per cent! Lebrun's heart – no one's heart – could sustain that demand. What had the pulse readings been of the Antarctic rescuers, before they'd died? She couldn't remember, although she was sure they would have been recorded, like Henri Lubrun's were being recorded, automatically, upon what could become an immediate computer print-out. If there was any comparison in the rapidity, they hadn't – she certainly hadn't – been professionally doing the job she'd been sent here to do. Neither – more culpably – had Pelham's teams if there had been matching readings from the Antarctic. The heart monitor pounded on, like a mocking drumbeat.

From behind the screen Pelham said: 'Can there be any useful purpose in this?'

Without looking in the unseen direction Geraldine said: 'That might be a question to put to your people, not to me!' She was scanning all the monitors now, looking for other readings, at once confused when she found the body temperature gauge. It was a normal average – 37 degrees – which was impossible with the heartbeat that was still registering mostly 165 beats a minute and with the positive warmth she could feel from the man's hand and wrist, through the glove. She said: 'How do you feel?'

'What sort of question is that!'

Geraldine winced at her own crassness. '*What* do you feel?'

'Nothing.'

'Are you hot?'

'Cold.'

Another impossibility. Why hadn't this all been picked up – brought to their attention – before now? Lebrun's wrist and arm remained unmoving when Geraldine released them, moving her hand to check the bed coverings. The room temperature would be as automatically recorded as everything else. And Lebrun was covered to the neck by two separate thermal blankets. With such an accelerated heartbeat, under two such blankets, the man should have been visibly perspiring but he was equally visibly totally dry skinned.

'What is it?' demanded Pelham.

Conscious of Lebrun's slow but obvious attention to the question, Geraldine once more didn't reply. Instead she said: 'I want to snip a little hair. That's OK, isn't it?'

'What is it?' echoed the Frenchman.

'I want to make some more tests,' said Geraldine, avoiding the question.

'Keep me alive! Please keep me alive!'

'Stop this!' came Dupuy's voice.

Geraldine's concentration was only upon the man before her. 'If I could . . . can . . .' she tried awkwardly, before stopping the clumsiness and abandoning the attempt. '. . . I can't . . .'

'Try . . . maybe . . .'

'Let me.'

The long-handled scissors on the instrument tray were specially adapted for protective suited use, the finger and thumb eyelets enlarged to accommodate gloved hands but Geraldine was unaccustomed to using them, unable to grasp them as she should have done. She finally picked them up between both hands, like shears, not needing any finesse to take her intended DNA sample, which was a mistake because trying to hold them that way was even more insecure. She

172

dropped them when she was bringing them over Lebrun's chest and her impeded attempt to keep them away from the man worsened the accident, tipping the blades to fall points first against the Frenchman's collar bone. There was no penetration but the force was sufficient to split the skin surface and there was a pinprick of blood, but Lebrun registered no reaction whatsoever.

Dupuy said: 'For God's sake, get out of there!'

To the Frenchman lying on the bed in front of her Geraldine said: 'Did you feel that?'

'What?'

Geraldine retrieved the scissors, pressing the points sufficiently to indent the skin but not break it further along the man's shoulder. 'Can you feel anything?'

'No.'

The blood spot on the collar bone had almost immediately coagulated. She eased the top of the smock away from the man's chest and four more times indented the skin. Lebrun felt nothing. Neither did he when she pricked both arms. Careful not to disturb any of the tubes and catheters to which he was linked, she eased aside the bed coverings and tested his unfeeling abdomen and legs. She finally took the hair clipping hurriedly, successfully at the second attempt, anxious to make the other tests she considered necessary. Wishing she could have used her bare fingers she instead utilized small surgical forceps to measure skin pinches in every part of Lebrun's body that had failed to respond to skin pricks and finally used a scalpel to scrape off what she considered sufficient skin from the man's forearms and thighs.

'Is it going to hurt when I die?' asked the man.

'No,' said Geraldine, sure that it wouldn't.

'How long?'

'Soon.'

'No one else would tell me.'

'It's your right to know; your dignity.'

'I hope I can maintain it.'

The two men were waiting for her outside the decontamination chamber, Dupuy hovering from foot to foot in red-faced

173

fury that nearly made it impossible for him to form the words and when they came they were at first disjointed. 'What the *hell* do you think you were doing in there?'

For the first time Geraldine saw Stoddart behind the other two and guessed he'd been summoned. She said: 'What should have been done before now: realizing and analysing what we did have, in front of our very eyes!'

'Good of you to call so regularly, Peter.'

'I'm planning to come back,' declared Reynell. Everything had to be timed to a watchmaker's precision but he was sure he could do it. The need was to feed – and predict – the man's perpetual anticipation and answer it for himself, ahead of anyone else, which made Cabinet meetings a one-man, self-operating puppet show. That and to let Buxton think there was a possibility in agreeing to his return to London.

There was a pause, before the jump from the London end. 'It's all turned out to be nothing then?'

Reynell smiled at the over-interpretation. 'Far from it. We could have a very serious situation here: one we need to be on record as having reacted to.'

'Are you absolutely sure you can afford to come back if it's that serious? Wouldn't it be better you stay there, on top of everything? But let me have a very full briefing overnight in the diplomatic bag.'

Imagining another opportunity to upstage him publicly in the House, in his absence, recognized Reynell. It was seed planting time. 'I accept that what I'm suggesting puts my credibility on the line, but as a science minister – although I suppose really it'll become a medical problem – I don't believe I can afford *not* to come back and personally address Cabinet. I've talked it through with Sir Alistair and also with Dr Rothman. They agree.' The name listing ensured Buxton knew there were independent witnesses to the call, people who would know if the man used prime ministerial authority to refuse the return. The fact that he hadn't been able to reach Geraldine Rothman was immaterial at the moment.

'What, exactly, is it?'

174

The unprovable moment of open deception, Reynell accepted: the moment, if he miscalculated by a hair's breadth, Buxton could isolate as the first positive move against him. 'British agriculture, tens of thousand of jobs, are still affected by the transmission of bovine spongiform encephalopathy into humans, as Creutzfeldt-Jakob disease . . .'

The hesitation was intentional and over-anxiously Buxton took it, as Reynell was sure the man would.

'What's the connection with mad cow disease and what you're doing there?' protested the prime minister.

'I'm using it as an example of a government miscalculation. I don't think we – you – should risk anything similar with what I've become aware of, since getting here. That's why I'm suggesting full Cabinet involvement . . .' The lure was feather light. 'I realize, of course, that Cabinet might go against me: consider I'm over-reacting, but I'm prepared to take that risk . . .'

'What is *it*?' insisted Buxton, impatiently.

'It could be an epidemic: a pandemic, even.'

'Confirmed?'

The bastard had bitten! 'No.'

'If you consider it's that serious, then of course you must.'

'Thank you, prime minister.' Before the failed coup meeting at the Carlton Club, Reynell had estimated his inner government support at just under half the Cabinet, with a sufficient number of uncommitted members to tip the balance either way in a direct leadership challenge. In just twenty-four hours – thirty-six at the most – he'd have changed the odds substantially.

'I've missed you,' said Henrietta, answering Reynell's next call.

'It'll only be a flying visit, literally: a day and a half maximum. Invite your father to dinner.'

'Are you making plans, Peter?'

'Serious plans.'

'Anything to tell me?'

Stoddart had been entering his office after the brief, dismissive

175

confrontation with Geraldine Rothman when Amanda's second call came. 'Could be the Brit's on to something. We won't know until she's finished re-examining some autopsy findings; maybe conducting secondaries herself. She's in the morgue now!

'Your McMurdo contract doesn't carry any third party liability insurance. Only if something happens to you, personally.' By telling her at the end of their meeting, as he had, Paul Spencer had obviously learned the intended lesson. Amanda hoped it lasted.

'Why are you telling me this?'

'I thought it was something important you should know.'

'Like the victims' families should know,' said Stoddart.

'Haven't you thought that by going solo you could screw up the special financial arrangements being planned here?'

'No,' admitted Stoddart.

'Think on it,' insisted Amanda. 'Think on it very hard indeed. What's more important, your conscience or the financial security of their wives and kids?'

'We've got trouble,' announced Sheldon Hartley, the Pentagon colonel who had jointly organized the security clampdown at McMurdo and Amunsden-Scott under the guise of medical concern.

'What?' demanded Spencer.

'Something approaching a rebellion in Antarctica,' said the soldier. 'They're not accepting any medical need without proof. My people don't know how much longer they can keep things under wraps. My team leader there talked this morning about needing to use force, which of course I forbade.'

'Of course,' agreed Spencer.

'I'm specifically asking for White House orders here.'

'I'll get back to you,' promised a lip-chewing Spencer.

His direct, private line rang again almost at once.

'Things are going badly wrong in the south,' said the Science Foundation's David Hoolihan.

'I've heard,' stopped Spencer.

Sixteen

Common as well as scientific sense made Geraldine accede to the authority and argument of Fort Detrick's stone-faced principal that she couldn't continue bulldozing on as a one-person medical investigation unit, either in the specially staffed laboratories or the mortuaries. But it took the entire foot-stomping journey to the research section for her to concede it.

The installation's chief pathologist, Barry Hooper, was a cautiously responsive black man who clearly hadn't expected – nor welcomed – direct involvement with anyone other than Walter Pelham. Neither, from his matching, quick blinking hesitation, had Duncan Littlejohn, the balding, pebble-spectacled head of scientific analysis. Pelham's unconcealed anger at her earlier, censorious dismissiveness completed the spring-tight unease. It was also too late – and the wrong place – to attempt to make amends, which in any case would only have been for Pelham's face-saving because Geraldine didn't genuinely think she had anything to apologize for. To have waited, as she believed the installation director had waited, for every test and analysis to be presented to their group as a comprehensive, end-of-term report, was ridiculous. The alarm-ringing, staring-in-the-face anomalies should have been presented for interpretation within minutes of their being isolated – presuming they had been isolated! – not held back until the arrival of the Alaskan survivors and victims and then further postponed until Raisa Orlov got there.

If they meant anything at all, came the echoing warning in Geraldine's mind. Instantly followed by a balancing – more than counterweighting – professional dogma. Fear of

177

being proved wrong was *never* scientifically a reason for not experimenting or asking, although courtesy to colleagues was an understood rule of engagement, which she'd badly failed to observe.

Geraldine shrugged aside the introspection, determined against wasting any more time, posing her questions without explaining why they needed to be asked. All stain tests on the tissue and blood of every victim – those barely surviving as well as those already dead – had failed to isolate any unknown bacterium, insisted Littlejohn. Nor had any antibodies or their formative antigens been detected, either microscopically or under electron microscopy.

'What about lymphoid cells?' demanded Geraldine. More Raisa Orlov's question than hers, the body-circulating lymph gland cells being those most usually and directly attacked by viruses. But she definitely didn't recognize any demarcations, although from that morning's encounter she imagined the Russian would try to erect electrified razor wire around her speciality.

'Lymphocytes were removed from every victim . . .' said Hooper. After quickly glancing at Pelham, the pathologist added: 'The most basic and obvious investigation, surely?'

Geraldine didn't respond to the patronizing defensiveness. 'Autolysis?'

'No evidence anywhere of disorder to indicate viral cell invasion,' responded Littlejohn, at once.

One hundred and sixty five beats a minute arrythmia, Geraldine remembered. 'Every one – those from both Antarctica and Alaska who were already dead – suffered massive heart failure, didn't they?'

For the first time the hostility eased. From Littlejohn there could even have been the vaguest admiration. Hooper said: 'My findings were general, massive organ failure.'

The positive professional clash, recognized Geraldine, expectantly. But she couldn't challenge yet, not until she'd conducted her own examinations. And not even challenge then. There'd still be time for the man to qualify the generalization, or rather to quantify it, which was what she foresaw

– hoped – to be able to do herself. 'But the heart failure was substantial?'

'Yes,' conceded Hooper.

'Manifested how?'

The pathologist's face stiffened, superciliously. 'How else? Muscle discolouration: infarction . . .'

'Softening,' pressed Geraldine. 'What about autolysis? In the brains, for instance?'

'Of course,' said the man. 'It's customary with normal ageing.'

'But this was anything but normal ageing,' Geraldine reminded. 'How much cerebal softening was there? Lique-faction?'

'There was liquefaction, yes.' Hooper's reluctance was easing.

'Pancreas?'

'Again, customarily one of the first organs most likely to fail.'

'Did it, in *every* case?' persisted Geraldine.

The looks this time were between Hooper and the man who'd headed the laboratory investigation and it was Littlejohn who replied. 'Not in every case. In Jane Horrocks, from Antarctica, we decided from their softness that her liver and kidneys went first. In Armstrong, the kidneys preceded the pancreas. In Ben Jordan, an Alaska victim, it was the spleen and gall bladder.'

Geraldine felt a warmth of satisfaction spread through-out her body. It was only when Pelham asked the signifi-cance of the reply that she realized she must have been smiling. She said: 'I don't know . . . don't know what it means, that is. But I think it's important – might give us a direction and prevent us taking the wrong path. Which I know is talking in more riddles than we already have and why I want to take it further before offering any-thing more . . .' She handed Littlejohn the slide contain-ing some of the skin she had pared from the still living body of Henri Lebrun. 'While I'm . . .' she began, stopping before the undiplomatic mistake, '. . . assisting Barry with

179

the secondary autopsies, I'd appreciate your running a test on this.'

'To establish what?' frowned Littlejohn.

'Whether it's living skin. Or skin that's already dead. From a dead man.'

Geraldine half-expected Walter Pelham to accompany them into the dissecting area but he didn't, although he came as far as the suiting room. The bodies of Buckland Jessup and George Bedall, the two Antarctic victims whose condition and symptoms had first aroused Geraldine's doubts, lay ready on adjoining dissecting tables, the skin still whitened by its recent refrigerated preservation. Geraldine considerately gave way to Hooper on the man's own territory, following several steps behind. There were two similarly suited attendants already there. At the tables the pathologist looked enquiringly at her through his vizor and because she hoped more quickly to find her answer – some answer at least – from the rodeo-riding Texan, she identified Buckland Jessup. The body had lost both the immediate after-death rigor and the effect of being climatically frozen and was fully outstretched, no longer squatted with the hands in an outstretched praying or entreating position.

'What are we looking for? Or at?' demanded Hooper.

'The vertebrae. Other bones later, but the easiest to reach first.'

The two attendants moved immediately, uncovering the already investigated body. The original entry from sternum to pelvis had been as neatly rejoined as would have been an incision on someone living. She'd always liked – admired – such courtesy upon the bodies of the already dead. The opening parted with Hooper's release of the sutures, exposing the organ-removed chest and intestinal cavities, with no obstruction to the spinal column.

'Well?' Hooper demanded.

Geraldine reached forward, but abruptly stopped, remembering that Pelham, who would be watching from the gallery, would be among the rest of the control group before which

180

she would later explain these practical experiments to support her theory. 'You before me,' she yielded. 'Try intruding your finger where the thoracic joins the cervical.'

Hooper's extended finger went maybe a millimetre into vertebrae and supporting trabeculae. 'Consistent with what I would expect.'

'Now try the sacrum, nearest to the coccygeal.'

The pathologist's forefinger virtually disappeared into the unresisting softness. Without commenting, Geraldine manually repeated the tests for herself. At the sacrum her forefinger penetrated almost to the second knuckle into the intra medullary canal.

Hooper said: 'Localised skeletal dying is recognized.'

'Spinal differences of this magnitude?' Geraldine challenged. She was right! she decided, feeling another burst of satisfaction. She didn't know about what, but she might have found an entrance into the maze.

'It's unusual.'

'Have you ever known spongoid as extreme as this, upon any examination you've ever conducted?'

'No, I haven't,' the man finally conceded.

From the reluctance, Geraldine guessed this hadn't been part of any autopsy finding, on any victim. 'Could we now expose a femur?'

'Both thighs?'

She needed to be as sure as she possibly could be, Geraldine decided. 'Please.'

It took far longer, because of the connected muscle and ligament encasement. In both, the finger-penetrating spongioses was as pronounced as at the spinal base, towards which, at the suggestion of the now fully co-operative American, they extended the incisions as far as the hips. In both, and at the knees, there were the pronounced bony outgrowths of osteoporosis. There was also sufficient cartiliginous mass in the right femur to suggest osteosarcoma.

'Where did you get the suggestion?' asked Hooper outright.

'The way they were found, in Antarctica. It was a guess.'

The second post mortem, upon George Bedall's forearms, found the same degree of spongiosis in both but although the bone was wafer thin – later tests showed it to be less than a third of the thickness it should have been – the two breaks in each, the first where the astrophysicist had fallen in the field station, the second intentionally broken by Morris Neilson to get the corpse into the sleeping bag, were distinctly sharp edged and separated, not joined greenstick fractures of bone that was soft.

Hooper said: 'We need second autopsies on every victim, for bone tests, don't we?'

'I think so,' said Geraldine. It was only when she straightened, supporting herself against the specially adapted support chair, that she realized she had been bent over dissecting tables for five hours. Her entire body throbbed. It didn't help when she tried to stretch the ache from her back and shoulders.

'Congratulations.'

'It doesn't prove anything.'

'It's more than anything my teams found so far. And we thought we'd finished.'

It was only when she was stripping off in the decontamination chamber that Geraldine discovered the tear in the forefinger of her left-hand glove. She hadn't been aware of it happening at any time during the autopsies and decided it was far more likely to have occurred unzipping and undoing the awkwardly stiff fastenings of the protective suit. In which case it had occurred after she'd safely passed through the sterilization process. She still intently studied the forefinger, satisfying herself there was no skin break or abrasion.

Walter Pelham and Duncan Littlejohn were waiting outside the chamber. The laboratory director said at once: 'Lebrun's outer skin, the coreum, was dead of course.'

'Of course?' urged Geraldine, expectantly now.

'But the layers below, the lucidum, gradulosum and both strata of the germinative, were dead, too! The man is literally only being contained – held together – by the last corium layer!'

182

'So you've established necrobiosis?' said Pelham. There was none of Hooper's earlier acknowledgement or Littlejohn's disbelief.

'The decay and death of the outer epidermis is a constant process,' said Geraldine, saddened by the man's resistance. 'The dying of the other strata in supposedly living people is unknown, wouldn't you agree?'.

Pelham flushed. 'There's an urgent message for you to return your minister's call, at the embassy,' said Pelham. 'And the Russian translations are ready. You OK for a late night meeting? You'd seem to be the person with most to say.'

Geraldine still ached, despite the shower. 'What time?'

'You're the one who's got to catch up. Midnight's been fixed, for your benefit.'

And with what she was already doing still unfinished. 'Midnight's fine.'

She spent a further full hour gratefully seated in the observation gallery individually questioning Harold Norris and Darryl Matthews, disappointed at not getting the replies she wanted from either Alaskan survivor. It was probably too much to expect to score ten out of ten, but it would still have been good. The Russian material waiting in her room didn't look too formidable and she took a hopefully relaxing bath before telephoning Washington. By the time she did – no longer aching so much – Peter Reynell had already flown out on the London-bound Concorde. The message was to ring him at his London home in four hours.

Perfect timing with an hour to spare before the scheduled scientific meeting, Geraldine calculated, finally settling down to read what Raisa Orlov had supplied.

'It was stupid! Arrogant, stupid and achieved nothing except belittling yourself!' accused Gregori Lyalian, intentionally stressing the contempt to puncture the woman's pomposity. 'It's entirely a matter for you if you want to make a fool of yourself. It's not, when you make a fool of me, your superior. And of your country, which you're supposed to be representing at an international forum. I've ordered everything, omitted in what you brought, sent immediately from the Institute and now I am giving you a direct order – which I'm placing on record here at the embassy with the ambassador – to co-operate totally with everyone with whom you are supposed to be working. You understand that better than when I told you virtually the same in Moscow?'

Raisa Orlov physically shook with fury at the rebuke, her hands – her entire body – so wet with perspiring anger that she had to use both to avoid dropping the telephone. It would have been the pig-fucking American, Stoddart, who'd complained direct. No doubt urged on by the British woman who he was probably fucking, in between pigs. 'There is an anti-Russian animosity here,' she tried. 'I was tricked into a discussion before I had the opportunity to study what was available here: to assess my responses.'

'It was nothing of the sort!' rejected Lyalin. 'It was preposterous arriving without a translation. And from what I read in the original, after that translation was made by the Americans, to have left out the material that I've now got on its way.'

'How have you explained the omissions?' The enforced humility rasped out, as if there was a physical obstruction in her throat.

Lyalin refused her any escape. 'You tell me how to explain it. You created the problem.'

'Not ready,' she said.

'Speak up! I didn't hear you.'

'I said that the complete written findings and the samples weren't ready when we left Moscow.'

'How are you going to explain specimens that clearly *were* taken, days ago, not being made available?'

'They were still being worked on.'

Would this humiliation – and this reprimand – bring her to her senses? wondered Lyalin. 'I'll support that story. This time. If there's any more totally justifiable criticism I shall order you back to Moscow and have someone replace you. And to ensure there isn't any misunderstanding, I'm going to put all this in writing and have it brought up to you at Fort Detrick.'

Criticism, isolated Raisa. So there had been a direct complaint! And Gregori Lyalin was siding with the Americans – with the West – against her. She would have to be very careful, she thought, although not thinking about any of the warnings she'd just received. She was the person with the international reputation, not the man who covered himself in so much hair he looked like a bird nesting inside an overgrown hedge. She couldn't risk making her calls to the Institute from here but that's what she had to do. Independently reach people she controlled and make sure the stories were spread about her abandonment. She'd also need to get some idea of Lyalin's strength, within the Kremlin and within the Moscow White House. No one was going to treat her as Lyalin imagined he could treat her. Neither him nor the people she was going to meet again, in just a few hours; meet and be totally prepared this time. Ready. And knowing full well that scientifically and medically none of them had the slightest clue what they were up against. Or, she thought with a smile, *whom* they were up against.

In his working part of the Detrick complex, Jack Stoddart was using the intervening hours as diligently as Geraldine. Although there was data still to correlate, the proof of warming from the robot gauges at Noatak and close to the destroyed Antarctic base was positively established. And the drafted-in paleobotanist had promised at least preliminary results of the protectively obtained permafrost cores from the same locations by eleven that night. Stoddart was impatient to know whatever Geraldine had discovered, and supposed as chairman of the group he could approach her in advance but decided instead to wait to hear it at the same time as the others. It was more important to assess the outbreaks of human influenza, and if what Amanda O'Connell had told him on the telephone about the infection in Lake Baikal fitted in with everything else the CIA and Science Foundation monitors were picking up. He was beginning to think that although there might be no direct connection

185

with the ageing disease, there might be a linking thread: two maybe.

Henrietta lay on her back, totally pleasured, needing only to bring her outstretched arms across to hold Reynell's head. 'If foreplay became a separate Olympic event as well as fucking, you could go for gold in both.' Reynell made to move but she anxiously tightened her grip, keeping his head where it was. 'No! . . . It's coming . . . coming . . . there!'

He moved up the bed, trailing his tongue over her stomach and breasts, until he was level with her. After several minutes Henrietta said: 'Who was that on your telephone?'

'The scientific advisor still in Washington.'

'You fucking her?'

'Did it sound like I was fucking her from what we said?'

'I hope you're not going to disappoint me, darling.'

'I haven't ever before, have I?'

Henrietta refused the *double entendre*. 'Daddy's very curious. So am I.'

'I want to clear the Cabinet meeting first.'

'Influenza!' she exclaimed, disbelievingly, having overheard Reynell's end of the conversation an hour before.

'You'd be surprised who's going to catch the cold!' Reynell enjoyed his own joke, sniggering at it, and decided to use it again so that Henrietta could appreciate it too, when she'd be better able to understand.

'My turn to welcome you home,' she said, sliding further down in the bed.

Seventeen

Jack Stoddart regarded that morning's false start and the later irritable frustration outside Henri Lebrun's isolation chamber as learning curves. From what Amanda had told him, the Russian awkwardness was limited to Raisa Orlov personally, not one of the woman performing to a Moscow script, which kept the problem localized for him to eradicate, and this was Amanda's judgment as well. If Raisa Orlov attempted a repetition tonight he had to confront it head on and get any black hat, white hat shit out of the way, even at the risk of further embarrassment.

Certainly the Russian woman had created the most obvious difficulty. But his major role (what the fuck *was* his full role?) had to be always to remain totally objective. And being objective, it was unfair to isolate Raisa as the only disruption. Stoddart understood Geraldine Rothman's frustration. And although in terms of normal scientific investigation they were moving at the speed of light, his sense, like Geraldine's, was that they'd wasted time waiting for every result to come in to be analysed and cross-checked and referenced with every other finding, instead of reacting at once to anything unexpected. But to have done so would have been to ignore their necessary level of professionalism. They'd followed established – internationally required – medical investigative methodology. Which made Geraldine's unthinking, lash-out-at-anyone impatience just as distracting as Raisa Orlov's initial, backfired condescension. And, completing the circle, justified Walter Pelham's complaint about the British scientist and her peremptory demands as she left Henri Lebrun's room for specific laboratory tests on organs removed from the dead, as well as upon specimens she'd taken from the Frenchman.

Thank God it had all happened so quickly, within a single half-intervening day. So far, only he knew – acknowledged – his own difficulty with the uninvited function politically imposed upon him. A very personal learning – realizing – curve indeed.

Because it was the initial formal session requiring a record-maintaining secretariat, they were assembling in a small conference room closer to Pelham's suite and Stoddart got there early enough to be the first – psychologically the person in control – although he only made it minutes ahead of Pelham himself, who was accompanied by one of the support staff with individual copies of the completed laboratory tests. Stoddart considered adding his assessment of the emergency team and robot sampling from both American sites, but decided the data was best kept separate to avoid its being overwhelmed. Stoddart still checked through the thick file and quickly located the transcripts of the earlier Blair House meeting at which Gregor Lyalin – as well as apologizing for the translation failure – disclosed the seal disease outbreak at Lake Baikal.

Watching Stoddart going through reports, Pelham said: 'Dr Rothman's late input is all that's missing.'

Diplomacy time, Stoddart at once recognized. Dr Rothman, not Geraldine, uttered in a voice as stiff as the man himself. Stoddart said: 'We're all a little strung out, Walt. I need your help keeping things as smooth as I can. As smooth as they need to be kept, for everything to stay on course. I'd appreciate a little slack.'

'So would I,' said the dry, unyielding man.

'I'll do what I can to see you get it. Your people are closer to what she's been doing today. You think she's got something?'

'Maybe.'

Stoddart didn't like the attitude: refusing to acknowledge the contribution of others – particularly when they formed part of the same working team – was the very apogee of

188

scientific protocol. 'If she has, so soon, we're all going to look good.'

'We'll see.'

It had been Amanda's suggestion that Paul Spencer sit in on the session, as he was doing in Washington, and the liaising American arrived at the same time as Guy Dupuy. Looking between the two men already there Dupuy said to Pelham: 'You told him?'

The installation director said: 'Lebrun died two hours ago. Much quicker than we believed he would.'

The reluctance of a misdiagnosis or continuing petulance? Stoddart felt able to confront both – or either – women if he had to, but he could hardly challenge openly the man in charge of the complex itself. If Pelham's attitude became a problem, the correction would have to come from Washington, an admission by inference that he couldn't properly hold the group together as he was expected to do.

The entry of the two women was almost simultaneous, too, Raisa ahead by maybe a minute. Each of them had been early, Stoddart noted, wondering if they'd all tried for the psychological first. If she had – but in fact been the last – it didn't appear to upset Geraldine. He hoped the tiredness he was sure he detected hadn't shortened her temper any further. She was wearing the same rumpled shirt and jeans of the morning. Raisa had changed into a fulsome but uncreased smock over trousers and she'd lightly made up. Geraldine hadn't bothered. Her face shone under the artificial light, hinting at freckles.

Moving at once to stamp his authority on to the gathering, Stoddart said: 'This is our first working session with everyone involved—' He patted the medical dossier in front of him. 'There's a lot here to digest and a lot more to talk about. If we're going to move forward, which we must, the input from each of us has got to be constructive . . .' He filled the staged pause looking at the blank faces around him. 'Which is what the disagreements have to be, as well: constructive, not divisive. Let's work – together – for points to be made, not scored . . .'

189

The pig-fucker was making a direct, personal attack upon her, Raisa knew, posturing in front of the rest of them, probably playing out some charade over which they'd already sniggered in preparation. Geraldine supposed the rebuke was in order but she hadn't expected it. Until that moment, without consciously calling it to mind, she hadn't put Stoddart down as a forceful man; not disinterested – how could he have been disinterested! – but aloofly distracted. The new emergence was interesting.

Too general, judged Pelham. This session had to be the test. He wasn't again going to be treated as the British woman imagined she could treat him – treat everyone – and if Stoddart couldn't run the operation better the problem had to be raised with Washington, direct, not through the liaison man beside him. Raised and solved. Fort Detrick was his complex and his was the supreme authority here. It hadn't been such a good idea after all to agree to Stoddart being the neutral controller because the words contradicted themselves. Stoddart was being too neutral, which prevented his being in control.

Guy Dupuy was locked into his own uncertainty, held there by Lebrun's death. The medical opinion had been that the climatolagist should have survived for twelve hours and he'd died in eight. Dupuy remained unsure whether he'd had the authority to prevent the British woman's examination, Lebrun himself being by then beyond any rational decision. If the autopsy currently being conducted found evidence that Lebrun's death had been accelerated, even by as little as a few hours, by Dr Rothman's intrusion then surely he had some culpability, for not forbidding it.

Paul Spencer cupped his hands over a stomach from which all university muscle tone had been melted by overindulgence and was surprised at the outspokenness, which hadn't been necessary down in Washington but from which there might conceivably be a morsel to bite at, which was why he'd argued so strongly to attend, relegating the unrest in Antarctica – for which he so far hadn't thought of a resolve anyway – until the following day. Had there been more friction here than that which he already knew about over the translation failure? Yet again he was at the right place at the right time.

'. . . bulk of what's before us comprises autopsy specimen analysis and that of organic and waste material recovered from the Antarctic and Alaska, all conducted here at Fort Detrick,' Stoddart was saying. 'So let's begin with a verbal summary if we can, Walt.' The christian name informality was intentional but Stoddart was at once unsure if he shouldn't have accorded the director his title as a reminder that they were guests in Pelham country. Too late now. Why the fuck should he have to worry about such irrelevance?

'Details which may have been overtaken by Dr Rothman's work today,' responded Pelham, at once. 'Perhaps it might be better if we heard the outcome of that first, our not having any written presentation to examine, for comparison or perspective.'

'It would risk confusion, by it being out of context, rather than move us forward,' refused Stoddart. 'Let's start with you. Then we'll come to Dr Rothman and after that I've got something to say about the climate monitors. And I think there's something to be gained by discussing these other sea life outbreaks and transmitted influenza that we've been asked to comment about . . .' At once contradicting himself, he said: 'You might like to consider the fact that the political group in Washington have decided to pass the influenza outbreaks on to the World Health Organization.'

'My own minister has returned, briefly, to London to do that,' added Geraldine.

What about my supposed liaison role, thought Spencer, who'd seen the human influenza outbreaks – outbreaks that wouldn't yet have been identified if it hadn't been for his establishing the global search – as his contribution to the meeting.

Raisa wondered why Gregori Lyalin hadn't told her about the influenza decision, when clearly their ministers had told Stoddart and Geraldine Rothman! A refusal to communicate could be a useful complaint to make to Moscow about the man.

191

The only outward sign of Pelham's inner turmoil at being overruled was the faintest flush to the man's cheeks, gone as quickly as it so briefly came. His hands were without the slightest tremor as he opened his master file, the previously prepared pandect now scrawled with updated notes from the examinations of Henri Lebrun and the two Antarctic victims. When he began to speak there wasn't any tremor in his voice, either. Every organ, tissue and the blood of every already dead victim – including that of Jane Horrocks's unborn foetus – had been subjected to every known pathology test, examination and evaluation. There had been no positive bacterial response to Gram staining. Neither had the serology isolated natural immunity interferon to indicate body resistance to a viral infection. From both Antarctica and Alaska there had been full recovery of faeces and urine, although there was disinfectant contamination from the storage systems. Despite which no bacteria, virus or parasite had been detected. Neither had there been any presence in the undischarged faeces or urine of the bodies brought back for examination. Every piece of garbage from discarded food tins, containers and debris had undergone every bacterialogical examination. Nothing had been found. None of the medical conditions discovered among five victims – gall stones, blood sugar level suggesting nascent diabetes, duodenum ulceration and a chlamydia venereal infection – had any relevance to the ageing phenomena from which they had died. Each had shown outward physical and inner organic deterioration consistent with extreme senility, the most obvious outward signs being hair discolouration or loss – in three cases total – skin wrinkling and brown keratoses markings and finger and toenail keratinzation. In four there had been glaucoma or macular degeneration and in three arthritis. The most predictable and common manifestation within the bodies of every victim had been the substantial bone thinning of osteoporosis.

Unexpectedly Pelham stopped, looking sideways to Geraldine. 'No doubt you'd like to come in at this stage?'

The woman appeared surprised. 'No,' she said, refusing, too, the condescension. 'Not at all. You're helping me. What, overall, was the extent of medullary spongiosis to the brain?'

Pelham's face briefly coloured again. 'Softening was extreme, in every case: even the foetus. Before his death Burke, the pilot of the Antarctic rescue plane, evidenced advanced Alzheimer's.' The man paused. 'Which might be an anomaly to point up. Burke unquestionably *was* suffering Alzheimer's, a condition that needs to manifest itself by a loss of reality in life. Apart from the medically recognized prematurely ageing diseases in children, there are a number of other age-related or associated conditions: Parkinson's, Huntington's chorea, polycystic kidney growth, pituitary inflammation, Shy-Drager Syndrome. . .' There was another pause, for Pelham mentally to ensure he'd completed the list. 'There is no scientific post-mortem evidence that any victim suffered any of those afflictions . . .'

There were other commonalities, Pelham suggested. It had been possible to make after-death comparisons with every victim from the detailed medical records available and again in every case – with the exception of the foetus, which was larger than it should have been – the bodies had lost size, weight and height, sometimes by as much as three inches. With another inviting glance at Geraldine, who shook her head, Pelham said that in every case the monitors upon those who had been alive when they arrived at Fort Detrick had over the last thirty-six hours of life registered grossly increased pulse rates: James Olsen's heart had been recorded pumping at 170 beats a minute, which should have been medically impossible to sustain over such a period.

'What we have,' concluded Pelham, in what appeared an unexpected admission, 'is an extremely comprehensive record of what we *don't* know against which there is far too little that we can claim *to* know . . .' Yet again the man deferred to Geraldine. 'As you all know specimens have already been made available to Dr Rothman specifically for DNA analysis. In anticipation of each of you needing them, I have arranged comparative samples of every serology and pathology examination conducted here for each of your own molecular and medical research facilities to conduct independent study.'

193

Stoddart was surprised by the gamble, but clearly Pelham was confident enough of his own installation's research to be certain that others in London, Paris and Moscow wouldn't isolate anything either. The risk remained that one of the other countries *would* make the breakthrough, which was clearly the thought mirrored by Spencer's briefly startled – and even more quickly covered – expression. The concealment was helped by the Russian's even quicker reaction.

'*I* didn't know of any DNA material being made available!' said Raisa Orlov.

'You weren't here when they were provided,' said Pelham. 'There was obviously a record kept of every specimen and sample. All of which can be duplicated, if you wish to conduct separate, repeated gene experimentation: any experimentation whatsoever.'

Paul Spencer made a note of what he saw as a further concession.

Geraldine said: 'Anything – and everything – my research centre might find will be made freely available.'

There was nothing confrontational in Geraldine's voice, any more than there had been in Pelham's, but Stoddart was anxious to bring the discussion back on scientific course and there was something close to irony that it was Raisa who provided it.

Coming up from the newly provided medical material she said: 'I can't find anything here about culture growths?'

'Because we haven't succeeded in growing any,' said Pelham. 'As I've already made clear, we didn't recover from any victim a single instance of viral cell invasion or mutation, from which we would obviously have attempted egg-fertilized cultures. Despite which, we've tried cultivation, from each victim, with lymph cells. Nothing whatsoever developed.'

'We've yet to hear today's work carried out by Dr Rothman,' prompted Guy Dupuy, anxious for any indication, however slight, absolving him from negligence in Lebrun's death.

'Which certainly – obviously – has links with what I have already outlined and is included in greater detail in the medical

194

file I've provided,' said Pelham, suspecting from those few of his forensic scientists who had been swept up in Geraldine Rothman's slipstream that what she had to say would appear more medically exciting than anything he'd offered and eager to get a connection established by the secretariat.

Stoddart had expected more discussion upon Pelham's presentation, inconclusive though it had been, but reminded himself that if there were factors common to both it made sense to consider Geraldine's contribution now and revert back and forth between the two as and when anyone had a point to make. They would be, in fact, maintaining his sequential insistence. It was so far going better than he'd hoped. Geraldine was actually looking at him, for his agreement. 'If you're ready, Gerry?' he invited.

Gerry, seized Raisa, actually the diminutive of the woman's given name! If he wasn't already screwing her – which he probably was – he clearly intended to. With much of her earlier anger gone – and what remained under tight control – it was a detached, uncritical reflection. Raisa's bisexual appetite matched her size and, as well as banqueting at any bedside table to satisfy it, Raisa had without hesitation enthusiastically used her sexual as well as scientific ability to progress her career whenever it had been necessary and sometimes even when it hadn't. Quite apart from very personally deriding the woman who had that morning far too publicly derided her, there could, Raisa accepted, be every professional benefit enclosing Jack Stoddart between her legs. He certainly looked the only likely candidate, compared against the stick-like installation director, a presidential aide who looked like one of those bulging children's toys that always returned upright when it was pushed over and a Frenchman with a buttoned jacket like about-to-burst skin and bagged trousers full of farts.

'Buckland Jessup couldn't have died kneeling, with his hands outstretched, which was how he was found in the Antarctic field station. The body would have collapsed,' Geraldine began. 'George Bedall's arms wouldn't have cleanly snapped, not once but twice, the first time when he

195

fell, the second when the rescue doctor had to break them to transport the body. Arm sections can only separate as positively as Bedall's were when they're shattered by a blow and even then that's not positive, edge from edge separation. The force of the blow creates fragments – fracturing – and there weren't any on the X-rays taken within the first hour of his body arriving here . . .'

There was every reason for her to give the explanation like this, beginning logically with the first incongruity that had occurred to her, but Geraldine consciously recognized that instead of a clinical recitation she was dramatizing the presentation, building towards a denouement as if it was a work of fiction. It was as if she wanted to impress someone with her medical deduction, which was ridiculous. She'd already talked through some of it – the beginning at least – with Jack Stoddart so what . . . Geraldine abruptly halted the drift. So what, indeed? What place did Jack Stoddart have in any reflection that she might be performing to impress anyone?

Hurriedly, strangely disconcerted, she went on: 'That's all I had this morning, something I didn't understand. Which I wanted to investigate further, with a second autopsy . . .' She turned briefly towards Pelham. 'But on the way I was told Henri Lebrun was about to die. What happened then – what I think we learned then – started as an accident, as discoveries so often do. I dropped an instrument, point first, and very superficially punctured the skin, at Lebrun's shoulder. He didn't feel it. Neither did he feel skin pricking over most of his body: only in his hands and the soles of his feet – the latter most often neurologically used for body sensitivity testing – was there any reaction. I took skin samples, as deep as the germinative strata. They were dead. His body temperature was quite normal, 37°C, but he complained of feeling cold. Yet his pulse rate was averaging 158, frequently peaking higher . . .'

'That's not possible!' protested Raisa. 'The readings are wrong!'

'I know it's not possible,' agreed Geraldine. 'But the instruments recording it as such are accurate and you've

196

heard from Walter that similar readings – higher even, at 170 – were taken over the last thirty-six hours of the lives of all those who briefly survived here.'

'You told him he was going to die,' accused Dupuy.

'I didn't tell all the rest whose hearts beat at the same rate. And the print-out of Lebrun's monitor shows it was averaging 158 for twelve hours before I entered his room. It wasn't a shock reaction.'

'What was it then?' asked Stoddart.

'I think it was the heart trying to do its job and keep him alive,' said Geraldine. She didn't have to dramatize anything for effect: impress anybody. All of them – all trained, experienced, unemotional scientists of various disciplines – were regarding her with various degrees of unease. 'I personally attended second autopsies upon Buckland Jessup and George Bedall, specifically to examine why Jessup was kneeling as he was and why Bedall's arms snapped, like dry sticks. Now, post rigor, Jessup's lower spine, femur and tibia are in advanced stages of medullar spongiosis, despite mortuary preservation. As are both of Bedall's arms. I've taken specimens –' She looked to Raisa – 'sufficient for all . . . for the genetic testing I want to carry out, as I wish to do upon Henri Lebrun's already dead skin samples. And that's what I expect to confirm orthopaedically from bone re-examination upon all the victims: that Jessup remained upright, arms outstretched, because his legs and arms were already dead and rigored. Where he died was as far as he could pitifully drag himself, towards the door. Before the rigor could dissipate, he froze. So that's how he stayed until he was found.'

Raisa shook her head in refusal. 'You're suggesting localized necrosis?'

'Not localized for long,' said Geraldine, in matching refusal. 'I believe – and I hoped to get some genetic as well as organic proof – that this ageing disease affects organs and tissue progressively, killing each off—'

'No!' rejected Raisa, although objectively. 'If that happened – certainly in the case of the man who was found to be kneeling – there would have been gangrene.' She tapped

197

her medical dossier. 'There's nothing here about gangrene.'

'There wasn't any,' agreed Geraldine. 'Degeneration occurs predominantly because of an interruption of blood supply and flow. There has been no blood interruption in any parts of the bodies upon which autopsies, first and secondary, have so far been completed. Although the organs, tissue and limbs died, blood still circulated – pumped around the body by increasingly overstrained hearts trying to keep up with metabolisms going completely haywire . . .'

There was a moment of deliberating silence. Uncertainly – denied the necessary scientific A-B-C progression – Pelham said: 'As a theory it fits the anomalies. But contravenes – contradicts – every accepted molecular principle . . .'

'. . . totally,' insisted Raisa.

Neither remark was personal, a dismissal of Geraldine Rothman. It was, judged Stoddart, a refusal to accept a deviation from the rules. After that morning, the Russian still very much needed to establish herself. 'This is something about which I could certainly do with more guidance, Raisa.'

'I think I could, too,' said Dupuy, in an unexpected bonus.

Now her given name, isolated the attentive Russian. They were patronizing her, as she'd known they would, which made her churn inside but which she had, for the moment, to accept: pretend she hadn't realized. To lecture would be patronizing them, in turn.

'Think of blood vessels, arteries, as the pathways through the body constantly travelled by blood itself. Which carries the oxygen to keep the organs of the body alive,' Raisa began, spacing the words for her own amusement at student dictation speed. 'Unless there's an infection – a virus or a bacteria – in the blood, as long as it flows organs stay alive. The only other way they can die is if there's a blockage, an infarction. Or a direct wound . . .'

Had Stoddart and Dupuy really wanted it like this, painting by numbers? wondered Geraldine. Or was the Russian . . . ? Geraldine stopped the thought, as well as holding back the temptation to interrupt with the insistence that the autopsies – most certainly that upon Henri Lebrun – would prove her right.

198

'So there has to be an explanation that complies with, not contravenes, medical and molecular science,' Raisa was continuing. 'Which logically brings us back to infection. I don't know of any bacterium that fails to respond to Gram staining. Which leaves us with a virus that has so far escaped detection by any recognized staining technique. Which it could easily do if it's a virus we haven't any previous experience of and which I think it is. As we're speculating, let's speculate further but more logically. A staphylococcu bacteria can be as small as a thousand nanometres and a nanometre is one thousand millionth of a metre. Viruses are usually enclosed in a capsid, a shell, of protective protein. Sometimes there's a second, protective envelope—' She looked directly at Pelham. 'Wouldn't you be happier thinking of a virus smaller than any science has ever encountered before, beating us for the moment by hiding perhaps behind a third protein layer?'

Pelham actually looked between the two women, aware he was being shepherded into a choice and unwilling to make either. 'We're into the realms of the unknown. It's a theory. Both are theories.'

Which could be expanded, thought Geraldine, professionally. 'At the moment, we have scientific – medical – proof without knowing what it proves of blood-supplied organs and tissue dying. Perhaps what you refer to as an indication in the blood of your victims will turn out to be the bacteria or antigen or antibodies or interferon that will lead us to a virus. Which would be a quantum leap. So it might, if examinations like I conducted upon Henri Lebrun could be carried out on those of your victims still surviving. Are they still alive?'

Bitch! thought Raisa. 'I'm waiting for a reply, through the embassy in Washington, about the survivors. Blood specimens are on their way, for repeat testing here.' There *was* something in the blood of two of those who'd died at Iultin. So she had to be right!

'A virus has a genetic structure,' stated Geraldine.

'A fact I'm sure we all know,' said Raisa. 'Just as I'm sure we'll benefit from your particular expertize when the virus is found.'

Shit! thought Stoddart, uneasily.

'I don't think the point I want to make need wait until then,' said Geraldine evenly. 'For the sake of the discussion, let's go for the moment with the virus theory. If it has DNA – deoxyribonucleic acid – we'll be lucky . . .' Allowing herself the balancing superciliousness she said: 'Another fact I'm sure we all know is that a virus invades a cell and feeds off it to reproduce more viruses which then infect the body. DNA checks itself; if there's a mutation, it repairs it. It stays as one virus and if your theory is right and we isolate it, we can raise a vaccine—'

'What *is* your point?' broke in Raisa.

'Ribonucleic acid,' said Geraldine and stopped. The Russian had herself sawn through the branch she had chosen to sit upon and pontificate, so fuck her.

Walter Pelham saved Raisa. He said: 'Do we really need to be any more frightened than we already are?'

'I don't want to slow anything down, but the rest of you understand molecular biology. I don't,' said Stoddart. 'I really would appreciate your making it as simple as possible, so I can keep up.'

'Ribonucleic acid – RNA – is another genetic structure of viruses. The influenza bug is one of them,' expanded Geraldine. 'RNA doesn't – can't – correct itself. If there is a gene mutation while it's replicating itself in a host cell, it can create an entirely new virus. So the vaccine we might cultivate against our first virus – if we find one – won't be effective against the second . . .'

'. . . Or the third or the fourth and so on and so on,' said Pelham.

'Jesus!' said Paul Spencer.

'We haven't established it's a virus yet,' cautioned Pelham, urgently.

'What *can* we establish?' asked the dispirited Dupuy.

'Temperature,' said Stoddart shortly.

More for Raisa Orlov than anyone else Stoddart offered what brief documentary material there was, but suggested that with

200

the Antarctic and Alaska monitoring covering only days they might prefer to wait for a complete month's readings. Because the now destroyed field station had not existed the previous winter, there was no direct day or week comparison, but against the previous year's records for the same period from the nearby Amundsen-Scott base there was a two-degree temperature increase, which climatically was remarkable. Even more remarkable was the five-degree rise for the same days at Noatak, for which direct comparison did exist. Because of the onset of winter at the South Pole, the existing hole in the ozone layer had closed, but there was every indication that a matching hole would form for the first time over the North Pole during the oncoming summer. If that occurred, the already unusually high early summer temperature would get higher still and cause even further ice sheet and tundra melting.

'Which is why I think we need to talk about the other incidents that we've become aware of. I believe it's a reasonable hypothesis that although pollution might be a contributing factor, the sea life diseases are being caused by the introduction into the oceans of organisms, microbes . . .' He shrugged, looking between the two women. 'Let's just call them bugs . . . the entry into the oceans of bugs that have been trapped and kept dormant in the ice of the Antarctic and the Arctic . . .'

Paul Spencer had been slumped, head forward reflectively on his chest, although listening intently. Now he straightened, aware of the presidential danger. If this idea was accepted – even without being linked to the ageing illness – America would be the country most criticised for ignoring international treaty emission agreements. 'It is, though, an unsubstantiated hypothesis?' he demanded, hopefully.

Stoddart was surprised at the man's intervention, although supposed Spencer had the right to clarification even though there seemed to be a direct channel opening up between himself and Amanda O'Connell. 'Not entirely unsubstantiated. From a permafrost core sample sunk at Noatak four days ago a palaeobotanist attached here to this investigation earlier today isolated calcivirus, an intestinal microbe that causes diarrhoea. The core was 2,500 years old.'

'Are you suggesting our ageing illness could be something like that . . . something that's been locked up for thousands of years and is now being released?' demanded Spencer.

'I'm suggesting there is sufficient evidence of global warming and ice sheet melting to put the theory forward to Washington,' said Stoddart.

'Transmission,' said Geraldine, almost to herself but thinking back to the conversation with Peter Reynell in London.

'What?' said Dupuy.

'The discussion we had about the ageing virus emerging at either Pole; that it could be wind borne,' reminded Geraldine. 'We've clearly got influenza mutating across species, from whales to humans. And it's moving inland, well away from coastal regions. A more obvious transmission than wind is seabirds – and other scavenging birds – feeding off infected carcases and spreading the infection inland through their droppings.'

'And if sea animals become infected by the ageing process it could be spread the same way?' said Pelham.

'Yes,' said Stoddart. 'That's my theory, to go with all the others.'

Three o'clock, Geraldine saw, looking at her watch; eight in London. Still time to call Reynell, which was what he'd asked her to do if anything emerged from the session.

Robert Stanswell had created several computer programmes specifically to analyse the disparate reports of unusual or inexplicable illnesses or occurrences throughout the world and decided that what was showing on the screen was definitely something that should be forwarded to the White House, as well as going back to the various sources, because what he was looking at now was at least a week old. The information came from Shiznoka in Japan, Palan, a US dependency in the Indonesian archipelago, and Dag Nang in Vietnam, and recounted people suddenly being stricken with debilitating senility that was defying diagnosis.

202

Eighteen

Peter Reynell knew that in a political lifetime of rarely stumbled high-wire performances, today was going to be his most difficult yet, without a balancing pole or safety net if he took just one misjudged step. And with probably many of the very selective audience, with Simon Buxton in their forefront, ready for him to fall. Reynell didn't think, though, that he was totally suspended over the abyss. The previous night's disclosure by the gossip-attuned Henrietta that the prime minister had infuriated those for whom he was a figurehead by an over-commitment at a European leaders' summit, had been useful. And the breakfast call from Geraldine Rothman was a technical bullshit bonus.

Reynell wondered how many of those fence-perched vultures Buxton had already tried to influence in the brief time there'd been, in anticipation of what the man thought was to come? Or – the more appropriate word – in *preparation* for what Buxton imagined to be his chance for a destructive encounter. There would certainly have been some search for allies after the European debacle. The more there'd been, the greater would be the rebound upon Buxton himself, further proof to his puppet masters of the man's incompetence and misjudgment.

Simon Buxton had fervently accepted the insisted-upon, string-tugging attachments to become the obedient marionette of the party's backroom manipulators for the unquestioned public and historical glory of being first minister. Reynell had no doubt that his caucus, banner-led by Henrietta's father, clearly imagined him being just as obedient. Maybe they'd look back upon this moment, when he quite determinedly hadn't approached Lord Ranleigh for advice, as the first unrealized hint of his being his own untethered, opportunistic manipulator, a dancing doll to no one's tune.

Although he believed he'd already thought, rethought and thought out again every twist and pitfall he might encounter, Reynell still timed and hopefully utilized the short walk beneath the very real shadow of the House of Commons on a brightly sunlit day from Lord North Street to Downing Street, the timing to get him there in the middle – neither uncertainly too early or uncaringly too late – of the rest of the cabinet.

Reynell was as careful inside Downing Street, greeting everyone but refusing alliances by stopping at any group, his first need to see if he was listed upon the prepared agenda. He wasn't. Reynell scored the first point to himself, minimal though it initially was; it could later be suggested that Buxton dismissed what his science minister wanted to raise as too unimportant for official entry.

So could the way Buxton conducted the meeting, calculated an increasingly confident Reynell. There was only the most cursory acknowledgement of his presence ('Good to see Peter back among us') before the supposedly detailed analysis, prompted and then led by Buxton himself, who attempted to admit his European summit debacle as a knowingly offered sacrifice, in order to later gain concessions. Freed by his absence – as well as by his unconnected portfolio – from any active participation, Reynell used the debate to balance the for and against attitudes towards the prime minister, at once discerning a distancing from the Chancellor of the Exchequor and the Foreign Secretary, both of whom, as Buxton's strongest supports, comprised his strongest opposition. Reynell calculated that a change of allegiance – even from just one of them – would bring enough in their wake to make his leadership bid practically unstoppable. The eventual endorsement of Buxton's account was unconvincing and Reynell was further encouraged that when invited the Foreign Secretary declined to add anything to Buxton's account, unwilling to be associated with the blatant apologia.

Buxton was an astute enough politician not to need a weather-vane to tell him the direction from which a cold wind was blowing and overcompensated in his greater than usual anxiety to deflect it, three times wrongly anticipating a point and having to be corrected, once by the Foreign Secretary who scarcely bothered to conceal his irritation. Buxton twice more got it wrong, on both occasions with health minister Roy Cox – someone Reynell suspected of being an undeclared Buxton ally – and Reynell concluded he couldn't have chosen a more advantageous moment even with Machiavelli and Lucretia Borgia as joint campaign managers.

Reynell was always to remain unsure if in his eagerness to escape the session Buxton hadn't for the briefest moment genuinely forgotten him at the very end curve of the elongated table, although it only required a sideways nod from the Cabinet Secretary to remind the man. Reynell's immediate thought was that it didn't matter if it were feigned or not, Buxton's apparent need to be prompted – the fact that others in the room might come to think that he had forgotten – could only be in his favour.

'Ah, Peter!' said the man, nodding himself in Reynell's direction, before going back to those grouped around the table. 'We have an unscheduled item, gentlemen.'

The haughtiness was all too obviously forced, judged Reynell. So the man was rattled. He had to further it as much as he could to tighten Buxton's over-commitment spring. Reynell said: 'In view of its importance I had hoped for it to be listed, Prime Minister . . .'

'Your show, Peter. No second thoughts then?'

If Buxton had stopped with the first sentence the onus would have been upon him, accepted Reynell. But the stupid man had to indicate that he knew, or thought he knew, what it was all about. 'No second thoughts whatsoever . . .' He looked directly at the health minister. 'And I'm sorry, Roy, that I haven't had time to speak to you in advance. I only got back from Washington late last night. I'm returning first thing tomorrow.'

Buxton's incompetent avidity broke through, as Reynell

205

had gambled it would, by his digressing to the health minister. 'Let's hear all about this mystery illness then, shall we!'

With every eye upon him Reynell allowed the slightest frown at the flippancy, although stopping just short of directing it positively at the prime minister. 'Hardly a mystery illness but still potentially a disastrous one. And frightening from the way it appears to be mutating and transmitting.'

'What is it?' demanded the health minister.

'Influenza,' announced Reynell, finding it difficult to avoid looking at Buxton to see what expression there would be on the man's face. Instead, straining every last particle from Geraldine Rothman's breakfast call, he launched into his earlier determined and shaving mirror-rehearsed medico bullshit. He identified the haemaglutinin and neuraminidase proteins comprising the outer skin of the fifteen strains of influenza currently known to medical science, each identified numerically against the protein's initial letter. Against Buxton's acknowledged tendency to exaggerate, Reynell presented himself as the fact-following non-alarmist, preferring forty million to one hundred to be the 1918 death toll from the disease, even correcting its source to be a French transit camp for American soldiers and not San Sebastian, which gave it the wrongly accusatory label of 'Spanish Flu'. The disease, Reynell lectured, had then as now been cross-species, as easily able to jump to humans from its swine fever pig host as it was to transmit from almost every bird.

'In 1997 there was an H5N1 flu transmission from chicken to humans in Hong Kong,' continued Reynell, chancing at last to look at the prime minister's blood-drained face. 'It led, you might remember, to the entire chicken population of the then British colony being destroyed, despite which some – fortunately very few – people died . . .' Time after all for a little hyperbole, Reynell decided. 'Affected chicken virtually melted from within into a bloody, infectious pulp. A new strain of infection I felt it my duty to return today to warn about seems to be carried at the moment by whales, but already it's mutated into a fatal human disease . . .'

Rather than lose the momentum by itemizing the global

206

outbreaks, Reynell took assuredly from his briefcase Paul Spencer's selectively copied report from the previous day, gesturing to one of the secretariat to distribute around the table. 'That, currently, is the extent of the infection, worldwide. At the moment so small and in parts of the world which lack the facilities or knowledge to comply with international regulations. Under those international treaty obligations, influenza is a notifiable disease to the World Health Organization. The United States, France and Russia, who also have these facts, are informing the WHO today. I think it is important – particularly as England is one of the four notification centres throughout the world and we already have isolated cases here – that we do the same.' He'd opened the trap jaws as wide as they would go and Buxton was remaining worryingly – unusually – silent! Reynell risked a second look at the man against whom he was at that moment making his first open move. Buxton remained fixed-faced, almost unblinking, his absolute concentration boring in, laser-like. Reynell looked blankly back.

It was the health minister, coming abruptly up from what Reynell had circulated, who responded. 'But of course it has to be notified. That goes without saying. But I don't understand why—?'

'Neither do I,' came in Buxton, the habitual need to anticipate a resurgence but knowing he had much from which to recover on this disastrous day.

He could choose his own reply! snatched Reynell, disbelievingly. 'I already have the prime minister's authority – and confidence – to be part of a group composed of ministers of the three countries I have mentioned examining unexplained occurrences, the majority sea-based. It was the decision of the prime minister – as it was by the leaders of the other three countries – that this examination be carried out in conditions of the utmost secrecy, to avoid public alarm. This influenza outbreak is just one such incident which I believe has, in the interest of public safety and protection, to be disclosed. But to avoid drawing attention to what else we are doing in Washington, the decision taken

207

there was that the notification should be through national capitals.'

Positioned where he was – he was sure at Buxton's insistence – at the runt end of the table, Reynell was denied a comprehensive view to anticipate visually the first of the eruptions, which came from the virtually unseen Foreign Secretary far to his right.

'What international examination is so secret and so essential to avoid public alarm that this Cabinet has been kept unaware of it?' demanded Ralph Prendergast, a beak-nosed man whose mastery of a speech impediment just failed to avoid it seeming as if he were tasting as well as uttering his words. The peculiarity made the demand sound even more outraged.

'There was an approach, from the US President. About things too vague to consider bringing before Cabinet,' floundered Buxton.

'A possible global pandemic doesn't strike me as being vague,' said Cox.

'I was unaware of a possible global pandemic until this morning!' protested Buxton.

Reynell allowed the affronted look to be briefly – but sufficiently – visible before becoming engrossed in the Cabinet agenda before him. Prendergast had been a Buxton man, Cox an uncommitted. Neither were any longer. Nor, from the quickness of the continued protests, were the Home Secretary or the Chancellor of the Exchequor. The demand from the Chancellor, Gordon Adams, for a fuller explanation of what was happening in Washington brought Reynell back into the discussion but satisfied – euphoric – though he was, Reynell refused to concede Buxton a millimetre.

'I find myself in difficulty, Prime Minister?' he invited, sure he could hear the jaws finally snap shut around the pompous, avuncular man.

Buxton's face wasn't rigid or colourless any more. He was flushed, blinking, for once robbed even of the half thoughts customarily sufficient for him to begin to speak. 'Yes,' he blurted, illogically. 'I mean I think it's time everything was discussed.'

208

'*Everything?*' persisted Reynell, relentlessly.

'Yes,' flustered Buxton. 'I suppose so.'

Reynell hadn't expected to get this far – hadn't in his wildest dreams expected it to have gone a half or a quarter as much to his benefit as it had. But he'd tried to prepare for every eventuality, providing himself with photocopies of everything the CIA and Science Foundation had discovered, with the addition of what Gregori Lyalin had disclosed about Lake Baikel. Reynell intently watched the distribution and reaction around the table, alert for the timing. It was the health minister who primed him. As Cox raised his head to speak, Reynell said: 'And that is not all. In fact, there is something conceivably even greater than any global influenza pandemic.'

Finally he circulated the photographs of the Antarctic and Alaskan victims. And then spoke, uninterrupted in a room numbed into silence, for a full thirty minutes, so totally sure of himself that on occasions he had the sensation of listening to himself, aware – and enjoying – his total control. 'I returned for this meeting today because I believed the proven development of a new influenza outbreak more than reason enough in itself to be discussed,' he concluded. 'I'd like to thank the prime minister for allowing everything else to be brought out, particularly and most importantly the ageing illness. I am, as I already told you, returning tomorrow to Washington but I think, with the prime minister's agreement, I should return at very frequent intervals to keep this Cabinet fully updated, not just medically but politically.'

'Yes,' said Ralph Prendergast, 'I think so, too.'

'Astonishing!' declared Lord Ranleigh, who was not given to verbal overstatement, despite a penchant for a dandified Edwardian dress preference always accompanied with a silver filagreed malacca cane rumoured to be a sword stick – which it was once, but the blade had been removed – mutton-chop whiskers and the financial independence to be able to support, with a staff of thirty, one of the few privately occupied castles, complete with ancestral ghost, in England.

209

'I hadn't imagined – hardly expected – that the stories would begin to circulate so quickly,' said Reynell. The servants had been dismissed and there had been no question of Henrietta withdrawing and now the three of them remained around the dinner table, the port decanter available but untouched between them. Neither men was smoking, either.

'In every corridor in Westminster and at every necessary dinner table in London,' insisted the mottled-faced viscount whose loss of an hereditary seat in the House of Lords in the turn-of-the-millenium reforms had not in the slightest diminished or interrupted his Svengali role within the party.

'What, exactly, *are* the stories?' asked Henrietta.

'Just one, in actual fact,' qualified the older man. 'That Buxton made an even greater mess of Cabinet than he managed at the Rome summit – largely by trying to convince everyone that Rome wasn't a disaster – and that in a later discussion with Peter he made himself look an even bigger idiot.'

'But nothing about the subject of that discussion?' pressed Reynell.

'Precisely what I was coming to,' smiled Ranleigh, at last reaching for the port. 'That's what's fuelling the story, no one truly knowing what it was all about. Just something to do with a possible epidemic. If we're going to go on from today – which believe me we are, from all the soundings I've got – I need to know chapter and verse about it.'

Reynell shook his head against the offered decanter. 'It's a possible pandemic. Influenza jumping from mammal – whales – to humans. Cabinet agreed to notify the WHO.'

Ranleigh sat with his port glass suspended before him, waiting. When Reynell didn't continue he said: 'What else?'

'Unexplained infections in sea life, most likely caused by global warming.'

The port remained untasted. 'And?'

He knew, Reynell decided. Probably not everything but enough to know there was something else, something more important and therefore, logically, something worse. So this was a test, as he guessed the Carlton Club had been a test to gauge his reaction to setback, but perhaps more importantly to judge Buxton's response to the prospect of overthrow. Which had been panic, in Rome. But wouldn't be his, here in London, Reynell determined. 'There is a potentially serious medical situation. Not, at the moment, a risk of an epidemic or a pandemic but a condition that needs to be identified and resolved. Which is as much as I feel able to tell you, Cabinet having today confirmed the decision that it should remain tightly restricted.'

Ranleigh snorted, disbelievingly. 'Peter! I'm talking about your future; a future to the very top, as high as you can get! I can't persuade people to support me – support you – without knowing what the hell it was you did in Cabinet to convince virtually everyone in the room that Buxton should be got rid of, as soon as possible.'

Had it been a mistake for Ranleigh to disclose that he had a definite Cabinet majority? Reynell wondered. Or was it a ruse, to get him to offer more in exchange? 'I know what we're talking about. Of the influence that you and others are exercising on my behalf. I am sincerely, truly grateful and I want to assure you that I will never forget it or fail any of you. But I feel I would be failing you – as Buxton has so often in the past failed his backers and supporters – by totally abnegating my integrity.' As you abnegated yours, you manipulative old bastard, leaving me high and dry at the Carlton Club to see how resilient I was.

'Are you seriously refusing to tell me?' Ranleigh's incredulity was absolutely genuine.

'I believe that if at this juncture any leaks were to be traced to me or to yourself – and let's not forget for a moment that as well as being an elder statesman of the party you are inextricably linked with me as my father-in-law – everything we are trying to achieve would be destroyed in an instant.'

'How could that conceivably happen?' demanded the affronted man.

'Simply by Buxton – or one of Buxton's people – trying to put his survival ahead of everything else and leaking it all to the media on condition that the information appeared to

211

come from us. It's your integrity as well as my own that I am protecting, sir. If there were to be a later investigatory tribunal or committee of enquiry – upon which we've enough support to insist being established to discover the leak – you could take an oath and truthfully attest that you had no knowledge of what I was doing in Washington. Just as I could honestly testify that I had told no one outside the Cabinet Room and in doing that I had obeyed Buxton's recorded instructions.'

Ranleigh's outrage seeped away. 'We can't make our bid while you're engaged on this. If there's the potential for success to be achieved, the credit goes to Buxton, the incumbent.'

'I know,' accepted Reynell.

'Can you overcome that?'

'That I don't know.' There was an odd easiness about total honesty.

'Let's speak daily, Peter.'

'I intend that we will.'

The aphrodisiac of political intrigue drove Henrietta's insistence that he share her bed for the second night far beyond invitation, so much so that Reynell only just matched her demand. After her third orgasm she fell back, exhausted, and said: 'You were totally magnificent tonight. Not here I don't mean, although you were. With Daddy. You're going to make a brilliant prime minister.'

'With you at my side,' said Reynell, dutifully.

'You wouldn't be in the running if I weren't, darling.'

'You're absolutely sure?' demanded Henry Partington.

'The positive connection with global warming is the most definite conclusion there is,' said Spencer.

'Then you're right, Paul,' agreed the president. 'We've got to move fast with some meaningful, catch-up legislation in the process of enactment if not actually on the statute books. High profile agenda, congressional leaders summoned down from the Hill to show our commitment, all that kind of stuff . . .'

'Tomorrow too soon, Mr President?'

'Can't be soon enough,' said Partington. 'There's a lot of

buttons to press. And Jack Stoddart: get him on board from the beginning.'

'There's another potential problem, Mr President. The military don't think they can keep the bases in Antarctica isolated for much longer.'

'But they've got to be, Paul.'

'I know that, Mr President.'

'So find me an answer, just as quickly. Don't let me down, Paul.'

Nineteen

There would have been room enough for four inside one car but a single boot wasn't large enough for the three separate, sealed containers of refrigerated sample and specimen which the three needed personally to deliver to their embassies to duplicate the Fort Detrick experiments in their respective countries. It was not until after Geraldine had packed her collection in the boot of his car that Stoddart realized it might have been better diplomacy for him to have driven Raisa Orlov into Washington, but to have changed over would have drawn unnecessary attention to something he didn't consider really important. Guy Dupuy insisted he was quite comfortable driving the second car and Stoddart promised he'd make sure they didn't get separated on the way. Today Geraldine had out-dressed Raisa, in a white skirt and polo-necked sweater under a Ralph Lauren badged blazer.

Stoddart drove through the Frederick township and as they did so Geraldine said: 'Doesn't look like there's much to explore but it would get us out of the complex for a couple of hours one night.'

'Stir crazy?'

'It's a little claustrophobic. Don't seem to notice it until I get outside.'

'Thanks for getting so personally involved. If you hadn't, we wouldn't have got as far as we have.' The repeated autopsies on all the victims had found degeneration in both bones and organs to support Geraldine's progressive dying theory.

'Raisa's still not going for it.' It was a comment, not a complaint.

'You think she's giving it her full input?' Dupuy was keeping close enough behind for him to be able to see them both in his rear view mirror. Raisa was staring fixedly ahead. Neither appeared to be talking.

Still uncritical, Geraldine said: 'And she had a lot to catch up with here. In between some of the preconceptions last night there was a contribution of sorts. She quite obviously knows her science.' Geraldine was silent for a moment. 'There's something that worries me about last night.'

'What?' demanded Stoddart.

Geraldine shook her head. 'I don't know. Just a feeling that we missed something. Maybe I'll pick it up going through the transcript when we get back.'

Enough shop talk, Stoddart decided. 'You got anything else to do in Washington apart from seeing your minister and arranging the shipment of all that stuff in the trunk?'

Geraldine supposed there'd be some tests – samples maybe – as well as an examination by the gynaecologist with whom the embassy doctor had arranged her afternoon appointment. 'I'm not sure how long I'll be, doing that.'

'Neither am I, with Amanda or at the White House. But I thought we'd be through by happy hour. Say five? I'm your ride back to Fort Detrick so we've got to meet somewhere.'

'Only on condition you can get the President to do his helicopter bit again,' she accepted. There still wasn't any awkwardness between them and she'd enjoyed the rooftop bar and, as he said, they had to meet somewhere. She swivelled, to look briefly through the back window. 'What about them?'

'You think I should invite them?'

She picked up the cell phone from the passenger shelf. 'You want me to call them?'

'That's my personal phone. They haven't got one, as far as I'm aware. I certainly don't have a number.'

'We'll do it when we stop.'

Stoddart began to descend the parkway and Geraldine got her first sight of the cathedral and then the needle point of the Washington monument. The Key bridge looked too congested so he continued on to take the Roosevelt, but in his mirror

215

saw a lot of arm-waving from Raisa and the Frenchman turning off, as directed. Stoddart said: 'I've lost them. She's made him go through Georgetown to get her on to Wisconsin for the Russian embassy. I didn't imagine Raisa knew Washington that well.'

'You could call them at their embassies.'

'Sure.'

Stoddart helped her out with the specimen containers at the British legation but still got to Blair House before the arranged meeting time with Amanda O'Connell. She was already waiting.

She said: 'Looks as if you've lit the fire.' She was trying to temper her annoyance at Paul Spencer getting to the President ahead of her by subjectively reasoning that the effect of America's disregard of global warming treaties was beyond her specific remit, but she had immediately acknowledged the need for a warning and resented losing the chance.

'It's taken long enough,' said Stoddart. What had he really been summoned for? The final, too long delayed acknowledgement that its inhabitants, led by an emission-fuelling America, were destroying their own planet and possibly themselves with it? Or yet again to play the stooge in a political shell game? Or something else entirely he couldn't anticipate? Whatever, he wouldn't be the willing stooge. It wasn't, particularly, the personal, professional credit he wanted, although the virtually unarguable indications were that he *was* vindicated. His primary hope was that at last politicians might be frightened into doing more than platform pontificating and agreeing international protocols they ignored before the ink was dry upon the paper. Stoddart admitted to himself for the first time that he'd come close to being overwhelmed by Antarctica, the days (could it still only be little more than days?) that followed and the responsibility – the political, stooge-role responsibility – imposed upon him. Today, this moment, was like waking up from being drunk or drugged. But without a hangover from either, having at last got to the far end of the already realized learning curve.

216

There must even have been some physical sign because Amanda said, frowning: 'What is it?'

'Nothing,' dismissed Stoddart. 'What's the agenda?'

'The President wants to be proactive rather than reactive.'

'How the hell can he be proactive?' demanded Stoddart.

'The alchemy of political science,' said Amanda, matching the cynicism. Was it an impression of Stoddart physically appearing the more positive, assertive person she remembered from television that had caught her curiosity?

'I'm close to being scienced-out, certainly politically.'

'Like the wise man said, you ain't seen nuthin' yet.'

Paul Spencer and Richard Morgan were already in the Oval Office when they were ushered in and, from the way papers were strewn across the president's desk, had been there for some time. The Chief of Staff was in shirtsleeves. Spencer avoided Amanda's look.

Henry Partington said at once: 'Congratulations, Jack! You've got it right. Which means America's got it right. That's good. That's how I want it.'

The feel-good, your-president-loves-and-admires-you approach, both aides recognized, settling back in their chairs to enjoy the show. Richard Morgan had read the previous night's transcript of the scientific group's discussion and was concentrating more upon his former deputy, who'd put everything planned for that day in motion without advising him in advance.

'It's the most obvious, logical theory, but still only a theory, Mr President,' cautioned Stoddart.

'That's why I wanted to see you personally. I want to be as sure as I can. Which means I need to know how sure you are.'

'The polar melting, and that of the Greenland ice cap, is unarguable. There's scientific data a foot high. The Antarctic ozone depletion is a scientific fact, too. The checks we've put in place at both disaster sites supports it.'

Partington cleared some papers immediately in front of him, to lean forward on the desk. 'Global warming's your baby, Jack. You've been crying in the wilderness for years . . .'

'Not totally unheard,' said Stoddart.

Morgan came around abruptly at the interruption. Partington's face closed but almost at once opened again, although the smile was bleak. Amanda thought, this *is* the no-shit Don Quixote she'd watched poking his lance into too many cogs of industry.

Partington said: 'I hadn't actually finished speaking, Jack.' *Watch your ass, son.*

'I'm sorry, Mr President,' said Stoddart, who wasn't. He didn't intend letting any of them, including Amanda, imagine he would roll over as he had about informing relatives of the dead. And that was nagging in his mind too, although there was still something he could do about it.

'As I was saying,' resumed Partington. 'Shouting in the wilderness for years with not enough people listening. Now they're going to and I intend seeing that you're well and truly heard.' *Here's your chance, Jack. Hitch your wagon up to mine and there's no end to where it might lead.*

'It's good to get your support,' said Stoddart. The son of a bitch *was* in some way trying to set him up as the stooge. Although he saw the president about to continue Stoddart said: 'How, exactly, do you intend achieving that, sir?'

'Do what other administrations should have done before me and I've been too slow doing myself,' declared Partington, in rare but safe admission. 'Appoint you special executive director of the Environmental Agency, reporting and directly responsible to me to ensure the United States takes the effect and seriousness of global warming – particularly gas emission – far beyond the Kyoto agreement. I want all these things that are happening brought to the attention of the public – except one, of course – and to show our commitment stage a conference here in America with a treaty on the table more stringent and binding than that which was agreed in Japan. How's that grab you, Jack?'

By the balls, thought Stoddart. There was a lot – almost too much – to assimilate and he couldn't afford to miss a single thing. The president was using him and his public reputation but then he'd already accepted the man had done

218

that from the beginning. But the situation had escalated, with the involvement of Britain and France through Alaska, the separate outbreak in Russia and the marine life discoveries, one of which at least was leading to an international health warning. *Special executive director*, reflected Stoddart. Bullshit title for a bullshit job. Partington's idea of being proactive was to blow enough smoke to blind everyone from seeing he was coming from behind, not already out there in front. Time to blow a little – or maybe more than a little – smoke of his own. 'It grabs me very well, Mr President. Just as I'm sure the declaration of American leadership will grab the public, not just here at home but abroad . . .'

Partington's smile remained uncertain at the qualifying tone of Stoddart's voice. Morgan and Spencer were attentive, too. Careful, thought Amanda.

'But I see some problems,' finished Stoddart. And didn't continue.

'What sort of problems?' came in Morgan, to spare the president appearing to get into a question and answer debate.

'I don't see how I could take over such a public role at the same time as doing what I am trying to do now.'

'Easily overcome!' dismissed Partington, the smile broadening. 'I announce the American commitment from here at a press conference with you beside me, naming you as the supremo to take over as soon as your current commitments allow, without saying what those commitments are. We go public together with all this other stuff we've found out, as well as the influenza – which the WHO will confirm – showing us ahead of the game. It'll take weeks, months, for a new environmental treaty to be framed and agreed by all the Kyoto signatories. Which you don't have to be bothered with, not until the very end. Yours – and mine – will be the final approval. Which gives you those weeks and months to go on heading up the Fort Detrick investigation and coming out ahead on that, too.'

The sheer cynicism was breathtaking both in its completeness and simplicity. 'So my being special executive director is largely symbolic: a recognizable figurehead?' demanded Stoddart, directly.

'You're somebody the public trusts,' said Spencer, taking his turn to relieve the president.

'And the job is what you make it,' added Morgan, falling back on cliche.

Indeed it would be, thought Stoddart. At that moment – and perhaps for some time to come – Partington needed him and his reputation more than he needed Partington. And when his usefulness was over, the man would discard him like the irritant he'd always been. So there was very little to lose. 'I think it's important, Mr President, that we agree the situation as it is. As I see it—'

'. . . We're looking at the general picture here, Jack,' Morgan broke in, hurriedly. 'The overall game plan . . . we can fill in the gaps later—'

'But some details we can flesh out now,' cut off Stoddart in turn, bothered by the persistent buddy use of his christian name. Intentionally echoing the president's earlier irritation, Stoddart repeated: 'As I see it, we're going responsibly to show ourselves – America – just a tad proactive to a lot of unsettling things brought about by global warming, although still keeping under wraps a horror illness until we can reassure everyone we've got the handle on it. Is that how you see it, Mr President?'

There was a stir among the two aides at the wafer thinness keeping the question away from open disrespect. Amanda was glad there was no way she could be associated with the suicidal climatologist.

Slowly – to indicate his displeasure – Partington said: 'Yes, I suppose that's how I see it.' *You're out of your league, little man; enjoy your moment and remember it when I bury you.*

'So when the ageing illness becomes public knowledge – most certainly if we *haven't* got a handle on it – we've got to stand up to public scrutiny to show that we really were proactive and that the principles we're going to announce have real, effective meaning. Prove to the critics that we're

220

genuinely intending to have enacted proper internal legislation to give a lead to the rest of the world.' Alert to Spencer's about-to-erupt interjection once more to deflect things from the president, Stoddart said urgently: 'Believe me, sir, I'm not talking about a bunch of organic-growing shitkickers. The green lobby's well organized. Clever. Unless you get it right from the beginning – *before* the beginning – you'll be accused of catch-up, of empty gestures.'

How, wondered Amanda, had she ever thought of Jack Stoddart as an ineffectual lost cause? She was witnessing political mud-wrestling the like of which she'd heard about but never seen. The bastard was even inferring that he was poacher turned gamekeeper to protect the president!

With teeth-grinding reluctance, Partington said: 'I understand the point you're making.'

'I'm an environmental scientist, not by any means a politician,' continued Stoddart, actually enjoying himself. 'And again I ask you to believe me when I say that I am in no way being presumptuous. But as an environmentalist who knows the lobby, I'm urging you as strongly as I can to announce – at the very beginning because there won't be a second chance – that there'll be punitive and enforced legislation against any American industry that doesn't adopt your proposals . . . And I think the Environment Agency should be given the watchdog role to ensure the legislation is properly observed.'

'We really are talking details here that we can't possibly—' Morgan began to protest.

'No!' stopped Partington, relaxed. 'Jack's right. We'll put forward the most stringent environmental and ecologically protective legislation on any statute book, anywhere in the world. Thank you, Jack. Thank you very much indeed.'

'There's something else that's worrying me: worrying me very much,' persisted Stoddart.

'What?' demanded Morgan, apprehensively.

'As *hugely* important as it is, global warming is only a part of what we are trying to understand. If, like the influenza and the other effects, the ageing illness . . .' He stopped. '. . .

If the Shangri-La strain is coming from the sea then there'll be situations we can't sit on. It'll break out – be discovered – in too many different places. We know there'll be a backlash for our keeping secret the deaths there have already been . . .'

'This has already been talked through,' said Spencer.

Stoddart ignored him. 'The backlash would be greatly ameliorated if, at the moment of it becoming public knowledge, there existed an Executive Order setting out the special – necessarily generous – compensation that I've already been told the families of each American victim were to receive.'

'Yes,' agreed Partington. 'I think that's another suggestion we could well take on board.'

'And I'd like to say, Mr President, that I'm honoured by your trust and your offer. Which I'll very seriously consider . . .'

'*Consider*?' blurted Morgan.

'I wouldn't be treating the position with the seriousness it deserves if I didn't give myself time to think about it, would I?' said Stoddart.

It was Amanda who insisted upon the drink and, because it was the most convenient to the White House, they used the Old Ebbitt Grill again. In the lull part of the day they didn't have to wait for a table. Amanda ordered doubles and after they were delivered said to Stoddart: 'You've virtually held the President of the United States to fucking ransom!' Amanda was conscious of a surge of sexually wetting excitement, which she couldn't remember experiencing for a long time. It felt good.

'No, I haven't,' denied Stoddart. 'Just made a few points that needed to be made.'

'Where'd you learn that?'

'From years of being shat on, from a great, hopefully smothering height.'

'Maybe it's your time.'

Was she coming on to him, with innuendo? 'Maybe.'

'You are going to take the job though, aren't you?'

How much and how well could he use this woman as she,

222

with equally suspended compunction, would use him if the personal ambitious need or benefit arose? 'If all the terms and conditions are provably established.'

'I think Partington spelled those out: direct responsibility to him?'

Stoddart shook his head. 'That's meaningless.'

'What would you want?'

'Probably twice as much as Partington is prepared to offer,' he generalized.

'So where's that leave you?'

'Waiting for the proper offer.'

Just over 500 yards away, meandering yet another unrecorded walk in the Rose Garden, Spencer said. 'That was outrageous!'

'No, it wasn't,' contradicted Partington, pragmatically. 'We'd underestimated him, that's all. He wants to bargain; imagines he's tough.'

Morgan was glad he'd waited to gauge the president's feeling. Calmly he said: 'How we going to get around restrictive legislation that'll affect so many of our major industry contributors?'

Yet again Partington smiled. 'We've got the White House but we haven't got Congress, have we?'

'No?' said Morgan, questioningly.

Partington looked to Spencer. 'And how long before our hostile congressional leaders get here?'

'An hour,' said Spencer.

Partington nodded, leading the way back towards the White House. 'I want the most swinging ideas you can come up with. We don't have time for details, obviously. What I want to do is give them as much warning as I can that we're going to propose something really draconian . . .' He shook his head at the frowns of the other two men, enjoying out-politicking them. 'Congress will wreck whatever bill I put forward for Stoddart's treaty, everyone worried about offending their own financial backers, and when the Shangri-La strain becomes public, following this flu business, we'll gain so many mid-term senate and representative seats that we'll get the

223

Hill – and the adulation of the party – for my second term . . .'
He smiled genuinely for the first time that day. 'That strikes
me as perfect. How's it strike you?'

'Perfect,' echoed Spencer.

'And our own big industry backers?' reminded Morgan.

'I've got all the home numbers,' reminded Partington. 'I'll
make the reassuring calls personally.'

'And the Executive Order to compensate the victims?'
asked Morgan.

'Another brilliant idea,' said the small man. 'We'll hit
Congress with the Executive Order while they're still reeling;
they'll have to agree whatever figure I set. Astonishing how
Jack and I thought on the same lines, all along the track. I
always knew we'd understand each other perfectly.'

Raisa Orlov had no doubt whatsoever that the separation at
Fort Detrick was planned for Stoddart and the woman not just
to travel cosily to Washington for some quick hotel-room fuck
but to work against her and the inconsequential slob beside
her whose shapeless trousers were probably full of farts,
because he smelled. She arrived at the Russian embassy tight
with impotent fury, which worsened by the minute. She was
greeted by a demand – not a request – to meet Gregori Lyalin
in an hour. She infuriatingly miscalculated the time difference
between Washington and Moscow and Sergei Grenkov, her
deputy and the ally with whom she intended establishing a
back-channel, had left for the day and wasn't at home when
she redirected the call. When she spoke a second time to her
institute department, Anatoli Lisin, the laboratory chief and
a man not sufficiently frightened of her, began awkwardly
by saying that every experiment they had conducted was
included in the material already shipped, at Lyalin's specific
instructions, to America. He had to be angrily pressed into
volunteering that there had been no unknown viral protein
or any other finding to lead to any understanding of what
the illness might be. He didn't sound sorry.

Intentionally to delay her encounter with her science minister, Raisa remained on the telephone for a further fifteen

minutes stipulating the tests and experiments she wanted conducted on the Fort Detrick specimens, even though they were to be accompanied by detailed written instructions, dictating and then correcting which made her a full thirty minutes late. She was initially glad they were meeting in the ambassador's office, for there to be a witness that even a minister had to respond to her commitments, not she to his.

Raisa didn't apologize or offer any explanation for her lateness. Lyalin thought she was a sad person although he didn't feel any pity for her. Having read the transcript of the scientific committee's midnight discussion, Lyalin said: 'So there could be a convincing connection with global warming, as there seems to be with the influenza?'

'And our supposed chairman is the renowned and foremost harbinger of global warming doom!'

Lyalin determined against becoming annoyed, aware of the ambassador looking confusedly between himself and the woman. Lyalin said: 'What's the importance of that remark, if it shows us the way to go?'

'It doesn't!' insisted Raisa. 'At best it suggests – not positively *shows* – a possible route for an infection that remains viral.'

'Nothing that's arrived from Moscow confirms a viral precursor,' challenged Lyalin.

'The investigation isn't completed.' Why was the sanctimonious bastard so obstructive! There were influential people in Moscow to be told – through Sergei Vasilevich Grenkov – that the Russian science minister had abandoned her in preference to his American hosts.

'Certainly not with what's to be exchanged today, from Fort Detrick,' agreed Lyalin. 'Do you really consider it necessary to duplicate everything the Americans have done?'

That was a remark that very necessarily had to be heard by a witness, Raisa thought, looking gratefully towards the ambassador. 'Of course! Didn't you actually lecture me that scientific progress is achieved by the work of one group being shared and examined by another!'

'Yes,' said Lyalin, who'd chosen the ambassador as a

225

witness way ahead of Raisa recognizing her believed benefit. 'I'm glad you remembered and are observing it. So is Moscow, with whom I've very fully discussed everything we've talked about and who totally agrees and supports the instructions I've already given you.' How childish it was to have to speak literally like this. Worse, to spy upon the woman, as everyone had spied upon everyone else in the ridiculous era of communism. But he had to protect himself. Which was, Lyalin sadly acknowledged, the justification of that aberrant era.

It wasn't essential for the gynaecologist to have been a woman – until she'd been shown into the surgery it hadn't even occurred to Geraldine – but she supposed it had been slightly easier because her English gynaecologist was female, too. Geraldine waited for the inferred medical criticism of a termination, no matter how slight, because she'd detected it in London. But she hadn't detected it here, even though she knew the strength – the actual terrorism, in fact – of the pro-life movement in America.

The doctor, who'd immediately addressed her as Gerry and told her to call her Rebecca, said: 'I'll obviously need to get the test results, but from the scan and the physical examination you're fine. There's no evidence at all of any tube damage. You had a simple staph infection that's been completely zapped by antibiotics. It would be nice to know that every infection could be treated so successfully.'

'Yes,' agreed Geraldine heavily. 'It certainly would.'

Her second, person-to-person encounter with Peter Reynell had been quite different from the first at Fort Detrick. Until then, she'd only been in her minister's company in group situations, at receptions or conferences or, once, when he'd chaired a London conference on AIDS research. He was, in fact, someone she'd known – or rather been aware of – more through gossip columns and personality magazines recounting the upper-echelon lifestyle of an ascending parliamentarian who had risen first – and determinedly again

226

– from the desperate impoverishment of a once secure and minor landed background into one of the most famous political families in the country.

The comparison between the meetings had been remarkable. At that first, there had been the practised, seemingly intense but actually blank attention with which Geraldine was familiar from members of parliament and politicians allowing just part of their concentration upon her with the rest splintered between a dozen other quite separate things. Today had been different. Sir Alistair Dowding hadn't been with them and Reynell's concentration had been total. She'd genuinely believed he'd been grateful for her briefings – particularly the early morning London call she'd been uncertain of making – and there hadn't been any insincerity in his demanding to go through the transcript of the scientific meeting in point-by-point detail. Because of the intensity of his interest, she'd expected him to reiterate the demand for them to talk daily ('it doesn't matter if you don't think there's anything to talk *about* or that I'm getting a transcript of everything') but she hadn't expected the end of the conversation, which surprised her. As well as warned her.

'You understand, of course, that all your dealings with London have to be through me. Even anything from here, from the embassy. I need to know about them.'

'You're not talking of all the samples I'm shipping back and forth?'

'Not the shipping, of course not. But very definitely any findings that arise from them. Only to me and through me.'

'Is it likely I will be asked by someone other than yourself?'

'It's possible. You're well enough aware of the sensitivity of what we're doing. That's why I'm insisting we do things this way; just you and I – not allowing any other intrusion – guarantees the security.'

'So what do I say if I get a direct call from London? Or from here, from someone other than yourself?'

'That you need to check out whatever their question is and that you'll relay the answer back through me.'

227

'What if I'm told to answer directly to whomever it is?'

'Tell me, before doing so.'

With time to spare before meeting Stoddart, Geraldine decided to walk to the downtown hotel. She didn't need prompt boards or neon signs to know that she was caught up in some political intrigue and in a virtually hopeless situation. Reynell was her superior, a minister to whom she was answerable and who, in fact, had assigned her the Fort Detrick job. But she was equally answerable to the health minister, without even bringing the prime minister himself into the equation. Where was she if the intrigue was between the two (or three or four) of them and Reynell – 3,500 miles away from any battleground, as she was – lost out? It wasn't difficult to understand why the British ambassador hadn't been included in today's session. Just work, she decided, dismissively. Far more important was what had happened earlier, the virtual assurance that there was no lasting damage from the abortion. How easy – although understandable – it seemed to have been these last few days to wipe any thought of Michael from her mind.

Geraldine was still at the Washington Hotel ahead of the American and managed to secure a table against the rail again. She was halfway through her first glass of wine, playing a game with herself that it was her own secret celebration at knowing she was quite well, when Stoddart arrived.

She nodded out towards the unseen White House and said: 'You didn't get the President to put on a show for me.'

'He put one on for me instead,' said Stoddart. There was no reason why she shouldn't know, in advance of something that was going to be made very public indeed.

He included his doubts and suspicions when he told her and when he finished she said: 'So what are you going to do?'

'Keep in mind what Morgan told me: that the job will be what I make it.'

'That sounds like a threat.'

'It is,' admitted Stoddart. 'But they don't know that.'

It was when Stoddart was ordering the second round that he admitted not bothering to contact the other two, insisting

228

the White House session had driven the thought from his mind, which it hadn't. He and Geraldine by themselves made it a pleasant, undemanding hour's relaxation. Including Dupuy and Raisa would have turned it into an organized, follow-my-leader outing with him as tour guide and he didn't want to be that.

'You mind?'

She shook her head. 'Maybe we should do it one night at Frederick?'

'Maybe,' he said, unenthusiastically. 'Any news from your genetic investigation?'

Geraldine shook her head. 'Still going through the sequential computers. I told you how it was.'

They had a third drink and served themselves give-away happy hour snacks and Geraldine said she supposed they shouldn't stay on in Washington for dinner and Stoddart said he supposed they shouldn't either, although it sounded like a good idea to do next time.

They drove not needing conversation, Stoddart for a long time unsure if the head-slumped Geraldine was dozing after their through-the-night session. He got off the Beltway as soon as he could, hoping the traffic would be freer on the 270, disappointed that it wasn't.

'We're going to be late getting back,' he said, more to himself than to her. 'Not that it matters.'

'Carriers!' declared Geraldine, uncoiling in her seat. 'That's it! Carriers!'

'What?' said Stoddart, bewildered, his first thought that she had awakened from a dream.

'The something that was worrying me this morning. It's not my science, but it's my understanding that a virus doesn't always infect the person it initially invades. Their body becomes a host, in which it can develop: live for months, years even. They become carriers, never falling ill themselves but passing it on to others . . .'

'But who . . . ?' started Stoddart and stopped. Then he said: 'No! I couldn't be. I had every test: was kept in isolation . . .'

229

'Did you have nose and throat swabs? Mucus tests?'

'I don't think so.' The car swerved as he snatched up the cellphone. 'Call Pelham!'

It was a short, staccato conversation. With the telephone cupped between both hands in her lap, not looking across the car to him, Geraldine said: 'He doesn't see how you could conceivably be—'

'Didn't I tell you—?' started Stoddart.

'But that it's possible,' she finished. She turned in her seat, to look directly across the car at him. 'You've been with the President, Jack! All through the White House. You could have made the rest of us carriers . . . We've been to the embassies . . . tonight at the bar . . . everywhere . . . that's how viral infections spread . . .'

230

Twenty

They alerted the complex to their arrival, as they'd been told to do, and Stoddart's car was identified from its registration and waved through, without any gatehouse contact. Their waiting escorts were protectively suited – close by the car in which Raisa and Dupuy had obviously arrived back ahead of them – but they remained in the street clothes they'd worn to Washington. If he were a carrier and Geraldine or anyone else in the group had contracted it, they were going to die and an entirely new unit would have to be created. It wouldn't actually put the scientific investigation back to square one but it wouldn't be far beyond. He wasn't thinking in the right sequences, he told himself, recalling – how could he have forgotten! – what Geraldine had blurted in the car. He'd been in close proximity – contagiously close – to the President and a lot of the White House staff. Amanda O'Connell and . . . He couldn't remember, count how many other people. With the sudden, physical sensation of nausea came what had to be the final, emptying thought. If he were a carrier he'd have to remain in permanent, goldfish-bowl confinement until a cure was found. And there was no possibility – no hope – so far of that being achieved.

At their separation in different isolation chambers Stoddart said: 'We're going to be OK.'

Geraldine didn't reply.

Stoddart wasn't sure, because the interiors were identical, but he thought it was the same room into which he'd been put after Antarctica. He looked up to the smoked glass observation window and said: 'Who's there?'

'Duncan. Duncan Littlejohn,' came a voice.

'And me, Barry Hooper,' said a second.

The Fort Detrick department heads he'd met when Geraldine had carried out her personal examination of Henri Lebrun, Stoddart remembered. 'Where are the others? Walt, Raisa, Guy . . . ?'

'All in isolation,' said Hooper.

'What's happening?'

'They've all tested negative. That, in itself, is a pretty simple pathology screening by swab, blood analysis and electron microscopy but all it establishes is that they're not carriers; it doesn't mean they haven't contracted the full blown disease from you,' said Littlejohn, the laboratory chief. 'The helicopter that took a unit up to the White House – and to test the Blair group – is already on its way back. There's another helo on standby to evacuate anyone here, if anything shows that we can't understand. The big test is to see how you check out. If you're clear, the panic's over.'

'I don't remember any throat or nose swabs being taken,' said Stoddart.

'There was every other test and examination,' said Hooper. 'Something would have shown.'

The defensiveness was obvious in the man's voice. Stoddart said: 'But swabs should have been taken, shouldn't they?'

Before an answer there was the hiss of the airlock to admit a suited figure anonymous behind the vizor.

'Hello again,' said the woman doctor who'd examined him the first time. 'This will only take a minute.'

He coughed, close to gagging, at the depth at which she took her swabs from his throat and the nose sample made him sneeze and his eyes water. She took two phials of blood. He went back to the unseen observers as the door sucked closed after the doctor. 'I didn't get an answer?'

'Yes,' conceded Hooper. 'It should have been done.'

Stoddart decided he was more frightened now than he'd been when he'd first returned from the Antarctic. Then he hadn't known that the others who'd been there with him were infected: not fully believed or imagined, even, that in some way it could be transmitted. Now he very definitely knew it

232

could happen and that he could have spread it to God knows how many people – the President himself – but most horrifying of all was knowing there was nothing that could be done to prevent or stop it. He bit off a half considered, angry demand to the men behind the glass; losing his temper, losing control, was pointless. Instead he said: 'How about the two guys who survived Alaska – Darryl Matthews and Harold Norris?'

'Both tested clear,' said Hooper.

Should he be encouraged by that? 'How long will it take to decide whether I'm a host or not?'

'A couple of hours,' promised Littlejohn. 'Maybe less. You're not actually in a queue.'

'How can you do it so quickly?'

'Elimination,' said Pelham shortly. 'A diagnostic template, if you like. We just go through the list.'

'So if I did have something you couldn't eliminate you'd isolate what's causing the ageing!' He'd become the guinea pig, as Patricia Jefferies had so willingly offered herself to be. Which he'd have to . . . Stoddart stopped the incomplete thought, his mind flooded by another. It wasn't the guinea pig recollection – or personal awareness – that startled him. It was that he hadn't thought for days of the woman he'd told he loved and watched die, making promises he hadn't kept. Stoddart was ashamed, all the submerged anger churning in him turned against himself. They'd both known it hadn't been love – Patricia, more openly honest, had actually acknowledged it wasn't – but he hadn't considered it a lie, wanting her to believe him at the end. But hadn't she – didn't she – deserve more than a final, almost automatic act of kindness? At least a memory, even occasionally. He had no right to despise the men in the White House for their self-serving hypocrisy, imagining – flattering himself – that he had more integrity.

'We haven't thought things through that far yet,' said Hooper. 'But yes, it could be that way.'

With difficulty Stoddart forced himself back to the bizarre, talking-to-the-wall conversation. 'What's to say the germ or bug or whatever couldn't somehow mutate from being

233

non-infectious in me to giving me the disease? That I couldn't become a victim myself, after having spread it around?'

'Nothing,' said Hooper flatly.

They were made irrationally hit-out angry, initially unthinking, in their fear, Partington pacing his small, private office off the larger public business – and tape monitored – oval room, repeating over and over that he couldn't believe it and asking how it could have been allowed to happen of two men as disbelieving as himself and who didn't, for once, have any answers.

'We could die! *Be* dying! That's the bottom line, right?'

'Pelham told me he doesn't think it's possible,' tried Spencer.

'And after that went into isolation in his own complex and there's a helicopter out on the lawn to evacuate us there as well and I've just had a probe stuck down my goddamned throat and given Christ knows how much blood to guys dressed up like something out of Star Wars!' *Someone had to answer for this. Suffer like I'm being made to suffer.*

Richard Morgan remained steadfastly silent, willingly surrendering the scapegoat search to the man who'd painted the target on his own chest. Spencer said: 'Pelham called it an outside precaution against a trillion to one possibility.' Which wasn't strictly true – the man hadn't given odds – but Spencer's sole intention at that moment was indelibly establishing Pelham as the expert who'd made the mistake.

'I'm the President of the United States of America! I shouldn't . . . we shouldn't . . . have been exposed to the goddamned man if there was a *zillion* to one risk!'

'No, sir,' agreed Spencer. 'Detrick fouled up big time. Theirs was the medical advice we had to rely on.'

'They're supposed to be solving the problem, not fouling up!' *If it turned out all right – had to turn out all right – Pelham was history. Spencer, too. The whole goddamned lot. How could they have let it happen to him? He couldn't believe it.*

'Yes, sir,' said Spencer, with nothing else to say.

Morgan knew he had to make some contribution, difficult though it was to think beyond the photographs he'd seen of wizened, monkey-small people the same age – some younger – than himself. 'The helicopter will be back at Detrick by now. They said our tests wouldn't take long. Stoddart's too.'

Partington stopped pacing, standing in front of his desk to face the two aides. Extending cupped fingers he said: 'It was all so good. We had it right there, in the palm of our hand.'

'Yes, Mr President,' said Spencer, dully.

'I've been let down,' complained Partington. 'I trusted people and I've been let down. Now I could die.'

At that moment Spencer thought that if it hadn't meant he'd almost certainly go too, he would have enjoyed watching the whining motherfucker wither away.

There was matching disbelief holding the four at Blair House, but it wasn't directed upon the need for an individual culprit. Within the first few minutes of them reassembling at Pennsylvania Avenue, Amanda had, without a choice she instinctively wished she'd had, acknowledged the seemingly inconceivable oversight at Fort Detrick and just as haplessly – and logically – accepted American responsibility. She'd actually been surprised, although perhaps more relieved, that the reaction had been so muted.

Gerard Buchemin had said virtually nothing, retreating within himself, his mind's eye blocked by the memory of Henri Lebrun's shrunken body and skeletal face, further horrified by the English scientist's insistence, relayed just hours before by Guy Dupuy, that victims died from within, an organ or a part at a time. He was not sure that if he fell ill – knowing now how it attacked and that it couldn't be stopped – if he had the courage to kill himself at the very onset, while he was still capable of doing so. He had to find the courage: make himself do it. Something painless. Pills. A lot of pills and alcohol and simply go to sleep and not wake up. He'd die with dignity, not as a freak.

Gregori Lyalin was also contemplating death, although far more rationally and philosophically than the Frenchman, his imagery uncluttered by mental pictures of dying victims. He was totally confident and supported by his religion and on that level could even find an anticipation in so early leaving a secular existence for what and to what he knew his soul if not his mortal body to be going. He was even able to find a comforting reassurance on a secular plane, knowing that although his wife and adored children would grieve – as he would grieve to leave them during the time it took him to die – their belief and devotion, as strong as his, would enable them to celebrate his death, not mourn it. The vision he did call to mind was actually comical: how he'd look at the end if all his hair remained after losing its colour, like a mole buried in a snowdrift. Lyalin actually sniggered, which the rest misunderstood as suppressed hysteria.

Peter Reynell's refusal to believe he could be infected, which he thought of more in terms of being interrupted, was not a mentally imbalanced rejection of reality, because he totally recognized the need to be medically tested. It was, rather, the consuming, overwhelming conviction – an arrogance that *did* come close to a mental imbalance – of a man who had no religious belief that his impending success was assured by something akin to supreme divine right and that nothing whatsoever could possibly prevent it happening.

He was careful with his approach to Amanda, leaving her what he considered the proper reflective time and space. As she looked up he said: 'I've calculated something. We can make a direct comparison between how long, either directly or through association, we've been exposed to Stoddart against how long it took for the other Antarctic rescuers very obviously to show signs of infection. They all became ill in days: the longest, three and a half. Stoddart's been out of isolation, meeting you direct or with Geraldine, with whom I've been in contact, three times that long. If any of us four were going to get it, it would have happened by now.'

Amanda smiled, wanly. 'He wouldn't have infected everyone. But we could have become carriers too, from him.'

Reynell shook his head, determinedly. 'And you've been tested and very shortly you're going to be told you're OK.

236

No one's got it! This will end up nothing more than a bad embarrassment, for what Detrick didn't do.'

'Embarrassment we can live with . . .' She stopped, smiling despite herself. 'I didn't intend it to sound like that, as if it was a joke . . .'

Reynell decided fear had melted the ice: softened it, at least. Stripping it away completely, along with that blue silk dress, would be an excellent end to what had most definitely been an unexpectedly traumatic day. 'I'm offering to buy the celebration champagne.'

Amanda decided, close to astonishment, that it wasn't bravado. Reynell genuinely wasn't frightened. 'Let's see if there's anything to celebrate, first.'

'Trust me.'

'Let's see about that, too.' Why had she said that! It had sounded like a come on: worse, a very gauche come on.

'Let's do that,' he said.

Shit, Amanda thought. But dinner hadn't been the problem she'd feared it might be and she'd need a drink when the decision came, whatever it was.

It was precisely 9:33 p.m. by the bureau clock in his isolation room when Barry Hooper told Stoddart: 'You're OK. You're clean. Congratulations,' and Stoddart hoped the permanent and automatic recording didn't pick up the whimper of relief that he at once tried to turn into a cough, actually bringing his hand up to his mouth. He made the pretence of needing the toilet further to compose himself and the rest – even Raisa – were already waiting in the outer corridor when he finally emerged.

Stoddart said: 'We originally planned to get together when we all got back. Why don't we do just that; talk a few things through?' He listened to the business-as-usual tone, pleased there was no tremor in his voice.

Unprotesting, each of them working to regain their mental – even physical – equilibrium, the group followed Stoddart back to his office. As he turned to face them he said: 'I'm sure as hell glad that's over!' That had sounded calm enough, too.

237

Immediately, tensed in a readiness that overrode any lingering concern, Raisa declared: 'What's just happened was utterly inconceivable and came from total incompetence. Why was a basic test like that not conducted?' It had to be capitalized upon – used totally to wash away her first day difficulties – and not allowed to be swept aside or forgotten. Moscow certainly needed to be told. And by her, ahead of Lyalin.

'A very bad and serious mistake was made,' sighed Pelham heavily, seemingly unable to look directly at anyone. 'I personally apologize to each of you. It most definitely shouldn't have arisen. The only good outcome is that Jack didn't turn out to be a carrier.'

'*Is* the danger entirely over?' queried Geraldine. 'If a virus is dormant within a cell, would a swab test give any indication of its hidden presence after all other tests failed to show it?'

The question was put specifically to Raisa and the Russian felt the warmth of long overdue professional recognition. 'Yes,' declared Raisa positively. 'There's definitely no longer any risk. But that doesn't excuse or remove the fact that the potential for an unimaginable catastrophe was absurdly allowed to arise.'

Stoddart's renewed blip of alarm at Geraldine's question went as quickly as it came. 'But it didn't turn out to be a catastrophe, potential or otherwise.' He looked invitingly to Raisa. 'So let's talk about what's come from Moscow?'

Raisa humped her shoulders in what she hoped was a resigned gesture. 'Since I left, all the surviving victims have died,' she announced, to get rid of her original lie. 'But there's everything else. All autopsy reports and research translations – and originals – and every specimen taken, from every victim, for comparison analysis here.'

'We're ready in the laboratories,' said Pelham, anxious for activity – anxious most of all to find something that would re-establish the credibility of himself and his scientists – after the failure for which he had to take personal responsibility.

After all that had happened in the last few hours it didn't seem to Stoddart to be the right moment to announce the

President's Environmental Agency intention, which in truth had very little to do with them in any practical term and for the moment actually seemed inconsequential. Time enough – better timing, in fact – to tell them later. He said: 'We've got a lot of reading, to bring ourselves completely up to date.'

Despite the isolation chamber interruption, Raisa was satisfied she'd filleted everything that was necessary from the Moscow material to prove her viral theory to be the cause of the disease without any supposed help – and certainly without any interference – from anyone here. She most certainly had to get the clock difference right the following day, to ensure she reached Sergei Grenkov at the Institute.

'Nothing like that's ever got to be allowed to happen again!' insisted Henry Partington. They were still in the unrecorded private office, the man already seeking advantages.

'No, sir,' said Spencer, his mind already going in the same direction.

'I think it would be an idea if Paul – and Amanda – cleared visits here through me, in advance,' tried Morgan.

Partington, locked in inner concentration, didn't respond and Spencer kept the smile long enough for the Chief of Staff to see it. Partington, who at the height of his terror had imagined a sacrificial hero's state funeral at Arlington rivalling that of JFK, but was glad now he hadn't mentioned it aloud, said: 'We really could have died.'

I really could have died, the other two men translated, simultaneously.

'Yes, Mr President,' agreed Morgan.

'It was a very real and serious possibility,' expanded Spencer.

'We'll let it be known what we went through, when everything gets into the public domain,' decided the man. *How I personally but willingly faced a horror death to protect my country and its people from a similar fate.*

'It's something that should be publicly known,' said Morgan.

'Taking the swab tests was a very necessary medical precaution,' said Spencer, the answer to another pressing problem coming to him.

'Yes?' prompted Partington, expectantly.

'It would be totally justified – an equally necessary medical precaution – for such tests to be carried out on the personnel at McMurdo and Amundsen-Scott,' stated Spencer. 'You'd be far more liable to criticism, Mr President, for not ordering such a mass examination than for keeping so many people there against their will when the reason does get into the public domain. Despite the time it will still take – added to by the swabs needing to be brought back here for analysis – it's essential the people are kept there, as you so rightly decided at the very beginning.'

Partington looked around the room, as if reminding himself there was no later historical risk in speaking openly. 'That's another neat solution,' he agreed.

'You weren't frightened, were you?' demanded Amanda, in the darkness.

'No,' said Reynell.

'How could you *not* have been!' She had needed the drink but she hadn't arrived at the Hay Adams intending to go to bed with him, although the thought that he might this time hit on her had always been in Amanda's mind. She wasn't sorry that she had. He'd made love to her dispassionately but considerately – with something, even, of a professionalism – ensuring she orgasmed twice before allowing himself to and just as dispassionately but experimentally she'd made sure he did. It had actually gone beyond pleasure. It had confirmed her impression that she and Reynell were so totally similar they could have been cast from the same dye, gender being the only difference.

'I knew – absolutely knew! – it wasn't my time,' he said. 'I've got far too far to go.'

'Asshole,' she said, trying to dent the vainglory.

'Your choice,' he said.

240

Twenty-One

R obin Turner alerted the Kyoto conference signatories to the forthcoming announcement and Partington personally sent official notes to the Russian and French leaders and the British premier. He ensured Amanda had sufficient time in advance of their being delivered to tell the three ministers working with her at Blair House and had the fervently rehabilitating Spencer issue Jack Stoddart with an ultimatum appointment. It wasn't, however, presented as such. It was actually a written and signed memorandum asking Stoddart to provide a definitive assessment as America's foremost environmentalist of such an historic proclamation. The officialdom – and the officialese – briefly bewildered Stoddart until he acknowledged that both was precisely that, official, produceable documentation of a president covering his ass against any unforeseen oversight, error, debacle or lightning bolt from an emission-fogged heaven. One or several of which, Stoddart judged – a number of decisions already reached – the man might have brought upon himself. Stoddart wondered if kamikaze pilots had felt as suspended from reality as he did, about to risk annihilation. On a far less immediate and practical level the presidential edict enabled him belatedly to disclose the president's plans – and his intended acceptance – to his Fort Detrick group. It was the only new and practical development of that day.

The overall reaction, both in DC and Maryland, was mixed, surprisingly limited and once more confused.

At Blair House the uncertainty was largely confined to Peter Reynell. Both Gerard Buchemin and Gregori Lyalin, assured by Amanda that the president was communicating personally and directly with their respective leaders, decided there was no need for their involvement beyond advising Paris and Moscow of their prior awareness. Reynell's priority was to use the American move to his maximum and further advantage, which required his getting his moves in precisely their right order. He timed his first embassy-routed call to Simon Buxton knowing the prime minister would be unavailable during Prime Minister's Questions in the House of Commons, instead leaving the vaguest of vague messages with Buxton's parliamentary secretary that he would supplement the direct presidential approach still to be made with an equally provable memorandum in the diplomatic pouch.

Reynell hurried away from the embassy to make himself unavailable for Buxton's return call, and from the greater comfort of his Hay Adams suite succeeded in reaching the instantly available Foreign Secretary before the man heard from the American Secretary of State – an unexpected bonus – and dominated the conversation assessing the American move to be an unquestionable criticism-limiting exercise. They should, insisted Reynell, ride on the back of it – and for the same reason – by having ready to coincide with the Washington invitation emission control statistics at least five per cent lower than those already agreed in Kyoto, knowing from what he'd researched since his return from London that Britain had already achieved its Japan-agreed target.

Reynell succeeded just as quickly in reaching Lord Ranleigh and again controlled the exchange, urging that in advance of the Washington media event, rumours be started that the British success in meeting the Kyoto agreement had been achieved despite, rather than because of, Simon Buxton's leadership, which could be supported by the lack of any publicly provable or quotable commitment by the man, which Reynell also knew from the checks he'd had made since arriving back in Washington.

'We're getting solid backing here,' assured Ranleigh.

'Let's hope we can maintain it.'

'We're going to build upon it until you're unassailable,' promised the older man.

'That sounds good,' said Reynell. None of them had any idea how unassailable he was going to make himself, once he got the job.

The connection to Simon Buxton was immediate when Reynell finally called, again from the embassy, and by then the American president's courtesy message had already been delivered from the Grosvenor Square embassy and Robin Turner had been in personal contact with an already alerted Ralph Prendergast. Unlike his earlier conversations with London, Reynell didn't attempt to lead, instead responding – always shortly – to Buxton's questions.

'They obviously expect a leak,' insisted Buxton. 'Partington's trying to cover himself.'

'That's fairly obvious.'

'We should do the same; be part of what Partington's going to do . . . make it joint . . .'

The man was lost without someone else to follow, thought Reynell, saying nothing.

'What do you think?' demanded Buxton, openly conceding his need.

'Partington communicated directly with you,' Reynell pointed out. 'It's a matter between leaders . . .' He smiled to himself at the intentional pause. 'I'm assuming, of course, that you wouldn't want me to take part in whatever event the man's planning to make the announcement . . . ?'

'No!' said Buxton, hurriedly. 'It's something I should discuss with him personally.'

'That's probably what you should do.' Buxton's refusal to let him become involved, which Reynell didn't for a moment imagine Partington would have even contemplated, was something to be remembered and used later as an example of the man putting personality ahead of proper political responsibility.

At Fort Detrick, Raisa Orlov was pulled by conflicting frustrations. She was impatient to reach Sergei Grenkov in Moscow, to discuss what had been detected in the blood of the two Russian victims, which she had held back, and discover if there were any comparable findings in the American specimens, although acknowledging if there were that they should have been detected by Fort Detrick analyses. But having had time to reflect more rationally beyond the fiasco that overwhelmingly compensated for her first day problems, Raisa thought that if Walter Pelham and his so-called top scientists could have allowed an oversight as appalling as not having taken carrier swabs – as well as failing to detect the necrosis the Englishwoman had isolated – then all their experiments could be suspect. Or at least justify secondary examination. Raisa's only conflict regarding this matter was yet again with Gregori Lyalin, who had said during their discussion of the American president's environmental intention that he saw no purpose diplomatically in exaggerating an oversight that caused no harm. Lyalin's failure – or refusal – to acknowledge that made his competence suspect, too. For her to do nothing – putting Lyalin's far less qualified opinion above her own – actually threatened her professional integrity. So there was every reason for her to go over Lyalin's head. Paramount in Raisa's mind was that properly presented – and with nothing else in the current hiatus to do except concentrate upon that presentation – such an account spared her and by inference Russia from any culpability for any medical investigatory lapse whatsoever, each and every one of which could be turned back upon America. So most unarguable of all was the need *for* Moscow to be fully informed. Completing her decision, Raisa decided that for her to be shown to be above any personality conflict she would actually copy everything to Gregori Lyalin. None of which could be achieved from provincial Maryland.

Stoddart's overdue social invitation that night to eat outside the complex in a plastic-beamed, gas-fired log-grated tavern – in which, contrastingly, the food was excellent – provided Raisa with the moment to passingly mention that she was returning to Washington the following day. Raisa was curious if Walter Pelham would be with them, which he wasn't and which gave her further although unnecessary confirmation of the American embarrassment, which she decided also had to be included in what went in the diplomatic pouch to Moscow.

It was an awkward and stilted evening, despite the efforts of Stoddart and Geraldine both individually and together – hardening Raisa's unfounded belief in a personal relationship – to make it the amicable evening it was intended to be. Dupuy very quickly stopped bothering to cover his disinterest and Raisa, who'd set out to enjoy her recovery and acceptance, gave up when the efforts of Stoddart and Geraldine ceased to be amusing.

There was a moment at the end of the evening when Raisa was in the rest room and Dupuy was collecting his coat when Stoddart was alone in the reception area with Geraldine.

'Cambridge – Cambridge, England – is taking too long on the original genetic tests. I'd appreciate a ride down with you tomorrow, to stir up some action through the embassy.'

'I was thinking of checking out my apartment at Fairfax that I closed up before going to McMurdo; of staying overnight maybe.'

'I'll get the embassy to check me in somewhere. You could pick me up on your way through in the morning.'

'Sure.' He should offer a ride to Raisa Orlov, too, although after tonight he didn't want to.

The preparation, in such a comparatively although necessarily short time, was impressive. Even on the briefing cards, credit was given to three of Stoddart's most apocalyptic warnings – with all of which he was now, strangely, uncomfortable – and in the text of the verbatim prompt to run unseen on his podium screen as Partington addressed the press conference, each was set out in full for the president to quote, if he chose. The supporting statistics stopped well short of making the presentation indigestable, but what at first surprised Stoddart most of all was the apparent apologetic tone of the speech until Stoddart recognized how cleverly the responsibility for America's failure to meet its Kyoto undertakings was very positively being made that of the previous White House incumbent, whose nonperformance

245

Partington was belatedly but dramatically setting out to correct and more than fulfil.

Despite his awareness of the motivation – despite, even, not wanting to be – Stoddart was impressed by the breadth of Partington's seeming although unspecific commitment, until he recognized how well it fitted his own undeclared intentions.

'What's been missed that needs to be added?' demanded Partington. Already with Paul Spencer in the private, unrecorded office when Stoddart arrived, had been the nervously thin, notebook-poised speechwriter who had been introduced as Barry Tilson. Stoddart hadn't personally met the press spokesman, Carson Boddington, although he recognized the man from countless televised White House media briefings.

'Nothing, I don't think,' said Stoddart, to the obvious relief of both Spencer and Tilson. 'Everything that needs to be has been properly covered.' He had another fleeting kamikaze impression.

Partington appeared disappointed. 'You don't think anything should be improved, pointed up more obviously?'

'I think it's all fine.' Stoddart made a mental note to tell Geraldine later how the president had physically held back from any greeting when he'd entered the small room.

Partington eased further, contentedly, into his chair. The other three men followed. The president said: 'Which only leaves you, Jack . . . ?'

Formally Stoddart said: 'I'll take the position you've offered me, Mr President—'

'Of course you will,' broke in Partington, not bothering to disguise his impatience at what he clearly saw to have been importance-building posturing about which, Stoddart supposed, the man was an expert.

'With some additional suggestions,' abruptly added Stoddart.

Partington instantly became wary. 'What?'

It would, thought Stoddart, be a rehearsal – even perhaps an excuse – of sorts for what he hoped to follow. Consciously – cynically – flattering, he said that by announcing the environmental conference in the wording of the speech, the president was making it a very positive, personal commitment. Which he, Stoddart assured, even more forcefully and publicly intended to match in every way possible. But they'd already acknowledged the problem of his being at Ford Detrick and he didn't believe they should rely upon the existing environmental and ecological agencies properly to combine to create in his absence the absolutely binding agenda necessary – and publicly expected – after what the president was going to say today. 'We've got two survivors from Alaska, now cleared. If they were given facilities here they could be my liaison, until I can take over more fully, to detail what we have to establish on an agenda they'll understand *without* my having to explain in detail. They already know. And because they know it won't be possible, in my absence, for them to be sidetracked or outmanoeuvred by environmentalists with their own, conflicting agendas or those whose colour preference is simply green . . .' Stoddart needed to pause, at the same time regretting the tail-off glibness. Quickly he picked up: 'And if they're my bridge, there'll be no danger of media curiosity at why I'm not as absolutely hands-on, which they know me always to have been in the past. And also be the barrier to anyone knowing why – and where – I am at Fort Detrick.'

Partington remained with his head slumped forward on his chest, paring the words and the arguments for hidden meaning, which he didn't find. 'Paul?'

'Some place has to be found for them until we've got a handle on this,' granted the still grateful Spencer. 'And Jack does need a secure link to Fort Detrick until it is. It sounds good to me, Mr President.'

Partington began gradually to nod his head, in agreement. 'It's neat. Tidy. Let's do that. There's room to set them up at Blair House.'

Where they'll be totally under my control, translated Spencer. 'I'll fix it,' he promised.

The Lincoln Room had been chosen for the conference because of its size and when they got there, forty-five

247

minutes early, the platform and podium had already been erected and the twitching Barry Tilson was checking a speed and clarity run-through of what he'd written on the podium prompt that would be in front of Partington. Technicians were running TV cables to electrical feeds and White House staff had started setting out rows of seating.

Boddington came across as they entered and said to Stoddart: 'You nervous?'

'No,' said Stoddart, honestly.

'No need to be,' said the professional, reassuring, you-can-trust-me man. 'You're not expected to say anything. I'm not allowing questions. It's just a photo opportunity, you and the President together after his declaration.'

'I understand,' said Stoddart. He decided the other man could probably sound sincere breaking wind.

'Smooth as clockwork,' declared a satisfied Tilson, from the podium.

Stoddart and Spencer withdrew at the pre-arranged gesture from the earpieced Secret Service attendant but remained in the expansive approach corridor along which Henry Partington, accompanied by the Secretary of State and Richard Morgan, appeared almost at once. The president had changed from the morning encounter into a subdued, dark-blue suit and muted, unpatterned tie.

'The President goes to the podium by himself,' guided Spencer, quietly. 'You stand with the rest of us to one side and only go up to join him when he signals.'

Precisely on time and as choreographed by more ear-pieced Secret Service men, the double doors swung open and Partington strode forward to the respectful standing ovation from a room that had become filled with people and whitened by intense TV lights. Only when he edged in, initially unrecognized, behind Robin Turner and the White House group, did Stoddart see a narrow, elevated platform was built directly behind the podium to give Partington the appearance of height to everyone in the room beyond.

Although he'd twice read the speech in its entirety and even wondered at some of the actual phrasing, Stoddart

248

had failed totally to anticipate how it would be performed – and performed, he decided, was the apposite word – by a politician as consummate as Henry Partington. The intonation was faultless and every pause, each a prelude to an empty but resounding sound bite, meticulously timed.

The world had for too long ignored its responsibilities to the young and the still unborn – to the planet itself – of global warming and America was the chief and guilty culprit. Today, this moment, he was calling a halt (delivered with a two-handed, palm outwards stopping gesture) by announcing the convening of a conference, the date yet unscheduled, at which all the industrialized countries of the world – with observers and representatives of the innocent but just as badly endangered Third World – were to be invited to commit themselves unequivocally to reduce emissions. Partington proposed that United Nations and world environmental auditing groups be given legally binding authority to enforce what it was essential to agree. For America, for its part, he intended a new environmental governing body, headed by someone whom people both within and beyond America would recognize as the man who for far too long had been warning, unheard, that the world was destroying itself. Here the delivery was accompanied by a gesture to Stoddart who made to move but felt his jacket held by Spencer, stopping him.

At the identification Stoddart abruptly became the attention of cameras and television and a lot of the hurriedly writing, seated journalists. Just as quickly Partington brought the focus back to himself, beginning to speak but then faltering, as if troubled by emotion or uncertainty. There was, the president resumed, a real and potentially frightening reason to move as quickly as possible to adopt the measures he was talking about today. There was evidence that ice-cap melting at both Poles was releasing into the oceans the disease of influenza, which America – with some other involved countries – had already notified to the global monitoring bodies. In the preparation Stoddart had earlier read the 1918 death toll had been kept at forty million, but now Partington quoted one hundred million with the hope that a pandemic of such proportions would not result from what he was disclosing. Partington waited for the stir to subside. The transmission of influenza from sea animals to humans was the most worrying and threatening. But there was more. Solemnly – prophetically – the man enumerated the other inexplicable marine manifestations, making the pause between each announcement like the chime of a warning bell.

'These are things – frightening, unanswerable things – that we so far know about,' concluded Partington in another departure from the text. 'There could be others even more horrifying, even more dangerous. That is why I am taking the lead I am today – urging the other nations of the world to follow me – and appointing this country's foremost advocate against man's destruction of his own planet to lead what I refuse to call an effort but instead pledge to be a determination . . .'

Spencer's restraint became an encouraging push and Stoddart's arrival beside Partington coincided perfectly with the man's gesture of invitation. There was an explosion of flash guns and the glare of television illumination. Stoddart was careful to avoid the elevated podium step keeping the president at his level for the renewed crackling of side by side photographs. Despite the earlier insistence that there would be no questions, there were isolated, unheard shouts, and from the corner of his eye Stoddart saw Boddington come up from the huddled, head-nodding conversation with Spencer, his wrist still bent from him obviously timing the camera access.

As the man moved towards the podium to quell the demands, Stoddart shouted above the hubbub: 'I want to say how honoured and pleased I am to accept the position I have been offered by the President . . .'

The noise faltered and so did the media spokesman, halted by the risk of appearing to cut Partington off if the man chose to go even further beyond his prepared speech.

Hurriedly Stoddart went on. '. . . I do so because I believe as fervently as the President that there is a need for urgent

250

and binding action, action to which no industrialized country has so far done anything more than pay meaningless lip service . . .' He was close enough to Partington to feel the man stiffening and Boddington was edging closer. '. . . Many of you here today will know how long I have been sounding the warnings that the President has endorsed here today. My record is a matter of *public* record and that is how I intend it to remain. Public. And I want to make a public promise about the responsibility I have today been accorded and today accepted . . .' Boddington was beside him now, fidgeting to intervene. Partington was rigid, fingers white where he was gripping the podium edge. '. . . With the complete backing and authority of the President of the United States I will evolve, with the Environmental Agency of the United Nations and of every involved country in the world, restrictions and conditions and monitoring to halt what is happening to the earth's resources—'

'I think . . .' tried Boddington, but the man was too far away for the microphone to pick up the interruption.

'. . . And here is my undertaking,' Stoddart forced on. 'If I come to the belief that the efforts that have been pledged today are being sabotaged or treated contemptuously by any of the bodies or countries invited to participate, then I will publicly name them at the time of my even more publicly resigning. And that resignation will be the signal and the proof that the pressure of industrialized commercialism has defeated the obligation that the President has so rightly identified today, to the newly born and the unborn, babies who might enter a world to diseases not yet known and others, like cancer, virtually inevitable from unfiltered sunlight . . .'

Partington actually stepped back from the podium to make room at the microphone for Boddington as Stoddart finished. The eruption of questions was so loud nothing was intelligible and Boddington stood with his hands outstretched to quell the noise. Partington was already off the dais, hurrying back towards the corridor and Stoddart followed. Almost at once

Turner, Morgan and Spencer created a protective cordon behind them.

Partington halted just beyond the quickly closed double doors, wheeling to confront Stoddart, white-faced, physically shaking in his fury. 'You smart-assed son of a bitch! I'll bury you, for what you've just done! Bury you without a trace . . .'

Twenty-Two

Richard Morgan physically intervened between Stoddart and the president – although touching neither – in an effort to stem the far too public tirade and Spencer grasped Stoddart's elbow to lead the man into the side corridor and the basement elevator.

'My office,' Morgan called after them. Partington's voice became indistinct but Stoddart heard 'son of a bitch' repeated and 'fix'. There were two cleaners in the lift and Spencer and Stoddart rode down unspeaking.

It wasn't until they were inside Morgan's suite that Spencer said: 'What the fuck do you think you're doing!' He was ashen and his voice trembled.

'Matching the President's determination is all,' said Stoddart. Partington's unrestrained fury astonished him.

'You knew you weren't to say anything! I told you!'

'The President's just made a long overdue commitment. I gave the man every credit for it and made one of my own.'

'Bull*shit*! You publicly trapped the President!'

'*That's* bullshit. Unless, of course, the President didn't mean anything he just said. Which I can't believe. You telling me something I need to know?'

Spencer looked steadily at Stoddart, visibly tensing to recover his own self-control. 'Let me tell you something you do need to know. You need to know you've just made one of the biggest mistakes of your life. I don't know – can't guess – what the President's going to do, but he's a bad man to cross and he sure as hell thinks you've crossed him. If there's any future for you in this thing after today, then you'd better listen to everything you're told and if you're told something

253

the President wants or doesn't want, you make damned sure you follow it to the letter. And—'

'Paul!' stopped Stoddart. 'Here's something I think you need to know. Or remember. I've been fucked over for years by people who refused to hear what I had to say because it affected their balance sheets, which I very well know fund political parties and political campaigns. Something else I very well know is *precisely* why Henry Partington wheeled me out today. And you know it, too. So let's be honest with each other, you and I. I respect the *office* of the presidency and I'll do nothing to show disrespect to it. What you regard as trapping the President I consider maintaining my own independent integrity and refusing to become anyone's talking doll . . .' Stoddart stopped at the entry into the room of Richard Morgan and Carson Boddington. '. . . We're clearing the air here. You think it might be an idea, Paul, if I repeated what I've just said . . . ?'

Before Spencer's shrug Stoddart said it again anyway and when he finished Morgan at once demanded: 'Who said anything about the President being trapped?'

There was an echoing pause before Spencer said: 'Maybe I said something like that.'

'I think there's been some misunderstandings,' calmed Morgan, looking at his former deputy. 'The President feels that maybe, Jack, you weren't properly briefed upon what was expected up there today.'

Spencer's face tightened again. 'Jack was told he wasn't expected to say anything.'

'Then maybe it's unfortunate it wasn't stressed strongly enough,' said Morgan, refusing to let go the blame he'd already planted firmly in Partington's mind. 'What's important now is to keep things in proportion.'

'I don't consider anything's *out* of proportion,' said Stoddart.

'That's good to hear, Jack,' said Boddington, easing into the soothing conversation. 'That's how we want to keep things, don't you agree?'

'What, exactly, is it you're asking me to agree with? Or to?' asked Stoddart.

It was Morgan who replied. 'The President didn't expect you to say anything. He was surprised—' Again looking directly at Spencer, the Chief of Staff went on. 'He's asked me to make sure there aren't any more misunderstandings.'

Go with the flow, decided Stoddart. He'd made his point far more forcefully than he'd imagined. 'I don't see why there should be. I'm clear on what I am supposed to do and until I can get fully involved there's Darryl Matthews and Harold Norris to get things up and running.' It was important – essential – to ensure there hadn't been a change of heart about that.

Boddington made a vague gesture in the direction of the outer corridor. 'We're being inundated with personal interview requests.'

'Which I'm not interested in doing at the moment,' said Stoddart.

The relief from the press spokesman was as muted as Stoddart's qualified refusal. Boddington said: 'You've been pretty approachable in the past. People have got your number. You'll be chased.'

'Not to Fort Detrick,' Stoddart pointed out. The Fairfax apartment was too well known to the media, so checking that out wouldn't be possible now. He was glad he'd arranged to meet Geraldine before setting out. He supposed there'd be a cancellation penalty for whatever hotel room had been booked for her but they could drive back to the installation that night. Even with the likelihood of rejection he should have suggested meeting Raisa Orlov.

'That would be better,' said Boddington, obscurely. 'Not talking to the media any more, I mean. Not until—'

'There's something to tell them,' provided Stoddart. 'Relax, guys. I'm not trapping anyone or holding anyone over a barrel. As long as the game's straight – or straight enough – I'll play by the rules. That make everybody happy?'

'There must be something!' insisted Henry Partington. In his continued fury he was stumping around the small, private office, all his calls held.

'Better to wait,' urged Morgan. 'He's on side now. Best to

let him have his moment, his fifteen minutes of glory, until we get a solution to whatever the damned Shangri-La strain is. Something goes wrong we need to offload, Jack Stoddart's there for us.'

'Okay, there's nothing we can do at the moment but when he's served his purpose I want Jack Stoddart buried . . . buried so deep he'll think it would have been better if he'd died, with all the rest. And screw him at Blair House. Give his two pet monkeys space and secretaries but no other support staff. They'll suffocate under paper.'

Morgan let the threat hang in the air.

'It's Paul's failure, more than anybody's,' continued Partington.

'Yes, sir,' said Morgan.

'Is there anything for him to talk to me about other than to save his ass?'

'I don't think so,' said Morgan.

'Then I won't see him.'

'You want me to tell him you're too busy?' offered Morgan, hopefully.

Partington considered the question. 'Not right away. Let him twist in the wind for a while.'

Gregori Lyalin actually laughed as he tossed his copy of Raisa's complaint on to the coffee table of his temporary office in the embassy. 'Very forcefully expressed.'

Surely the bastard wasn't patronising her! 'It was your right to be told my professional opinion.'

'And your right to express it direct to Moscow,' agreed Lyalin, easily.

It *was* condescension. It wouldn't have been if he'd known – which he wouldn't, until she was well and truly ready to tell him – what Sergei Grenkov had just told her: that in the tissue sample she'd held back from everyone at Fort Detrick there was a stain trace which her deputy was virtually sure had to be an antibody. Which meant she was right about the infection being viral and they had a route to follow. 'I'm glad you accept that.'

256

It wasn't difficult, thought Lyalin, to suspect the woman had a genuine mental problem. He gestured towards the paper. 'You haven't said you've given me a copy, as a matter of courtesy.'

Raisa hesitated, feeling the irritation. She'd intended to but had been distracted by her conversation with Grenkov. 'An oversight. The importance is that I did show it to you.'

Lyalin smiled again. 'An oversight about an oversight! So they do occur. And like that of the Americans, no harm's been done.'

Bastard! 'I think that's a facile comparison, scarcely worth suggesting.'

'So do I,' said Lyalin readily. 'You going to add to what you've already written to Moscow that you've copied me your note. The impression might be that we're openly disagreeing.'

'Aren't we?' seized Raisa.

'Not on the importance,' qualified Lyalin. 'Just on whether something that turned out to be a false alarm was worth commenting about as strongly as this.'

'It illustrates the American inadequacy.'

Lyalin nodded towards the television upon which they'd just watched the White House announcement. 'If he's right, about how this thing is getting into the environment, Stoddart isn't proving to be inadequate.'

'*If*,' said Raisa heavily.

'I'll leave it up to you whether you add to your message,' dismissed Lyalin. 'I won't bother to comment unless I'm asked. I'm more interested in the positive than the negative.'

Peter Reynell had also watched the environmental declaration from his embassy, his concentration not directly upon the White House event but upon the CNN transmission of Simon Buxton's closely timed and matching British commitment from which he'd been further deflected by Geraldine Rothman's totally unexpected and hopeful news. Until she received the detailed Cambridge findings overnight – and

257

more importantly had the woman explain them to him in terms he could better understand – it was obviously premature to try to take any early advantage, but it was enough upon which to base another telephone call to Ralph Prendergast at the Foreign Office and to the now always-receptive Lord Ranleigh. Reynell stopped short of using a word like breakthrough – limiting himself to suggesting a possible but by no means certain development – more intent upon filtering from both conversations that Buxton's anxiously proposed overnight flight to Washington to appear with the American president had been rejected by the White House. Striving to remain impartial, Reynell still judged Buxton's performance lacklustre, too obviously a tagged-on effort made even more obvious by neither the Russian nor French leader trying to compete with a personal appearance.

Which was Henrietta's – and therefore clearly her father's – opinion when they spoke. She said: 'Buxton looked panicked, I thought.'

'I'd liked to have seen a longer excerpt than CNN,' said Reynell.

'I taped it, for when you get back. Any idea when that might be?'

'None.'

'So who you going to screw tonight?'

'I'm actually having dinner with a man,' said Reynell, which was true.

'You into fucking men now?'

'Only figuratively.' Believing he'd sufficiently seduced Amanda – in every definition of the word – that night's dinner was with Gerard Buchemin.

The rooftop bar of the Washington hotel had become their place and Geraldine was already at a table when Stoddart arrived. He thought he detected two signs of recognition as he moved past the line waiting to be seated and was glad they were tonight to the side and not in the front, where they'd managed to sit on previous evenings.

As he sat she said: 'I saw the television. You were terrific.'

'A lot of people don't think so.' There was definite recognition from the waitress taking their order. 'I was supposed to stay mute.'

'You certainly weren't that.'

'I'm in media demand. So I'm not going to Fairfax after all: it'll be surrounded. But we can have dinner before we go back.'

'I'm not going back,' Geraldine announced. 'We've found something, genetically.'

Stoddart looked hurriedly around the noisy verandah and was at once embarrassed by the theatricality. 'What?'

'I need to wait until the full research material gets here tomorrow, but it seems to involve telomeres. They're the sealing-off caps at the end of each DNA molecule; essential, to keep chromosomes intact. In all our victims their telomeres were either abnormally short or didn't exist at all.'

'I don't understand the significance,' protested Stoddart.

'You will.'

They went again to Georgetown, Stoddart relieved to escape the growing attention at the hotel, and this time found a smaller French restaurant just off Wisconsin's join with M Street. Stoddart was more comfortable with a table near the large, plant-filled fireplace. Geraldine changed from Chardonnay to gin martinis – although restricting herself to two, remembering her arrival flight – and tried in general terms to explain the importance of DNA telomeres until Stoddart said maybe he should wait until the following day. They drank imported Pomerol with the quail and Stoddart admitted to planning that afternoon's intervention.

'It's borrowed time but as long as I can stretch it out maybe there can be some legislation that can come halfway near to being complied with.'

'Just halfway near?'

'That will be a damned sight better than anything that's being achieved at the moment.'

Geraldine raised her wine glass. 'Here's to a brave, committed man.'

259

'Or a stupid one.' He raised his glass in return. 'Here's to the person who found the answer to our problem.'

'I'm not even going to drink to that,' refused Geraldine.

Stoddart examined his near empty glass. 'I've drunk too much to consider driving all the way back to Frederick. You have any difficulty in getting a room?'

Geraldine shook her head, solemnly.

'I can call from here, see if they've got another.'

'It needn't matter, if they haven't.' She felt as if her face was burning and hoped it wasn't.

Stoddart was confused, not sure what his sensation was. 'You sure?'

'No,' she answered, honestly.

'You can change your mind.' What about his mind? He wasn't sure either.

'Let's not go into deep subconscious analysis.'

Geraldine's reservation was at the downtown Marriott on 14th Street, just a block behind where they'd earlier been, at the Washington Hotel. They crossed the huge foyer and rode the elevator unspeaking and untouching and halted just inside her door, looking uncertainly at each other.

Trying to lighten things, Stoddart said: 'Raisa wouldn't like this.'

'She might, given the opportunity.'

They kissed awkwardly, fumbling with buttons until Geraldine pulled away and said: 'We'd be better doing it ourselves.'

She was very full busted, her breasts freckled, and flat stomached and naturally red haired. Her thighs were freckled, too, at their very tops. The kiss was better when they tried again and he explored her with his mouth, urging himself to respond. He remained flaccid and tried to disguise the failure with his mouth again before becoming aware of her rigid unresponsiveness.

'I'm sorry,' she said.

'So am I.'

'Patricia?'

It hadn't been such a secret after all, he accepted. 'I guess so. It wasn't anything long term but I saw her die.' He wasn't sure what he was trying to say.

'There was someone, Michael, just before I came here. It was a mess. Ugly.'

Stoddart extended his arm and she came into its crook, snuggling against his chest and shoulder. 'I'm not,' she said, her voice muffled.

'Not what?'

'Sorry. Better to give ourselves time.'

'Not too much, though.'

'Not too much,' she agreed.

It was two hours later, on the far side of the city, when the telephone jarred into Gregori Lyalin's embassy compound room, waking him from the sleep he didn't regain for the rest of that night.

Twenty-Three

They made love sometime in the early morning, each for the first few seconds surprised to find someone next to them, and afterwards Geraldine said: 'There, that wasn't so difficult after all, was it?' and Stoddart laughed because she was making their discovery of each other fun.

They slept afterwards with her body cupped against his, always vaguely conscience of each other – each wanting to be conscious of each other – in the half dream between sleep and wakefulness. And when they finally did awake, they made love again and she said they had to be careful it didn't become habit forming and he asked why and she said she needed time to think of an answer.

It continued for both of them to be an adventure without any unexpected abyss. He was able to gift her a second toothbrush from his travel bag and she promised that the shaving head of her cosmetic razor hadn't been used, even though he said it wouldn't have mattered if it had.

They flicked between morning television channels, all three majors of which remained dominated by the environmental declaration and all three of which concentrated – with separate panel discussion, supplemented by footage of ecologically-claimed disasters – more upon the importance of Jack Stoddart's personal involvement and even more positively upon the man's integrity pledge than they did, regretfully (even forgetfully), upon the president's supposed ecological awakening, although that, even more regretfully, was the actual word used to describe Henry Partington's statement in an accompanying *New York Times* editorial they discovered later, at breakfast. The concentration was equally upon Stoddart in the *Washington Post* and *USA Today*.

Stoddart remained secure in the anonymity of a room reserved in Geraldine Rothman's name when she left for the British embassy. His first call was to Walter Pelham ('Where the hell have you been, posing for a commemorative statue?') to fix a meeting for that afternoon ('Geraldine's got something; I don't know how good it is') and separately – but individually – to the no longer isolated Darryl Matthews and Harold Norris, to outline briefly the environmental offer and arrange a meeting with them, even later. Stoddart turned the television off at the second repetition of CNN's White House coverage of the previous day to introduce that morning's news-of-the-moment footage of his many earlier televised criticisms of industries' ecological disregard and sat alone, momentarily uninvolved and disconnected, wondering what had happened between himself and Geraldine Rothman.

Nothing, he decided. They'd had a lot – too much – to drink and their individual adrenaline had been high and eventually they'd spent a mutually satisfactory night together, which had certainly been good for him and which, from the very little she'd said about someone named Michael, had been good for her, too. It was ridiculous, artificial, for him to imagine that what had happened between them in any way affected what there'd been with Patricia. He found it even more difficult now than he had less than twenty-four hours earlier invoking Patricia's memory to excuse his embarrassment. He was humiliated by using her to cover his inadequacy. If there'd been a way – if he'd believed in God and prayer, maybe – he thought at that moment he would have prayed for her forgiveness and at once felt even more embarrassed and humiliated because he *didn't* believe, which made the reflection even less respectful to the dead woman.

Geraldine returned just before eleven, flushed and smiling. She said at once: 'I've outlined it to Reynell but I don't think he fully understood, so I want to read through it all again on the way back and do a better comparison on the tissue Raisa

263

made available from the Russian victims. In a nutshell, I think we've found the effect but not the cause.'

Stoddart frowned, disappointed. 'We know the effect. Everyone gets old and dies.'

'*How* they get old,' said Geraldine. 'What have you told Fort Detrick?'

'To be ready for a two o'clock meeting. We talking breakthrough here?'

'How about something close to a giant step forward?'

'That'll do.'

Geraldine pushed her passenger seat back as far as it would go to make room on the floor in front of her for papers and diagrams and what looked like surreal positive prints taken from what he guessed to be some specialized microscope images. She kept the Russian file separate on the back seat. Her concentration was absolute and Stoddart didn't attempt any conversation, instead formulating in his own mind what – or how – he would discuss with Matthews and Norris about the previous day.

Occasionally, beside him, Geraldine mumbled to herself. Once, consulting something she took from the rear seat, she said: 'Shit!' although again not addressing him. They had almost reached Frederick, the landmarks becoming familiar, before she said, softly at first but then repeated, finally, to him: 'I'm right! And it accounts for the necrosis, too.'

He jerked his head towards the rear seat and said: 'What's wrong with the Russian stuff?'

'There's not enough to take it any further.'

Because Geraldine suggested display screens and a blackboard might help, they arranged to meet in the improvised conference room, but before they did Geraldine huddled specifically with the two virologists on Pelham's staff, comparing the British and American analyses of the Russian material. She told Raisa Orlov before doing so, accurately anticipating the woman's insistence upon taking part, which effectively rehearsed Raisa for what was to follow.

By the time they finally assembled, only fifteen minutes

behind schedule, Geraldine had her surreal prints displayed and had ensured complete duplicates were available of what had arrived that morning from England.

'There's unarguable proof that our disease is attacking its victims' genes,' declared Geraldine. 'And the effect of it doing so confirms the theory of organs dying – technically necrosis – that we found in our victims and is evident, too, in the Russian tissue samples.' She indicated what looked to Stoddart nothing more than dark markings against a lighter background on three of her illustrations, continuing on to her blackboard. 'Those are chromosomes, more precisely 5, 8 and 14 of the 23 that make up the molecular structure of cells in the human body; in this case those of Harry Armstrong and George Bedall, who died in the Antarctic, and Henri Lebrun, the French glaciologist at Noatak, in Alaska, who died here . . . They're samples, chosen at random. The packs you have in front of you contain tissue readings identical to those I've pinned up here . . .'

Raisa shifted, looking neither at the material in front of her nor at Geraldine, who on her blackboard drew a sausage shape. 'There's a chromosome, packed with thousands of genes.' Very positively she chalked in both ends. 'And they're telomeres. They don't contain genes, as such, but are a special sort of DNA which—' Geraldine waved her hands, as if seizing an analogy from the air. 'Let's think of them as sealing wax. That's their function, to act as a sealant or cap at the end of each chromosome for a very specific and necessary purpose . . .'

Geraldine's voice grated and she moved away from the blackboard to pour herself water. 'The human body is made up of millions of thousands of cells, a lot of which are constantly renewing themselves. Those in the skin and gut, for instance, do so every three days. They do that by dividing, but prior to that division each DNA makes a complete replica of itself, giving the new cell the genes it needs. Which is where – and why – telomeres are vital. During the division process, they cap each end of the chromosome to prevent the DNA from being eroded or frayed—' Abruptly Geraldine

265

wiped away her chalked-in ends. 'No telomeres, no seal. All the beads – the DNA – can just fall out the tube, erode, go to hell, whatever. Which is what the indications are, in all our victims. In *every* case with *every* victim the chromosome telomeres are three, in some cases five times shorter than they should be. There are twenty instances overall, among all the victims, of there being no telomeres remaining at all . . .'

She gulped water and during the pause Pelham said: 'I accept the genetic findings, but why is it that only the genes that bring about rapid ageing are being affected . . . falling out, to continue your analogy? That doesn't have any scientific logic.'

'I agree it doesn't,' said Geraldine. 'And I don't know the answer. We don't fully know, genetically, which or what genes cause ageing: only that there are obviously several. Those affecting skin, others causing hair loss or discolouration, still more resulting in bone depletion, sight loss, hearing impairment . . . There is, though, sufficient indication from cells developed in culture that telomere shortening is an intrinsic part of the ageing process. If cells can't regenerate themselves they die. And we already know that the organs of our victims here progressively died . . .' She hesitated. '. . . At an astonishingly accelerated rate . . . a rate I'm not aware of in any other disease, causing organs to die as we now know the organs of the victims died, one after the other. It's as if . . .' She spoke to Raisa. 'And here we need your input . . . it's as if we're not dealing with *one* infection – one virus or one bacterium – but several attacking different targets like an army . . .'

Dupuy said: 'You've discovered this *post* mortem, like it's only possible to diagnose a lot of diseases – brain sectioning for Creutzfeldt Jakob, for instance – after death. How are we going to find a preventative or a cure if there aren't recognizable pre-death symptoms to treat . . .'

'We're not even in sight of that question yet, let alone an answer to it,' said Geraldine. 'Let's try to understand where we are with what we do know.'

266

'But you've been right so far,' smiled Dupuy, in intended congratulation.

Quickly, without looking at Raisa, Geraldine said: 'A lot of science is luck and coincidence.' She tapped one of the prints, without bothering to look at it. 'That's happened. I can't tell you why it's happened, how to stop it happening again or even – as I've already admitted – why it's having the specific effect that it has—' She went to Raisa again. 'Which was why I was hopeful about the tissue register in your one victim . . . ?'

'Oleg Vasilevich,' identified the Russian, reluctant to concede the unquestionable British progress. 'It *is* a register and brings us back to viruses.'

'A register of what, though?' demanded Geraldine. 'It's too faint – indistinct – to recognize as an antibody or an enzyme . . .'

Not on my more positive sample, thought Raisa. That was clearly an antibody and very shortly Grenkov, using immunofluorescent staining and electron microscopy, would establish the antigen to which it had been trying to attach itself and give them the alien protein. And when he did that, she'd have her viral proof and the simpering Frenchman would have to acknowledge who deserved the real credit. To Pelham she said: 'Don't your virologists consider it enzymal evidence?'

'They can't be certain,' said the uncomfortable director.

'Nor are our virologists in England,' said Geraldine

'What about Geraldine's theory of it being a multiple infection, to account for the speed of the infection?' pressed Dupuy.

Raisa easily covered her satisfaction at the double admission that the separate viral tests had failed. 'All we've got so far is the one example.'

'How then could it have the multiple effect that is has?' pressed Dupuy.

'Remember what you've just been told,' Raisa escaped easily. 'We're far too far away to understand that yet . . .'

'Werner's Syndrome,' said Geraldine, uttering her thought aloud.

'What?' asked Raisa, presciently.

'Werner's Syndrome,' repeated Geraldine, coming up to Pelham. 'That's a condition brought about from an inherited protein deficiency, right?'

'As far as we know,' agreed the installation director, still obviously hesitant.

'But we *do* know – the scientific coding is known – of which proteins are lacking?'

'I'd need to check,' sidestepped the man.

'I'm sure it's known.' declared Geraldine. 'Why don't we run a comparison – even though we can't decide what the Russian slide shows – against the acknowledged protein deficiency in people suffering Werner's Syndrome?'

It would be a route march in the wrong, uphill direction, Raisa instantly recognized. Which they – Geraldine Rothman most of all – should not for a moment be dissuaded or deflected from following. The problem was the attentive, fart-and-cough-noting secretariat. 'I'm not sure that it follows,' she lured, cautiously.

'But you're not ruling it out as a potential way forward?' persisted Geraldine.

'At this stage – which isn't really any stage at all because we know so little – I'm not ruling anything out.' That didn't endanger her scientific credentials, Raisa assured herself.

'So why don't we compare against what there is on the Russian slide, the recognizable – but missing – proteins affecting sufferers of Werner's Syndrome?'

There was a moment of silence which Raisa made no move to fill, happy for them to wander off theoretically into the hazy distance. It was the Frenchman who spoke. 'To achieve what?'

'Werner's Syndrome is an ageing condition,' Geraldine reminded, pedantically. 'If there was anything approaching a match – no matter how indistinct – we could reasonably suggest it was the Werner's Syndrome proteins being destroyed. Knowing what those missing proteins are, we could re-introduce them into our next victim, hopefully to arrest – even reverse – the condition.'

Raisa was abruptly glad of the attentive secretariat. 'Where's the ethical validity in that?' she demanded. 'In Russia we have a medical code against scientifically using human guinea pigs.'

Geraldine went to speak – her first instinctive reaction to challenge that medical assertion, which she didn't believe – but for once held herself back. Instead, more tellingly, she said: 'We tried progesterone on Henri Lebrun, with even less scientifically proven validity. I'm only putting the comparison forward as an idea: throwing stones into the pool to see where the ripples will go. You got a better proposal, I'll listen and if it *is* better – halfway better – I'll go with it.'

The unexpected opening of the door saved Raisa trying for an answer she didn't have. And it was to Raisa that Pelham's personal assistant, a matronly large, grey-haired black woman, spoke. 'It's your minister. I said you were in conference but he insisted it was sufficiently urgent for me to interrupt.'

Stoddart turned the interruption into a formal break and used it to bring forward the encounter with Darryl Matthews and Harold Norris. As they entered the office Norris, a crewcut, arm-tattooed man, remarked that getting out of isolation was like being released from prison, as if he was speaking from personal experience and Matthews said he was probably at the end of a long line but wanted to congratulate Stoddart on his White House declaration.

'Which I'm asking you guys to keep up the momentum for me,' announced Stoddart. Succinctly, prepared during the drive up from Washington, he set out the offer for them to establish the early administration apparatus of the intended environmental ombudsman's function, bluntly acknowledging why he in turn had been invited to be part of the previous day's White House ceremony.

It was Norris who queried Stoddart's choice of word. 'In England an ombudsman is the person you complain to, usually against some official administration.'

'Which is precisely why I used it,' said Stoddart. 'Yesterday was photo-opportunity bullshit which I want to turn into something positive—' He swept his hand around the office. 'You know what I'm doing – trying to do – here, which is why I can't set myself up immediately in Washington and why I'm asking you to do it initially in my place. Because if I don't start moving right away, it's all going to get shunted quietly into the background, like it always has in the past, the administration having covered its ass against the public eventually learning of the illness you escaped catching . . .'

'This time I hoped it would be different,' said Matthews, accepting the cynicism. He was a thin man, made thinner by his ordeal, and his clothes sagged about him.

'This time it's going to be,' insisted Stoddart. 'Like I said, we need to keep the momentum – the public awareness – going all the time. I want all the environmental agencies told we're bringing them together, under one cohesive, *working* organization. And I'm not just talking America. The United Nations has an environmental programme, with a staffed division in New York to implement it. With the declared commitment of the US President, the UN won't be able to get on the bandwagon fast enough. And the UN gives us access, worldwide, to all the other groups . . . And don't restrict your spread to environmental groups. It was the President who brought disease into the frame because he wants to appear ahead when the ageing illness becomes known. Involve the Centre for Disease Control in Atlanta. And the WHO, who've already been warned about the influenza outbreaks. Go to the other international disease control co-ordinators.'

'You're going to need a bureaucracy as *big* as the United Nations,' protested Norris, mildly.

'Maybe not,' refused Stoddart. 'We've always got that self-proclaimed, all important power of the press. You make the sort of high profile list I've suggested and then you *invite* their participation. And let it be known that they've been asked—' He made rolling motions with his hands. 'You're playing the charity game, getting on your letterhead a lot of high-sounding sponsors that don't really have to do anything.

270

Our only need is to keep the publicity groundswell going so that no one invited to the environmental conference – and remember the responsibility for organizing *that* is the White House's, not ours – can back away from the commitment.'

'What about the agenda?' asked Norris.

'I could write that now, without any input,' said Stoddart. 'First we've got to publicly back everyone into a corner from which they can't escape.'

Matthews' cynicism remained. 'Seems you've thought a lot through in a short time.'

'I've got a lifetime's experience of government opportunism,' said Stoddart. 'Now I'm playing by their rules.'

'You really mean it, about resigning if it doesn't work?'

'Absolutely,' guaranteed Stoddart. 'Which is something you've got to understand fully. You agree to do what I'm asking and you're tarred with the same brush as I am.' He looked to Norris. 'Maybe not so much a problem for you, being British. But it might not be a wise career move for either of you. It's something for both of you to think about, before making a decision. No hard feelings or recriminations if you don't want to come along.'

'There's another side to the coin, using the same criteria,' pointed out the American paleobotanist, sardonically. 'You achieve something worthwhile – as well as being recognized for correctly establishing how this infection's getting into the system – and there'll be a lot of public credit for anyone riding the bandwagon with you.'

Stoddart smiled, to both of them. 'That's the choice you've got to make.'

'I haven't got a better job offer,' Norris smiled back. 'My workplace got burned down, remember?'

'I was looking for something to do, too,' accepted Matthews.

In her assigned private quarters on the floor below, Raisa Orlov remained standing, rigid, although no longer from the disappointment at not hearing from Gregori Lyalin about what she'd speculated could have even been the man's recall to Moscow.

271

'This should not be shared under any circumstances what-soever!' she insisted.

'That's not your decision.'

'I want a ruling from Moscow.'

'I've already told you what that is.'

'I want it reversed. To speak to Moscow myself.'

'I am going direct from the embassy here to tell the rest of the group,' said Lyalin. 'I am ordering you to do the same with your group.'

'No!' said Raisa, desperately.

'You will do as I ask,' said Lyalin, replacing the telephone before she could speak again.

Peter Reynell hadn't fully understood Geraldine's explanation, although he'd assimilated enough generally to brief the others in Blair House, but during the time between their embassy encounter and his arrival at Pennsylvania Avenue he'd evolved a way to turn his difficulty into a continuing advantage. To delay speaking to Simon Buxton in London until the following day – until he'd tested the water with Lord Ranleigh and possibly with the now obvious ally he had in the Foreign Secretary – Reynell admitted at once that some of Geraldine's explanation had been too scientifically esoteric for him. Geraldine herself had anticipated the need for a simpler clarification and promised to provide it as an addendum to the transcript they would automatically get under the existing discussion exchange between themselves and Fort Detrick. In the interim, he insisted it was an important and positive genetic discovery, talking of telomeres and their erosion although apologizing for being unsure of their function or importance.

'As essential as it is for us to totally understand what the breakthrough is – and what it represents – I propose we wait until we get my scientific advisor's definitive account, as well as the additional help from all the other experts at Fort Detrick, before alerting our respective governments. We can't risk the slightest misunderstanding or misconception.'

'I think you're right,' accepted Amanda, to immediate nods

of agreement from the other two men around the table. 'But it's clearly some sort of progress—'

'That we'll only have to wait a few more hours to learn properly,' finished Reynell, wanting to cut the discussion before there were any second thoughts about a delay.

'There's something else I want to raise,' said Gregori Lyalin. 'Something quite incredible has been happening in eastern, as opposed to northern, Siberia.'

'What we know is very limited,' said Raisa, tightly, unsure how much more she could restrict what the hairy bastard Lyalin was making her disclose. 'You'll remember from an early Blair House transcript my colleague talking about adding the distemper infection in the unique seals of Lake Baikal to the other marine illness outbreaks?'

Everyone was looking at her expectantly and Raisa wondered if Lyalin had intentionally timed his call to interrupt the Fort Detrick discussion to heighten – as well as forcing her compliance in – the drama of what she was being made to say.

'There's been something else?' frowned Stoddart.

Lyalin would be revealing everything, Raisa accepted. So she couldn't withhold anything. 'There is a volcanically active island in the lake.'

'Ol'khon,' identified Stoddart, at once and unexpectedly.

Raisa's look was a combination of curiosity and irritation. 'There hasn't been a positive eruption for over a hundred years. In the winter the lake freezes over to such a depth that it becomes a road, capable of supporting heavy vehicles, but sometimes the tremors are sufficient to break apart ice even that thick . . . that's how severe they are. There were a series of such tremors three days ago . . .' Briefly the final revelation stuck in Raisa's throat. 'The permanent research institute at Listvyanka has discovered that what was believed to be a solid cliff face above the permanent freeze line of the Barguzin mountains has sheered off uncovering a cave complex. Inside there is what's described as a Neolithic colony of perfectly preserved human beings . . .'

'And?' anticipated Dupuy.

'The majority died from what appeared to be premature old age,' completed Raisa. 'But some very young children died from malnutrition because the adults hadn't been able to provide food for them . . .'

'What's happened now?' demanded Stoddart.

'On orders from Moscow –' Raisa stopped short of admitting that they had been issued personally and directly to Listvyanka by Gregori Lyalin, '– the area has been sealed and everything has been left, as it was found.'

'We need to go there!' declared Geraldine, at once.

'I don't think that will be at all possible,' rejected Raisa, snatching at the faint chance of keeping it to herself. 'It's an extremely remote area, difficult to obtain permission to get into.'

'It wasn't the last time I was there,' said Stoddart.

At that moment, at Blair House, Peter Reynell, his mind yet again far ahead of what he'd also just been told, said: 'One of us at least has to go there personally.'

Twenty-Four

It took less than twenty-four hours to organize because Gregori Lyalin was on the spot instantly to authorize a lot of the arrangements he'd anticipated and stayed up most of the previous night getting into place, and in Washington there was the power of the president to gain unobstructed access to military transportation and whatever specialized material was considered essential. Ironically it was Jack Stoddart, an American, who was the only one of them with personal experience of the unique Russian region, who made up the equipment list – the detail to which took longer than getting an aircraft put on standby – and whom Lyalin asked to give an orientation briefing. Both stoked another layer to Raisa Orlov's controlled frustration because she'd avoided a lot of initial questioning pleading – honestly – that she had no local knowledge, even though it made her appear lacking. Overnight she'd realized how to turn the entire situation to her benefit though, despite what she now regarded as Lyalin's opposition.

The entire Fort Detrick group, including Walter Pelham, despite his not being included in the Siberian party, were at Blair House by seven the following morning. The Blair group was already waiting, with an anxious Paul Spencer hoping for miracles to restore his acceptance by the president.

It would be wrong, Stoddart decided, to paint a sunset picture, although in fact he recalled the sunsets at Lake Baikal were spectacular. They were, he began, going to a place different from any other they'd ever heard of or imagined. He'd worked there – knew the Limnological Institute of the Siberian Academy of Science at Listvyanka – because its climatic variation, unlike anywhere else on the globe, was one of its several exceptional features. Held as it was – and as large as it was – in the Barguzin mountains, only in the freezing winter was the lake spared hurricane force winds capable of blowing animals and houses – and even more easily people – off cliffsides and shorelines into the water.

'And if an animal or a person drowns, their remains are never recovered,' Stoddart continued. 'You know already of the infected *nerpa* seals, the only species of its type capable of living in the fresh water of the lake. They're not its sole endemic life form. There's estimated to be around 1,200 species of mammal and fish and 600 different types of plant found only there. But they *are* endemic. Nothing from outside the lake can survive in it.' He stopped, searching for a comparison. 'Nothing can live in the Dead Sea because of the toxicity of its salt content. Nothing – apart from its own evolved species that have adjusted and mutated over millenia – can exist in Lake Baikal because of the intensity of its oxygenization. Which isn't its only purification. One of the particular lake species is a crab that eats anything – including animal and human bones – alien to the water. The only foreign intrusion that can touch the lake and leave it again are migratory birds.'

There were shifts around the table, the most obvious from Paul Spencer, although he remained professionally expressionless. It had been the ice tomb discovery that had finally gained him readmission to Henry Partington and briefly he'd thought going to Siberia might continue his desperately needed recovery. The decision to remain the co-ordinator in Washington had been further to avoid political ice entombment but he was fucked if he liked the idea of becoming crab food.

'None of which, I don't think, is our immediate or even necessary consideration, just a background fill-in,' Stoddart was saying. 'There are other things that well might be, though.' Addressing the politicians, he said: 'From our transcripts you'll know some of our discussions at Fort Detrick have revolved around the possibility of a virus or a germ or a bug being unlocked from the ice after a very long time. Just as you know Baikal dates from the Paleocene era. Another of its claims to uniqueness is that Baikal is the deepest continental body of water in the world: at its basin it's over 1,600 metres or more than a mile deep. Research at the Institute has estimated that under that huge volume of water, possible more than a further mile deep, is sediment which logically has to date back twenty-five million years . . .'

'You think there could be buried in all that sediment whatever's caused the illness?' demanded Reynell. Having thought it through overnight in its entirety – although still to talk to London – he was convinced Siberia was a brilliant political opportunity, as well as a heaven-sent excuse to postpone any discussion with Buxton.

'I'm just tagging things,' said Stoddart. 'Baikal's enormous. In the Paleocene and Lower Neocene periods, it was part of an even larger sea that covered all of Siberia. And that would have included Ilutin.'

'There'll be every precaution?' demanded Gerard Buchemin, the most relaxed among the group because he'd excluded himself from the expedition, but needed to go on record showing responsible concern for fellow countryman Guy Dupuy, whom he'd insisted should go.

Stoddart dealt out his already prepared equipment list. 'That's everything we'll be taking with us, already ordered and on its way to our aircraft. There's still time – one of the main reasons for meeting as early in the day as this – to have anything added that anyone here feels I've overlooked.' He let several moments elapse, for it to be scrutinized. No one, certainly not Raisa, offered suggestions.

'One or two items might be worthwhile explaining,' resumed Stoddart. 'There'll be seven in our group from here. We're taking three sets each – and by each I mean the closest to individual height and build – of the totally protective, internal oxygen-supplied and air-conditioned suits to enter the caves. That's one primary suit and two back-ups each, in the event of damage to the first.' He nodded towards Lyalin. 'I understand from the minister that we will be supported and

277

assisted on site by personnel from the Listvyanka complex. So I'm adding another thirty suits, in various sizes, for them.'

'I'm sure from local experience the staff at the academy are sufficiently provided with all the protective clothing they might need,' intruded Raisa, xenophobically.

'I'm sure they are, too, for what I am about to come to,' said Stoddart, briefly giving way to annoyance at the constant obstructiveness of the Russian woman. 'But I'm talking – and thinking – specifically about a cave colony in which there appear to be perfectly preserved prehistoric people who died from a disease that could have re-emerged to infect now and which still might be possible to transmit, as it was in the three instances that we are so far aware of. Which, as far as I know, *isn't* a local experience with which they will be familiar and therefore they might appreciate our including them in our planning.'

Raisa flushed, embarrassed not just by the total logic of the rejection but by it being delivered in front of Gregori Lyalin.

'. . . Which I want to talk more about,' Stoddart hurried on. 'You'll see I've included an even greater number of jungle-adapted long johns –' momentarily he deferred to Raisa, to lessen the rejection –'the need for which will be local knowledge. These aren't long johns for warmth. They're protective all-in-ones against insects and parasites.'

'What insects and parasites?' broke in an increasingly unsettled Guy Dupuy.

'The most prevalent in the region is a skin-burrowing tick from the Ixodidas genus, which exists worldwide,' replied Stoddart. 'It's probably as common here in America as it is there. Around Baikal they exist in great concentrations. And carry a slew of infections. Here and in Europe it's Lyme Disease. At Lake Baikal it's encephalitis. At this time of the year the locals usually wear two layers of clothing to keep them out. The long johns we're taking will hopefully make life more comfortable as well as safer for us. You'll also see the hat and cap allocation. We'll have to cover our heads at all times, they drop off trees, roof overhangs, places like that . . .'

278

'What about inoculation?' asked Dupuy.

'There isn't one that's effective, or worth trying even,' said Raisa. 'If a tick gets into you, there's a ninety per cent chance of infection. At least if anyone becomes ill there'll be an instant diagnosis and treatment. For which the Institute *will* be prepared.' It was amusing, generating the unease.

'You'll also see on the list a variety of insect repellents including smoke candles, room sprays and the finest mesh mosquito netting,' Stoddart pointed out. 'Everything is recommended by jungle incursion medics, with additional guidance from entomologists—' He indicated Lyalin again. 'On the subject of which, we're promised at least one local entomologist from the Listvyanka Institute when we go into the colony, to avoid increasing the size of our party any more.'

'We're getting insect specimen from Noatak and where the McMurdo field station was,' came in Pelham. 'The entomologists assigned to me at Fort Detrick have asked for comparisons.'

'What's the risk of the discovery leaking out?' asked Spencer. 'It would attract a hell of a lot of publicity.'

'Small,' said Lyalin at once. 'It's one of the most isolated places in Russia, let alone the world. And I've told the institute it's not to be talked about.'

It was, Stoddart realized, the second time in a very few hours that he'd set out the downside of a situation, although unlike the encounter with Darryl Matthews and Harold Norris today wasn't a no-hard-feelings choice. He guessed his team, with the possible exception of Guy Dupuy, remained committed. It would be hardly possible, either, for Gregori Lyalin – the man who after all had made the trip possible – to withdraw. Would either Amanda O'Connell or Peter Reynell make a last minute excuse?

There were closely similar, although not dissuading, thoughts in the minds of both Reynell and Amanda.

Just as Reynell hadn't believed he'd been at risk from Jack Stoddart being a carrier, he couldn't contemplate any danger now. He had his own camera and spare film packed

279

in case there weren't any official photographers and wondered how spectacular the space-suited image of him would be in a mountain cave with a lot of preserved, prehistoric ape-men. When the declaring moment came, the media hysteria at his having personally faced horrifying, certain death to investigate a mystery, primeval disease would be phenomenal. He'd be acknowledged as the bravest party leader and premier since Winston Churchill, whose army valour was questionable anyway. Wanting a fitting – and later quotable – remark for the record busily being made by the secretariat, he said: 'It certainly isn't going to be a walk in the park, is it?'

'No,' agreed Stoddart, expectantly.

'But then I never considered my role simply to be that of sitting behind a desk. And I most certainly don't now.'

Amanda wondered curiously, although uncritically, whether Reynell always looked at his own reflection walking past shop windows. Tensed to get her own selfless attitude – and complete understanding – even better documented, she said: 'Phenomenal winds?'

'Yes,' agreed Stoddart. 'Ferocious from every point of the compass, almost as if they're in competition.

'As well as migrating birds and easily carried parasites?'

'Yes,' he agreed again, wondering at the direction of her questions.

'West Nile encephalitis was introduced for the first time into the Western hemisphere – into New York – in August 1999 by migrating birds infected by mosquitoes,' she reminded. 'An airborne virus resistant to sunlight could be lifted into the upper atmosphere to be carried for hundreds – thousands – of miles by hurricane force winds. Either way – either route – we could be looking at a source for the biggest transmission yet, if indeed the ageing illness is endemic at Lake Baikal.'

It was, Stoddart supposed, a summation of the obvious. 'Yes,' he agreed for the third time. No one was going to back down.

'It's not the influenza, is it?' demanded Lord Ranleigh.

280

'No,' allowed Reynell. He was still holding back from being specific about the disease, wanting even his father-in-law's later admiration for what he was about to do. There were few people better at creating legends than Ranleigh, particularly if he were somehow connected.

'Worse?'

'Far worse.' Not by any means an exaggeration, Reynell judged, building up his later-to-be acknowledged integrity.

'There'll be a full, publishable record?'

'Of course.' Reynell was aware, in passing, that the other man was concentrating entirely upon the later benefits rather than upon any present physical risk.

'And the medical breakthrough is British?'

'Absolutely.' Falling back upon his earlier excuse to the Washington group, Reynell added: 'This has come up too quickly for me to get the full explanation of how important that is from our scientific officer.'

'No urgency,' assured Ranleigh.

'As I'm going into Russia, I thought I should perhaps advise Prendergast. He should be informed, as Foreign Secretary, shouldn't he?'

There was momentary silence from the London end. 'I think he's strongly enough committed to be trusted,' agreed the older man at last. 'It brings him into the inner fold, where we need him.' There was another pause. 'I'm sure of our strength now. All we really need is you back here.'

'There'll be a development to justify it soon.' The public revelation would be sufficient now that a British discovery could be heralded. There was an amusing reverse that the leak he'd initially feared might destroy him could so soon actually be utilized in his favour, if it were timed carefully enough.

His manipulative mind obviously tuned to the same wavelength, Ranleigh said: 'Maybe a question should be cultivated?'

Reynell laughed. 'Wait until I get back, with photographs and a story to tell.'

When he told Henrietta where he was going she said: 'Is it dangerous?'

'Potentially.'

'Don't do anything silly, will you?'

It was, he supposed, Henrietta's way of telling him to be careful. 'Have I ever?'

'What can you bring me back?'

'How about the key to 10 Downing Street?'

'Just what I've always wanted.'

There was no hindrance in his being connected to Prendergast at the Foreign Office. Pushing the urgency into his voice, Reynell said: 'I've only got a few minutes, Ralph. I'm going into Russia: Siberia. Everything's up in the air but I thought you should know. There's not enough to talk sensibly to the PM about, though . . .'

'I understand perfectly,' said Prendergast.

They got to Andrews Air Force base by mid-afternoon and Stoddart was relieved that their transport was a militarized, passenger-carrying Boeing 727 and not a canvas-seated, flying warehouse C-130, although as they settled aboard he had the discomforting recollection that the last time he'd flown had been with a different, now dead lover beside him. If the thought occurred to Geraldine, it wasn't obvious. The group split without any discussion, Geraldine with Stoddart, Reynell next to Amanda and the two Russians – quietly although intently speaking Russian – together. They spread themselves around the aircraft but the apprehensive Guy Dupuy chose his solitary seat furthest from any of them, as if already seeking protective isolation.

Quietly to the man beside her, Amanda said: 'You've been working the room more closely than I have. You think Lyalin's a straight arrow?'

'Absolutely,' said Reynell. 'I think he's as unique as this time warp we're going to.'

'And you and I completely understand each other?'

'Even more absolutely,' he agreed.

'No reason for us not to trust each other?'

'None,' Reynell agreed. Unless, he mentally qualified, a reason arose that at the moment he couldn't anticipate.

282

'That's good,' said Amanda. She hoped she wouldn't have to screw him in any other than the strictly physical and pleasurable way. And she wasn't sure how that was going to be possible, wearing all-in-ones she didn't intend taking off, even at night. Maybe there was a flap, although it still wouldn't be the same.

Gregori Lyalin had patiently heard out Raisa's latest protests but refused a repetition by yet again invoking his official seniority, relieved that very soon after take-off she'd relapsed into a hostile silence. He felt, upon reflection, that he'd personally handled Raisa Orlov very badly. He shouldn't have needed to contemplate letting her know the political reality of his conducting himself the way he had – it was politically far above and beyond her permitted level of knowledge – but belatedly, far too belatedly, he wondered if it wouldn't have been better at least to have taken her partially into his confidence.

Raisa Orlov decided there was no purpose in arguing any further with the man. She had to dismiss him and his clearly imagined importance from her thinking, as she was sure he would be even more literally and quickly dismissed from his ministry by what she intended. Until now – this droning, long haul chance to rationalize – she hadn't properly calculated all the advantages of returning to Russia, despite Siberia being remote, virtually a continent away, from government and power. Now she did and the most positive awareness was that it gave her the opportunity personally to correct a situation instead of trying to achieve it long distance, by telephone and through surrogates. And there would be the additional advantage of whatever she might be able to discover – but still needed to confirm – at Lake Baikal.

She said: 'The bodies must be taken to Moscow.'

'I'll decide how and when – and *if* – when we find out what we've got,' sighed Lyalin.

'Whatever that decision is, I intend going back to Moscow! To consult!'

'We can go together,' smiled Lyalin.

*   *   *

283

The acknowledgement of Russian sovereignty required that they transfer in Alaska to an already waiting Russian military aircraft. They slept, although fitfully, for most of the flight down the eastern Siberian seaboard. Lyalin awoke them when the Illushin turned inland for them to get their first sight of Lake Baikal, which appeared out of the early morning Siberian mist from its mountain surround as abruptly as it was startling.

Geraldine said: 'It's so blue! It's incredible!'

'So's the visibility which causes it to be that colour,' said Stoddart. 'I told you the crabs eat everything. That includes algae and plankton.'

On the final approach to Irkutsk they flew low enough to see the lake surface hugely churned and torn. Stoddart said: 'That's what the wind does.'

Geraldine shuddered and said: 'I actually saw the Shangri-La movie once; a film institute showing. It was set in a place just like this, hidden away among mountains. Scary!'

'You'd made your mind up what it was going to look like,' refused Stoddart.

'It's still open about what I'm going to find here, though. The only thing I've already decided is how Raisa's going to try to stop us finding any answers ahead of her.'

The story that was going to engulf the world's media broke in Japan.

It began with the account of the deaths, from an ageing condition doctors couldn't identity or cure, of five people – two men and three woman, none over the age of forty – in the Hokkaida edition of the *Asahi Shimbun*. When eight people died in Tokyo, there was reference to the Hokkaida deaths in their *Asahi* edition but it was the *Daily Yomiuri* which illustrated the Tokyo outbreak with a photograph of a thirty-year-old mother of two children who died, actually on the day of publication, a wizened old lady of at least eighty. When newspapers in New Delhi, Bombay, Sydney, Santiago, Caracas, San Diego, Charleston, Ottawa, Paris, Naples, Moscow, Vienna, Newcastle and Madrid picked up

284

on localized cases, Associated Press compiled a round-up that was later to win the news organization the award for journalistic excellence in eight of the western countries in which, along with the other thirty-three worldwide, the story exploded within the space of twenty-four hours.

It did so, at various times around the globe, as Stoddart was hurrying his group off the aircraft at Irkutsk, but Paul Spencer had been alerted overnight by his CIA monitors at Langley and blitzkrieged Henry Partington into such a pre-breakfast meeting that the man appeared in a dressing gown stained with the previous morning's menu. Egg was an obvious favourite.

'It's out,' announced Spencer.

'We ahead?' demanded Partington, at once.

'No American newspaper or television channel has picked up on it yet,' assured Spencer, who'd stayed up the entire night, bypassing Boddington, to check. 'You could segment each of this morning's three television majors with an immediate statement to run over your ecology footage and go live tonight, for combined television and print.'

'You're back on track, Paul,' smiled Partington.

Back was where he wanted to be, reflected Spencer, tingling with relief.

Twenty-Five

D espite Jack Stoddart's Blair House briefing, none of them was properly prepared and all were disoriented, some more than others. Their most immediate unpreparedness – a political failure – was not to have realized that the arrival of a Russian minister and his foreign counterparts would be considered a civic event by the Irkutsk authorities. The mayor, heading the entire town council, was waiting on the single airstrip inevitably claimed to be an international airport, to deliver a welcoming speech directly beneath a windsock blown horizontal, like an accusing finger, by a wind that flattened their clothing around them. Stiffly beside the council was the local police commissioner flanked by his attendant officers – quite a lot of whom had the mongolian features of the local Buryat population – and directly after the speech a man almost as expansively bearded as Gregori Lyalin introduced himself as the director of the Listvyanka Institute. His name was Vladimir Bobin and he was the only one with any English, which he spoke slowly after obviously mentally rehearsing the words. Lyalin took on the role of interpreter, explaining that the two photographers shepherding them together for group pictures were from the town's newspaper.

'We're going to look like shit,' whispered a travel-crumpled, wind-tossed Geraldine to Stoddart, as they were jockeyed into position.

'I *feel* like shit,' complained Stoddart. He still had his watch on DC time. He couldn't understand why, but at that moment they'd been travelling one hour and twenty minutes longer than it had taken him to get back from McMurdo. They

286

were permitted – feted – guests in another country, so they had to go with the local flow but he'd imagined their being able to go at once to the caves. Over the photographers' heads he saw their luggage being unloaded into two battered trucks and wished the equipment was being handled more gently.

The newly polished official cars were in better condition, each with its own Buryat driver. They travelled separately to the surprisingly named, but fittingly baroque Grand Hotel on what, even more surprisingly after the demise of communism, was still called Marx Street. Lyalin was in the lead vehicle with the mayor and institute director. Continuing the unexpected, the main streets were wide, several multi-laned boulevards bordered by imposing houses and orderly although wind-rattled trees.

Geraldine said: 'This doesn't look at all primeval to me.'

Stoddart said: 'This was one of the gold mining centres of Siberia *before* the revolution. Once it competed with St Petersburg for grandeur.'

Guy Dupuy, who had started out withdrawn from them in the corner of the rear seat, said: 'You think ticks could be in those trees?'

'I wouldn't have thought so, in this wind,' reassured Stoddart. Away from the openness of the airport it didn't, in fact, seem so strong. Dupuy was already wearing one of the protective hats which he'd kept firmly on during the photographs and Stoddart wondered if the man had changed into his long johns as well.

'You think our gear's going to be all right in those trucks?' asked Geraldine.

'Everything's well packed but it might be an idea to check your suit for snags,' suggested Stoddart, remembering the unloading.

Unaware of what was developing in Washington, Geraldine said: 'You really believe Lyalin's right about this place being too remote for our being here – and why – to leak out?'

Equally unaware, Stoddart said: 'Who knows?' A political question, not his problem.

When they reassembled in the foyer, Lyalin said at once

that according to Bobin there was no local history of an ageing disease nor any recent cases of which the man was aware.

'So you've told him?' challenged Amanda, joining the group.

'In English. And warned him it's the equivalent of a state secret, although it's shared with the represented countries.'

'What about the local mayor?'

'Just that there's the danger of infection, without saying what it is.'

'Is the site still sealed?' asked Geraldine.

Lyalin nodded. 'There's a police guard but from what I was told on the way from the airport it hardly seems necessary. Shamanism is a stronger local religion than Christianity, despite the churches and the Epiphany Cathedral we passed. Ol'khon is the virtual centre of it. The volcano makes a lot of audible noise, apparently. The people think it's the actual voice of the spirits, warning them away.'

Reynell indicated the still hovering cameramen. 'Have they been allowed up?'

'No. They want to come with us.'

Virtually the entire fourth floor of the hotel had been allocated to them. Geraldine's room was next to Stoddart's, but there was no connecting door. There was a smell of dampness and the bed felt wetly cold. She sprayed it with the insecticide before erecting the mosquito net on its tent-like frame and sprayed that, too, before moving on to the windows which overlooked the Marx boulevard of imposing, mansion-like houses and reminded her of Paris, another unexpected comparison. There were some small flies, already dead, on the sill and even more on the bathroom window ledge. She doused everything with spray, the bathroom most heavily of all, and flushed the brown-rimed toilet twice but failed to get rid of the staining. The water was barely warm and the bath filled with a black-flecked scum, despite her having rinsed it twice. She didn't sit, instead standing completely to wash away the grime of the journey if not its physical ache. She must, she realized, have smelled to the people among whom she'd been crushed for the arrival photographs but then they had, too. Uncomfortably naked – straining for the sound of a flying insect although knowing full well that ticks didn't make a sound – Geraldine liberally smeared herself completely with the repelling unguent which at once made her smell far worse than she had before bathing but which acted as a lubricant of sorts to help put on the off-white but instantly marked all-in-one body stocking, which was a surprisingly good fit. Careful not to pad about the room in her bare feet – remembering having read somewhere of ticks burrowing under toenails – she followed Stoddart's advice and checked the first of her three protective suits before packing it in the large sports-type holdall Stoddart had included in the equipment. She experimented fitting in as well the portable medical case but decided it risked damaging the suit so she resigned herself to having to carry two cases.

The trouser suit she'd travelled in was concertinaed from such prolonged wear and she rolled it up and tossed it into the bottom of the wardrobe. There, for the first time, she saw more dead flies and insects and she resprayed the entire closet after hanging up her spare clothes. She decided against putting her underwear, shirts or sweaters in the unlined drawers but sprayed the case in which she left them, accepting everything would probably be permanently stained and have to be thrown away. She dressed, finally, in jeans, shirt and zip-up jerkin and decided on a bill cap under which she managed to coil her hair tightly. She greased her face with repellent, which made make-up pointless.

Stoddart and Lyalin were the only two ahead of her in the foyer. Both had their sports bags beside them. There was also a bag beside Vladimir Bobin. The photographers were with uniformed policemen in an adjoining lounge.

Bobin prepared himself like a clock winding up to strike before saying: 'There are some wall paintings, in the caves. But just stick people, as they invariably are: nothing to indicate an ageing condition.'

Apprehensively, Geraldine said at once: 'You've been inside?'

289

Bobin shook his head. 'An anthropologist from the institute.'

Lyalin hesitated. 'He should be put into isolation immediately.'

It was unravelling, thought Geraldine. From Stoddart's expression he was thinking the same thing.

Bobin swallowed, heavily. 'It's a woman. She's been in contact with everyone for two days. What diagnostic tests are there?'

'None that we know of,' said Geraldine.

'Oh God!' said the man.

Geraldine wondered if he was praying to the one to whom the cathedral was dedicated or the growling presence on Ol'khon island. It was probably a good idea to insure with both.

Amanda O'Connell and Peter Reynell, who also had adjoining rooms, arrived shiny-faced together. Guy Dupuy was next, his features so heavily greased there were globules of repellent under his chin and behind his ears, where he'd smeared it on the back of his neck. His ski hat was pulled low enough to cover his ears but sprigs of lank hair escaped all around. Even his jeans and ski jacket seemed creased from wear, like his always buttoned suits. At the arrival of the mayor, who'd clearly come in the same car as the police chief, the two local press photographers emerged.

Echoing Geraldine's earlier doubt, Amanda said: 'We're not going to be able to keep a lid on this!'

Geraldine said: 'If we can find an answer here, it won't matter.'

'It will if we don't,' countered the American woman.

As three more people, a woman and two men, came expectantly towards them Bobin said: 'My people, from the institute.'

The anthropologist, Lyudmilla Vlasov, was a short-cropped, slightly built, white-blonde, Caucasian-featured woman of about thirty-five. Any hair colour change would have been difficult to detect – and might anyway have been natural –

290

but there was no obvious brown-spotting keratosis or skin wrinkling.

Stoddart said to Lyalin: 'You must ask her about any symptoms.'

In far better English than the institute director, Lyudmilla said: 'Why don't you? What symptoms?'

'How many days ago were you in the caves?' said the discomfited Stoddart.

'Four,' replied the woman.

'How long were you inside? And what about the people who found the bodies originally?'

'I was the only one to go inside. The cave was found by a Buryat hunting party. They ran, immediately, thinking they were spirits. They described them as monkeys. They reported it to the police in Irkutsk, who contacted the institute. There's one exposed cave; you'll understand what I mean when you get there. I got up into a gallery and saw the group, male and female. All wizened. Very hirsute. I could see other galleries – passages – leading off into the mountain. I didn't have any equipment: no lights. It was incredibly cold. I knew it had to be a proper investigation – anthropologically, I mean – so I got out and went back to the institute and then we got the orders from Moscow not to touch anything.'

'Did you physically touch any of the bodies? Touch anything at all?' seized Stoddart.

'I told you, I wasn't properly equipped,' said Lyudmilla, indignantly. 'Of course I didn't touch the bodies or anything around them. The site has to be photographed; precise records made of how everything is . . . as it was when they died . . .'

'You been conscious of any physical change: tiredness, losing your hair or its colour, generally feeling unwell as if you might be going down with flu?' asked Geraldine.

'You think they died from an infection that made them like that?' demanded the woman, instantly prescient.

Stoddart hesitated before saying: 'Yes. We're anxious not to frighten anyone, though.'

'Except me!'

291

Stoddart realized, relieved, that apart from Bobin, who already knew, none of the other locals gathered intently around were able to understand the conversation, including Lyudmilla's two blank-faced entomologist colleagues. 'What's the answer to my question?'

'No,' said the woman. 'Nothing at all. Would something have shown, by now?'

'We think so,' said Geraldine.

'Is there an antidote?'

'No,' said Geraldine bluntly.

'Fuck!' said the woman.

Geraldine said: 'There've been other victims. All have registered visible symptoms under four days.'

'What's your discipline?' asked the Russian.

'Genetics. And forensic pathology.'

'So you're medically qualified?'

'There aren't any diagnostic tests,' anticipated Geraldine. 'But if you'd like me to check you out then of course I will.'

There was an impatient eruption of Russian and Lyalin said: 'They want to know what's going on.'

Stoddart said: 'I could make it take a while getting the right-sized suits for those who are coming with us.'

'All I can literally do is examine you externally, for any signs,' Geraldine told the other woman.

'Please,' said Lyudmilla.

Raisa Orlov emerged from the elevator as they approached it and at once demanded: 'What's happening?'

'You can come too,' invited Geraldine.

Lyudmilla Vlasov's actual age was thirty-three. Her hair colouring was natural and both Geraldine and Raisa concentrated upon it – under-arm and pubic, as well as head – when she told them she hadn't yet detected any discolouration. Neither did they. Nor was there any indication of loss. Completely – and unashamedly – naked Lyudmilla was remarkably firm bodied, with no breast sag. There appeared no elasticity weakening when the skin was pinch-tested, which both Geraldine and Raisa did separately.

292

Examining separately again, neither Geraldine nor Raisa located any liver spots on any part of Lyudmilla's naked body. While Lyudmilla dressed, Raisa used Geraldine's room and telephoned to call the pathology department of Irkutsk hospital, feigning the anger with which she slammed down the telephone.

'There say they haven't the equipment for swab testing,' she declared.

'We have at the institute,' announced Lyudmilla, at once.

'We'll organize it on the way,' said Geraldine.

'It'll involve a detour,' warned Lyudmilla.

'Then it'll have to be made,' said Geraldine.

They were back in the foyer before Stoddart finished issuing the protective suits, carrying one down the same size as Geraldine's for the Russian anthropologist. The local officials stood uncertainly with their allocated suits still in their packs.

The Listvyanka Institute is on the headland tip where the Angara river flows into Lake Baikal and there the river-bordering road ends instead of continuing northwards along the lakeside to Ol'khon. The only way to reach the island and the overshadowing Primorskiy Khrebet mountains is by an entirely different road leading directly from Irkutsk and when Geraldine insisted the swab test was essential, Stoddart accepted they had to split.

'We'll wait for you at Shara-Togot,' promised Stoddart, who knew from his earlier research visit, as well as by studying a map with Bobin while they waited, that Shara-Togot was the port village from which boats crossed the narrow strip of water to the island.

The buffeting wind increased when they began to clear the city and on the side roads they saw for the first time how some of the insufficiently stilted houses were cracked – some even lopsided – and subsiding from their bricks and concrete thawing the permanently winter-frozen tundra upon which they were too directly built. Raisa chose the front passenger seat for unshared comfort, but twisted at once to look at Geraldine and Lyudmilla in the rear. The driver was a creased-suited, oil-haired, Asiatic-featured Buryat whose dashboard swung and tinkled with shaman amulets.

Geraldine said: 'Tell me what sort of people they are, in the caves.'

Me, not us, isolated Raisa.

Lyudmilla made the vaguest gesture towards the driver. 'Certainly some facial similarities.'

'Neolithic or Neanderthal!' seized Geraldine.

Lyudmilla smiled, apologetically. 'I can't be positive from the ones I saw, so briefly.'

Wind constantly hammered against the car, despite the summer brightness of the sun which struck constant sparks off the snow of the surrounding mountains. Geraldine wondered how the head-shaking trees kept their leaves. The body stocking that had seemed so comfortable when she'd first put it on was now cutting her, too tight under the arms and in her groin.

'Tell me about the illness,' said Lyudmilla.

'I wish we could,' sighed Geraldine. 'The infection, when it's contracted, spreads astonishingly quickly –' she smiled sideways – 'which is a major factor in your favour.' Uncaringly crossing professional boundaries, she went on: 'Viruses are very choosey, for self-protection. If they destroy their host cells too quickly they destroy their chances to replicate.' To the woman in the front seat, Geraldine said: 'Isn't that molecular and biochemical fact, Raisa?'

'Yes,' begrudged the Russian virologist.

'So how about, in some way we've never known before and don't understand, a non-selective virus or a bacterium exploding like a shotgun cartridge and hitting lots of different genetic targets at the same time?' asked Geraldine. 'That would result in what we're looking at, wouldn't it?'

Raisa Orlov said: 'That's scientifically impossible.'

'So's a forty-year-old person becoming eighty years old in days, and we've watched it happen,' said Geraldine.

The institute complex emerged suddenly ahead of them, against the brilliant azure-blue background of the furrowed lake, a range of low, single-storey buildings clustered around a central, five-floored building. A lighthouse would have completed the scene, but Geraldine acknowledged there was no flashing light capable of warning against the unseen hazards of the water. The driver followed Lyudmilla's over-the-shoulder directions to the furthest, prefabricated block.

'I might as well do the test myself,' offered the abruptly friendly Raisa Orlov.

The designated laboratory was far better equipped with much more modern equipment than Geraldine had at best anticipated, even to the extent of having an electron-microscope. There were three white-coated assistants who at once deferred to Raisa's superior authority when Lyudmilla introduced the Moscow virologist. It was the first time Geraldine had seen Raisa work and she was impressed; the Russian had the sure-fingered nimbleness of a large person intent on proving herself. In seconds she took both throat and nasal swabs without appearing to cause Lyudmilla any choking discomfort. Just as quickly Raisa prepared four slides from each source, staining them one by one in the order in which she slid them beneath the visual microscope. Only then did she slow, with the intensity by which she examined every slide. She came up shaking her head to announce, theatrically: 'Nothing!'

The tension visibly leaked from the Russian anthropologist.

Raisa smiled at Geraldine and said: 'Want to take a look?'

Geraldine did so, curious at the abrupt change of attitude. Every slide was totally clear. Straightening, she said to Lyudmilla: 'We had to be confident to have travelled this far in such an enclosed space with you. But it's good to be doubly sure.'

The time difference between the two capitals meant Henry Partington's early morning statement in Washington DC disclosing the pandemic extent of the ageing illness – which he insisted upon identifying as the Shangri-La strain – exploded four hours before Prime Minister's Question Time in London.

Lord Ranleigh had already succeeded in planting his 'where's the minister for science?' question in the parliamentary sketch columns of that day's *Daily Telegraph* and *The Times* but on the back of the Washington announcement propelled it into front page speculation in the main edition of the London *Evening Standard*.

Ranleigh still tried to reach his son-in-law through the Washington embassy, despite his previous day's conversation with Reynell, and when he was unsuccessful reluctantly decided that the opportunity had to be seized without Reynell knowing about it. Ranleigh lunched discreetly at his South Audley Street townhouse with the Foreign Secretary and the coterie of backbenchers who had supported Reynell's campaign from the beginning. All agreed that Reynell's absence was unfortunate but that they had no alternative but to move.

It was later calculated that there were only two MPs – both seriously ill in hospital – absent from the House of Commons when a visibly disarrayed Simon Buxton entered the green-leathered chamber. Because it was part of the lunchtime planning, the Foreign Secretary was minutes behind, virtually at the moment when the Speaker was calling the House to order.

Buxton, who'd frantically – and personally – tried to reach Reynell in Washington after Prendergast had told him Reynell was unavailable, leaned anxiously along the bench and said: 'Anything since we last spoke?'

'I've talked to Washington . . .' Prendergast whispered back, although concentrating upon the Speaker's opening and stopping at the call to order.

At once the first three of Ranleigh's seeded questioners competed for the Speaker's eye to pose the same entrapping question. Buxton's uncertainty was obvious as he rose at the Dispatch Box to insist that he had been aware of the American declaration before it had been made, that he'd had prior indication of a virulent, fatal disease and that his government was taking every precaution to protect the population. It was such a trite, daisy-chain of meaningless cliches that momentarily there was a hushed silence of disbelief.

The next skirmisher deputed by Ranleigh used the hiatus

to get the Speaker's nod. 'Could the Prime Minister inform the House of the whereabouts of the Minister for Science?

Buxton hauled himself to his feet. 'At the moment the Minister for Science is out of the country.'

There was an eruption of discordant noise for which the next of Ranleigh's troops was prepared, gaining permission for the next encircling question. 'Could the Prime Minister confirm that the Minister of Science is at this moment personally involved in an expedition specifically connected with the pandemic that this House – this country – has only today become aware of?'

There was more resignation than weariness in the way Buxton rose. 'I can confirm that the Minister for Science is part of an international group of ministers actively involved in the investigation of this matter.'

At his positive moment of commitment, Ralph Prendergast almost hesitated too long with his planned interjection, close to missing the staged tug at the prime minister's elbow, the moment saved only by the second shocked hiatus at Buxton's ineptitude. The disorientated, confused man turned, bewildered, at Prendergast's touch, didn't hear the Foreign Secretary's words – because he wasn't intended to – and visibly shrugged in accepted defeat.

The vociferous groundswell of protest stilled as Prendergast rose, the moment sufficient for him to command the chamber. He said: 'I have this afternoon – literally only minutes before entering this chamber – been in contact with the American Secretary of State and the Russian ambassador to London. As a result of those conversations I can inform this House that our minister of science is currently in Siberia personally exploring, as part of the international team to which the Prime Minister has referred, what can only be described as potentially – and I stress the word potentially – an incredible development in the disease that has become public knowledge today.'

Briefly the shouted demands and questions prevented Prendergast continuing and he stopped until the Speaker's shouts for order lessened the row.

297

'I cannot help this House any further, upon the specifics of what the minister for science is doing, apart from telling this House that there is a high degree of personal danger which might become better known in the weeks ahead . . . What I can tell this House, however, is that a brilliant British scientist has already made a major and significant contribution in finding the cause, cure and prevention of this terrible, fatal condition.'

Lord Ranleigh was in the drawing room at Lord North Street, watching the live television coverage. He turned to Henrietta and said: 'Your husband's the next prime minister, my darling.'

Henrietta said: 'Are you sure he's up to it?'

'It doesn't matter if he isn't,' said her father. 'We are.'

The president's address to the nation was televised live from the Oval Office, Partington sombre-suited and grave behind a desk specifically measured to appear in proportion to his diminutive stature.

'My fellow Americans, it is my duty to speak to you tonight . . .' he began, having to concentrate upon the teleprompt because the speech had needed to be rewritten after the son of a bitch in the English parliament had claimed that the British scientist had achieved a breakthrough.

It was not until after they had retraced their journey into Irkutsk and turned on to the foothills road towards Ust-Ordynskiy that Geraldine started noticing the coloured twists in the trees and on bushes, like artificial flowers.

'Prayer ribbons – prayers themselves on the pieces of paper – to the spirits,' explained Lyudmilla. 'Shamanism is a very seriously observed religion.' She pointed to an approaching cluster of houses and unnecessarily said: 'All blue. Blue's the colour that defeats the evil eye.'

In startling contrast, far below now, the azure of Lake Baikal glittered to their right. They turned at Bayanday and began to descend towards the lake, just able to see the rooftops of Yelantsy as the road turned for the final approach to Shara-Togot.

The cars were neatly parked just before the entrance to the village itself and their driver carefully joined the line. Stoddart approached as Geraldine climbed gratefully out of the car.

Geraldine said: 'Everything's OK.' She stretched. 'I'm stiff.'

'You won't be,' warned Stoddart. 'From here on we hike.'

Twenty-Six

The spirits snarled and the ground shuddered.

Or rather, deep in the churning meltingness of Ol'khan's volcanic core, sulphurous gases exploded to vent noisily through ground level fissures, but in the brooding presence of the cliff-skirted, prehistoric lake it was easy – easier – to imagine the supernatural. They all stopped, startled, and the Buryat driver dropped Geraldine's medical satchel with a tinkling clatter. For the briefest moment even Raisa Orlov looked uncertain. There was a dialect babble from all the drivers which Vladimir Bobin stopped with curt Russian but the men drew together, nervously.

Lyudmilla translated. 'They're saying they have been told to keep away.'

They had been climbing unsteadily for more than an hour, although inexplicably the wide track – practically a road – was relatively firm, rocks and stones hammered into a proper surface, and nearly all the shrubs and stunted trees they passed were garlanded in prayer sprigs.

'Do we have suits for them?' asked Geraldine.

'No,' admitted Stoddart. 'I didn't know they were going to act as bearers.' To both Bobin and Lyalin he said: 'There's a limit to how close we can safely let them get to the caves.'

Lyudmilla said: 'It's still more than two kilometres: maybe nearer three. The track ends about 400 metres up ahead; gets really hard after that.'

'To the track's end,' decided Lyalin. 'They can wait for us there.'

There were resentful mutterings when the order was relayed, two of the locals – the Listvyanka driver one of

300

them – initially shaking their heads in refusal until another sharp burst in Russian, this time from the mayor. Geraldine's medical case clattered again when it was angrily picked up.

The wind was at their backs and sides, becoming colder as they climbed, but in her now chafing body stocking Geraldine still sweated and flying things swarmed, despite the repellent. While they'd paused, Dupuy had smeared more upon his face, making sweat-marked lines, like a Hallowe'en mask. Starting off again he bustled into the very middle of the track, clear of overhanging branches and shrubs, flapping his free hand more often and more wildly than the rest of them. The locals didn't bother at all, seemingly untroubled by the insects. The apprehensive Buryats lingered at the rear of the straggled line. No one spoke, needing their breath.

The abrupt sight of buildings as they rounded a bend was another near-halting shock, although this time the locals continued on, carrying the visitors with them. 'A Stalin gulag mine,' identified Lyudmilla. 'Mica, which was used for electrical insulation. Closed down a long time ago.'

Closer they could see the rusting skeletons of conveyor equipment, although no longer with their carrying belts, and open, rock-moving trucks still neatly parked in a sentry line. After so long the forest and undergrowth that had begun to reclaim everything had intruded or fallen into their inviting openness and flourished with greenery and white and blue flowers so that they now looked like a garden display for giants. Ribboning off to the left were the prisoners' wood-rotting barracks gradually crumbling under the encroaching trees and shrubs. Strangely barren, in the middle of so much ready growth, was the cemetery where nothing grew except stunted crosses, some of those collapsed, marked simply by the numbers that had been the only identity of the nameless who lay forgotten in their graves. Geraldine guessed that at its busiest the gulag would have held hundreds of long dead slave prisoners and wondered why the locals did not fear their ghosts.

The disgruntled Buryats shuffled, heads lowered at the instruction to wait. Geraldine said: 'We're going to need

301

them eventually – more of them, in fact – to get the bodies down.'

Lyudmilla said: 'They won't do it. To them, bodies like those hold spirits that are only sleeping. To move the bodies wake the spirit.'

'Let's confront the problem when we get to it,' said Stoddart.

To Raisa's smirk, Stoddart reached for Geraldine's medical case, which after the slightest hesitation she gratefully surrendered.

It was the opportunistic Reynell who'd seized the gulag backdrop, posing himself quite alone as if he were its discoverer, but now he was photographing Amanda against the black-holed mine entrance. Further back, the press photographers made a photo opportunity out of a photo opportunity.

Stoddart called: 'We've still got a long way to go when you're ready.'

The change in terrain was immediate just a few steps beyond the hard core of the old mine approach. There was no proper route, little more than an occasional tight gap between trees and underfoot the ground was a greasy mix of ever shifting shale and decades' mulch of autumn-dropped leaves. Dupuy struggled upwards, head bowed, his collar pulled up against his ski hat to cover his neck, his free hand in constant movement although the insect problem seemed to be lessening. Once, when she slipped suddenly sideways into a thicket, Stoddart freed a hand to offer to Raisa who at first made as if to ignore it, but then took it to be hauled out. Just as reluctantly she stopped when Stoddart told her to, halting the entire line, while he inspected her neck, face and hands – even though she'd checked her hands – and from her left ear lobe and the nape of her neck flicked black spots that could have been ticks. One such was certainly something that was alive.

Gradually the forest fringe changed, from thick-leafed maple and narrower birch to needle-tipped conifers. It took a further hour of constantly sliding to finally clear the tree-line and as soon as they did Stoddart called another halt for each of them to examine the exposed skin of their own

302

hands and faces before doing it for each other. No one found it amusing, although the monkey-cleaning comparison occurred to Geraldine. Away from the protection of the trees, the wind hit them again, freezing now, and before the positive snowline there were white, unthawed oases of previous falls. Underfoot the increasingly frozen ground ironically became firmer and briefly easier to walk upon. Geraldine felt the perspiration chilling upon her, not just against her skin but where it had permeated her clothing to create a second discomfiting layer. They fanned out, no longer in a rough line but spreading sideways, each making their own path. Geraldine wondered how much higher there was to climb; there would soon be a need for thermal protection, although she didn't believe, from the list Stoddart had produced in Washington, that there was cold weather protection. She doubted sufficient would be available locally. She supposed there would be clothing in Moscow, but that would still take days to ship. The air was definitely thinner, having to be dragged into their lungs in short, panting breaths. Lyudmilla was walking beside her.

Geraldine said: 'How much further?'

The anthropologist pointed slightly upwards and ahead. 'It's the other side of that bluff. We're looking virtually at the back of the cave system. We should suit up.'

'Your call,' said Geraldine. Cold weather gear wasn't necessary after all although she guessed Amanda and Reynell would have liked it even for such a short distance.

'We should use our suits from here on,' declared Lyudmilla, more loudly.

'Where are the caves?' demanded Reynell.

Lyudmilla pointed ahead again. 'Directly around that outcrop.'

There wasn't another backdrop – the very much intended backdrop – for the minister's photographs, Geraldine guessed. And suited and helmeted he – and Amanda – would be anonymous behind their vizors. Life's a bitch and then you're dead, she thought, recalling the old cliche that until so very recently had seemed so personally appropriate. What would the diplomats choose, the bitching disappointment or the risk of death?

'We can't see the caves,' protested Reynell.

'They're there,' promised the unwitting Lyudmilla.

'This is near enough, unprotected,' frowned Stoddart.

Everyone was milling around, although keeping to their own space, unsure what was expected. Even with an elevation this high it was difficult to see the far side of the huge expanse of water, more an inland sea than a lake. Until that moment, Geraldine hadn't thought about it but she hadn't expected to undress on the side of a wind-blasted, sub-zero Siberian mountain. She did so, though, unconcerned in her body stocking which Lyudmilla immediately noted and nodded at, approvingly. It was abruptly so cold that the breath gasped out of Geraldine. The anthropologist stripped, even less embarrassed – and apparently less discomfited – to bra and pants but then quickly into her allocated suit, as good an estimated fit as Geraldine's all-in-one earlier. Geraldine was aware of her body stocking being oddly ringed by sweat bands, like the skin of some exotic snake, and wished she was as hard bodied as the Russian anthropologist. Despite her height and stature, Raisa Orlov appeared to carry little excess weight, although the all-in-one underwear that she wore obviously with nothing beneath accentuated her heavy, big-nippled breasts. Despite the rasping wind, Raisa didn't hurry to get into her suit, actually turning clad only in the stocking to look in Rubens-bodied profile over the lake and Geraldine decided at once that the virologist was posing, although she was unsure for whose benefit. Herself zipped and enclosed to the neck, Geraldine left the head cowl hanging over the bulge of the oxygen supply like everyone else at that moment and was aware of Stoddart beside her, closely studying her suit for damage.

The suited, although head-free photographers were circling, taking pictures to Amanda O'Connell and Peter Reynell's posed unawareness. Stoddart said loudly: 'This isn't a freak show. There's no initial need – maybe no need at all – for everyone here to go through whatever we're going to find

304

on the other side of that bluff. We're here to conduct the best scientific examination possible on site: tests, too, if they're feasible. That means only those for whom it's actually necessary may enter the caves: the Listvyanka institute director, its anthropologist and two entomologists and Geraldine Rothman, Raisa Orlov and Guy Dupuy from the visiting group . . .' He hesitated. 'Are we agreed on that?'

Reynell said: 'I'd like to see for myself.'

Amanda said: 'So would I.'

'If it's not possible for everyone to see for themselves today, there's always tomorrow,' said Stoddart. 'Or the day after that.' For some it *was* a freak show, he thought, irritated. The difficulty was deciding if the freaks were the long dead or the opportunistic still alive.

'I think what you're suggesting makes sense,' said Lyalin.

'Let's talk about precautions,' stopped Stoddart, at the general movement to go on. 'Everyone complete their suiting here, now. And check the communication links, which should activate automatically. If anyone snags their suit – even if it isn't a positive tear – get out of the caves and come immediately back to this spot. We'll leave the bags here, as markers. And each watch the person next to you to warn if their suits become damaged without their realizing it. Everything quite clear so far?'

They were mutterings and head nods of agreement.

'Those of you going in remember your main oxygen will last precisely one hour,' continued Stoddart, the compiler of the equipment. 'If it runs out, it'll switch automatically to ten minutes of reserve. By then you've got to be out and back here, where you can breathe normally and fit new bottles you've all been provided with, in your equipment bags . . .' He paused. 'The suits are completely hermetically sealed; that's their entire protective purpose and why the wind isn't cold to your bodies any more. If your oxygen runs out – and remember you can't risk taking your helmets off – you'll suffocate. So constantly check your supply time, whatever happens inside. Remember it's going to take you as long to get out as it takes you to get in. All clearly understood . . . ?'

There were more nods and mutters.

Although the face masks and vizors were designed to be as panoramic as possible there was still a severe visual restriction once the helmets were in place and secured. They straggled forward in a vague, follow-my-leader line again, Stoddart at the head. The ground unexpectedly became loose, uncertain boulders and shale they couldn't properly look down to anticipate shifting beneath them. Lyalin and the institute director separately started brief rock slides where they stumbled. Stoddart had provided large, high-powered rubber-protected flashlights, with wrist straps, which only gave one completely free hand, none for those with other equipment to carry.

Stoddart rounded the outcrop first, jerking abruptly to a stop as he did so. Over the headsets echoed a sharp intake of breath and the word: 'Jesus!' At once he said: 'Sorry,' a pause and then: 'Be very careful. The rocks are even looser here, where the fall's most obvious. We could even be caught up in an avalanche.'

The entire side of the mountain, for as high up the cliff as they could see and for more than a hundred metres across, had simply split away to create the unstable rock and boulder-strewn scree. In doing so it had exposed, as the facade of a completely furnished and occupied dolls' house is exposed when its side is opened, at least two cave tunnels and the beginning of a third connecting high-ceilinged, intermittent chambers in each of which there were easily visible perfectly preserved figures in what had once been their cave homes.

The whispered disbelief of the deeply devout Gregori Lyalin was picked up and relayed over their headset links. 'It's a miracle of God that we are being allowed to see such a thing.'

'Let's hope these can rise again like Lazarus, at least for us to learn what they died from,' said the more practical and agnostic Peter Reynell.

The desperation to catch up or draw level in the first twenty-four hours after the American president's revelation was like a lemming rush in reverse and Henry Partington felt himself close to being obliterated in the dust cloud of the stampede.

In his own desperation to match the British Foreign Secretary's assertion of an English medical breakthrough, Partington too quickly had Boddington disclose that Jack Stoddart was among the Siberian group, but it was Darryl Matthews – deciding with a quickly agreeing Harold Norris against their own personal experience becoming known – who just as swiftly leaked through the United Nations environmental division that Stoddart was an Antarctic disaster survivor. The instant media interpretation was that Stoddart – whose White House declaration was re-run – was knowingly risking death for the second time to discover the cause of the ageing illness. The overwhelmed Partington's knee-jerk reaction was to announce a $500,000 compensation package for the relatives of the dead Americans as well as an airlift of all American personnel from McMurdo after their having been quaratined and medically declared free of infection. He followed that with a demand to Congress for a budgetary allocation of one hundred million dollars.

Moscow's overnight response to the exploding furore was to release every available detail – which wasn't a lot – of the Lake Baikal discovery as well as the Iultin catastrophe, reveal that the Russian science minister as well as the country's famed virologist were in Siberia and to promise that travel permission to the site for the three hundred television, radio and print applications that were received in the space of four hours would be considered as soon as it had been possible to speak to Gregori Lyalin.

After he was identified on French television, live from Washington, as a member of the political crisis group, the world media descent upon Gerard Buchemin was so enormous that he was forced to take refuge in the French embassy. It was there that he named Guy Dupuy as one of the Siberian group at a hurriedly convened press conference at which he was panicked and confused by journalists posing questions as intended headlines or sound bites and provided, not just far more medical detail than had so far been given,

307

but in far too hysterically dramatic a manner. People of thirty years old became eighty overnight. Irreversible death occurred in days. Bones melted. Organs died, progressively, unstoppably. It was a pandemic worse than AIDS. A blacker than Black Death.

It was largely the Domesday pronouncements of Gerard Buchemin, a supposedly responsible minister of the French government, that led to the United Nation's Secretary-General announcing an emergency General Assembly debate to formulate an international response. Before which he was asking member countries to provide immediate finance and aid agency personnel to work under the co-ordinating aegis of the UN. A belated, half-thought-out hint that armed forces might be necessary to keep civil order was a far too exaggerated suggestion which did nothing to allay the hysteria and everything to feed it.

The World Health Organization, from its Geneva headquarters, announced within those first twenty-four hours that it was monitoring worldwide the outbreaks of the ageing illness at the same time as estimating, from the information so far and so rapidly accumulated, a death toll of 25,000, with the possibility of it being twice as high as that. Any true figure would be impossible until sufficient diagnostic information was made available for doctors and medical services properly to recognize the illness.

And Simon Buxton conducted the inquest upon his own political mortality.

'How many are still loyal?'

'I'm guessing at forty but some of those might haemorrhage away in the next few days,' said William Dempsey, the party chairman.

Buxton winced. 'What about the cabinet?'

'No more than four.'

'Bastards!' exclaimed Buxton. 'I never expected to get ambushed during Question Time by members of my own party! And Prendergast is the biggest bastard of all.'

'I checked. He was on the phone to Washington only five

308

minutes before coming into the chamber. And he says he tried to tell you but you didn't hear.'

'Conniving liar,' accused Buxton again. 'It's Ranleigh, obviously.'

'Sees himself as the surrogate premier,' agreed Dempsey.

'When do you think Reynell will openly declare?'

The other man shrugged. 'Any time. It's going to be a hell of a re-emergence, isn't it: out of the wastes of Siberia, where he's risked life and limb returning to pre-historic times! Today's papers are already making the Wellington and Churchill comparisons.'

'I know what today's papers are saying,' said Buxton, testily. He was silent for several moments. 'Have I got anything to fight with?'

'No,' said Dempsey, honestly.

'I deserve more loyalty than this!' declared Buxton.

Dempsey didn't reply because he didn't believe Buxton did. He was disappointed he hadn't already had an approach from Ranleigh.

'I don't want to be humiliated,' insisted Buxton. 'I want to go with some honour intact.'

'Of course.'

'You know what I hope?'

'What?'

'That Reynell catches whatever the hell this thing is. Catches it and dies.'

It was an enormous pity, reflected Dempsey, that there were only the two of them in the prime minister's office, which would make him the too easily identifiable source if he leaked that remark. It was something Ranleigh's group could have made good use of.

Lyudmilla Vlasov led, knowing the way from before, followed by the two entomologists carrying slide cases. Raisa Orlov had forced herself next into the line. They kept to the very edge of the scree but it was still unstable, first one of the entomologists and then Raisa stumbling to create a small rock slide. Geraldine was unbalanced by the weight

309

of her case and the flashlight dangling from her other wrist and once almost fell more heavily than the other two. There was no positive entrance to the cave complex – that was obviously still hidden somewhere in the part of the cliff that hadn't broken away – so Lyudmilla approached the lowest part of the first tunnel in the cut-away facade. One of the entomologists clambered in first, needing to lever himself up and then kneel, to swivel his body in. Obedient to Stoddart's translated instructions, the man examined the knee and shin part of his suit to ensure it was undamaged and Lyudmilla, at whose eye level the man's legs were, double checked. With someone inside offering a hand it was easier for the rest to get in.

Lyudmilla said: 'We've literally stepped back millions of years.'

Twenty-Seven

B ut no one moved, wanting someone else to take that first step.

Finally Geraldine forced herself, aware of the tremble in her voice as she said: 'We all of us know what we're here to find; let's keep talking to each other. We've got to decide whether there's any point in us being here or whether this comes down to Lyudmilla's unbelievable lucky break.'

Without the outside perspective of the dolls' house facade, she needed to orientate herself to remember the direction of the first corpse-occupied chamber – realizing that to Stoddart and the outside astronaut-suited audience they would appear a moving, living tableau against a background of the dead – and set out positively to her right, in her absolute concentration driving from her mind everything but her surroundings and what she hoped to learn from them.

Her illogical impression was that as living accommodation it was filthy. The height of the open-sided corridor she was traversing was far lower than it had appeared from outside and Geraldine had to bend, which by lowering her head concentrated her vizor-limited vision upon the ground directly in front of her. There was, in rare places, a hard and clean rock floor but more often the surface was littered not just by understandable rock shards and stones but by clean-picked but discarded bones and twigs and plant stems and leaves and what, astonishingly, looked like corn husks and straw stalks. Everything was sheened with ice. At one point she bent even closer to confirm a cluster of fruit stones. She might have missed the faeces if the first and then several turds to follow hadn't been trodden upon, at least three of

311

which even more astonishingly still held the frozen imprint of the careless or uncaring foot that had made it. There were a lot of fish bones. Following her own suggestion she relayed the finds and asked Vladmimir Bobin or Lyudmilla if the specimen-prepared entomologists had sufficient containers to go beyond their insect gathering to pouch the dropped bones, plant debris and dung. There was a spurt of Russian before Lyudmilla's translation, that they thought they had. She added that she was following Geraldine. The institute director and one of the entomologists had split from Raisa, the Frenchman and the other insect specialist, although both groups were initially moving off in the opposite direction. At once Raisa reported that they'd found a shaft apparently leading deeper into the mountain and she and the two men were following it.

Geraldine couldn't remember seeing from the outside the first belling out of the tunnel to which she came, although it was still insufficient to be a habitable cave or cavern. Its importance, Geraldine felt, was the few although comparatively orderly arranged straw stalks and seed husk strands, as well as a separate pile of berries which she could not immediately identify. Just beyond, there were more turds and then, abruptly and surprising because again it hadn't been obvious from outside, the perfectly preserved body of a large animal, most obviously wolf-like but hugely furred, its tangled coat so long it came more than halfway down its legs. It had frozen to fix the grimace with which it had died, exposing extraordinarily long-toothed incisors halfway along its overlapped jaw. Geraldine was sure the black spots in its matted fur were insects and said so, to alert the entomologists.

Raisa responded at once that the scientist with her had already collected some from an animal they'd discovered with five dead adults and two dead children, in an inhabited chamber. Raisa actually described the animal as a wolf, and also thought a lot of the bones came from fish. The adults were visibly aged, similar to their modern victims. The children, one maybe six, the other younger, perhaps five, were emaciated but unmarked by any sign of premature ageing.

Bobin's voice crackled over their communication system, warning of splits and gaps in the rock floor.

Geraldine moved further along the corridor, jumping at Lyudmilla's voice that she was directly behind now, but stopping to look at the animal. Geraldine promised to wait at the first chamber. When she reached it she recognized at once that the impression from outside was misleading. At least half the cavern was still hidden by its rock wall and too dark to see by natural light and she needed the flashlight which until now had been an encumbrance. The projecting wall shielded her from the near gale but the coldness of the cave permeated the windproofed protective suit.

There were five adults, three men and two women, and three children, the youngest little more than a baby of perhaps two, the eldest possibly seven, although she didn't try to guess an age. The division was virtually the same as Raisa reported, the adults very obviously and visibly old, the children skeletal from starvation. Closer, she saw – briefly revulsed – that the eldest child had died against the body of another long-haired animal; sinews and flesh of its rear left leg were exposed where the children had gnawed at it.

All the adults – and the children – were heavily haired, even the women with a matted covering over their breasts and all of them with pubic growth that began at their navels and extended down their thighs almost to their knees. At its thickest, around the pubis, their genitalia were virtually concealed. Only the childrens' retained its brown colour. All the head, beard and body hair of the adults was grey or white and two of the men were bald. One of the women had died and frozen squatted in a remarkably similar position to George Bedall, in the Antarctic station.

They were all naked and there was no evidence of clothes although two of the men and one of the women had died lying on or beneath skins of a slightly shorter-coated animal than the two so far found inside the colony. There was also a lot of grass stalks and straw around the bodies: the baby

313

appeared to be lying on a bed of dried grasses. Again there were a lot of fish remains.

Geraldine turned, attracted by the movement of Lyudmilla entering the chamber. When the Russian spoke her voice was thin with disbelief. 'There hasn't ever been an anthropological discovery like this. I don't know where to begin. How to begin.'

Into their helmets Bobin said: 'Scientifically, this is phenomenal.'

Geraldine looked down at her case, which she'd rested on the floor. She had come ill equipped by preconceived expectations and wasn't sure what she was going to be able to do or achieve on this first visit. Actually kneeling to get closer to one of the dead adult males – for the first time aware of the milky opaqueness of blindness behind half-closed lids – she tested the right arm and found it solidly rigid, quickly stopping to avoid snapping the frozen limb from the body. She'd tested by putting pressure against the claw-fingered hand and noticed at once a thick crust of filth beneath the taloned nails. She took a sharp-pointed probe from her case and tried to prise some of the nail debris into a specimen bag.

Lyudmilla, who'd moved further into the darkest part of the chamber, saw what Geraldine was doing and said: 'We're going to be here for days . . . weeks . . .' and Geradine wished her group had the luxury of time.

What she managed to dislodge from beneath fingers that were concretely frozen was scarcely sufficient to be considered a specimen, as it was from a woman and another male. Geraldine took a scalpel from her box and tried to pare away finger and toenail samples but the bone was so frozen it shattered under pressure, although the debris was still worth putting into a glassine envelope. She didn't bother for skin scrapes. Hair strands deep frozen over hundreds of thousands of years snapped off, like dried twigs, under the slightest pressure.

Geraldine confronted the fact that there was nothing practical – nothing here, cast back as she was into a prehistoric time warp – she could do to advance her own individual science. Lyudmilla was moving around the cave, gently but meticulously exploring, lifting but not moving, making self-absorbed sounds to herself.

'Incredible!' said the still awed Russian anthropologist.

'Tell me how,' encouraged Geraldine. There might be something important to Lyudmilla's specific expertise that she could pick up on. Touched by the disbelief of the other woman, Geraldine acknowledged the wonderment of being a scientific fact-and-rule realist who disdained miracles, suddenly finding herself in a miraculous situation.

'Definitely not Neanderthal,' determined the Russian. 'Early Neolithic.'

So the genetic coding should be the same as the other victims, snatched Geraldine, at once. 'You're positive?'

'Sufficiently, from what I can see,' said Lyudmilla. 'We've got domesticated dogs, which is Neothilic. An established, tribal community. That fits—' She pointed to a recess that Geraldine couldn't properly see. 'There's more grass and straw and berry pips. That's positive storage: a prehistoric larder . . . !' Lyudmilla reached the furthest edge of the cave, from where a tunnel led deeper into the mountain. She turned and came back. 'No fire or evidence of burning: not in this chamber, anyway. That's consistent. No clothes, as such. Wearing or covering themselves with skins would have been for warmth, not dignity. And there should be . . . ah . . . !' She reached into a fissure in the rock wall. 'Here we are—' She offered what appeared to be a handful of thin, much curled and distorted sticks. 'Pieces of creeper or stalks, malleable enough when they aren't frozen solid like this to be ties, binding the straw around their legs unprotected by the animal skins.' She knelt, fingering the partially covered man Geraldine had already tried to examine. 'There'll be tools somewhere, for them to have skinned as well as this . . .' There was another satisfied exclamation. 'We're looking at the head of the family . . . maybe even the head of the colony. Here's his authority . . .' From beneath the animal skin blanket

315

Lyudmilla produced a wooden spear shaft approximately five foot long, with an instantly recognizable triangular shaped flint tip bound into place by the sort of thong she'd found earlier. Still more in conversation with herself, the Russian woman continued: 'But that isn't all there should be, so . . . ? And here it is . . . !' Smiling triumphantly she produced from beneath the skin another matching wooden length, this one with a grooved notch where the previous one had the flint tip. For Geraldine's benefit, Lyudmilla stood and fitted the blunt end of the spear into the notch. 'This is the very later Palaeolithic, early Neolithic equivalent of the Smart Bomb.' She used the notch as the fulcrum against which to open and close both pieces like a set of jaws. 'They held the spear in one hand, to direct it, and the throwing stick in the other to propel it. Using it like that, as a lever, they got at least twice as much velocity and distance as they would throwing it in what's today regarded as the conventional over-arm, spear hurling way.' She jerked the notched stick towards the long-haired, partially gnawed dog. 'And they needed as much force as they could get to penetrate that amount of fur and bring their quarry down . . . And more!' she announced, holding up something Geraldine at first couldn't identify. 'Hooks, to catch their fish. Fashioned from fish bones themselves. We might even find the hair weave they'd have used for a line . . .'

The Russian began intently studying the darkened inside walls, holding her torch close against the rock face. 'Here!' she said.

Geraldine came to the other woman's shoulder, not at first sure what she was seeing. Lyudmilla physically pointed to red and brown marks and said: 'Finger painting. Literally. The beginning of cave art. They crushed berries between their fingers, for the juice, and daubed. With luck we might find something better.'

Abruptly, into their headsets, came Raisa's voice. 'We've found a total of twelve bodies, in their chambers. All the adults seem to have been infected and two children, as well. Five other children appeared unaffected. Again they appear

316

to have died from starvation. There's some flint tools, an adze and skinning knives and a bow and three arrows.'

Geraldine knelt again, glad the protective gloves were thin enough for her to test the rocklike hardness of the deeply frozen bodies. The trip to the Listvyanka Institute had been necessary to confirm Lyudmilla wasn't a carrier, but Geraldine was beginning to doubt whether the isolation and autopsy provisions there or at the Irkutsk hospital would be good enough. What was available locally would fall far too far short of what was totally necessary to examine and analyze, not just these prehistoric specimens, but everything else that made up the colony and which might very well provide the vital lead they were seeking. She needed the state of the art facilities of Fort Detrick and the support and combined expertize, not just of the drafted-in scientists but of the genome team at Cambridge who had already discovered the telomere erosion.

Lyudmilla said: 'Let's go on.'

Geraldine's movement was instinctive – as it was to lead – but at the mouth of the tunnel leading further into the mountain she recognized she was frightened, a physical, stomach-dropping sensation, and at her hesitation Lyudmilla collided lightly into her back. Bending quickly to provide the excuse she said: 'There's no point in my taking my case.'

'I'm right behind you,' said Lyudmilla, presciently.

Stoddart's voice said: 'You've got fifty minutes of oxygen time. Keep checking.'

The wide reflector torches were the most powerful Stoddart had been able to get but the beams didn't seem sufficient. Geraldine felt the pressure on her arm from behind and adjusted to Lyudmilla's unspoken suggestion, shining her flashlight from the middle upwards while the Russian concentrated her's downwards, giving them the maximum spread of light. Everything sparkled with the ice reflection from the walls and it was slippery at every step, Geraldine's feet several times skidding off stones or ruts. The passageway was high ceilinged, enabling them to walk upright and because that was the level at which her torch was directed

317

Geraldine saw the blotched whiteness before they found the cause.

'Bats!' guessed Lyudmilla.

'There!' confirmed Geraldine.

There were eight tiny bodies littering a head-high ledge to their left, frozen like everything else, in every case their lips grimaced back to expose sharp-pointed fangs.

'Vampire species?' suggested Lyudmilla.

A possible transmission cause, acknowledged Geraldine, remembering Amanda O'Connell's account of how West Nile disease reached New York by mosquito-infested birds. There had to be as detailed an autopsy on the bats and whatever parasites there were as upon the humanoid bodies. And upon the droppings splattered all around. She said: 'We've found a bat colony. Any sightings where you are?'

There was no response and Geraldine repeated herself, feeling another lurch of uncertainty.

Lyudmilla said: 'The mountain is too solid and we're too deeply into it for anything to be transmitted now.'

They scuffed on, their bodies touching, but came to another quick halt as they rounded a corner into a much more intense jewelled glitter of a stalagmite and stalactite gallery, the downward and upward white calcium carbonate cones almost touching at their tips in several places.

Geraldine said: 'There would have once had to be water percolating through to have formed these.'

'Look!' ordered Lyudmilla, again. On the wall behind the calcium icicles were very obvious paintings, stick-figured men throwing spears with the launch stick at what looked like humped-back bison. There were also long-legged, elongated-beaked birds and a fish which had been drawn with two rear legs.

'These stalagmites and stalagtites would have seemed magical: some sort of shrine?'

'Possibly,' Lyudmilla accepted. 'Your voice is breaking up, even as close as we are,' and her sound was intermittent. Geraldine did, though, manage to hear: 'We've been down for twenty minutes now.'

The stalagmites narrowed the passage and Lyudmilla lowered her torch even further and in doing so saved Geraldine's life, although it wasn't Geraldine who saw the gaping abyss. Her first awareness was the snatch of the Russian's hand, pulling her back before she saw the hole into which she would have plunged if she'd taken one further step. The opening appeared strangely eroded from beneath the painted rock face and continued on to have eaten away all but maybe a half a metre of the tunnel floor. At its widest, the hole was at least a metre and a half wide and would, Geraldine realized, have swallowed her completely. The fear whimpered from her and she began to shake more than she was already doing from the penetrating cold, uncaring that the other woman, who still held her arm, would feel it.

The simple words wouldn't form at her first attempt but she swallowed and managed: 'Thank you,' at the second.

'You all right?' crackled Lyudmilla.

Geraldine nodded. 'Yes. OK.'

'Do you want to go back?'

'No,' refused Geraldine, stronger voice. 'We need to go on. See everything.'

'Make sure what's survived is sound. Tread carefully.'

Geraldine felt out tentatively with her foot and then stamped. Immediately her foot slid sideways towards the hole. Swallowing, needing again to say it twice, she said: 'It's firm but it slopes towards the gap.' She edged out sideways, the abyss seeming to gape almost at her toe's edge, back pressed against the wall, her own torch directed down to join the illumination from Lyudmilla's flashlight to her right. Her too-easily skating foot scuffed against a rock and then two bat corpses both of which skidded over the edge of the hole. Geraldine stopped, biting her lip hard to prevent any further whimper. She eased herself on, a millimetre at a time, letting out a gasp of relief when she got to where the passage floor widened again.

She directed her light back to help Lyudmilla and said: 'Use the stalactites to push yourself back against the wall.'

'If one snaps off, I'll fall,' rejected Lyudmilla.

She was halfway along the narrow ledge when her left foot went from under her and she screamed, steadying herself at the very lip, almost throwing herself sideways to get back to the solid floor.

Geraldine said: 'We've got to find another way out.'

Lyudmilla clutched Geraldine's arm for several moments and Geraldine held her in return. There were unconnected sounds, not possible to identify as words, breaking into their headsets. The Russian woman said: 'Could be we're close to the others?'

The two women formed up closely again, needing the continued reassurance of physical contact. It was so cold it was impossible for either to stop shaking permanently. Geraldine remembered the other woman didn't have the double protection of a body stocking, just bra and pants. They came across the corpses of two emaciated, fur skin covered babies who had died in each other's arms in a shallow sided chamber with the remains of five bats on the floor, and two metres further on hesitated again at a very obvious change in the total blackness ahead, where the rock face appeared to end in total emptiness.

They advanced a groping step at a time. Their flashlights picked up the sparkle of more stalagmite and stalactite formations against the ice glitter, at first as if they were suspended in space. Closer, the formations emerged to be row after row of shimmering white pillars, in themselves breathtaking but the cavern they decorated was even more spectacular, high vaulted – in two places with proper rock pillars from floor to an unseen roof – and clearly the central communal room of the Neolithic colony. It appeared to be full of the dead – the later count came to twenty-two – with what must have been families drawn apart in groups to die. Again all the hair – apart from five young children of varying ages, two only babies – was greyish white, the skin puckered and withered with age. There was a lot of straw floor covering and close to every body – nearly always protecting or partially protecting – were animal skins. There was a lot of faeces and one of the two wolf-like dogs had died close to the body of a man at whose leg it had been chewing. There were hunting scene inscriptions and finger painting on two of the walls, in far more detail than before. There were several depictions of what were clearly woolly mammoths and more legged fish, four with elongated beaks. Quite separately was what appeared to be a war or fight scene. There were animal and fish bones everywhere but no skeletons intact enough to look like the creatures on the walls.

Lyudmilla said, thin voiced again: 'I have never seen – know of – anything like this, anywhere in the world. There's nothing like this at Lascaux, Les Combarelles or Font-de-Gaume, which are supposed to be the best and most well preserved prehistoric art there is.'

'What are they?' demanded Geraldine, bending closer over a family of five – two adults and three children, all girls – unusually side by side, as if they had been properly laid out in death.

'Arctic roses,' identified Lyudmilla, understanding Geraldine's question.

Even in the wavering light the pink and red colouring of the tight flower buds was obvious. Their stems had been split to be threaded one into the other, to make chains. Two of the girls wore them as wristlet bands, the woman as a crowned head-dress.

'Funeral tributes, from those who survived?' queried Geraldine.

'More likely decoration: these are their jewellery.'

There was a sudden blare of Russian – Bobin's voice – into their headsets so loudly that both women jumped. Almost at once they saw the approaching flashlights of the institute director and his entomologist and unnecessarily – forgetting that their torches would be equally obvious – Geraldine called: 'We're over here.'

As the two men approached Bobin said: 'We were worried. Have you seen the others?'

'No,' said Lyudmilla.

'They might have turned back,' suggested Geraldine.

'I hope they have,' said Bobin.

321

Geraldine physically shuddered at the thought of being lost, incredulous that she'd actually set off alone, unsure how long she would have continued if Lyudmilla hadn't caught her up. With the extra light, concentrated at Bobin's direction, they more fully explored the communal cavern. Each family had its cache of weapons, some spears longer than those they had so far found without throwing sticks, and bows with bird-feather flights, and all seemed to have stores of grasses and stalks and usually corn husks. There were more paintings on a far wall, behind a separate outcrop of stalactites, one a hunting scene with a woolly mammoth in a pit, being speared from above by a group of men, which Lyudmilla explained was one of the ways the behemoths were stampeded into traps where they would be helpless. Immediately after, beyond a cleft in which a lot more grass, straw and plants were stored, they found what Lyudmilla identified as the hide of such an animal huge enough to be divided to cover two separate groups of dead. They pinpointed all their light for the entomologist to probe the fur and recover several insect specimen. Bobin thought the cavern might once have had natural light through openings or fissures closed over the millenias by volcanic shifts and they actually shone their pooled light upwards but the beams were too weak to reach the roof, although ice walls sparkled back at them.

'People from around the world will want to see this . . . become involved . . .' Bobin said.

'Not if there's a source of infection,' warned Geraldine.

Bobin visibly shivered at the cold permeating his suit, checking his watch. 'Just over twenty minutes. We should get out.'

The institute director said they'd encountered two boreholes in the passages along which they'd reached the cavern – quoting them as evidence of volcanic shift – when Lyudmilla cautioned about the danger of the other approach and they initially chose what looked to be a third tunnel out, no one voicing the shared thought that Raisa, Dupuy and the other entomologist might have fallen into such a crevasse. Bobin led, Lyudmilla and Geraldine at the rear behind the other Russian man. After only about five metres the tunnel divided into two. Bobin hesitated momentarily before going to the right but almost at once the passage became narrower and lower and finally ended. Briefly, until it widened sufficiently, Geraldine had to lead the retreat. They found another dog and a small colony of bat carcases in the other tunnel, which very quickly became so low they had to bend double. Bobin hit a rock spur with his head and Lyudmilla cried out when she slipped on ice and turned her ankle. Even as close as they were their sentences broke up when they tried to speak, so dense was the rock, despite which Bobin every few moments called out, in Russian, for Raisa and her companion and then in English, for Dupuy. There was never a reply.

Geraldine, who'd never before known of claustrophobia, began to feel uneasy at the tight, enclosing constriction and consciously tried to subdue it, breathing deeply in and out, at once wondering at the level of her oxygen supply. She extended her arm into the beam of her torch. Eighteen minutes before the switch to the emergency reserve. They should have given themselves more time: prepared properly for the increasingly funnelling passage to become impassable and for their having to retrace their steps for one of the already explored, dangerous routes. Whose heavy, measured breathing was she hearing over the communication link? More than one person. Measured, for conservation? Or against the discomfort she was barely managing to control? There was a grunt, a man's tone, and gratefully she saw them straightening ahead and did so herself, relieved, entering a sudden chamber. Geraldine was the last to enter and by the time she did Bobin was calling again for the missing group. There were two more adult bodies, flint-cutting tools and a spear and its launch stick but no furs, and there were a lot of flower fronds she didn't recognize. There looked to be a continuation of the passageway on the far side of the chamber, with another tunnel exit to the left side.

Geraldine said: 'I'd say we've got another ten minutes from our main oxygen supply.'

Bobin said: 'I'm sure we're going back in the right direction.'

Geraldine wasn't. 'There's time for us to go back and take one of the routes we know.'

'It's your choice,' accepted Bobin.

Geraldine didn't want to try alone.

Lyudmilla said: 'We're using up our oxygen, talking. I'll give myself five minutes, going on this way. At the first problem I'm going back to the main cavern to the way out I know.'

'So will I,' agreed Geraldine, at once.

'We all will,' concurred Bobin.

The apparent continuation on the other side of the chamber turned out to be nothing more than a recess, containing more grass and fronds. The other ice-shimmering passage was high enough for them to walk erect although it was little more than a body width, so at the rear Geraldine couldn't see the reason for Bobin's next abrupt exclamation. The man said: 'I think we can get by,' and Geraldine finally saw the institute director and the entomologist pressing themselves through what couldn't have been more than a half a metre gap between the rock wall and a series of stalactite icicles hanging like long-fanged teeth.

Lyudmilla said: 'Let's go back. Hurry!'

Geraldine turned without argument, but at once Bobin said: 'Don't! I can feel wind, blowing against me,' and there was a burst of Russian from the other man.

The ice, against the rock and coating the stalactite, acted as a lubricant and it was easier than Geraldine expected to get past the obstruction. She felt the wind pressure directly beyond and the anxiousness to get to wherever it was coming from – to try to run even – surged through her, as difficult to curb as the earlier claustrophobia. She did it, though, swallowing as if physically to keep it down, conscious that they were moving faster and knowing she hadn't been the only one to be frightened. The darkness broken only by the

324

yellowness of the flashlights abruptly lightened, at first into greyness and then even lighter, making the torches unnecessary, and Bobin said: 'I can see daylight,' and Geraldine did too, finally, an oblong beacon of sun and blueness growing bigger and bigger.

At once Stoddart's voice came into their headsets, urgently but calm. 'You've got seven minutes on your main supplies. Plenty of time. Glad to get you back. I'm where you went in . . .'

They didn't emerge directly on to the exposed facade of the cave dwellings but from the side, where part of the cliff still remained to conceal them. Geraldine wasn't sure if she let out any sound of relief, but thought she probably had. The American acted as a support for each of them to jump down from the ledge, easing each of them away from the scree to the firmer ground, repeating as he did so: 'Don't stop. All the way down to where the bags are, where it'll be safe to get out of the helmets.'

Geraldine felt his reassuring pressure against her arm and back where he helped her and said, uncaring that everyone would hear: 'Jesus, am I glad to see you.'

Her oxygen began to go as she rounded the bluff – immediately seeing Guy Dupuy already by the equipment bags – and she was actually holding her last breath when she reached him. Stoddart had to help her unfasten her mask and as it fell away from her face she gasped: 'Where's Raisa and Vadim Ivanovich, the other Russian? Are they out?'

'No,' said Stoddart. 'Still inside.'

From Gregori Lyalin, still at the point of the bluff, there was a shout.

It was Paul Spencer's suggestion that Henry Partington helicopter to Andrews Air Force base personally to welcome back the first of the returning scientists from the US Antarctic stations at McMurdo and Scott-Amundsen and Spencer again who evolved what came close to being a disastrous idea how to turn the media event into one of international statesmanship because he hadn't calculated Partington would have to speak individually to eleven global leaders from the VIP lounge. They were lucky the military C-130 encountered delaying head winds. Partington was actually finishing his last conversation with Tokyo when the plane touched down and only had five minutes to scan what Spencer and Carson Boddington had hurriedly briefed the speechwriter to create.

Partington insisted upon shaking hands with the first twenty to get off the plane before leading Hank Brownlow, the McMurdo director, to stand beside him on the podium. He called the group that Brownlow led 'brave men and women' and thanked God that none of them had contracted what he referred to as 'a scourge sweeping the globe'. America had taken the lead alerting the world to the pandemic and that's how he intended the country he was proud to lead to remain. He had personally ordered the evacuation of all American facilities in the Antarctic and only thirty minutes earlier had concluded, with the Japanese premier, conversations with heads of the eleven countries with research and scientific stations in the Antarctic.

'My message – and plea – was that until we find a cause and a cure for this dreadful illness, that they withdraw their people to safety as I have today begun to withdraw Americans.' With an excuse to consult his printed list – and at the same time remind himself of the target points to flag – Partington pedantically recited the titles and the nationalities of the stations. 'The Russian president, with whom I have been closely working since we first learned of the disease, agreed at once to pull out from their five stations. So has the United Kingdom from its Halley base. And Japan from Mizuho and Showa. Argentina already has transport en route to airlift its personnel from their General Belgrano station. New Zealand, Australia and South Africa are convening cabinet meetings. India, France and Germany have promised a decision by tonight.'

No contact had yet been possible with those ('true heroes') in Siberia but he had authorized officials at Fort Detrick, Maryland, where all the medical research had so far been attempted, to release to the WHO and all other involved scientific groups, the known symptoms and indications of the Shangri-La Strain.

'No one – certainly not me, personally – is going to rest until this terrible scourge has been defeated,' concluded Partington, stentoriously.

On the return flight to the White House, Partington said: 'What's my next shot?'

You're back in favour, translated Spencer. 'How about you photographed on the telephone, talking to Amanda and Stoddart in Siberia?'

'I like that a lot. Make it work.'

Which was very much the thought at that moment in the mind of Lord Ranleigh. The stories were already beginning to run that Simon Buxton had lost the confidence of the parliamentary party. The drama of a telephone interview with Reynell would be the ideal launch pad for his name to be leaked as the most likely successor.

For several minutes Raisa was unable to talk, the helmet link to the collar of her suit ripped where she'd torn it away, as she slumped uncontrollably shaking on the ground where she'd been stumblingly helped by Lyalin. When she did speak she did so accusingly, directly to Guy Dupuy.

'He came back, looking for you!'

'I lost you. Didn't know which direction you'd taken,' protested the Frenchman.

'What happened?' demanded Lyalin.

'We set off together,' said Dupuy. 'I was the last . . . got separated. I didn't see which way they'd gone ahead of me, where the shaft divided. I carried on, looking for them. Realizing I'd lost them, I went on for a while, saw some of the bodies and an animal, like a dog. Then the passageway just ended. I came back, calling for them. Couldn't find them so I made my way out . . .' It sounded like the defensive plea it was.

'I heard Vadim fall,' broke in Raisa. 'His scream. He'd

gone back about five minutes before, when he realized Dupuy wasn't up with us. I went back, after the scream. There was a side passage he must have taken, that we'd passed. It opened out into a cavern with a lot of boreholes. I went to each one, calling. There wasn't a reply. I couldn't hear him breathing even.'

'We've got to go back!' declared Stoddart.

'We don't have the equipment!' said Bobin. 'Nothing that we need. Certainly nothing to get him out of a crevasse.'

'He might have recovered consciousness,' argued Stoddart. 'We could drop fresh oxygen bottles. Take the risk even of his taking his helmet off, so he could survive until we can get proper help. Could you take us back to the place where you think he fell?'

Raisa nodded, still looking at Dupuy. 'Where the shaft divided, which way did you go, to the left or to the right!'

Dupuy hesitated. 'The left, I think.'

'You *think*!

'If he's still alive he's got five minutes left on his reserve,' cut off Stoddart. 'We need to move, right now!'

'Someone has to go back to where the drivers are. Get ropes and more people to help, from the institute,' said Bobin.

'You,' ordered Lyalin. 'Your authority.'

The other entomologist said something. Lyudmilla said: 'Vadim Ivanovich . . . that's his name, Vadim Ivanovich Karelin . . . is married. They're having their second child in two months. He wanted a boy.'

Her attention unwavering, Raisa said to the Frenchman: 'You're coming back, too. To look for the man who went back for you.'

'We're wasting time!' insisted Stoddart.

Lyalin said: 'We'll all go.'

Only when she tried to do just that – to move – did Geraldine recognize how total her exhaustion was. Raisa had to be helped to her feet and into her spare, untorn suit. Stoddart insisted on minutely examining all the protection of those who had already been into the colony before replacing everyone's oxygen pack and cupping two spare packs beneath his free arm. He led the trudge back up the incline towards the bluff and as he turned it, toward the cliff face, he exclaimed: 'Fuck me!'

Peter Reynell and Amanda O'Connell were on the exposed facade terrace, appearing to look and examine for the benefit of the forgotten photographers. Stoddart said: 'We've got someone lost in there – most likely down a borehole – so get the fuck off your stage so we can go in to look for him . . . get him out . . .'

The suited, posed figure briefly stiffened. Reynell said: 'If it's a search party I want to be part of it.'

Amanda said: 'So do I.'

Stumping up beside the shifting scree Stoddart, outraged, shouted: 'I'm talking rescue, not photo opportunity! Get the fuck out of the way!'

'You haven't been inside, any more than I have,' said Reynell, evenly, controlled. 'So you don't know what the fuck you're talking about. You got someone lost in there – in difficulty – you're possibly going to need all the brute manpower you've got. And at the moment we're it!'

Stoddart was at the broken cliff face, the ledge upon which they had to climb just above head height with Reynell and Amanda far to his right and the two local media men stuttering their camera exposures just behind him. He said: 'You're right. I'm wrong. You could make all the difference. Let's hope to Christ you do.'

When they'd all clambered up, Geraldine said: 'It's an ice tomb. Nowhere you're going to step is safe. There's boreholes and crevasses everywhere. Slide your feet: don't try to take steps. If you do that and slip when you put your foot down, you could go into a hole none of us saw . . .' She paused, unsure whether to continue. 'If you do see filth – shit – on the ground, step over it. We're going to need it, forensically, uncontaminated by whatever we might have trodden in from outside. You're possibly going to see some unusual-looking people, most of them dead from what I think we're investigating. Don't touch them: don't touch anything. And don't get separated; hold

329

on to the person in front. Under the mountain, the voice link goes . . .'

Unasked, Lyudmilla provided the Russian translation.

Raisa, insisting that Dupuy be the next in line behind her, set off along a passage that broke away from a larger opening almost directly inside the open facade walkway. Everyone did hold on to the person in front of them and scuffed flat footed along the ice-greased floor, necessarily in step because of their front-to-back closeness, like a crocodile of cross-country skiers. They came upon two recesses, one with two geriatric adults, the other with a similarly aged couple and their daughter surrounded by the paraphernalia of their lives, and there was a variety of grunts and breath intakes. Only when there was a near blinding flash from behind did Geraldine realize the two photographers had tagged themselves on to the end.

'We're going into the borehole cavern,' announced Raisa, first in Russian, then in English. The transmission broke up and she repeated it several times to ensure everyone heard and remained just inside the entrance to fan everyone out around the absolute edge of a floor pockmarked by sinks.

There was a murmur of horror, at the thought of what could have happened to the lost entomologist, and curtly Lyalin said, in both languages: 'Be quiet! Only I will speak. Our only chance of locating him is by the voice link. Help me, with light . . .'

The Russian stepped delicately out on to the holed surface, the centre of everyone else's spotlight. Despite Lyalin's injunction Geraldine said: 'Test where the separation is narrow, between the holes! A rock bridge could collapse.'

The Russian grunted in acknowledgement but noticeably altered his step, adopting something close to a tip-toeing gait. At each hole he stooped, trying to peer down by the light of his own flashlight, repeatedly calling the name of Vadim Ivanovich. From the far side of the cavern, Lyalin told them all to take a deep breath and hold it and for them all to listen for the faintest sound of unconscious breathing. They heard nothing.

'Maybe a photographic flash would go deeper,' urged Bobin, in sad desperation.

At the very obvious hesitation, Stoddart said: 'I know how to fire a flashgun,' and took equipment off the unprotesting local cameraman. He edged out as cautiously as the Russian institute director, sure as he did so that it was Geraldine's whimper when he dislodged some unseen rock into a hole. It felt as if everything was in constant, shifting movement beneath his feet. He exploded the flash-gun into eight holes, seeing nothing but impenetrable darkness, before the battery began to give out. Stoddart didn't see the rock large enough momentarily to bruise his foot that he unintentionally kicked into a hole slowly making his way back and this time Geraldine cried out.

'I'm OK,' he said.

From where he stood, still on the far side of the cavern and addressing Raisa by name, Lyalin said: 'You sure this is the only way he could have come?'

There was a moment's silence, broken by Lyalin's sonorous Russian which Geraldine guessed at once to be a prayer. She was surprised to hear Raisa's intermittent voice among the responses dominated by the other entomologist.

Raisa made a point of insisting that Dupuy lead the line outside and it wasn't until Stoddart was again helping everyone from the ledge, instinctively counting, that he realized she wasn't with them and called for a halt, grateful for Reynell's help at once to climb yet again back on to the ledge. He was at the mouth of the tunnel before he detected the light of her approaching flashlight.

'Where were you?'

'Checking that the tunnel Dupuy says he took was a dead end.'

'Was it?'

'Yes. But I know the frightened bastard backed off. Vadim Ivanovich died going back to look for him.'

Vladimir Bobin was waiting around the cliff outcrop, with at least ten men brought up with ropes and ladders from the institute.

331

'I need to be shown where the cavern is,' insisted the bearded man.

'I'll show you,' offered Stoddart.

Bobin said: 'Irkutsk – the institute – is in uproar. Calls from everyone, from everywhere. The illness has become public. And what's been discovered here—' He looked around the group. 'You've all got to call your governments . . . whoever . . . right away . . .'

'Great timing,' said Geraldine, curious at the openness with which Reynell laughed at the remark.

Twenty-Eight

W ithout genetically counting – too physically and mentally drained to count, let alone *think* genetically – Geraldine ached throughout every DNA molecule, strand, thread and fibre of her being into one agonized, heartbeat-throbbing amalgam of near total exhaustion. It was genuinely a physical, hurting pain and there were abrupt awakenings from eye-open gaps of mental blankness, one moment knowing where she was and what she was saying, seconds later, seconds that seemed like hours, finding herself in a sentence she couldn't remember beginning.

A separate ache was to sleep properly, but she wasn't allowed to. Peter Reynell came close to invoking his official, superior authority by insisting she travel back to Irkutsk with him and Amanda O'Connell. He made her go step by prodding, questioning step through her exploration of the Neolithic cave complex and recount everything that she and Lyudmilla Vlasov had seen and what ('not just your own impression – your remit – but what everyone else felt as well') they'd concluded before the failed rescue attempt, which she'd left Stoddart desperately guiding the Listvyanka party back to resume.

They were twelve kilometres from Irkutsk – although Geraldine had no awareness of where she was – before they finally allowed her to slump into the rear seat corner and Geraldine had almost an hour to sleep. She had to be roughly shaken awake when they reached the Grand Hotel. She was conscious of slips of paper being thrust into her hand from her key slot – and of Reynell taking them from her, saying he'd handle the messages – but not of actually

333

getting into her room. She left it momentarily to slide a shaking note beneath Stoddart's door, saying she was leaving hers unlocked, and remembered to respray the mosquito net with insecticide before getting beneath it, taking off only her boots and ski-jacket.

Geraldine fought against being awakened, actually trying to push Stoddart's shoulder-shaking hand away, for a long time refusing to respond, wanting only to be left and when she finally regained some awareness she still tried to resist. It was Stoddart's gently persistent voice that eventually roused her and when it did she came together at once, anxiously.

'Did you find him?'

'No,' said Stoddart. 'They brought harnesses from the institute to lower men down the holes. There wasn't rope long enough to reach the bottom of any of them. None of the men on the lines could see the bottom either, with their lights.'

Geraldine swung out from under the netting. 'What else?'

'An enormous number of media are trying to get here, apparently. Lyalin's asked Moscow to refuse permission. He's flying army specialists and equipment in overnight: engineers to chart and map the complex, generators to provide the lighting we'll need and an official film crew and stills cameramen. The Russians have got body bags developed for radiation victims that we're going to use to prevent any disease transmission. There's also going to be soldiers to seal the mountain off.'

'What about Washington? London?'

'Our intrepid politicians have given telephone interviews to let the world know how brave they've been, leading an ongoing rescue attempt. I was five minutes into a conversation with Partington before I realized he was being filmed talking to me.'

'Those people in the caves died from our illness,' stated Geraldine.

'I know.'

'I don't want to work here. It was ridiculous of me to imagine I could. I want to collect everything I think could be relevant and take it all back to Detrick with some of the bodies, some that have obviously died from ageing and the youngsters who didn't. That's what could show us the way, discovering why some were resistant and others weren't.' Geraldine smiled, wanly. 'I don't want to sleep by myself tonight. Not for anything else but to sleep. I just don't want to be alone.'

Stoddart smiled back, just as bleakly. 'At this moment all I'm capable of is sleeping.'

'Couldn't have gone better!' insisted Partington. To show his satisfaction he'd had drinks – Scotch and bourbon and a pitcher of martini, which was his drink – set up in the small, private room off the Oval Office, and partying, glasses in hand, they'd watched the specially extended main evening news on all three major channels. Partington had, in combined total, filled an unprecedented one hour and ten minutes of television screen time – with constant CNN repeats – and Boddington had stopped at two hundred trying to keep count of the number of radio stations across the country running extended air time segments. He sipped his drink.

'Pity Stoddart tried to dominate your reference to global warming,' said Richard Morgan.

'Our legal people have had some approaches from lawyers representing the relatives of those who died in Antarctica . . . wanting more details of the compensation and pension package I announced on television . . .'

Million-plus litigation, read Morgan and Spencer together. Morgan examined the contents of his glass, leaving Spencer to wade through the morass alone.

'And personal effects?' anticipated Spencer, lapsing easily into double-speak.

'That too, I'm sure,' said the president. *Exactly what I'm talking about.*

'I've got it all together.'

'All of it?' *I'm talking James Olsen's diatribe.*

'Maybe one or two things got mislaid in the initial days.'

'Nothing to worry the family about, though?' *Get rid of it, if you haven't already.*

335

'The point surely is to cause the bereaved families as little distress as possible?'

'That's what I want to avoid. See it doesn't happen, Paul. OK?'

'Of course, Mr President. I understand,' said Spencer, who did. *My fingerprints on the smoking gun, if there's a copy I don't destroy.*

'Let's have another drink!' declared Partington. 'I think there's every reason to celebrate tonight.'

'So do I,' said Morgan, getting up quickly to pour.

It was another hour before Spencer could get away to cross Pennsylvania Avenue to Blair House and his personal safe.

'It was an excellent meal,' thanked William Dempsey.

'Shot the grouse myself,' said Ranleigh. 'Good season this year.'

There were only two of them at the South Audley Street townhouse and the servants had long been dismissed. The cigars were almost finished and the port decanter between them had dwindled to half.

'Peter sounded magnificent,' embarked Dempsey, knowing the opening had to come from him.

'Showed the calibre of the man,' encouraged Ranleigh, contentedly acknowledging it was the party chairman's place to make the running. Every television and radio news channel had been cleared for the telephone interview with Reynell, his photograph mostly dominating the screens apart from some library footage of a three-year-old natural world documentary on Lake Baikal. Channel 4 had replaced a scheduled hour-long slot on the Christmas Island giant carvings with a compilation of the Lake Baikal film, another on the imagined origins and appearance of prehistoric man with Reynell's description of the cave dwellers as a voice-over and a studio discussion by a selected group of anthropologists and epidemiologists.

'Buxton wants to go with dignity,' announced Dempsey. From his sources in the parliamentary lobby he knew that virtually every newspaper the following morning was naming Reynell as the successor to the leadership.

'He doesn't deserve it.' Ranleigh's uncompromising philosophy was that no prisoners should be taken or allowed in political victory.

Dempsey said: 'Peter's a hero now. And will be built up into an even bigger one. He doesn't need blood. He'll be judged by the public at large as well as by the party in general by how magnanimous he is.'

Ranleigh nodded, finally extinguishing the cigar, an instinctive manipulator recognizing the benefit of the argument. 'You imagining a life peerage?'

'I think a knighthood would be sufficient.'

'No attempted spoiling, last minute opposition?' bargained Ranleigh.

'I can guarantee there won't be.'

Ranleigh offered the decanter, which Dempsey accepted, both men knowing the negotiation wasn't over. Ranleigh said: 'You've served as a good party chairman, William.'

Dempsey smiled, gratefully. 'It's to the party, not individuals, to which I've always committed my loyalty.'

'That's well recognized,' said Ranleigh, honest himself. Dempsey ran an efficient machine and under his stewardship the finances were stronger than they'd been for a decade: with two years still to go there was already a war chest sufficient for the next general election.

'That's good to hear,' encouraged Dempsey.

'I know, from conversations with Peter, that he'd like you to continue if you'd see fit to do so.'

'That's even better to hear,' accepted the satisfied other man.

They did make love, in the early morning half light, and afterwards held each other. Stoddart said: 'The way I felt last night I never thought I was going to be able to do that again.'

Geraldine replied: 'I'm glad you made such a quick recovery.'

'So am I,' he agreed.

Geraldine snuggled comfortably into the crook of his arm. 'Do you think Dupuy ran?'

337

Stoddart shrugged. 'Something we're never going to know.'

'It'll be interesting if he comes back inside today.'

'I'm coming in with you this time,' announced Stoddart.

'I want you to.' She decided not to tell him how close she'd been to the sort of disaster that appeared to have befallen Vadim Ivanovich.

'Raisa seemed very different yesterday to how she has been,' he said.

'Long may it last,' said Geraldine, sincerely.

Stoddart went back to his own room to bathe and change. Her bathwater was hot and Geraldine soaked herself, immediately spoiling the effort to get clean and stop smelling by smearing herself with repellent. She put on her second, clean body stocking next to her skin, but remembering the bone-chilling cold struggled into her dirty one as well for double insulation before getting back into the same jeans, shirt and ski-jacket of the previous day.

Directly outside her bedroom door she hesitated on her way to Stoddart's room, remembering his remark about Raisa's changed demeanour. Perhaps it would be helped by offering her a ride with them back to the caves. Raisa opened her door almost immediately to Geraldine's knock.

'I don't know if—' Geraldine started but stopped at the sight further into the tousled bedroom of a smiling Lyudmilla Vlaslov, as proudly naked as she had been the previous day, her body shining from the unguent very obviously on Raisa's hands. 'I was going to suggest we go out to the caves together,' Geraldine finished.

'Lyudmilla and I are going to share a car,' said Raisa.

How much she'd misunderstood all that closeness in the caves, thought Geraldine, on her own way down in the elevator with Stoddart. Now she knew for whose benefit the two women had posed the previous day. She hoped it ensured Raisa's continued good mood.

The speed of the organization was remarkable.

The military security against intrusion began with tyre-bursting spike pads and an already erected prefabricated control post at the end of the snaking road to Shara-Togot and there were two more checkpoints up the rock-hammered road to the abandoned gulag. A lot of the rusting, flower-filled memorials had been bulldozed away to provide parking for canvassed and hard-topped supply trucks. Where they had the previous day had to force their own way through insect and tick infested trees and undergrowth, was now a cleared route with metal-matted strips sufficient for the heavy vehicles that would have been necessary to transport the gale-flapping tented encampment already in place where yesterday they'd simply dropped their hand-hauled equipment. There was a command post in which the officers from the earlier conference were already ensconced, a field kitchen alongside a trestle-tabled canteen and rest area and beyond that a separately tented latrine block. Some way from the main compound was another canvas-covered lean-to beneath which a battery of heavy duty generators throbbed noisily, their supply lines snaking further up the mountain towards the identifying bluff at which there was another prefabricated control position manned by guards completely encompassed in helmeted protective suits.

There were even separate tents for them to change, which Raisa and Lyudmilla did to each other's undisguised admiration and to Geraldine's unconcerned acceptance. The two Moscow arrivals appeared troubled by modesty, both undressing with their backs turned. Geraldine saw that both wore thermal underwear, which they'd need. She guessed both to be in their late fifties and hoped they had the stamina for what was to come. It wasn't until they were suiting up that Geraldine realized that Raisa and Lyudmilla, who today also wore thermals, were getting into Russian protective gear which looked far thicker and heavier than the American outfits. The Russian oxygen supply looked far bigger, too, and was harnessed on the outside of the tunics.

There was a two-man unit at the bluff, filming them as they approached, and when they rounded it Geraldine saw a board-walk had been laid along the edge of the shifting scree, leading up to steps into the initially exposed gallery. The entire, visible length of the open cave passage was brightly strung with lights and there were more inside the only cave that could be partially seen from the outside. Geraldine's immediate impression was of a fairy-lighted Christmas scene and it became even stronger inside where, despite the cowling, the lights struck a sparkling dazzle off the ice-clad walls.

The newcomers had unconsciously deferred to those who'd been into the complex the previous day. Bobin and Lyalin led, with Stoddart and Geraldine immediately behind. Turning once, Geraldine saw Reynell and Amanda had bustled their way into the forefront, where they could be most clearly and consistently filmed making their first penetration into the mountain. The posing became less obvious when the sound link began to break up and disappeared at the entry into the boreholed cavern.

Under lighting rigged to reveal every part of the chamber, the sight was far more sensational than Geraldine had remembered from the previous day. Concentrating as they had been upon finding the missing entomologist, she'd thought this room to be bare and unremarkable, apart from the holed floor. It wasn't. Encircling the whole chamber and reaching so high up that it would have required some type of scaffolding to achieve, was a wall-painted frieze that at once reminded Geraldine of the Bayeux Tapestry. Just as quickly she wondered whether this depiction would be judged more important globally than the woven recreation of the Norman invasion of England. Actually turning to follow the inscriptions around the wall, Geraldine decided they portrayed the entire existence and lifestyle of the Neolithic colony. They were hunting scenes with stick figures herding upended woolly mammoths into depressions or launching at animals, bear-like in body with elongated necks, spears and throwing sticks. There were more recognizable bears and bison and a lot more of the long-necked, beaked fish with rear legs and huge-billed birds with wings grossly out of proportion to their bodies. There were also what appeared to be battle scenes, stick figures intertwined and grappling, interspersed with the neatly lying dead.

340

And there were the solidly frozen bodies of the ageing illness victims – probably, thought Geraldine, the very artists themselves – just as neatly arranged in what was most likely three separate family groups, a total of ten afflicted adults and three starved children upon a ledge that also ran most of the way around the wall. The ledge was also too high to have been reached without steps or a climbing frame but there was no obvious way they could have got there.

Lyalin had to repeat himself several times, in both languages, to tell them to make way for the search party and as they filed out, turning right to go deeper into the system, the mountain rescue group approached from the left burdened with equipment.

The Christmas fairy tale imagery grew the deeper they penetrated, the lights throwing up the milky – or snowy – whiteness of the stalgmites and stalactites against their frozen backgrounds, the ice itself appearing to form a glassed frame for wall painting after wall painting.

There were also more bodies than they'd counted the previous day, and with better lighting Geraldine began to find not just grass and fauna storage but food as well: berries and fruit – what looked like crab apples and apricots and grapes – and at the entrance to the huge, communal cavern on a ledge by three carefully laid out dead bodies, there was the leg of an animal still covered with fur and with some meat still adhering. On the same ledge Geraldine found the first carcase of a rat-like creature, with elongated incisor teeth. Very quickly she found a lot more, as well as bats, in the cathedral-like chamber. She stopped counting weapons and fish bones and hooks.

The party was no longer in any order, split up and divided, and Geraldine was grateful that Stoddart remained close by her, although the improved illumination greatly lessened the dangers it still chilled her to think about.

Stoddart held up the watch strapped to the outside of his suit and said, brokenly: 'Let's give ourselves more time to replace our oxygen than yesterday.'

Geraldine started to follow him back the way they had

341

come, passing the sort of wall painting that by now was so familiar she scarcely glanced at it but then she did and stopped, abruptly. 'No!'

'What!' demanded Stoddart, stopping just as abruptly.

'We've got time!'

'What?' he repeated but she didn't answer.

Instead, Stoddart following, Geraldine studied each wall painting they passed, every time jabbing out a finger and then going back to check the families where they'd found food stores. Because they had to pass the holed cavern she went in there, too, although remaining at the edge to avoid the rescue teams lowering audio-sensor and harnessed men attached to metal, length-extendable hawsers. She ignored what was happening on the ground, again urgently pointing to the frieze. She said: 'I'm right! It's the same every time.'

'Out! Now!' ordered Stoddart and obediently Geraldine finally followed, light headed from excitement rather than her depleting oxygen, although she still hadn't gone on to her emergency supply when they reached the tents.

Helmets thrown back Stoddart said: 'You going to tell me now?'

'They're not battle scenes! They've got weapons: spears and bows and arrows, but they're not using them. They're trying to help each other, when they're dying. And look how they're laid out in there, when they die. In the family groups as they're displayed in the paintings. That's what they're telling us, in those paintings. That to die as they did was a recognized, accepted thing . . .'

Stoddart looked at her doubtfully. 'Helping each other . . . laying each other out . . . you're suggesting a structured society, of sorts . . . ?'

'It *was* structured!' insisted Geraldine. 'They lived together, as a tribal group. That's structured. And each family had its own space. That's structured. And what about the food we found? Food that those youngsters who weren't ill could have eaten, to stay alive. Come outside, to pick more berries and fruit even!'

'So why didn't they?'

'Because in a communal society . . . a society without walls or separation . . . the worst crime is to steal. Any child obedient enough *not* to steal when it's starving wouldn't disobey its parents by going outside where there were animals like the sort we've seen painted in there.'

'What's the significance?'

'For me, just one. If I'm right about premature ageing being endemic here, however many millions of years ago, it'll be in their genes. And I can find it.'

Geraldine and Stoddart went into the colony twice more that day and by the last time Stoddart allowed himself to be persuaded. Neither Raisa nor Lyudmilla were, although Geraldine was aware of the locally-based anthropologist delaying her assessment until after Raisa expressed an opinion before offering the same one herself.

The repeated question to the Moscow group when they assembled at the end of the day in one of the larger tents, was greeted with shrugs of dismissal and Lyalin's translation of a short burst of Russian from one of the Moscow women that such an assumption would take years to reach, if at all.

'It might not, if Geraldine were allowed to take back everything she wants,' said Stoddart.

'She can,' announced Lyalin, gesturing towards the canvassed radio tent. 'I've spoken to Moscow. You can take every sort of specimen you consider necessary, including bodies, on condition that they are returned outwardly intact.'

'Which I'm giving you here and now,' said a relieved Geraldine.

'And which I'm officially guaranteeing on behalf of the United Kingdom,' said Reynell.

'And which I'm further endorsing on behalf of America,' said Amanda, as aware as Reynell of the media sound bite for that evening's already planned telephone link-up with Washington.

Raisa's translation of the science minister's agreement created fresh protests from the Moscow scientists, from

343

which Stoddart eased Geraldine away. 'You know what you want from inside there?'

'To the very last specimen,' assured Geraldine, who'd occupied the second and third entries, apart from trying to convince people of her theories, isolating everything she believed she needed.

'How long to collect it all, once the cartography and filming is finished?'

'Three hours, maximum. All I need is to bag it.'

'Recording and mapping everything will be finished by late tonight, according to Lyalin,' said Reynell, who'd also moved away from the quarrelling group.

'We could be away from here by tomorrow if you can arrange the transport,' promised Geraldine.

'We can arrange the transport,' promised Amanda, in return. The sound bites were getting better by the minute.

They all turned at the entry into the tent of the shoulder-sagged mountain rescue team. The voice of the major in command was as weak as the man looked. For the westerners' benefit Bobin said: 'They got to the bottom of every hole. In five there were just a lot of dead bats and rats. The other four dropped straight into a river running into the lake. That means the body's been in Baikal for twenty hours now. There won't be anything left.'

Twenty-Nine

$\mathbf{S}$ toddart remarked later to Geraldine that he supposed they should have expected it because they'd each spent more than an hour the previous evening performing in officially staged media circuses – and there was the in-flight warning going over the Bering Sea – but none of it prepared them for what awaited in Anchorage.

Their first indication came through the window of the Aeroflot plane taxiing to its meticulously designated place that symbolically put it in the same frame as Air Force One in every film, television and camera shot.

Geraldine said: 'Oh my God!'

Stoddart said: 'God's probably the only one not here.'

Henry Partington was centre stage on the podium, with Robin Turner and Gerard Buchemin and the ambassadors of France, Britain and Russia sufficiently in the background not to divert any attention. The first pen to the president's left held 150 squabbling cameramen; twenty TV stations alone – including all three American majors – were running live satellite coverage. The second was occupied by 200 print and sound journalists. Paul Spencer and Carson Boddington scurried up the ramp practically before it was properly in place. With them was an ear-pieced, lapel-miked Secret Service officer.

Spencer, who'd arranged this ceremony as he'd set up the McMurdo greeting to exclude Richard Morgan, proudly said: 'What about this? A presidential welcome!'

Geraldine said: 'We asked for refrigerated transportation.'

'You got it!' assured Boddington. 'Nothing's been over-looked.'

'You won't need me out there,' said Geraldine. 'I want to supervise the transfer.'

'I think we do need you,' corrected Reynell, delighted by the preparations.

Geraldine had worked with Stoddart since three that morning organizing the specimen and body collection and flown still wearing the repellent-stained and crumpled jeans and ski-jacket she'd worn every day. Abruptly she realized the unshaven, unkempt Reynell and the tousle-haired Amanda O'Connell, without make-up, were in what they'd worn for every visit to the Neolithic colony, too. Oddly, both appeared dirtier and more wrinkled than hers. The creases in Guy Dupuy's formal suit seemed to match everyone else's dishevelment.

The Secret Service man cocked his head and said: 'They're wondering out there how it's going.'

Boddington said: 'We thought you'd like to transfer what you've brought back first,' turning at the arrival of an army squad in cowled safety suits identical to those they had worn to go into the caves, although these were camouflaged.

'Everything's packed in what the Russians developed to protect against radiation leaks during highly toxic nuclear movement,' sighed Stoddart. 'All that's needed is the refrigeration.'

Boddington said: 'They're suited up now. No point in wasting time, undressing.'

'Or spoiling the picture,' commented Stoddart.

'Jack!' soothed Spencer. 'You've got to be exhausted. But you've no idea what it's been like here, particularly after the photographs those local guys took inside the caves. Everything we're doing is to maintain calm: reassure people we've got a handle on things. Let's all stay on the same side, OK?'

'Who said we've got a handle on things?' demanded Geraldine, at once.

'You found the telomere fraying, didn't you?' said Reynell.

Geraldine regarded the man steadily for several long moments. 'You talked about that as a cure? How to control it?'

'I referred to it as progress,' insisted Reynell. 'I don't know how it was interpreted.'

The leader of the protected handlers shifted, impatiently. Without speaking further Geraldine led the American soldiers to the sealed-off rear of the plane, to a frowned and sniggered reception from the waiting, cotton-overalled Russians. It wasn't until she was returning after the second necessary trip that Geraldine acknowledged that dressed as she was she'd made the photo-staged precautions look ridiculous. Boddington didn't appear to have noticed.

'Ready?' urged Spencer and as they moved the Secret Service man mumbled into his microphone that they were on their way.

They disembarked abreast, Amanda beside Reynell, Stoddart with Geraldine and Dupuy shambling by himself at the rear. As they stepped on to the tarmac, Partington began to clap loudly, prompting applause from airport onlookers. He pulled the five of them up on to the podium with individual handshakes and Buchemin broke ranks to embrace Dupuy.

Partington launched into a word perfect eulogy about bravery and heroes and selflessness and horrific legacies from the beginning of time. Having proved his own bravery by standing in the Alaskan cold, he led them into the largest but barely adequate lounge of the airport, where more cameras and lights were already rigged and a dais had been assembled for a table and strictly rationed seating for the international press conference. There was an enviromentally green back-cloth and green-leafed potted plants at either end.

Initially few of the questions substantially varied from those they'd already answered by telephone over the preceding two days and Geraldine found herself concentrating more upon Reynell's orchestration of the event than upon its content. It would have been impossible, later, to have accused the man of superseding the pontificating American president ('I can confirm it was I who named the disease the Shangri-La Strain: Shangri-La existed in a lost continent, didn't it?') but there was rarely an answer to which Reynell didn't make a contribution. Although the preceding day's worldwide use of what the local Irkutsk photographers had taken had been phenomenal – whole editions given over entirely in at least twelve countries – it was Reynell who dominated the verbal description, although deferring to Amanda for confirmation and elaboration. Reynell's account of the pothole search for Vadim Ivanovich Karelin was vivid enough to imagine it had been Reynell who had been lowered into the unknown, unexplored blackness instead of the Russians. Amanda O'Connell came close to matching him with her tight-voiced drama of coming to within inches of an unseen, gaping hole as she made her way through the galleries, describing the never before seen images of the cave-painted monsters as if they still might have been lurking somewhere in the boreholes. It was Amanda who suggested some of the depictions were of dinosaur birds.

It was a full half hour before either Stoddart or Geraldine were drawn into any prolonged discussion, Geraldine actually introduced by Reynell as the person ('a scientist of near genius') who had made the genetic connection. Reynell came in at once, to smother Geraldine's quick correction that it hadn't been her personal finding and that it didn't take them any further towards a cause or a cure, by insisting she publicly confirm that the prehistoric Siberian bodies had definitely died from the same illness.

'That would seem to be so, from the external examination that I've been able to carry out so far,' Geraldine had to agree. 'There's an enormous amount of pathology still to be conducted but I believe Siberia could show us the direction in which to go.'

So specific were some of the demands, that Geraldine accepted there were specialist medical correspondents among her questioners who were able to ask and understand telomere shortening. To isolated nods of understanding from the packed room, Geraldine said: 'It's a recognized manifestation in old age, not its cause.' There was a long exchange about contagion, Geraldine needing to repeat several times that they did not yet know how the infection was transmitted. Although a comparison with AIDS had been made, the illness they were investigating was certainly not sexually passed on.

Encouraged by Amanda and Reynell's account of the Neolithic colony, the concentration was very clearly upon the lost world environment of Lake Baikal, which Stoddart strived to keep factual and in scientific perspective, but his mentioning that anything alien to the lake could not survive in it caused an immediate flurry of overlapping questions, almost at once repeated when he talked of a mile thick sludge of primeval sediment at its bottom. Pointing out that he lacked any medical competence, Stoddart agreed that outwardly the Siberian dead appeared to have died from the same illness that killed the Antarctic rescue group of which he was the only survivor and that it confirmed that the global warming depletion of the north and south ice sheets were somehow releasing a disease unknown since the pre-dawn of civilisation. While the medical and scientific research continued at Fort Detrick he intended taking up more fully the responsibilities entrusted to him by the president to ensure the environmental agencies, under the aegis of the United Nations, were co-ordinating with the necessary urgency.

Boddington's first attempt to end the conference was howled down, but after a further thirty minutes he succeeded on the second attempt. There were instant demands for individual interviews from every television crew, all of which were refused with the exception of Guy Dupuy who compensated for making the smallest contribution to the main encounter – responding in French to just five questions from the French contingent – by giving three separate personalized interviews, each in his own language.

As they were escorted from the room, leaving Dupuy briefly behind, Geraldine said: 'I wonder how brave he's sounding, now that it's all over?'

Only when they were being led by Partington towards the presidential plane did they see the Secretary of State escorting the ambassadors separately to Air Force Two parked well out of camera shot. Aboard, Partington at once adopted the role of genial magnanimous host. 'This is the White House with wings,' he said, encompassing with an arm wave the expansive mid-section lounge, complete with sink-in leather easy chairs and sofas, a steward-attended bar, television and telephones. 'Whatever you want, we've got.'

'How about a shower?' challenged Geraldine.

'For'ard, next to the sleeping quarters,' defeated the small man.

'With enough sweatsuits for everyone,' completed Spencer. 'Figured you might like to freshen up on the way east.'

'Plenty of time before dinner,' assured Partington. 'Thought you'd appreciate some good old Texas steak.'

Geraldine had actually showered – embarrassed by the scum that took a lot of hosing to disperse – and put on a lounging suit before the plane took off. There was no insistence upon safety belts and indulging herself with the technological luxury, like a child with a new toy, Geraldine asked for Walter Pelham's direct line at Fort Detrick and was instantly connected on the telephone beside her armchair.

'Everything we brought back left Anchorage an hour ago,' she said, relaying Spencer's information.

'I've already been advised by Andrews. It's being heli-coptered here.'

'Anything new from your end?'

'There's a common difference in how people are dying now from how those died in the ice stations,' said the man. 'I think it's significant. And there's something else . . .'

Raisa Orlov's satisfaction at finally being left professionally alone lasted only a few short hours. She'd also gone to the site at three that morning, to monitor – and later to duplicate – everything taken for Fort Detrick examination. Afterwards she remained with Lyudmilla Vlasov supervising the removal and refrigerated storage of the remaining forty-six bodies. The immediate transfer, to two waiting transport aircraft, was completed by mid-afternoon. Leaving Vladimir Bobin and specialists from the institute staff to finish the packing of what remained, the two women arrived back at the hotel coincidently just as the Alaskan press conference was being transmitted, live, into the packed lounge of the Grand Hotel. Raisa, who was recognized at once, shook her head against the offer to go closer to the television. Instead she remained statued just inside the door, not needing the voice-over translation, seething at the posturing of Amanda and Reynell, snorting in contempt at the word genius and sneering at the artifice of their filthy work clothes, and grew even angrier at what she saw and believed others would see as Geraldine's confirmation that the cause and cure would be found by Britain and America.

Because no one had bothered beyond trying to delay it, the media invasion had always been expected from the north-west, from the massed ranks in Moscow, but it actually came – although still in force – in a squadron of chartered planes from a closer and more convenient Japan. Raisa was lying, still stiff and unresponsive, beside a sympathetically comforting Lyudmilla when the first telephone call came from the lobby below.

Raisa went down wearing her stained and soiled outfit and was happily engulfed. She had to arrange her own conference but was commanding enough to do it, actually in the same lounge in which she'd so recently watched the more orderly affair from Anchorage, consciously using what she'd seen and heard from there as a rehearsal to stage manage her own solo performance. She was content for everything to appear disorganized, because it suited her intention, letting the pre-history questions ramble so that she could establish doubt at the bodies positively being Neolithic. When the discussion became medical she implied the British telomere findings had been made virtually in parallel with Russian research before, carefully timing her moment, she declared: 'As head of the Russian scientific research I am confident – in fact I think I can promise – that I am on the point of making the medical breakthrough we're looking for.'

Raisa picked her way through the deluge of questions, coming close to confirming that she was indicating a cause and implying that from it would emerge a cure. Carefully waiting for the question to come from an American reporter, she said that of course the research was being conducted jointly, although as she was returning to Moscow,

351

not Maryland, and would have been out of contact for almost a week by the time she got there, she'd need a period to bring herself up to date with the latest from her Moscow team.

Raisa was concluding her third personal interview with an NBC correspondent when Vladimir Lyalin finally returned from the airstrip where he'd been officially accepting signed responsibility for what was being shipped to Moscow. She at once identified him as the minister with the authority to allow protectively suited entry into the caves and as she was escorting him to where she'd initially sat, for the conference to resume, Lyalin demanded, soft voiced: 'What have you said?'

'Only what I believe to be true: that the breakthrough's going to come from us, in Moscow.'

Under questioning, the unprepared Lyalin tried to avoid confirming Raisa's statement by insisting upon the need for consultation – which unfortunately from what Raisa had said earlier appeared to *be* confirmation – and even more adamantly denied the abruptly voiced suspicion that his going back to Moscow as well as Raisa indicated a breakdown in the international co-operation.

He also categorically refused to let anyone near the caves, protected or otherwise. Anyone who tried would be arrested and, in the unlikely event of anyone getting past the military cordon, risked becoming infected and dying.

Much later, lying in the darkness in the crook of Raisa's arm, Lyudmilla said: 'You were magnificent. At the conference and later, standing up to the minister like that.'

'Lyalin's a fool,' dismissed Raisa. She'd avoided the man's closed-door demands to explain her remark by insisting that her own laboratory's research since she'd been away needed to be co-ordinated with that of Fort Detrick and put against what she was already sure she'd find from the cave victims, carefully quoting herself that she was *on the point of*, not that she'd actually made the breakthrough.

'You're certainly not,' flattered Lyudmilla.

'I want to go through the anthropology once more,' said

Raisa. 'The Neanderthal, which preceded the Neolithic, was the origin of man?'

'Yes,' agreed Lyudmilla.

'And the Neanderthal completely died out, as a species?'

'Yes,' the anthropologist agreed again.

'What killed them off?'

'No one knows.'

I do, decided Raisa.

'It's been good, meeting like we have,' said Lyudmilla, after a pause.

'Wonderful,' agreed Raisa, only half listening.

'I've been talking to the people – the director himself – from the Moscow institute. He thinks there's going to be years of anthropological work upon the cave people.'

Unseen in the darkness, Raisa frowned in suddenly concentrated anticipation. 'I should imagine there will be.'

'How would you feel about my applying for a transfer to Moscow?'

'That's an exciting thought.'

'I hoped you'd think that.'

'I've got a tremendous amount to do, when I get back myself,' said Raisa. 'Might even have to go back to America for a long time. Don't do anything until you hear from me.'

'I won't. But make it soon.'

'As soon as I can.'

Stoddart told Geraldine she couldn't wait until there was definite confirmation of what she'd discussed with Walter Pelham because all in-flight conversations from Air Force One were automatically recorded and not to do so would be construed from the playback as her withholding something.

For convenience she waited until they were all around the large oval table, being served individually grilled steak cooked by a White House chef.

'You're absolutely sure?' demanded Partington at once, preparing for the following day's headlines.

'No,' cautioned Geraldine. 'What seems to be emerging from hospital records is that it's taking longer – up to a month, sometimes even a week or two more than that – for people to die.'

'What's your interpretation?' asked Reynell, his mind running parallel with the president's.

Geraldine shook her head. 'There could be several. The most obvious is that the strain is mutating: becoming less virulent.'

'What's the potential significance?' asked Amanda.

'If we've got more time between the onset of the disease and death from it, we might be able to intercede and block its development: give the body's immune system time to fight,' said Geraldine.

'What about the birds?' questioned Partington, coming to Geraldine's second relayed Fort Detrick development.

'There could be a connection between the large number of dead birds and a lot of the locations where the illness has broken out—' Geraldine began to explain.

'I was right!' Amanda interceded, with the benefit of a presidential audience. 'Birds could be how it's transmitted, just like West Nile encephalitis in New York!'

'Yes,' agreed Geraldine. 'Birds could be a carrier.' Protectively refusing to let the woman take the credit she added: 'You'll remember Jack suggested that a while back.'

Thirty

Raisa Ivanova Orlov was unconcerned – happy even – that behind her back her staff accused her of running her institute by the same principles with which Stalin governed the Soviet Union, believing fear of dismissal, which from an institute as prestigious as hers effectively guaranteed any sacked scientist was unemployable elsewhere, brought the best dedication and that the very fact of her knowing the condemnation proved an eager-informer intelligence service matching the Stalin-period NKVD, which made her total master of her empire. Her original accuser, a senior botanist, had made the complaint to agreeing laughter at lunchtime and been fired by five that evening. He now sold *matroyshka* dolls to tourists on the Arbat. One of the laboratory technicians who'd thought the remark funny collected pleasure boat tickets for cruise boats on the Moskva river and the other drove for a minor mafia brigade leader.

There was still a discernible *frisson* when Raisa swept on to her working floor, even though she knew a warning would have already been given of her arrival from the reception area. She nodded to the dutiful greetings, not smiling until she reached Sergei Vasilevich Grenkov, dutifully waiting outside his deputy's office adjoining hers. She didn't pause, continuing past the two politely standing secretaries, knowing he would unquestioningly follow, which he did.

She turned at the sound of his closing the door, holding out her arms to be obediently embraced.

'Good to have you back,' said Grenkov. He was a big man, muscled in proportion to being just under two metres

355

tall, with the thick black hair and dark complexion of his Georgian birth.

'Good to be back.' She led the way to the lounge area of her expansive, corner building office and said: 'Get us some drinks. I'm exhausted.'

'You're famous,' smiled the man at the cabinet.

'I was before.'

Grenkov, who was cautious of the woman although believing he was probably the only person in the building without reason to be afraid, continued smiling on his way back with vodka for both of them. 'Not like this. All the western press have discovered you work here. We've been inundated.'

Raisa paused, her glass in front of her. 'Are there call back numbers?'

'I instructed the switchboard.' The operator would have logged the names and numbers without being told, but it had been automatic for the man to issue the order.

'That's good,' said Raisa, her mind in the future.

'I thought there would have been a press conference when you arrived, certainly after what the Americans put on in Alaska and what happened in Irkutsk,' said the man.

Raisa's face closed, her never totally lost anger bubbling up. 'It was proposed. Lyalin cancelled it.' Their unspeaking hostility during the trip from Irkutsk had exploded into a shouting climax just before their arrival at Moscow's Domodedovo airport at her learning for the first time, from a casual remark from the anthropology institute director, of the minister's refusal. He'd insisted there was nothing new or important to be announced, but Raisa knew the true reason was Lyalin's pique at her going ahead with the media encounter without his authority and the man's jealous determination not to allow her the public recognition she rightfully deserved.

Grenkov frowned, attuning to her mood. 'Why?'

'The man's a toadying fool, happy to kiss the ass of anyone in the west who drops their trousers. He's quite happy for us to appear to be following everyone else's lead –' she thrust out her glass, for it to be refilled – 'which I'm not.'

356

'I saw – heard – what you said in Irkutsk,' prompted Grenkov, holding back from directly asking what break-through she had been promising.

'Do you know what it is in the tissue sample of Gennardi Varlomovich Markelov?' demanded Raisa, instead of answering the implied question.

'An enzyme,' declared her deputy.

'Viral protein?'

'Not from any virus we can identify. It might be parasitic but we haven't found any parasite trace . . .' He paused. 'We have confirmed telomere loss, in all our victims.'

Raisa's face clouded again. 'When?'

'As soon as the guidance came from Washington. Two days after, to be precise: the time it took us to carry out our own specific genome tests.'

'Rough data?'

'That's how you ordered things to be kept, before you left,' reminded Grenkov.

'I want the written-up telomere results dated the 18th.'

'The day *before* the British announcement?' queried Grenkov.

Raisa nodded, sipping her replenished drink.

Grenkov remained silent too, for several moments. 'What explanation is there for our not passing them on to you and your having announced the gene discovery first?'

'There was a delay in your being told, by the genetic institute. As Britain made the announcement – as you already knew we had the information in Washington – the duplication would have been pointless.'

'I understand,' said Grenkov, uncomfortably.

'I've marked the bodies I want immediately autopsied tonight,' ordered Raisa briskly. 'Have the tests on both the obvious victim and the youngster who clearly isn't affected, apart from malnutrition, concentrated for the same enzyme you found in Gennardi Varlomovich. If it can't be found in them, it must be continued through the rest of the forty-four, if necessary. I want everyone else – every science – working throughout the nights as well as days, on a shift system. I want you now, verbally, to warn every department head and every outside institute and academy we're utilising, that I'm going to confirm those instructions by written, hand-delivered memoranda, within two hours.' It was good – exhilarating – to be back in total control.

Grenkov didn't immediately get up. 'What about the media calls?'

'I'll also give written instructions to the switchboard. But when you speak to everyone about the work schedule – particularly those outside this building – tell them that I'll instantly dismiss anyone talking to the media. Everything's got to come through me.'

Grenkov nodded. 'You going home tonight?'

Raisa looked surprised at the question. 'I'll stay with you. I've travelled a long way and I want you to bath me, before we decide what else to do.'

'You're going to come out of this ahead, aren't you?' said Grenkov.

Raisa's expression of surprise remained. 'Of course,' she said. 'I always intended to. I'm not losing out again.'

It took the woman almost two hours to dictate all her memoranda. Her penultimate note was to the institute switchboard that the standard response to every media enquiry had to be that Raisa Ivanova Orlov was too busy but that she would personally return calls as soon as she was able.

Her last, most carefully drafted, memo was to the president, asking for an interview.

Gregori Lyalin's invitation was for dinner, just the two of them in the president's private Kremlin dining room. Lyalin left the ministry with time to bathe and change at home and have an hour with his wife and daughters. The oldest girl was twelve, the youngest seven, and Lyalin spent most of the hour with Elaina smiling on indulgently while he told stories even more exaggerated than either Reynell or Amanda, of fanged dinosaurs and giant fish that walked on legs and huge mammoths and ice caves in which strange people had lived millions of years ago. Sasha accepted with the grave wisdom of a seven-year-old her father's regret that they couldn't have as a pet one of the dogs she'd seen pictured on television, because they were as big as a horse.

Lyalin told Elaina not to wait up but she said she would. 'I shouldn't neglect a husband as brave and as famous as you.'

'You never have,' he said.

It was only when he was escorted away from the president's private apartment to the Kremlin's small viewing theatre, where Ilya Savich was waiting, that Lyalin realized they were going to watch the premier of the official film of the Baikal caves. They did so with champagne already poured and the open bottle on the table between them, but neither finished their first glass. They didn't speak, either, until the end when the president said: 'That is almost totally beyond belief!'

'It was astonishing,' agreed Lyalin. During the film he'd actually thought his story to the children scarcely seemed an exaggeration after all.

'Tell me about it as we walk,' ordered Savich.

They didn't hurry through the echoing corridors, with only occasional attendants or guards, and Lyalin had virtually finished his account by the time they reached the dining room and the already prepared table. There was vodka with the beluga and Georgian red with the quail.

'What's the latest situation?' demanded the president.

'Possibly 300 cases here, in Moscow,' reported Lyalin. 'About the same, maybe a little more, in Odessa. Could be as high as 1,500 in Gorky. More than that, an estimated 2,000, in Novosikirsk. What we don't have even the vaguest estimate of is how many there might be out in the countryside. It could be thousands more.'

'And there's no precautions that can be taken?'

'None.'

Savich said: 'The IMF and the World Bank are insisting on auditing the Finance Ministry's figures. They're clearly suspicious that the inflation figures have been manipulated.'

'Can we meet their target?'

'Not by about two per cent. We're going to need all the pressure America can exert.'

'Do we have any promises from Washington?'

'No commitment I can rely on. I'm sending a finance delegation, headed by the minister, to try to get more from their Treasury Secretary next week.'

'Publicly announced?'

'Definitely not! Which brings me to what I didn't want to happen. How was the situation in Irkutsk allowed to arise?'

'I was at the caves, organizing their clearing. I didn't know any media had arrived – or that she'd organized a conference – until I walked in on it.'

'What's the impending breakthrough she promised?'

'There was something that couldn't be understood from two of the Iultin victims, before we went to Washington . . .' began Lyalin, but abruptly stopped, disjointed recollections flooding in upon him. Intertwined with all the arguments he'd endured with Raisa Orlov about what should and should not be shared, the names of those two victims, Oleg Vasilevich Nedorub and Gennardi Varlomovich Markelov, kept recurring until his memory wasn't disjointed any more.

'What is it?' frowned Savich.

'Something I've remembered: need to check further,' apologized Lyalin. 'As I was saying, there was something in those two she left her staff here trying to analyse and identify. She's being very secretive but as I understand it she expects to find a guide to what it was from the bodies we brought back.'

The other man remained frowning. 'By "being very secretive" are you suggesting she's refusing to tell you, the minister to whom she's responsible?'

'It's not a harmonious relationship,' allowed Lyalin, reluctant to concede the woman's rejection of his authority.

The president pushed his plate away, sipping his wine. 'She's written, asking to see me personally.'

To suggest the president agree and directly order Raisa Orlov to conform would be a *total* admission of her rejection, Lyalin accepted. 'What are you going to do?'

'What would you have me do?

'I haven't given her the financial reasons for our co-operating as fully as we are. Which in my opinion – in the

360

circumstances of this disease – we'd scientifically need to do whether there was a financial pressure or not,' said Lyalin.

'Neither should you. Nor will I,' decided the other man. 'Her function is strictly scientific. Ours is political. The division should remain that way. I'll tell her any contact with the presidency has to be through you. I'll copy the reply to you, so there won't be any misunderstanding.'

The man was supporting him and his position, Lyalin recognized. 'I think I should return to Washington as soon as possible. I only regard this as a short briefing visit.'

Savich nodded. 'Stay long enough to address Cabinet tomorrow. First I'll show them the film.'

'I'd like to take copies back with me to America. To distribute before we make it publicly available.'

'Yes,' agreed Savich. 'Let's not have any more premature releases.'

Fort Detrick came under siege within two hours of its identification and helicopter became the only convenient, uninterrupted way of their getting in or out. It was, anyway, how they came in from Andrews Air Force base. Without any discussion, Geraldine moved into Stoddart's quarters, relegating hers to being a dressing room with an additional spare shower. Despite the tiredness from nothing more than half sleep throughout the non-stop journey from Siberia, Geraldine only managed four hours proper rest, leaving their bed and Stoddart, bubbling soft snores, before dawn.

Accepting that he was probably trying to compensate for past failings, Geraldine very quickly acknowledged that Walter Pelham didn't appear to have overlooked anything during their absence. There were case history precis from within the United States, Japan, Australia, Austria and France, where the fatality period of the illness was unquestionably extending – with total files upon those victims for whom he'd ordered autopsy tissue samples sent for precisely dedicated research – and progress notes where he'd asked for comparable information from India, Canada and America. He'd also ordered ornithological autopsies from all the sites

361

within the affected countries where there was a correlation between human outbreaks and large-scale bird deaths.

Geraldine was fully up to date by the time Pelham arrived, able to discuss in detail the cases he'd specifically chosen for further Fort Detrick examination, and agreed with the austere director that the evidence of the illness becoming prolonged was significant. She, in turn, went through in matching minutiae what she hoped to learn from what had come from Siberia, welcoming his assurance that there were specialists among his now greatly expanded staff for virtually every test and experiment she was initially suggesting. Pelham remained with her, occasionally offering suggestions, when she dictated her various requests to the various scientific dedications from which she hoped they would at last be able to create a composite. She triplicated the examination she wanted on the bats, rats and dog-like carcase between ornithology, veterinary and entomology and duplicated the faeces and bat-dropping samples between the bird and animal experts. There was also duplication between botanists and entomologists in the tests she asked for on the grasses and vegetation she'd recovered. Her final instruction was to orthodontists and orthopaedists to whom she sent the bones that had littered the cave floor.

With self-imposed deadlines she began her own autopsies at once, initially seeking confirmation, not quick discoveries. Pathology director Barry Hooper and Duncan Littlejohn, the laboratory chief, worked with her and from the audible murmur through the sound-connected observation gallery she knew it was crowded with people wanting their first physical sight of the prehistoric bodies.

The elementary concentration was external. Geraldine took no longer frozen scrapings from beneath the toe as well as the fingernails of a male, illness-aged body before paring away bone from each hand and foot. She cut away a lot of the abundant hair, clearing space from which to scalpel off her skin specimens, and extended the hair sampling from the nasal and ear passages. She hesitated, remembering the undertaking eventually to return her four bodies visually externally intact,

362

and removed two unseen, rear molars, as well as taking a lot of mouth and nasal passage swabs. The grinding function teeth were greatly worn away from what she guessed to be gnawing on the cave bones.

As the body fell open with her thorax to pubis incision, Hooper beside her said: 'There's no question it's the same,' which Geraldine thought scientifically premature although not in any doubt herself, visibly confronted by the obvious osteoporosis. Each of the organs – commencing with the heart – that she placed into the specimen containers offered in sequence by Littlejohn was sponged by age and once again her probing finger went easily into spinal and shoulder bone. So rapidly had the body frozen that no blood had dissipated or separated into serum. It remained puddled in post-mortem lividity at the shoulders and buttocks where the man had died lying upon his back, enabling Geraldine to drain at least a litre. It was only when Geraldine was taking undischarged faeces from the bowel that it occurred to her to take semen from both testes, reflecting on the sort of cloning, lost-world-Tarzan-meets-Frankenstein hysteria that the encircling paparazzi would generate if they ever discovered the sampling.

Geraldine worked just as methodically – although just as quickly – upon the remains of a skeletal male child who had been in the same group and was therefore most likely the son of the adult upon whom she had just operated. The relationship would be the easiest genetic comparison. She matched the removal of every organ with that of the adult male and recorded that there was no spongeousness in any bone she tested, before removing some for further analyses.

Her timetable dictated that Geraldine stop after obtaining sufficient comparable organs, although she remained suited when they moved to the adjoining laboratories for her to take and pack the slides and tissue samples to ship back, with her dictated instructions, to England.

She emerged from the research buildings fifteen minutes ahead of the estimate she'd given Stoddart in her pre-dawn note. Stoddart was waiting. So was the helicopter, its engines whining on warm up. Built to be conveniently – and safely – away from the main buildings, the helicopter pad was in faraway view of the cameramen and there was a surge of movement at their recognized appearance. They were too far away for the shouted questions to reach them, drowned anyway by the rotor noise. It took three journeys and the help of two porters to load everything aboard.

As they lifted off Stoddart said: 'Find anything you didn't expect?'

'We obviously didn't expose ourselves directly,' said Geraldine. 'But there was a remotely measured olfactory test: they've got a gizmo normally used to detect poison gas. Seems the smell of these guys was indescribable.'

'Always a bastard getting efficient showers in prehistoric caves,' said Stoddart.

The panoply of power fitted Peter Reynell as perfectly as his Savile Row suits, which he was profoundly glad to be wearing again instead of the sometimes odorous but supremely effective fancy dress of the past week. It was a waistcoated dark-blue pinstripe when he emerged on to a journalist-crushed Lord North Street refusing any questions ('What I have to say today has to be said to Parliament') but allowing ample time for the photographers for whom he staged a doorstep kiss on the cheek of the immaculately coiffeured, Dior-dressed Henrietta. Science was not a portfolio which warranted armed protection, but as much as in anticipation of impending change as against demented attention, the personal detective whom he so far only knew as John and who had been at Heathrow airport after the overnight flight was ready beside the waiting ministry Rover, keeping the jostling throng at bay. The chauffeur who had replaced his regular driver also belonged to the police protection unit, trained in high-speed pursuit evasion and avoidance. As they drove out in front of the parliament building Reynell thought, gratefully, that the days of his walking or running in the hope of being recognized and snapped were gone forever. But with man-of-the-street modesty prominent on his already planned

364

public persona, he filled the short journey discovering the new driver's name to be Charles and that both he and John were married and made a mental note to get their children's birthdays, for cards and small presents to be sent.

He used the congestion of ministerial cars to disembark from his own at the gated Whitehall entrance to walk the final short length of Downing Street, intentionally hesitating on the doorstep of the prime minister's official – and soon to be his – residence for more photographers and film crews, smilingly shaking his head to all but one of the shouted queries, fortunately recognizing the TV questioner and able to flatter the man by addressing him by name to thank him for the enquiry and assure him that he felt absolutely fine.

There was a surge of welcome-back handshakes in the antechamber to the Cabinet Room and those who missed him there surrounded him inside before the entrance of Simon Buxton, whose first act was also to offer his hand. There was no other item on the Cabinet agenda. With so much rehearsal Reynell was able to make his word perfect presentation at the same time as examining and reflecting upon the men around the huge, appropriately coffin-shaped table, aware how frightened of surviving so many would be once his leadership was confirmed. A wholesale, even bloody purge would be necessary, both to rid himself of Buxton's ineffective sycophants and show from the very beginning how unyieldingly ruthless he was going to be.

Buxton's suggestion for them to drive together to the House of Commons was an obvious and desperate effort by the man to gain fading recognition by association, but Reynell agreed. One of the major decisions reached during an hour-long telephone strategy conversation that morning with Lord Ranleigh was the initial benefit of continued magnanimity.

During the short drive, using the Foreign Office exit, Buxton said: 'I've talked with Dempsey.'

'Yes,' said Reynell, non-committally.

'I'm grateful.'

'It's very satisfactory, all round.'

365

'How long, do you imagine?'

'I don't know. It should be very smooth, now that everyone understands.'

'I'm glad,' said Buxton. 'That everyone understands, I mean.'

Having made what he considered one concession, Reynell delayed his entry into the actual chamber until after the other man, refusing to share a moment rare in parliamentary history of unanimous, all-party admiration and respect. There was a confetti of waved Order Papers from every side of the House and a rumble of 'Hear, Hear's' and 'Aye's' that reminded Reynell of the muttering of Ol'khon's volcano and even, against tradition, a scattering of open applause which the Speaker did nothing to curb. Reynell glanced up to see Henrietta had changed into more colourful Versace and accepted that when he became premier his wife would elect herself to be even more of a fashion icon than she already was.

His statement to the House was longer than that he'd earlier given to Cabinet and, anticipating the question, Reynell made the point that he did not, at that moment, know precisely what the Russian scientific advisor had been referring to by her Irkutsk remark. 'Conditions, as you will have appreciated by what you have already seen and heard, were extremely difficult: it will take a little time for all the findings and research to be brought together.' He was flying back to Washington the following day to rejoin the returning Russian minister and the rest of the crisis committee and would inform the House – here he turned, indicating James Buxton – as soon as there was an explanation. What he could assure the House was that under the supervision of the country's chief scientific officer, Professor Geraldine Rothman, an enormous amount of material and information had been collected from the prehistoric complex and was at that moment under examination. He refused to offer any false promises, but personally believed progress would be made from what had been found in Siberia.

The rush to go publicly on record congratulating and

praising Reynell ('great bravery . . . statesman . . . selfless commitment . . . gratitude not just of this country but of the world') was practically as fervent as it had been in the Cabinet Room antechamber, and knowing she would want it, Reynell waited for Henrietta to come down from the public gallery for them to leave the House together in shared glory.

William Dempsey and Ralph Prendergast were among the guests at that night's celebration dinner at Lord North Street, their arrival noted by political rune readers as evidence of their survival. Henrietta was brilliantly in charge and during the meal Reynell guessed that being London's leading society hostess was another role Henrietta saw for herself.

It was Henrietta who asked if she could come to his bedroom that night, as she had when he'd arrived in the early hours of that same morning, and after orchestrating their sexual performance she said: 'How would you feel about my coming back to Washington with you?'

Reynell looked sideways at her, genuinely surprised. 'I don't think so. I'm working.'

'You fucking that woman, Amanda whatever-her-name-is?'

'Henrietta! What *is* this!' If it hadn't been so unthinkable he would have imagined there was some jealousy.

She shrugged. 'We're going to have to be even more discreet, aren't we? Respectable, even. Now that we've made it we don't want to spoil it by becoming careless and being caught out.'

Whose view was that, her's or her father's, wondered Reynell. He hoped neither of them were going to become tiresome.

An entire first floor wing of Blair House had been given over to a secretariat for the much proclaimed environmental conference, although Darryl Matthews and Harold Norris had so far remained the only operational officers of the president's special task force that Stoddart officially headed. Which was the major – virtually the only – problem that confronted Stoddart when he arrived.

'We've got the best bureaucratic swamp you've ever seen,' complained Matthews. 'We've got no chiefs but twice as many Indians as beat Custer, firing off faxes and memos and emails that we've initiated, in every which way around the world and an answering blizzard blowing back at us. We're buried, Jack. We don't get some more people, the world's going to be burned to a cinder by global warming before we can start talking about it.'

'What happened to the promised middle level staff?' asked Stoddart, with enforced quietness.

'We were hoping you could tell us,' said Norris.

'What's Spencer say?'

'That it's in hand but that there's got to be budgetary agreement. That it can't be put against any presidential contingency funding.'

Stoddart was more outraged at the blatant obviousness of the sideways shunting arrogance than at the obstruction itself, which he'd anyway expected in some form or another. A secretary answered Spencer's direct line but Spencer took the telephone the moment he knew who was calling.

'The President must be pleased with the coverage?' opened Stoddart, conversationally.

'There's never been anything like it,' enthused Spencer. 'Phenomenal. We need to keep it going. You got something new?'

'That's why I'm calling,' said Stoddart. 'I'm across at Blair. You think you and Carson can run over?'

'Give us ten,' said Spencer, the lift audible in his voice.

Stoddart later decided they must literally have run at least part of the way because the two men arrived in under Spencer's estimate, despite the delay in locating Stoddart on the upper floor, not downstairs where they'd expected him to be.

'What have we got?' demanded Carson Boddington, eagerly.

'We're up and running globally now, right?' said Stoddart.

'Cosmically,' smiled Spencer.

'So here's how I think we beef up the President's environmental commitment,' said Stoddart. 'I want you, Carson, to call a press conference, right now! They'll come running, just like you guys, when they know it's me. We'll make the main evening news, every channel. I'll point out the budgetary problems Darryl's told me about and invite other countries to contribute, not just money, but people in the numbers we need to get the conference off the ground, because at the moment we don't stand a chance of getting anything set up this side of nowhere, nowhen. And the delay will get even longer, waiting for congressional allocation. This way it'll be truly international! How's that sound?' Stoddart saw both Matthews and Norris were remaining impassive.

'Whoa!' said Spencer, urgently. 'We gotta lot to talk about here.'

'What?' demanded Stoddart, ingenuously. 'There's no contingency funding and without contingency funding we can't put into place a publicly proclaimed presidential commitment. I've just suggested a way around it, although it'll dilute America's leadership but like you said, Paul, everything's being shared cosmically now so that scarcely matters.'

'You only just got back,' reminded Spencer. 'I haven't had time to tell you. Or Darryl. The President knows what you're saying, about congressional delays; doesn't like it any more than you . . .'

'. . . So what's he going to do about it?' persisted Stoddart.

'Re-allocate,' improvised the presidential advisor. 'That's the route he's going, re-allocation.'

'So there *is* going to be funding available!'

'That's the last I heard. The President's been flat out on this, coming to Alaska like he did . . .'

'When do you think you can concentrate his mind on this?' pressed Stoddart.

'When I know the needs—' started Spencer.

'Nothing's changed since the memorandum we sent you specifically setting out our staffing needs,' cut off Matthews.

'I'll get back to you,' promised Spencer.

'Tomorrow,' suggested Stoddart. 'We could really get things underway as early as tomorrow if we knew the money was available, couldn't we, Darryl? You know the people you want to bring aboard, don't you?'

'I've got the list ready and waiting,' agreed Matthews. 'Tomorrow would be real good.'

'Tomorrow,' agreed a tight-faced Spencer, blinking against the brief fog of anger at being so totally backed into a cul de sac.

In Moscow Raisa Orlov's eyes also blurred, although in far greater anger in her natural predisposition to find conspiracy in every opposition. Her immediate reaction was to rip the president's refusal into as many pieces as she could, but reason – and calculation – prevailed. Gregori Lyalin was on his way back to Washington and over such a distance communication and misunderstandings were inevitable.

Thirty-One

Henry Partington didn't like his carefully polished plans backfiring and from the sound of it this one was mistiming far too loudly. 'He'd do it, of course.' *Anyone any ideas how to stop the son of a bitch?*

'Stoddart knows his publicity value; has done for years,' said Richard Morgan, before Spencer could answer. 'He'll do it just like that –' he snapped his fingers – 'unless Paul's got some idea he hasn't shared with us beyond apparently offering the funding already.'

'I said what I did to stall him,' insisted Spencer. 'And there might be one way.'

'What?' demanded the president. *It better be good: you shouldn't have committed me.*

'You do it first: pre-empt him,' suggested Spencer, cautiously. 'We put the request to Congress the day after you announced the conference. Now accuse them of prevaricating up on the Hill: playing financial politics instead of reacting with the speed you're showing, giving industrialized countries the lead.'

'What's the general feeling?' asked Partington. *I'm not convinced: persuade me.*

'That would bring you down to their level,' said Morgan. 'Your stance has got to be way above political squabbling. You're the world's leader, leading. Everyone else has to follow.'

Partington nodded, enjoying the phrasing. 'Carson?'

'It's negative. Messy,' judged Boddington. 'The only thing Mr and Mrs Six Pack in Des Moines are thinking about is how you're going to stop them waking up tomorrow

371

morning one hundred and ten years old and dying by the end of the week.'

'I think you're right.' *Not a good one, Paul.*

'Make the same journey by a different route,' said Spencer. 'Declare the funding from contingency *because* Congress haven't responded. Say the need to get things moving *is* too great to wait. Congress gets the flak and sure as hell will rush through whatever budget is asked, and the President's the man who whipped them into line. All that and a platform for our people in the gubernatorials to argue that Congress needs to be put under the control of the party of responsibility.'

'I like that! That's very good. What do you think, Carson?' *This is the way I want to go.*

'Very positive. Precisely the right message,' said the press spokesman.

'Dick?'

'It'll work, I guess,' begrudged the Chief of Staff, acknowledging defeat.

'That's how we'll do it,' decided Partington. 'Anything else?'

'Lyalin's getting in later, with copies of the official film.'

'We going to get a steer on what that woman meant?'

'That's the way we're supposed to be working,' said Spencer.

'Don't like the fact that the Fort Detrick group have split up,' complained the president. 'Get Lyalin's thinking on that.' Bringing the meeting to a close, the man added: 'Stay for a moment, will you Paul?'

As the door closed behind everyone else, Partington said: 'Relatives' lawyers don't seem to think our compensation package is good enough.'

'Usual arm wrestling?' suggested Spencer.

'Unless they come up with something to make a case.'

James Olsen sounded loud and clear in Spencer's mind. 'I'm sure that's not going to happen.'

'How sure are you sure?'

'Very sure indeed, Mr President.'

Partington smiled the smile of a contented man.

*   *   *

Gregori Lyalin gave specific instructions throughout the
embassy, including the switchboard, that he didn't want
to be disturbed and even locked the door of the allocated
office in which, carefully annotated, he'd retained copies of
everything that had come originally from Russia, as well as all
the records of the Fort Detrick scientists and the Blair House
sessions, up to the moment of their leaving Washington for
Siberia.

He first found what he wanted in the transcript of the last
combined meeting before their departure, when the scientific
group had come down from Maryland. There were three
further references – or rather a lack of references – in
the transcript of Fort Detrick sessions and he got his final
confirmation from going back to what he and Raisa Orlov
had originally brought with them from Moscow.

In every exchange, Raisa Orlov had only ever talked about
the tissue finding on Oleg Vasilevich Nedorub, too indistinct
to be identifiable. Nowhere had she spoken – or offered
specimen for Fort Detrick analysis – of the much more
positive trace from the aged body of the other Iultin victim,
project leader Gennardi Varlomovich Markelov.

Lyalin eased the cramp from his back, gazing down at the
incontrovertible evidence of the woman's blatant, deceptive
obstruction. It had to be the basis for her publicly promised
breakthrough, progress she had lyingly denied from him. To
say nothing would condone what she had done, as if he were a
party to it. Worse if she and her team *didn't* develop whatever
she believed her discovery to be or to delay other scientists
with better facilities or different approaches in finding the key
to what had become a global pandemic. Lyalin had never before
felt such a confusion of emotions, swinging the pendulum from
guilt, embarrassment, remorse, anger and responsibility.

He was careful to use the Russian embassy's secure communication link to reach Raisa Orlov's institute in Moscow
and because it was a minister personally calling, the permanently apprehensive switchboard put the call through to
Raisa's working level.

373

Raisa was engrossed and physically enclosed in the protection necessary for the autopsy upon the fifth of the Baikal recovered bodies and initially refused even to listen to the words coming into her headset from the observation gallery. When the imploring demand finally penetrated, she snapped back: 'Tell him I'll call him back, like I'm going to call everybody back when I'm ready.' She hadn't planned it to be, but such dismissal of an actual minister contributed another anecdote to the Raisa Orlov legend.

A disbelieving Darryl Matthews and Harold Norris were still going through the names of their intended and now financially approved organizational level when Paul Spencer thrust bleak-faced into their Blair House environmental enclave for the second time in less than an hour.

'More good news?' greeted Stoddart, lightly.

'No,' said Spencer. 'There's just been a message from Detrick, for the French minister. Guy Dupuy's collapsed . . .'

Thirty-Two

B y the time Stoddart's helicopter returned to Fort Detrick, with the French science minister an unexpected additional passenger, Guy Dupuy was in isolation and the brain swelling established by an MRI scan had confirmed the encephalitis for which he was already on fluid replacement treatment. The prognosis was for a full recovery, although any future working involvement with the science group was doubtful. The virus had also been stain-located in Dupuy's blood and urine. Everything he'd taken and worn during the Baikal expedition had been scientifically scoured for the Ixodas tick that infected the man. None had been found, but there had been other discoveries within Fort Detrick as intriguing as the intestinal infestation.

Geraldine asked for the meeting to talk about her concern at their now further reduced research assessment capabilities, but before she could Walter Pelham hurried in with his fresh disclosure.

'Ticks?' queried Stoddart.

'Two separate species our entomologists have never encountered before, although they're sure they're of the Ixodas genus,' confirmed Pelham. 'We've gone back to the Smithsonian and to London.'

'Where – how – were they found?' asked Stoddart.

'One was among the specimens the Listvyanka entomologist collected from the caves,' said the director.

'The other?' persisted Stoddart.

'On the nasal and ear hair Geraldine removed yesterday from the Baikal males. Both species are microscopic: they were only detected under electron magnification. They're certainly too minute to consider any sort of dissection. We're looking for more on the female bodies now, of course.'

'How many of these unknown ticks have your people lifted, so far?' asked Geraldine.

'Eight,' replied the man at once. 'Five of one, three of another. And there's the three that you brought back, with the other specimens.'

'That's enough,' prompted Geraldine.

'For what?' asked Stoddart

It was Geraldine who answered. 'They would have been frozen, like everything else at Baikal. So would any infection they carry. They can be introduced into laboratory animals.'

'Already being done,' assured Pelham.

'You said you'd found some more worms, in the females?' said Stoddart, picking up on what else Pelham had told them. 'You got enough to test those the same way?'

'That's being done, too,' said the director.

'We're talking only about Baikal,' reminded Stoddart. 'Even if it is important, it can't help with Alaska or the Antarctic, can it?'

'The special teams we sent to both did lift plant and insect material,' said Pelham. 'They're still sending stuff back. We're repeating every experiment – going back through everything we've already done – to see if we've missed anything.'

'The climatic conditions in both would be close enough to what Baikal was like when our cave colony became infected and died,' reflected Stoddart.

'This could be real progress: and we're on top of it, right here,' said Pelham, unusually animated and anxious to ensure it was well established that the discoveries had been made at Fort Detrick.

'Which brings us to something that's worrying me,' said Geraldine. 'If it is significant, we've been lucky: incredibly so. But now that Dupuy's out and Raisa's in Moscow, how are we from now on going to be able to cope with everything coming in from outside?'

'Not at all if we try to do it ourselves, which would

376

be unscientifically stupid because we wouldn't know what we're looking for, beyond our own disciplines,' frowned Pelham, wondering if he'd missed whatever point the woman was making. 'It was helminthology which picked up the infestation, entomology that found the microscopic ticks. We've got to go on filtering specifics through their individual specialisations: let them isolate the inconsistencies or the comparisons, before passing it on.'

The logic was embarrassingly obvious and Geraldine *was* embarrassed. She'd let herself get too close: too hands-on, imagining only she and the inner group capable of reaching a judgment. Relentlessly Geraldine forced the honesty on. Not her *and* the inner group. Only her. Subconsciously – maybe not even as unaware as that – she'd conceitedly promoted herself the indispensable arbiter of everything: a scientific Solomon. She said: 'You sure there's enough people here to handle the amount of delegation?'

'We've got *carte blanche*,' said Pelham. 'If one particular section starts being overwhelmed, we'll bring in more people. As simple as that.'

'Seems the obvious way to handle the workload,' said Stoddart.

Pelham said: 'Anything yet from Washington about Raisa's claims?'

'Lyalin hadn't shown by the time we left and she hasn't responded to any of the direct messages to Moscow,' said Stoddart. 'Amanda is going to call if Lyalin makes contact tonight.'

'We still supposedly working together or has Moscow pulled out?' demanded the installation director.

'Lyalin wouldn't be back if they'd pulled out,' judged Stoddart.

'What are we going to do about what we've turned up here in the last twenty-four hours?' asked Pelham.

'Let Blair House know, so Lyalin can be told,' proposed Geraldine at once. 'Nothing's happened to change this being a combined investigation.' It was good to be responding properly, as part of a team. It wasn't to be long before she realized how similar her thinking had initially been to that of Raisa Orlov.

In the thirty-two hours since her return the autopsies had been completed on all the Siberian bodies and the unspecific enzyme discovered in eighteen of them, all but three more pronounced than it had been in Gennardi Markelov.

'The enzyme's the key,' Raisa insisted, using the sexually as well as the professionally-dependant Grenkov as her sounding board; he knew better than anyone the danger of re-telling anything she ever told him.

'We don't know *how* it attacks,' argued Sergei Grenkov. 'Let's test it on animals before you make any public announcement. You've not got enough to make any claims yet.'

'It caused the complete annihilation of the Neanderthal species,' dramatically declared Raisa.

Grenkov gazed at her in total astonishment. '*What!*'

'The Neanderthal became extinct,' said Raisa. 'No one, until now, knows why.'

'What's that got to do with what we're involved in now?' groped the worried Grenkov.

Raisa looked at him, pityingly. 'Everything! This illness is what destroyed an entire ancestral species!'

'You've got no scientific justification – no evidence – for saying that,' disputed the man, with rare courage. This was irrational: deluded.

'The world's seen the Baikal bodies.'

'Neolithic, not Neanderthal.'

'There's no scientific evidence to contradict me.'

'It'll be enough just to identify the enzyme and how it works, so that we can reverse the infection,' pleaded Grenkov.

'No!' rejected Raisa. It was time she dispensed with Sergei Grenkov. He'd even become disappointing in bed. 'I've no intention whatsoever of letting this be taken away from me.'

Grenkov jerked his head towards the stacked, unopened folders on the two side tables of Raisa's office. 'There's an enormous amount to do. Let's try to do it – see what's here – while we give the animal tests time.'

'Only until we get the test results,' conceded Raisa, acknowledging the sense in at least looking through what had come in from outside. 'If they're inconclusive I'll make the announcement.'

'I want to make it clear – and I wish you to make it even clearer to your respective governments – that this had no official sanction,' said Gregori Lyalin. He spoke as if personally addressing Peter Reynell.

No one responded, although Reynell's mind was leapfrogging ahead.

'All I can do, on behalf of my own government, is apologize,' Lyalin stumbled on. Lying on the table between them, like a taunt, was the Moscow-intended research that Gerard Buchemin had personally brought back on an early morning helicopter from Fort Detrick.

'It would reflect very badly upon your government if it were to become public,' said Reynell. It had to be turned into an advantage – a favour – that he could call upon to be returned sometime in the future.

'I fully understand that,' accepted Lyalin.

'I'm not sure how much trust Dr Rothman will have in any future working relationship; if there can *be* any future professional relationship,' persisted Reynell.

'Which compounds a problem,' said Amanda, following Reynell's lead. 'Dr Orlov's remarks in Irkutsk – and her having gone back to Moscow instead of returning here – have already attracted a lot of media speculation about the co-operation.'

'Had you intended her eventually to come back here?' asked Reynell, seeing his opening. He supposed Amanda would need the president's approval and Buchemin would have to consult with Paris, but a diplomatic difficulty would be avoided by their agreeing to the woman's return.

'I think it depends upon your acceptance rather than my intention,' said Lyalin.

379

Perfect, thought Reynell. 'What has occurred has been unfortunate but I don't think it should be worsened by allowing the media speculation to intensify. Professor Orlov should be told not to make any more public statements without the knowledge of colleagues with whom she is supposed to be liaising – colleagues to whom an apology is owed – and brought back here as soon as possible to share the importance of whatever it is she believes she has discovered. As a measure of our good faith, I also suggest that the material that Monsieur Buchemin brought back with him from Fort Detrick should be relayed to Moscow, in case it contributes to that discovery.'

Lyalin looked uneasily towards the head-bent notetakers. Moscow was being patronized and Reynell would emerge in the records as the broad-thinking statesman befitting his soon-to-be-crowned leadership. It was still, Lyalin acknowledged, far better than their attitude might have been and hopefully wouldn't endanger the impending visit of the Russian financial delegation. He guessed it would require a positive directive from the Russian White House to make Raisa Orlov apologize, but what she'd done justified being put before the president. 'I think I can say my government would be grateful if that were to be the feeling of everyone represented here.'

'But I agree that the situation should not be allowed to get out of proportion,' said Buchemin.

'Why don't we convene again later today?' suggested Amanda.

Neither Henry Partington nor the Elysée Palace were prepared to agree so quickly – both seeking reciprocal advantage, which Reynell used for further benefit – but there were a lot of separate developments, which by initially remaining unconnected caused some excitement, conflicting confusion and even despair.

The most immediate came the afternoon of the Blair House meeting, when haematologists at Fort Detrick isolated from the recovered blood of the Siberian bodies an

380

enzyme that matched that in the newly provided tissue of Gennardi Markelov, which kept Geraldine Rothman on the telephone to geneticists in England for thirty minutes before helicoptering yet again to Washington to fly specimens back, this time for very specific analysis.

Thirty-Three

The first bit of what was eventually to become an important piece of the scattered jigsaw arrived at Fort Detrick more as a correction. The doubt of a brilliant twenty-seven-year-old sea mammal expert at Japan's Oceanography Institute that the whales washed up at Kita-Kyushu, Hamamatsu and Kanazawa and found floating off the island of Shikoku had all, in fact, died from influenza. Detailed autopsies conducted on three found evidence consistent with the disease but in two there were also indications of organ and bone degeneration that had caused the animals to suffocate where their frames had become too weakened to support their body weight, even supported by the sea's buoyancy.

The response to Pelham's requests for case history proof of death from the illness taking longer had been so great – from a total of eleven countries – that it needed computer analysis spread over days to confirm that the duration had definitely lengthened to an average of one month. That alone justified Geraldine's Air Force One hope of an intervention treatment period, but another commonality thrown up by computer comparison was that, additionally, eighty-five per cent of the victims suffered respiratory difficulties, up to and including pneumonia. At Geraldine's urging, requests were sent back to hospitals in Canberra, Tokyo, New Delhi, Vienna and Rome for body tissue specimens to be collected for further, specific medical comparison.

Quite separately, but from every one of those eleven responding countries, there also came matching ornithological reports of bird mortality so extensive that the term epidemic was common to all. So were the symptoms, among a wide

382

variety of species, of organ and bone ageing, and to a sufficient number of countries went new requests for tissue specimens.

To Walter Pelham's increasing satisfaction – although not immediately to any of their better understanding – a lot of the unexplained continued to be detected within Fort Detrick. The majority of the turds recovered from the cave floor proved to be animal and in all of them whole or parts of the unknown worm species were recovered. From the fur of the animal carcase, specially briefed veterinarians who might otherwise have overlooked them lifted both species of the microscopic tick, and in the bat droppings was located an enzyme practically indistinguishable from that in the blood of the cave dwellers. Strictly following their remit to search for the incongruous or unexplained, drafted-in paleobotanists matched unknown nothofagal pollen and seeds from bores sunk in the Antarctica and Alaska with unidentified seeds and actual, although never-before-seen, plants from the Baikail caves.

Although it was another first time oversight, Pelham's greatest satisfaction came from his pathologists' re-examination of the Antarctic and Alaskan victims. There were microscopic ticks on nine of the victims, including Morris Neilson and Chip Burke, both of whom had gone into the Antarctic field station with Jack Stoddart.

In every case they were in the nasal or respiratory passages.

'What's it amount to?' asked Stoddart, when Pelham announced the finding in the rescue party victims.

'What it always has been,' said Geraldine. 'A puzzle we haven't yet solved. But we're getting there.'

Henry Partington took the longest to agree the response to Raisa Orlov's withholding; his every move – or lack of it – calculated in staged priorities. It was essential to ratchet Russian nervousness up to its maximum to make Moscow beholden when he made what would appear not one but two sweeping gestures of political co-operation and into that carefully crafted scheme neatly fitted the opportunity finally to meet Peter Reynell on a future leader-to-leader basis as well as ensuring Amanda O'Connell's total and future loyalty.

An unwitting Paul Spencer was the initial cog, used to extend the invitation in front of Gregori Lyalin at the Blair House session at which Gerard Buchemin announced the Elysée acceptance, which left the equally unwitting Amanda to explain uncomfortably that she'd had no instruction from the White House and to convey the impression – heightened by the summons – that there remained serious American reluctance.

The official Russian film of the Baikal caves had either in part or in full occupied television and film channels over the preceding days – the French loudly proclaimed news of Guy Dupuy's illness the most recent replay reason – but although he'd been named, Peter Reynell had not been visibly identifiable from far too many others in his protective suit. To arrive separately from Amanda at the White House precisely at the time the Washington-based British journalists and television crews had been given, he excused himself from her by claiming a need to consult with London from the British embassy. Reynell entered grave-faced and head-shaking against the shouted questions. Amanda was already inside, in the Oval Office ante-room. They'd inventively slept together every night since Reynell's return from London and from her having kept nothing imaginable back from him in bed, he believed she would have at least hinted at the hidden purpose for this encounter if she'd known it.

Amanda said: 'Anything I should know about London's thinking?'

He shook his head, not having spoken to anyone apart from the embassy's dutifully media-alerting press section. 'What about you?'

She shook her head in return, not bothering to reply. Over the last few days she'd actually fantasized what a formidable political, as well as sexual couple, she and Reynell would have made. It would, she decided, have been a world-conquering combination. The cooling realism, confirmed

384

by watching his actions before his White House arrival on live CNN, was that Peter Reynell didn't want anyone sharing his parade.

The president wasn't at his specially adapted desk, backing on to the gardens, but deeper into the room, already seated in the high-backed, comfortably armed easy chair just as carefully carpentered to put him upon the same level as anyone seated in the lower, softer armchairs and sofas. He rose, briefly, to position them in their assigned seats.

'There'd seem to be more than one reason for our first meeting,' he opened, to Reynell. If the man's elevation to British premier was as inevitable as the London ambassador, as well as all the media, were predicting, it was important Reynell recognize from the outset who in the future would always occupy the master chair.

'Although not by any means our last, I hope,' said Reynell. It wasn't beyond speculation that he could have sat the man on his lap and innovated a world leader ventriloquist act.

'I hope that too.'

Your territory, your posturing, thought Reynell: so you lead.

Extremely confident, judged Partington. 'But before then we have more immediate things to discuss.'

'We have indeed,' agreed Reynell, unhelpfully. From the Nixon debacle he was very aware that he was talking in voice-recorded surroundings.

Clever, as well as confident, conceded Partington. It had been wise, quite apart from her other, future use, to have included Amanda. To her he said: 'What's your feeling about the withholding?'

'It went totally against the spirit and intent of what we were brought together to achieve,' said Amanda, as completely prepared and confident as Reynell. 'But I believe the Russian minister that it was personal, professional ambition, not officially sanctioned or ordered obstruction. Fort Detrick have not only caught up on that particular discovery but learned substantially more.' She nodded towards Reynell. 'I agree with the English minister that nothing worthwhile

385

could be achieved – indeed, it would fuel already over-fuelled public disquiet – if it were to become an open, diplomatic dispute.'

Reynell was tempted to come back into the discussion but decided he didn't have anything to prove to this man. Better – more productive – instead to let Amanda mark out the ground where hidden mines might be laid. He had, after all, to get Partington's agreement if there was going to be later, personal gratitude from Moscow.

Partington said: 'What about insisting the woman apologize?'

'No!' rejected Amanda, to the surprise of Reynell to whom she hadn't expressed the objection earlier. 'There'll be humiliation enough in her having to return, knowing that she's been caught like some exam-cheating kid. Making her apologize really is reducing it to school-yard level and Raisa Orlov *is* a world renowned scientist. Fort Detrick are getting a lot they don't understand and we might need her help, not her resentment.'

Time to come back in, judged Reynell. 'I totally agree. We might very well need whatever additionally the Russians get from their analysis of the cave findings. They might have something – the very catalyst – to make sense of everything that we're isolating here.' All this was obvious: school-yard level, to use Amanda's analogy. So what was the real reason for their being there? It hardly mattered. For the moment he'd benefited enough by being recognized as the future British leader by the President of the United States of America.

'So we just welcome her back, like nothing ever happened?' pressed Partington.

'No,' seized Reynell at once, eager to let the other man realize that he finally understood. 'She hasn't just been caught out here. She's been caught out in her own country and by delaying this long you've let Moscow know your . . .' he intentionally hesitated, for the heavy qualification, '. . . *our* feelings. Like Amanda says, Raisa Orlov's been humiliated enough.'

Partington shifted imperceptibly in his special seat, uncomfortable at being caught out himself. It was important to remember that the Englishman wasn't someone to be taken lightly. 'OK, then I agree,' he said, which he'd always intended to do. He smiled towards Reynell. 'I'm glad it's given us the opportunity to meet.'

'So am I,' said Reynell. 'I hope it's a long and successful relationship.'

'I hope so, too. I always think personal contact is important, particularly between our two countries. I'm going to enjoy our working together.'

As he left the White House, alone again and on foot for the benefit of an even greater number of cameras than there had been for his arrival, Reynell decided that he was at least an equal and probably a more adept manipulator than Henry Partington. He wondered why the man had asked Amanda to remain, but was sure he'd find out either in or out of bed later that night.

'What do you think of Britain's future leader?'

'We work well together,' Amanda said, amusing herself by her choice of words. She hadn't been led into this private study to provide a character reference for Peter Reynell. Why then?

'There doesn't seem to be any doubt that he'll get it.'

'That's what I understand.' Come on, give me a steer!

'So his future's decided, when this is all over.'

Better, thought Amanda, cautiously. 'It would seem so.'

'Have you considered yours?'

At last! 'Any thoughts I might have had are on the back burner, until this *is* over. It's far too important to be deflected from.'

Liar, thought Partington, unimpressed by the claimed dedication. 'Where did you see yourself, in those back-burner thoughts?'

Amanda's concentration was absolute. Partington wasn't a man to make offers without wanting something in return. His wife looked like Mother America at a weenie roast but there'd

387

never been any extra-marital rumours. There was always the first time, she supposed. 'State,' she said, bluntly. You want it, Mr President, you got it.

Partington nodded. 'That's where I see you, too. Particularly after how well you've conducted yourself over this.'

Don't be shy, Henry, thought Amanda. 'I appreciate your confidence. And this conversation.'

'There's a Russian delegation, lobbying our support for an IMF and World Bank bail-out.'

'Are we going to give it?' Amanda enjoyed the 'we'. She wasn't even going to have to get down on her knees!

'What do you think of the current Russian leadership?'

Testing time, Amanda recognized. 'Sound, given time. But it hasn't had that time, not yet. The alternative is a further slide back to communism, which I don't think is in our interests.'

'That's my feeling, too,' said Partington. 'You get on well with Lyalin?'

'Very.'

'I think Moscow should know we're doing them the favour they've asked for. Discreetly, of course.'

'Of course.'

'But that it wasn't an easy decision, after what their woman did.'

'I understand,' assured Amanda. 'So will Lyalin.'

The incumbent Secretary of State did not come to mind until Amanda was practically at Blair House and then her thought was that Robin Turner was a lucky asshole to have survived as long as he had. The difference, when she was in charge at Foggy Bottom, was going to be dramatic.

'So far, so good,' said Geraldine.

'We've only just ordered,' warned Stoddart.

'The waitress didn't recognize us.' It had been easier for Geraldine, getting unseen out of the British embassy. Stoddart had got through the media cordon around Blair House in the enclosed rear of a laundry truck. They'd arrived in Georgetown separately, the Italian restaurant corner table

388

booked by Geraldine in the name of Barton, her mother's maiden name.

Stoddart said: 'What are you going to do if someone asks for an autograph?'

'Give it, I suppose. And be bloody embarrassed doing it,' said Geraldine, responding to touch her wine glass against his. 'How's the conference agenda going?'

'We're calculating the necessary emission control targets for each country, before inviting their individual proposals. Then we'll work out agreeable compromises.'

'You're the greatest culprit.'

'We've set two and a half times what America agreed in Kyoto.'

'And promptly ignored. What's the point of bothering?'

'The President wants to make an environmental statement,' said Stoddart. 'It can be negotiated down by a third to satisfy industry, which will give us exactly the figure we want. That's how we'll make everyone happy.'

Geraldine grinned, raising her glass again. 'Here's to it working.'

'This time I've got the platform to see that it does: well enough, at least.'

Geraldine kept her glass raised. 'Here's to that, too.'

Both were aware of the closer attention when the waitress returned with their salads. Stoddart said: 'I warned you!'

'She's not sure.'

'It won't be the same girl next time: it'll be someone else, checking,' predicted Stoddart. 'Anything from England?'

Stoddart's environmental meeting had been the reason for that day's helicopter trip: Geraldine had hitched a ride to check for responses to what now numbered twenty-three separate but specific test analyses she'd demanded. She said: 'I spoke, by telephone. Three more days at the earliest.'

The man who served their steaks was obviously the manager. He smiled in recognition and said: 'Hi! Good to have you with us.'

Stoddart said: 'We're trying for a quiet meal. You think you can help us?'

'I'll do my best,' said the man. 'Could we get a photograph, before you go?'

'Providing we don't have to leave in a hurry,' said Geraldine.

After the man left, nodding confirmation to the staff gathered at the serving area, Stoddart said: 'I told you!'

'I can live with it,' said Geraldine.

'That's become pretty easy, hasn't it?' said Stoddart. 'Living with it, I mean.'

Geraldine stopped eating. 'What, exactly, *do* you mean?'

'Our living together,' qualified Stoddart.

'Emergency circumstances,' said Geraldine.

'Is that how you think it is? Why it's easy?'

'No,' she said, holding his look.

'Neither do I. You think it will be the same when the emergency's over?'

'I don't know. Maybe we should give it a try, to find out?'

'That sounds a good idea to me,' said Stoddart.

'You quite sure?'

'Sure enough.'

'I think I am, too.'

They didn't make a lot of conversation for the rest of the meal. It was only when they posed for Polaroids – swapping around so that each missed-out photographer could be included – that they were recognized by other diners. As Stoddart hurried Geraldine out, someone began to clap and at once every occupied table joined in but they managed to reach the door without being intercepted.

Geraldine said: 'Jesus! That was *embarrassing*!'

Stoddart said: 'Think what the wedding will be like,' and immediately wished he hadn't.

Soberly, Geraldine said: 'Let's take things a step at a time, shall we?'

Amanda lay with her head cushioned on Reynell's naked stomach, although she'd turned to look up at him. 'I thought that was what Partington was going to ask me to do.'

'Would you have done?'

'Of course,' she said, honestly.

'You didn't tell me why he asked you to stay?'

'No, I didn't,' she agreed.

Reynell waited. When she didn't continue he said: 'You happy with it?'

'I think so.'

'Good. Anything I can do?'

'In the future, maybe.'

'Any time.' He'd been wrong, believing he could seduce her in every way.

'Will I have all the telephone numbers?'

'Oh yes,' promised Reynell. 'You'll have all the numbers.' Sexually each was as innovative as the other, but there were some things that he preferred in Amanda over Henrietta.

Raisa's entomology department had only detected the second of the two unidentified ticks and the bowel and gut infestation from re-examination prompted by the passed on Fort Detrick analysis and Gregori Lyalin's written – and copied to the president – summons for her to return to America to rejoin the scientific investigation.

'They're getting ahead!' she declared.

'Raisa!' implored Grenkov. 'We've found unknown ticks in vegetation our paleobotanists have never seen before. Using the enzyme from the bodies we've synthesized the illness into three chimpanzees and our geneticists think it's attacking genes to a pattern . . .'

'It's not genetic! It's viral!' insisted the woman.

'Wait until we've finished the tests!'

'No!' refused Raisa.

The synthesized enzyme had also been introduced into five chimpanzees at Fort Detrick, all of which were at varying stages of carefully monitored death. The daily shipment of tissue samples for genetic testing in England were additional to the twenty-three already ordered by Geraldine. They were also being duplicated by American geneticists.

391

From its Geneva headquarters, the World Health Organisation warned that the global figure of two and a half million people having already died from the ageing illness should be considered a conservative estimate.

Thirty-Four

I t took a full day for two specifically assigned switchboard operators to return all the logged calls. Raisa Orlov selected the publications and Moscow-based TV bureaux – predominantly American and English – to contact personally. She chose the largest of the institute's lecture rooms. Every seat was occupied and nearer the podium journalists were standing two deep.

Raisa prepared her presentation with the care she'd given to her personal invitations. There were huge drawings as well as greatly enhanced laboratory photographs of the octagonally shaped, green stain reactive enzyme recovered from the body of Gennardi Varlomovich Markelov matching the samples from the cave bodies, actual photographs of which, enlarged to twice life size, were on display stands at the rear of the dais she occupied, quite alone. There were also illustrations of the intertwined DNA double helix and quite separately three drawn representations of telomeres in the process of age degeneration to supplement more greatly enhanced laboratory photographs of the actual gene cap. The only break in the illustration and photographic backcloth was for the enormous slide screen Raisa could operate from the lectern at which she stood, laser wand in hand to point up examples she intended to make.

'A short while ago, near the site of the most important discovery in anthropological history, I promised important revelations,' began Raisa, quietening the room. 'Today I intend to make them.'

There was total, expectant silence.

At the press of her operating button, an artist's impression of a Neanderthal appeared on the screen behind her. Raisa declared: 'The world is being infected by the disease that totally wiped out man's first ancestor.'

Raisa had a teleprompt running against her lectern screen but she scarcely needed it. She called up the official still photographs inside the Baikal caves, interspersing them with the enlarged slides of the enzyme from the bodies there and that recovered from Gennardi Varlomovich Markelov. Her prepared slides showed the two side by side, visibly proving a perfect match. It was evidence, she asserted, of a virus already being replicated under laboratory control. She quickly switched to the double helix and telomere illustrations, insisting the degeneration was being caused by virus invasion. That could – and would – be stopped by a vaccine that would be the logical result of their current laboratory experimentation, although she could not give a time frame in which it might be achieved.

'What I can say is that we are moving properly – and as quickly as is scientifically possible – in the right direction. And that I'll develop it.'

There was the briefest hiatus, of people who'd expected her to talk longer, before the explosion of conflicting sounds not recognizable as questions through which Raisa remained relaxed at her pedestal, unresponsive but alert to the cameras. When the demands did become intelligible she chose only those she wished to answer. Prepared – and happy to titilate although not to be shown directly responsible – for the sensationalism she confirmed to a *New York Times* questioner that she was indeed claiming that the Neanderthal species had been totally wiped out by the ageing illness, but insisted she was not suggesting the current world population ran the risk of total annihilation as well.

'The Neanderthal didn't have science and people trained how to use it. We have now. But there is something that is essential to understand. The latest World Health Organization mortality figures for this plague are in excess of two million. AIDS has already claimed more than thirty times that number. I anticipate – although I wish I didn't – that we have to prepare ourselves for fatalities in such number before there is any hope of arresting this new illness, let alone developing an effective cure.'

Raisa allowed herself to be led again through most of the questions she'd faced in Irkutsk – grateful for the rehearsal – and frequently used the laser pointer to simplify answers she feared might be too esoteric. It was only towards the end and from American reporters that the questioning switched to the speculation of disputes between herself and the rest of the Fort Detrick team. There were no such difficulties, she insisted. They'd recall the British science minister independently announcing what he'd described as a breakthrough, which as she understood was still being evaluated, and once more threw up the telomere representations to discuss viral infection of cells, although not actually mentioning that it was the telomere shortening that was the British discovery. She expected very shortly to be rejoining the scientists at Fort Detrick, although there remained some experiments in Moscow she intended to supervise first.

'I am sure there is ongoing research in America, of which I am at the moment unaware, that will contribute every bit as much to the final solution to this devastating disease as the progress I've been able to disclose here today.'

Raisa agreed to separate, one-to-one interviews with the BBC and all three American national stations as well as CNN. BBC, ABC and CNN even agreed to repeat their sessions in front of her illustrations and photographs which would be edited into the final report with what she'd initially said, as well as her general remarks, to be dubbed as her voice-over.

Television segments of the general conference itself were satellite relayed live for midday news bulletins, which was the first indication outside Moscow of what was happening, but it was not until the evening that the Fort Detrick group, on call-back instructions from Washington, were able to watch the complete, channel-cleared transmission. With the excuse yet again to show the cave footage, the concentration was upon Raisa's Neanderthal assertion.

Stoddart said: 'She even used some of the words you did, to explain telomere fraying.'

'Yes,' accepted Geraldine. There wasn't any anger; not even irritation.

'She's wrong,' insisted Pelham. 'It's definitely *not* viral.'

'That's not a distinction the public will understand,' cautioned Geraldine. 'She handled it all very cleverly, apart from one thing.'

'What?' demanded Stoddart.

'The Neanderthal is not our ancestor,' insisted Geraldine. 'It was proved from finds within her own country, for God's sake! There were some remains of a fossilised Neanderthal baby recovered from the Mezmaiskaya caves, in the Caucasus. DNA was extracted from the mitochondria. There was a seven per cent difference between the Neanderthal DNA and modern man.'

'You think the public will bother with that distinction?' demanded Stoddart.

'Anthropologists will,' argued Geraldine. 'Raisa's claiming still to be working with us, so we'll be judged with her.'

'As we are already being judged, mostly critically, by every scientific body in the world not included in our investigation,' agreed Pelham.

'I don't like the credit being taken from Geraldine,' stated Stoddart, defensively.

'If we directly challenge it, it'll look like sour grapes,' Geraldine pointed out.

'So what do we tell Washington?' asked Pelham.

'Shouldn't it be the truth?' said Geraldine. 'That's what we're here for.'

When they did give Washington their assessment, the virtually simultaneous thought throughout Blair House and across the avenue in the White House was that a lot of political advantages had been skewed, but even worse that there was a possibility of their being made individually and collectively to look foolish. Gregori Lyalin was the exception. He'd already accepted that what Raisa Ivanova Orlov had done had reduced him to a political and personal laughing stock, both in Washington and Moscow. For once, in an otherwise obedient christian life, he allowed himself to feel hatred and was uncomfortable that he wasn't ashamed by it.

'I didn't expect us to be meeting again quite so soon,' greeted Partington.

'Nor I,' agreed Peter Reynell. The inner study, with personally served drinks and no witnessing staff apart from Amanda, was interesting.

'Fort Detrick – your scientific advisor in particular – are adamant that this woman is wrong?'

'Absolutely,' said Reynell. 'She also expects the Neanderthal claim to be publicly challenged.'

Amanda said: 'Raisa Orlov was playing personal politics and went too far staking the ancestral claim.'

Partington's political concern was personal, domestic and international which rounded the circle to come back always to his first consideration: how badly – or well – it was going to affect him. What the goddamned woman had done, at least nine thousand miles from where the medical investigation was supposedly being conducted, virtually confirmed the already speculated scientific dispute. And without the slightest guilt at his own hypocrisy, Partington determined that if there was going to be the open impression of professional squabbling, and pride being more important than the cure for a global plague, the future British prime minister had to be the one in the public limelight, taking all the flak. 'It could become a mess.'

'Which we've got to prevent,' parried Reynell. 'The priority is to distance Fort Detrick and ourselves from wrong scientific claims.' The Tom Thumb lookalike wanted to follow, not lead. It was going to be an instructive conga-line.

This really was her testing time, Amanda recognized. 'There's still no doubt in my mind that what she did was neither sanctioned nor condoned by Moscow.' Not good enough! She should have offered more than that.

'Again, I agree,' said Reynell, with no cause to hurry.

Son of a bitch! thought Amanda. But she'd held back – rightly at the time but wrongly now – from telling him why Partington had kept her after their previous shared encounter. 'It was getting too much momentum before but now, after this, we've got to get a lid on the dispute speculation.'

'What about her returning, which is what she said she intended to do?' asked Partington, topping up Reynell's Scotch and pouring more mineral water for Amanda.

'Dr Rothman doesn't think there can be any working relationship: it'll all be one way, to the Russian's advantage,' said Reynell.

'We can't openly refuse her entry!' protested the president.

Reynell confronted the choice of either going alone or taking Partington with him. Or, he added in afterthought, chivalrously steering the answer to come from Amanda. '*We* can't.'

'But Moscow can!' snatched Amanda, alertly.

'The collapse is still there,' protested Partington.

Reynell smothered the sigh. 'Not if she was replaced by another Russian scientist; one who, perhaps, has been involved in the independent research there.'

Amanda took the offer seconds before Partington. 'Which would be Moscow's decision – Moscow's internal condemnation – and nothing whatsoever to do with us!'

He'd been generous enough to his lover, Reynell decided. 'Raisa Orlov did make a very important point. We don't have a cure – any treatment even – and there could be fifty million dead before we get close to it: a hundred million if we don't. If it becomes so bad, people will demand to know why the scientific research is so slow, but no one here can be accused when the wilful obstruction was Russian, can they?'

'No.' Partington acknowledged that in any future shared situation he had to work very closely with this Englishman. If he didn't, he'd be left behind: maybe even discarded. To Amanda, consciously to show the other man he wasn't included in everything, Partington said: 'Have you been able yet to speak to Lyalin about the other matter?'

'No,' she said.

'Good,' said the president. 'I think you should now, though. As soon as possible.'

Needing on this occasion to avoid the media cordon, Reynell and Amanda used the linked basement corridors between the two buildings. As they walked Reynell said: 'What other matter?'

Although she tried to limit her answer, Reynell said at once: 'So you've been offered the State Department?'

Amanda said: 'You know what would frighten me? I'd be frightened to be against you, in any negotiation.'

'Easy answer. Don't be.'

'I'll try to avoid it.'

Gregori Lyalin had imagined his unannounced recall was to be dismissed, not for consultations which extended over the course of the first day to the Foreign and Finance Ministers to discuss the western offer. The Russian conclusion was that Washington had in the circumstances shown remarkable restraint and equally remarkable good faith in its back-channel diplomacy to achieve the IMF and World Bank concessions. There was also the realistic but unavoidable acceptance that in the future they would be called upon to repay the generosity, at far greater interest than that being imposed by genuine financiers. Lyalin thanked the president for his offer but insisted the following day's confrontation was his responsibility. He'd not thought it possible to get this second – or was it third or fourth? – chance.

Lyalin's return had not been publicly announced but Raisa allowed only the briefest frown of surprise at being ushered into his suite at the Science Ministry.

'You've embarrassed the country,' declared Lyalin, at once.

Raisa Orlov gazed contemptuously across the separating desk. 'Scientific jealousy! I'll take the viral proof back with me to Washington when it's confirmed, which it will be in days.'

'You're not going back to Washington,' announced Lyalin.

He was as uncomfortable with the feeling of satisfaction as he had been with that of hatred.

'What are you saying!'

'It's very clear what I'm saying.'

'There can't be anyone else!'

'Your place will be filled by Sergei Grenkov.'

'I won't allow it!'

'You're no longer in a position to allow or disallow. You're no longer a director of the institute.'

'That's absurd!'

'You're the one who allowed yourself to become absurd, Raisa Ivanova. And by doing so you put at risk events and situations at the very highest level of government until finally exposing yourself and your country to ridicule.'

'No!' refused Raisa, the arrogance faltering. 'I won't have this . . . won't accept it . . . I'll demand to see the president . . . protest publicly . . .'

'You will not see the president,' refused Lyalin. 'You can, however, protest as publicly as you wish. If you do, then equally publicly it will be announced that you have been dismissed as institute director for making unsubstantiated scientific claims. Alternatively, to avoid public disquiet, the announcement will be that you are remaining here to continue your researches, which you can in fact do although not any longer in any position of authority. Yours is the reputation at stake, nothing else.'

The woman's head shook, but loosely, as if she couldn't control it, and for a long time there were no words and when they did come they were unconnected. 'No . . . that's . . . I won't . . .' and then, finally, anguished: *'Please!'*

'There's no other way . . . no appeal,' said Lyalin. And no sympathy, he thought. He wished there could have been.

The irony of Raisa Ivanova Orlov's disgrace and dismissal was that her replacement, Sergei Grenkov, took with him to Washington the one piece of evidence missing from what the Fort Detrick scientists had from the Baikal caves. It was to prove the key with which Geraldine unlocked so much.

But not immediately.

400

Thirty-Five

The challenge came first from a Japanese geneticist who quoted the scientifically recognized seven per cent difference between the DNA of Neanderthal fossils and that of modern man and within twenty-four hours there was condemnation from Europe, America, Australia and Asia. Gregori Lyalin forbade Raisa Orlov being named in the Moscow Natural History Museum's denial that the director who'd led the anthropological investigation at Baikal had ever agreed the assertion and ordered Vladimir Bobin, at the Listvyanka Institute there, to refuse any comment. Lyalin also ignored the demands for explanation that avalanched the Science Ministry.

Henry Partington determined upon remaining as far removed as possible from the controversy, insisting the response come from Blair House, although not anticipating Peter Reynell would make it personally or that Amanda would be beside him when he did so. Reynell apologized for not being able to offer any clarification. Fort Detrick did not understand the Russian claim, about which there had been no prior discussion, and were waiting to hear from Moscow. It appeared to be very specifically a Russian matter, with no bearing or influence whatsoever upon the quite separate research being conducted at the Maryland installation.

It was also Reynell's idea, quickly taken up by Amanda, to go out to Dulles personally for the return of the unsuspecting Gregori Lyalin, which gave the intended impression of their demanding answers as well as identifying Sergei Grenkov as Raisa Orlov's replacement to the alerted but angrily distanced press corps. Neither passed through the terminal buildings. Grenkov was helicoptered immediately to Fort Detrick and Lyalin spared any landing formalities – and journalist interception – to be swept by a waiting American, not Russian, limousine directly to Blair House, continuing the perception of Lyalin being called to account. There was no attempt to shield the man from the antagonized media ambush in Pennsylvania Avenue, and having so successfully separated themselves and their governments, Reynell and Amanda shook their heads against any questions. In the time it took him to shoulder his way through the resisting crowd, Lyalin insisted there was no collapse in the international co-operation, but suggested there may have been a misunderstanding, which was why Raisa Orlov was remaining in Moscow to review her particular research while her deputy had returned with him to resume work with the other scientists at Fort Detrick.

The melee was transmitted live by CNN and at Fort Detrick a watching Geraldine Rothman said: 'Poor bastard.'

Pelham said: 'His problem, not ours. Which was what had to be established.'

'Now that it has, perhaps we can start working properly again,' said Geraldine.

'Let's hope Raisa's successor feels the same,' said Stoddart, watching through the window as Sergei Grenkov's helicopter came in to land on the faraway pad.

Henry Partington, who was also watching the television coverage, said to Paul Spencer: 'Amanda and Reynell are sure as hell milking it, aren't they?'

I'm missing out here, translated Spencer. There'd be so many presidential stories to tell his grandchildren: a published memoir even to pay for the vacations in his old age. 'It wouldn't have been protocol for you to greet a minister, not unless you wanted to. Still best you stay apart from this situation.'

'What about another president-to-president telephone call, with a statement that I'm assuring him everything's OK?' *Get me back on the screen and on the front pages.*

'Too easy to construe that's what you're not telling him, despite any statement,' rejected Spencer, pleased at what he saw as an expansion of his role into wider political advice. 'And I think we've pushed Moscow as far as we should. Let's see if their new guy causes any problems.'

'We've got another guy closer to home who's doing that,' said Partington, nodding to the proposed emission control figures that had arrived that morning from Jack Stoddart's environmental executive and which now lay on the table between them.

'It's a discussion paper,' reminded Spencer.

'We consider anything remotely as high as this we'll be riding around in pony and traps and living in caves, like those goddamned hairy apes.' *I'm already getting flak from the money men.*

'You want me to start thinking about that other thing?'

'It's high risk.' *I've got to be bomb proof and Teflon coated.*

'There'll be the need for an environmental watchdog after this is over, won't there?' suggested Spencer.

Partington smiled. 'You're right, Paul. Good shot. Right about me staying out of things at this stage, too.'

Grenkov said: 'I've studied everything that was sent to Moscow from here, up to maybe four or five days ago. And being in charge of the institute during Raisa Ivanova's absence, I know everything that was being done there –' he hefted two briefcases on to the table around which they sat in Pelham's office – 'duplicate findings and details of which I've brought with me. My instructions are to co-operate – and operate – according to any schedule you've already evolved but in view of what happened and because of my overview I'm suggesting I start by making a total comparison, to ensure nothing else was . . .' again he hesitated, '. . . overlooked.'

He hadn't known what to expect – Lyalin hadn't been able to guide him, either – but there certainly wasn't the hostility there could have been. Compared to the hysterical, raging parting from Raisa Ivanova – culminating in the face-slapping charge that he'd betrayed her for which she'd ensure he'd never occupy another scientific position – this was almost amicable.

His accented English was as good, if not better than Raisa's and Geraldine hoped the others would allow the man the diplomatic effort of the final pause. 'As far as you know, at this moment, was the enzyme discovery the only thing withheld?'

'As far as I know,' said Grenkov.

'We got it, from the cave bodies,' said Pelham. 'Having had more time than us, from your Iultin victim, have you succeeded in totally crystalizing it?'

'Not totally,' said Grenkov. There was another word-selecting hesitation. 'I think it's parasitic.'

'*Not* viral?' demanded Geraldine. It wasn't a bullying accusation. It was the essential question to be answered for them to be able to dismiss entirely what Raisa Ivanova Orlov had claimed and move on, without any doubt of the woman knowing or having something else of which they were unaware.

'It was the direction in which the research was ordered in Moscow. We weren't getting the right results.'

'Why, if you weren't getting the readings, did she go on insisting it *was* a virus?' demanded Pelham, giving way to exasperation.

'She wanted it to be,' said the Russian, glad to get this inevitable conversation out of the way. 'She didn't allow herself to think properly: scientifically.' He breathed in, deeply. 'I believe Raisa Ivanova is unwell.'

Pelham said: 'In those circumstances we're lucky not to have been misdirected far worse than we might have been. Not at all, in fact.'

'She could have got away in the end, sticking to the theory that it's a virus,' reflected Geraldine, distantly. 'It would have been corrected, in the final analysis, but no one outside of here would have remembered. How on earth could she have made that Neanderthal suggestion, with your leading anthropologists with us in Irkutsk!'

'They weren't the people who agreed it was possible,' said Grenkov, who'd overheard Raisa's screaming telephone tirade. 'It was someone whose name I don't know, from the Listvyanka Institute.'

Lyudmilla Vlasov would have had a very personal reason for supporting the theory, Geraldine remembered. It was unfortunate she hadn't kept up with the genetic advances in her science. To the Russian she said: 'We don't know your specialization?'

'Virology, the same as Raisa Ivanova,' said Grenkov.

'In theory the perfect partnership with genetics,' said Geraldine. 'Let's hope this time it turns out to be the same in practice.'

It did, initially, Grenkov assessing the research already assembled and Geraldine sifting through newly incoming material, most of it prompted by earlier queries.

'It's drifting on,' complained Lord Ranleigh.

'I know,' accepted Reynell. It was a nuisance having to come all the way to the embassy for these secure telephone conversations but he supposed it was necessary.

'We don't want to give Buxton's people time to regroup.'

'It's too late for that, surely?'

'I'm uneasy, with you so far away,' said the older man.

'How about my coming back to make another statement to the House?'

'About this Russian thing?'

'No,' refused Reynell. 'That's run its course. I'll have to deal with Moscow in the future.'

'Good point,' accepted Ranleigh. 'What then?'

'I'll find something,' promised Reynell.

Geraldine's first excitement was from the English findings. There was a positive link between two specific genes – p21 and p53 – in tissues from the cave bodies and those from the current victims in Canberra, Tokyo, New Delhi, Vienna and Rome. She judged the most important to be p21, the gene scientifically proved to block the division of damaged or

405

infected cells to enable them to self-repair. Its known and connected secondary effect was to prevent division when cells aged. In each of the senility-illness cases p21 had been activated and when taken from recent victims and reactivated in laboratory cultures, it exploded through as many as forty other genes, at least fifteen of which in chromosomes 5, 16 and 19 were believed to cause or accelerate ageing or age-related conditions. One of the genetic team, in the covering summary, referred to p21 as 'going mad'. What was unclear, although obviously related, was the contribution – or lack of it – from p53, the proper function of which was closely allied to the other, a 'gate-keeper' gene to repel cell invaders. Again, in every victim test, p53 had been turned off, unable or stopped from performing its purpose.

Although genetics was her specific science Geraldine refused to let the DNA developments deflect or overinfluence her from the other re-examinations the Fort Detrick specialists, as a team, had asked for and conceded with the proper scientific objectivity that the sea mammal and ornithological pathology was probably as significant, although neither she nor anyone else could suggest how or where that significance might fit in to a pattern they still hadn't begun to see.

The gut infestation by the unidentified worms was found in rorqual, sei, bow-head and humpback whales and independently – from more detailed analysis of suffocated carcases from Tasmania, Japan and the coastal regions of the Indian sub-continent – came secondary, qualifying autopsy reports that no identifiable virus had been located confirming influenza to be the cause of death. Because every request from Fort Detrick urged cross-referencing, they began receiving bewildering oceanographic and fishery authority accounts, primarily from Scandanavia, Britain's North Sea coast and from Spanish deep sea fleets, of huge shoals of floating dead fish, thousands entrapped in the weed-mass breeding grounds of the North Atlantic's Sargasso Sea. When they split open, which they did upon touch, their digestive tracts were jellified. Intestinal jellification – melting was how it was described in some post mortem analysis – was also

406

reported by ornithologists dissecting birds collected from human outbreak locations of the ageing illness in America, Austria, Spain and India.

The in-house botanists at Fort Detrick, whose more regular occupation was to find antidotes to natural sourced toxins, subjected the nothofagus-type vegetation from Baikal and both polar regions to a series of experiments, including caterpillar, house-fly and bee exposure. All three insect species died, although the botanists could not extract an identifiable poison from the plants. There was, however, a heavy pungency which was still being tested for mephitism.

It took four full days from Sergei Grenkov's Washington arrival for the Russian to complete his re-examination of the existing material, although that correlation did not include what had come in during that time and which was kept separate, to finally bring the man completely up to date. The last two additions came the day Grenkov declared himself satisfied that everything was now fully shared.

From external microscopic study of the intestinal worms, helminthologists at the Smithsonian isolated an almost undetectable proboscis, although no positive head. Under higher magnification it proved to be pointed and hollow. Maintaining that increased magnification, they confirmed that the creature had an elementary digestive tract. And entomologists again working from within Fort Detrick noted that the ticks recovered from the caves, the bore samples and from the bodies of the Antarctic victims shared the Ixodidas characteristic of being soft skinned.

'So what do you think?' asked Stoddart, when they finished talking everything through in anticipation of the following day's first full discussion with Sergei Grenkov.

'I think it's like trying to wade through that mile-deep primeval mud at the bottom of Lake Baikal,' said Geraldine. 'Millions of tiny separate pieces, sucking us down to nowhere.'

That night the last of the six chimpanzees subjected to the measured, heat-diminished enzyme died, making the immunization experiment a failure.

*   *   *

407

But one out of a matching number in Moscow was still alive, after three weeks, and actually showing signs of recovery, moving around the cage in which five days earlier it had slumped near-comatose in a corner, now eating everything it was offered and grabbing for more.

It had been a rigidly controlled experiment, every piece of data recorded, and Raisa Orlov didn't have the slightest doubt that she was vindicated, even though she'd failed to isolate the virus. That could follow: would follow, with the next experiment. Which was to extend that control beyond an anthropoid from the very introduction of the infection. Then the sneering, jealous derision would stop. She'd be reinstated by title, although the official lack of it hadn't changed anything, and the first thing she'd do would be to dismiss Sergei Grenkov, the second to demand the dismissal of Gregori Lyalin. She hoped she didn't have to wait too long for the international acknowledgement.

Thirty-Six

Geraldine Rothman finally argued – openly – that the varied sciences had become too widely divided at their ultimate, four-person level and that the assessment should be expanded to the specially seconded department and division heads to guarantee the essential interchange, which furthered Pelham's determination to totally rehabilitate himself and Fort Detrick in the president's eyes. It also covered Jack Stoddart's self-admitted limitations.

At a pre-conference gathering of just the four of them they also agreed Pelham's suggestion that it should be a general, point-making review for every division director hopefully to slot his or her particular contribution wherever they felt it fitted. Despite that prior discussion about patterns and schemes and shapes, Geraldine was surprised when the normally undemonstrative, word-pedantic Pelham opened the full gathering by describing their problem as having the spilled and jumbled pieces of a smashed mosaic without the picture from which to reconstruct it.

'We've got to find how – and why – piece A is followed by piece B and B by piece C. And having got that, how to halt the progression long enough to stop the dying.'

Although she'd read everything more times than she could now count, Geraldine very quickly decided that having all the known facts and findings and opinions verbally recapitulated, as Pelham was setting them out, gave her a clearer, better perception. She might, she conceded, have even dulled herself by the constant eye-aching, mind-aching reading.

'There are too many gaps,' complained Pelham. 'Why did some children survive in the caves when adults didn't?

Why is most of the sea life that's dying infested, like those cave victims were infested, by parasitic worms unknown to helminthologists which aren't in the bodies of any of the victims from the Antarctic or Noatak or Iultin? But why is it that the worms – and we've now tested more than four hundred recovered from mammals or humans – are not in any way toxic, which they would need to be to have caused the deaths, if indeed they were the carrier of whatever caused their deaths? Why, in some but not all, of those polar victims are there non-toxic microscopic ticks not found anywhere else in the world? But *were* found in the caves, in the fur of the dog-like creature and the rats? Why, though, in *all* the victims is there the same enzyme – an enzyme defying every effort to purify, let alone crystallize – that destroys their internal organs? And liquifies the intestines of birds and fish? What, if any, is the significance of the unknown genus of nothofagus that was found in the caves as well as in bores sunk in Noatak and the Antarctic . . . ?' Pelham paused, for effect. 'I started by asking you to interrupt: fill gaps. No one has. So I'm asking you again: what are we missing? What aren't we seeing clearly enough, analysing enough . . . ?' He allowed another unfilled hesitation. 'We, in this room, are the leaders in our respective scientific fields in the United States of America, with unrestricted back-up from every institute, academy and research facility throughout the world. There's no other more highly qualified or better equipped group. We're *it*! So . . . ?'

No one spoke.

It wasn't the room-quietening histrionic that stirred Geraldine. She had the same feeling she'd experienced when she'd abruptly guessed that Henri Lebrun was progressively dying internally, although this time she didn't have as much – anything – upon which to substantiate the hope of a further step forward, let alone a breakthrough. It wasn't entirely what Pelham had said. She was sure there was a connection with something she'd read. Or was it what she'd expected to read, but hadn't? She was suddenly aware of Pelham's attention and hurried to her feet, to pick up on the medical and genetic details.

Stoddart was only belatedly aware of her rising from beside him, his mind working very similarly to hers. It quite obviously had to have been triggered by a remark of Pelham's, a reference closer to his own more physical science than to Geraldine's mysteries, too small to see and too abstruse properly to comprehend, despite her patient layman's translation. Gaps, conceded Stoddart, using Pelham's description. Or perhaps missing links. It all had to be linked to get to the same horrifying end, capable of killing humans and animals and mammals and birds alike. But *how* could the same enzyme cause that same end, transmitting and transmuting through so many species? Concentrate on his own science, Stoddart told himself. There was a partial, easy answer to how microscopic, prehistoric worms were infesting sea life. Global warming melting ice sheets in which they'd been preserved for millenia, multiplying parthenogenetically in their trillions and entering the marine food chain. But they were harmless, scientifically proved to be totally non-toxic. A broken link. A climatic route perhaps? The hurricane winds of Lake Baikal were unique, capable of lifting virus and spores into the upper atmosphere but it was inconceivable – like so much else remained inconceivable – that Baikal could be the source of the global pandemic. If it had been, the first cases would have occurred there, Irkutsk would be the city of the dead, the Listvyanka Institute would have isolated it long before the collapse of the cliff-face and most important of all there was no consistent, all embracing wind-stream in either the upper or lower atmosphere blowing over all the now affected countries. Another broken link. So what was it, scratching at his mind's door? He had to stop listening for what he couldn't hear but pay attention to what he could: hadn't he already decided that he more than anyone else needed as much help as possible?

He came back into the meeting as Geraldine reached their most recent genetic results from England, aware that for the benefit of all she was still trying for layman's simplicity.

At that moment – and at last – there was the interruption Pelham had invited, from the grey-haired, fat female anthropologist brought into the investigation from the conveniently close Smithsonian. 'You haven't given your opinion why young kids in the caves weren't infected?'

'Because I don't have anything upon which to base an opinion.'

'But they had worm infestation?'

'The two we examined,' confirmed Geraldine, turning invitingly to Sergei Grenkov.

'In all but two of the children we examined in Moscow,' agreed the Russian. 'We couldn't find anything to explain it, either.'

'What about the presence of the enzyme?' asked the black, surprisingly young entomologist from California's Berkeley University.

'None, in our cave children,' said Geraldine.

'The faintest traces in only three of ours in Russia,' said Grenkov. 'Our only conclusion so far is the most obvious, that they had a natural resistance.'

'Which the adults didn't have?' pressed the anthropologist.

'Or had lost,' said Geraldine.

'I need guidance,' interjected Paul Spencer, truthfully but at the same time anxious to have his position recognized by the wider audience. 'I'm the only guy here who doesn't have the degree to help me understand. And I've got to liaise on all of this with Blair House and maybe even the President, which means answering questions beyond what they can read from the transcript. The only way I can imagine so much physical damage being caused to genes and organs and God knows what else is by our not looking for one bug – one virus or bacterium or enzyme – but for several. Anyone want to help me on that?'

Geraldine paused, automatically looking to Pelham. She was about to respond when the director didn't speak but unexpectedly Grenkov said: 'I'm not sure that any of us can provide a complete answer, but it comes down to the enzyme.

A virus or a bacteria usually attacks a specific target with a specific effect. A cold virus gives you a cold, an influenza virus gives you influenza, although both can develop into other respiratory infections like pneumonia . . .'

'The majority of the victims now have respiratory complications,' broke in another woman, a middle-aged toxicologist permanently attached to Fort Detrick.

'But we haven't isolated a virus,' said Grenkov. 'We've got an enzyme and enzymes can have multiple effects. They're catalysts, protein that controls and motivates the body's metabolism. Everyone's body contains thousands and each cell produces several varieties. Science has so far only isolated a very few, mostly connected with the gut and digestion, particularly turning starch into sugar.'

'Let's explore that,' persisted the toxicologist. 'Dr Rothman's told us that it's the existing body genes that are going into accelerated overdrive.' She snapped her fingers. 'Overnight senility. And you've just told us science only knows a few hundreds of the many thousands of enzymes we have. Could what you're finding not be an outside intrusion at all but an enzyme we already have within us, being activated to affect the genes in some way?'

Grenkov frowned. Keeping any surprise from his voice at the question he said: 'The enzymes in the human body are different from those in other animals and mammals and birds that have died.'

The toxicologist didn't appear embarrassed. 'Poisons can cause different metabolic changes in different creatures. As I understand it from what's already been said, the enzyme in animals and mammals is different?'

Grenkov nodded, reluctantly. 'It's a very slight variation. In my opinion – and it's a personal opinion – I think all the indications are that it's an outside intrusion.'

'What about poison?' came in Duncan Littlejohn. 'Do these unknown ticks carry the encephalitis the Frenchman caught?'

The middle-aged woman shook her head. 'We're only three days into animal testing. There's a lot of skin irritation: lung and nasal congestion.'

'Respiratory again!' seized Pelham. 'There's got to be a fit there somewhere!'

The toxicologist gave another head shake. 'It's controlled experimentation, obviously. Eight chimpanzees, divided in twos. Measured doses, all the same food and liquid nourishment. Only four of them are showing any signs of infection. The other four are perfectly healthy. We don't know why some are getting sick and some are not.'

'Talking poisons, there's something positive that came in overnight,' announced the blonde-haired, in-house botanist. 'The nothofagus we got from the caves and the bores is definitely mephitistic.'

'What's that?' demanded Spencer, pained.

'It can emit an odour poisonous to small insects. A lot of plants do. It's a protective mechanism, against becoming an insect food source. It was the odour, not the plants themselves, that killed the insect we tested.'

'There's something!' exclaimed Grenkov. 'Give me a moment!' It took more than a moment and the impatient foot shuffling and chair scraping began before the man came up from the file he'd created. Talking more to the inner group than the division leaders, Grenkov said: 'It wasn't all shared, although it wasn't withheld. We collected all the vegetation that remained after what you took from the caves.' He looked out into the room, to include the botanist. 'There's nothing in the reports assembled here about tick colonies?'

'There weren't any, in what was brought back from Siberia,' said the botanist.

'What about the polar bores?' pressed the Russian.

'No.'

'In total, we received in Moscow just short of four kilos of plant and vegetable matter from Siberia,' recorded Grenkov. 'There were tick colonies on at least half of the nothofagus.'

'They under experimentation?' demanded Pelham.

'It hadn't been started before I left Moscow. Some of the colonized plants could be shipped here, for comparable testing.'

'I think I should come in here,' intruded the Berkeley ento-mologist, a towering, bull-chested man. 'We're comparing, with helminthology. Maybe the ticks are puparial.'

The reaction was a contrast between sudden realization among a very few – Pelham and Geraldine among them – and total incomprehension.

Spencer began. 'I need some more—' but Geraldine over-rode him.

Looking between the two museum experts, she said urgently: 'When?'

The huge man made an uncertain movement. 'Today, sometime.'

'Make it now!' insisted Geraldine.

Amanda O'Connell took the call at Blair House, aware of Reynell's concentration as she spoke. She included Lyalin in the smile as she replaced the telephone. 'They've taken a break. Spencer says something's come up they're very excited about but he can't understand it yet.'

'We talking breakthrough?' demanded Reynell.

'Excitement was Spencer's word.' Amanda looked at Lyalin. 'Seems it all began with something Sergei Grenkov said.'

'What are you going to tell the President?' asked Reynell. If Fort Detrick was excited, then so should they be. There was no way he could physically get back to London to compete with a White House announcement if it really did mark a breakthrough. He could easily speak to the British press here in Washington, as a build up for the personal House of Commons statement tomorrow.

'Nothing until I know what I'm talking *about*,' said Amanda. 'If it's good it's got to be right first time.'

Raisa Orlov personally conducted the preparation experiment, most of them duplicated and sometimes repeated for a third time, with her customary meticulousness. She paid the closest attention to the weight differentiation, calculating to 200th of a gram against dosage, and adjusted the heat treatment ratio of that accordingly. She monitored the surviving chimpanzee

415

on an hourly basis, taking blood samples as regularly, and on the last full day the haemal tests achieved twelve consecutive enzyme-free readings.

It was to the institute's chief haematologist that Raisa finally disclosed her intention, timing it to avoid any official intervention, and for several moments he stared at her in disbelief.

'No!' he said, finally. It was the first time in fifteen years he had ever contradicted her even though, several years before, he had been one of her ordered lovers.

'There are times I may be relying on you. I'm trusting you.' It was another first for Raisa to concede a need for help.

'You should not do this!'

'It's not the first time it's been done.'

'It was luck more than proper science!'

'You questioning my science?'

'I'm sorry,' the man immediately retreated.

'You know what I want you to do?'

'Please don't,' he said, and winced when she did.

Knowing she could not as successfully evade official intervention – and prevention – of another full scale media event, Raisa this time limited herself to just one telephone call, to the Moscow bureau of the *New York Times*, which would guarantee the necessary exposure. Then everyone could come begging to her.

It was an hour before the insect and worm experts returned together and by then Geraldine had listened to the stenographer reading back the notes of what Sergei Grenkov had said, found the missed remark and checked it with the Russian. She'd also managed, just, to babble what she was thinking to Stoddart.

There was an anxiousness to sit and before everyone had done so Pelham said: 'You got it?'

'Positive,' said the helminthologist.

'It's a gap filled in,' said the insect expert.

'More,' insisted Geraldine. 'Much more.'

'We going to get some help here?' asked Spencer.

There was a hesitation between Pelham and Geraldine. Pelham shook his head and said: 'I'll come in, if I think you miss something.'

'The killer – the cause of the disease that kills – is the enzyme we can't encode,' said Geraldine. 'It's the catalyst that's causing everything to go wrong with the genes. As you've heard, the majority of the enzymes that have been scientifically isolated are in the gut and the intestines, converting food into energy. Most whales, the largest sea mammals, exist on the smallest of sea life. Other fish do, as well. And other fish eat other fish—' She indicated the entomologist. 'The ticks that were found in the Antarctic and Noatak victims – and at Baikal – begin life as pupae, one form of life that mutates into another. You want an example, you've got a caterpillar that grows into a butterfly. Our microscopic worms become microscopic ticks. Puparial means that the last larval skin becomes the skin of its new existence. That shared skin might contain the enzyme: it might not show as poisonous under laboratory testing but *become* poisonous when it enters a body and comes into contact with other enzymes, as a protective system in both forms against predators. That's common in all sorts of life forms. Or the enzyme might exist within the gut of both. The worms have a digestive system, so whatever it ingests for food needs to be broken up. And any creature that ingests, excretes. The worms themselves could be harmless, its excretion the poison. And we've got the enzyme in the droppings of the cave bats but far more importantly from birds – a lot of them dead – in every place where we've now got outbreaks . . .' She stopped, dry-throated, looking enquiringly to Pelham.

'It's all there,' said the installation director.

'It still isn't for me!' protested Spencer. 'You got something with stick men?'

'Try a food chain,' said Stoddart, soberly. 'The worms are getting into the oceans from melting base ice. Fish eat the worms or already infected fish. The carcases that get washed up on shorelines are scavenged by migratory birds, dead fish that aren't eaten by other fish float and are scavenged by

417

sea birds. Before all those birds die, to be consumed by other carrion-eaters, they excrete over land. Their droppings infecting crops would explain how the epidemics are striking inland, hundreds of miles from any sea or water. Animals will eat the dead birds and become infected. Their excreta will go on spreading the disease.'

'We're looking for cures. You've just given us a situation twice as bad as it was,' said Spencer. And he'd told Amanda O'Connell it was looking good!

'Much more than twice,' said Stoddart. 'Try ten times.'

They reached Blair House, by helicopter, by early evening. Jack Stoddart did most of the talking, there and later in the White House, which they reached by the tunnel to avoid the permanent press cordon. They agreed every one of Stoddart's suggestions and the need to inform the World Health Organisation and the United Nations' Environmental Division overnight gave Peter Reynell time to get back to London for a House of Commons statement timed simultaneously with Henry Partington's television address. For that the president insisted Stoddart appear with him.

It was midnight before everything was in place and by then the first editions of the *New York Times* had broken the story of Raisa Ivanova Orlov intentionally infecting herself with the ageing illness to prove she had a vaccine against it.

Thirty-Seven

The identification of a contagion chain physically divided Stoddart and Geraldine. Blair House is more normally the government guest house for visiting dignitaries, so there was accommodation there for him that night and for nights – and days – that followed co-ordinating state by state responses and extending that liaison – and consultation – internationally. Apart from this time there being no purpose, it would have been impractical for Stoddart to try to hijack the president's televised address, but Partington personally voiced the warning ('let's keep the surprises to what we've got to tell the people, OK Jack?') although establishing responsibility for unforeseen problems by having Stoddart be the one to talk about unspecified precautions.

'He'll get the glory, you'll get the shit,' predicted Geraldine, unhappy from the outset with a long-distance telephone relationship.

'He's promising Cabinet-level appointment, a budget up there with Defence and State and department staffing at whatever figure I ask for.'

'You'll be his man, in his cage.'

'I can always leave by the same door I go in by. With the official authority I can achieve a lot more than by staying outside.'

'I hope you're right.'

'I am.'

Stoddart used his opening address in the United Nations in New York to describe the gathering as an agenda-preparing forum for every participating nation's environmental and public health group to contribute improved, better or new

419

suggestions. The proposals he was listing were provisional, an instant response to an instant emergency. Washed-up carcases of all sea mammals and fish should be burned where they lay and the pyres afterwards doused with the strongest available insecticide. Naval and coastguard services should spread and ignite oil slicks to incinerate floating, rotting shoals at sea. The corpses of infected birds and animals – domestic and wild – should also be burned. Without naming Geraldine he said Fort Detrick had advised every affected country to have their agronomy and agricultural authorities test all food crops for genetic mutation possibly caused by the droppings of diseased birds and animals. That advice extended to there being held a separate, agricultural science conference to consider the wholesale introduction and consumption of genetically modified crops to replace those found to be poisoned. There was the obvious risk of herbivores ingesting contaminated grass, which could possibly pass into the human food chain through their meat or milk. Any country discovering the infection in farm animals should report it immediately to the UN monitoring agencies and again those animals should be burned. No carcases should be buried because of the danger of the germ entering the soil as bodies decomposed. Bird egest had possibly polluted reservoirs, the water from which should be constantly analysed. In areas already affected by the ageing disease, all drinking water should be boiled and bird-scaring noise systems installed at sewage plants. Street cleaning departments should heavily douse bird-soiled public places with insecticide before scouring it away.

The totally compatible working relationship between Geraldine Rothman and Sergei Grenkov began within hours of their learning of Raisa Orlov's self-experimentation, by which time Raisa was already in an isolation chamber. She'd entered under protested duress from a drafted-in medical team, whose arrival finally broke the woman's rule-by-fear authority and reversed her edict that there should be no further exchange with Washington, most specifically about what she had done to herself. Raisa's full medical case history arrived in the same – although protectively separate – shipment of

420

tick-infested nothofagus and Geraldine said at once: 'It's her choice, even if it wasn't intended for our research use.' Two of the chimpanzees in that day's renewed tests were infected with precisely the same enzyme dosage that Raisa had self-administered, as well as being injected with the same measured, heat-treated inoculation of the same protein. It was also arranged for daily samples of Raisa's tissue, blood, faeces and urine to be flown from Moscow to Washington, for Fort Detrick analysis.

There appeared an immediate – literally within hours – result from the colonized vegetation tests that Geraldine spread with detailed but shared instructions between the no longer compartmented sciences concentrated at Fort Detrick. Entomologists were asked for a molecular comparison between those mites recovered from the Antarctic, Iultin and Noatak victims. Toxicologists, already attempting to refine components from the gaseous discharge, were brought in with paleobotanists to reduce the plant to its base chemical elements.

There were other developments which Geraldine and Grenkov agreed could have a connected relevance without being able to fit them into Walter Pelham's mosaic. The Fort Detrick director couldn't, either. Immunology analysis from the nasal and upper air passages of the unaffected cave children showed a high level of glutathione, a naturally occurring antioxidising enzyme medically acknowledged to lessen the effects of respiratory infection. And geneticists in England found the tissues of both prehistoric and modern victims lacked the non-coding cytokine gene.

By the time that information arrived, the United States' navy and coastguard had set up the daily collection of helicopter-delivered Arctic and Antarctic sea water from which it was hoped to extract undigested microscopic worms. From Moscow came reports of Raisa Orlov suffering hair loss and discolouration, with keratosis developing on the skin of her arms, hands and back. She'd also developed a bronchial infection. At Geraldine's suggestion, Grenkov telephoned the institute to suggest they determine the woman's antioxidant level before administering booster dosages of glutathione. The chimpanzee infected with the same dosage that Raisa had given herself developed severe influenza that glutathione failed to relieve.

The day Geraldine heard from England of the dyskerin gene mutation in the prehistoric as well as modern victims, she moved into Fort Detrick's genetic laboratory to work full time alongside the team there.

Peter Reynell was very satisfied with the way everything went. He'd limited himself to the House of Commons statement that coincided with Partington and Stoddart's television appearance, insisting in advance that all he had was the likeliest explanation for how the disease was spreading, not yet answers to any of the questions it naturally prompted. He pleaded pressure to find those answers for refusing any press interviews or statements ('the seriousness demands that the House is the only right and proper place from which to address the people of this country') and stayed in daily contact both with Amanda O'Connell at Blair House and with Geraldine Rothman in Maryland, although he spent much longer closeted in Cabinet-formation discussion with Ranleigh, evincing more strongly than before his later intended independence. Ranleigh argued that they'd maximized the benefit of Reynell's personal involvement and that he should succeed to the leadership in the already smoothly prepared power transfer and let a new science minister take over in Washington. 'Staying with it will become a burden if a cure and prevention isn't found and there's no guarantee of that.'

Reynell's counter-argument was that the public perception would be of his putting personal ambition and career above a declared and pledged commitment. 'A medical failure won't be put against me; abandoning ship at this moment would. Things are moving forward, at last. It's too soon for me to leave.'

Reynell had scheduled to the specific day his return to Washington, although telling no one – not even Henrietta

422

– because he wanted the last minute adjustment to the parliamentary order paper to create the drama, but learning from Geraldine of the large number of microscopic worms recovered from Arctic and Antarctic oceans heightened his departure announcement. It would, he told a hushed House, always have been necessary for him to be involved personally in the prevention precautions for which a team from his science ministry were already moving to New York to join other detailed UN planners. But now he understood there were rapid scientific developments that he could not at that time divulge but which made it even more essential for him to go back.

He and Henrietta that night lingered over brandy in the drawing room at Lord North Street after the departure of their dinner guests, one of whom had inevitably been her father. Henrietta said: 'You *are* going to work closely with Daddy, aren't you?'

'I hope so,' said Reynell, guardedly.

'He's done an enormous amount to bring all this about.'

'I thought we both had.' The old bastard was already sniffing the wind.

'I wouldn't like there to be a schism.'

'There's no cause for you to imagine there could be.'

'Guess what he asked me tonight?'

'What?'

'When we're going to start a family.'

Reynell laughed, outright. 'What did you tell him!'

'That it's your decision.'

Reynell said: 'Not even I believed your father would try to be with us in the bedroom.'

Henrietta remained serious. 'That's not an answer.'

'I didn't think I was being asked a question.' When Reynell refused Henrietta joining him that night because of the early morning flight she said she understood and Reynell hoped she did. He hoped even more strongly she'd make her father understand, too.

'You put a whole bunch of foxes in the chicken coop up there

423

in New York; it was all too much for people to take on board.'
It had to be an easy beginning.

'The purpose was to generate ideas,' said Stoddart, who'd
come directly to the White House from the airport. 'Every
proposal got on to the agenda. At least eight countries –
and fifteen states here so far – are adopting some of the
precautions ahead of any legislation or finance allocation.
I want to talk specifically about an Executive Order, to get
the navy and coastguards involved.'

Partington frowned at Stoddart apparently believing he
could set the Oval Office agenda, as well. 'I don't think we
took things slow enough before you went to New York.'

'You seemed happy with the ideas I sketched out,' insisted
Stoddart. He thought, you want the glory, you risk the heat.

'We've got to get things costed, budgets agreed to put
forward to Congress. And then some. The navy aren't going
to agree to their involvement coming from their current
allocation. Neither are coastguards.'

The Congress carousel, Stoddart recognized, expectantly.
'I'll have costed figures ready in a week. Contingency extras,
too. What I'm asking for is an interim Executive Order,
between now and Congress approval. With other countries
moving right away – and us the environmental hosts – it
wouldn't look very good if we lagged behind, would it?'

It was too late to move to the other office, away from
those goddamned revolving tapes, but Partington was sure
he could make the reality of life clear to Stoddart without
it becoming a rebounding problem. 'You're talking billions
for a department that hasn't properly been created yet. And
the hindrance there is your not making up your mind whether
you're going to accept the appointment. A lot of people might
be confused by that reluctance. I admit to being so myself.'

'It would bring me officially – responsibly – into the
Executive?'

Partington allowed the token smile, and thought, and just
you wait until it does. 'You got a problem working with the
President of the United States and being a member of the
Cabinet?'

424

'I can't imagine how there could be,' lied Stoddart easily.

It won't take you long to find out, Partington promised himself.

Stoddart was told Geraldine was unavailable when he telephoned from Blair House and it was an hour before she returned his call, her exhilaration audible. She said: 'We've got something! Too soon to talk about it but it's looking good!'

It was Geraldine's idea to come down to Washington and Stoddart's to move from Blair House to a suite at the Georgetown Four Seasons and the first night they ordered room service to avoid any interruption. He'd also ordered French champagne and she said: 'How did you know there might be something to celebrate?'

'I'm hoping.'

Geraldine visibly breathed in, composing herself. 'I've crystallized an enzyme, in culture. I'm as sure as I can be it's from uncoded ribonucleic acid, RNA, and its protein is almost homologous to an already encoded protein, dyskerin. And dyskerin has been cloned from mutated cells in people suffering Dyskeratosis Congenita, one of the known premature ageing illnesses that we've already talked about but until now has only affected children. I don't know – perhaps we never will – but maybe modern Dyskeratosis Congenita is a rare but weaker mutation of the much more virulent disease we've got now, suddenly activating a host RNA which over thousands of years most humans developed a natural immunity against, like the children in the caves. It's been dormant until whatever the chemical is, in these mites and worms, woke it up.'

'So Raisa was wrong?' said Stoddart.

Geraldine smiled, shaking her head. 'She always was. As Sergei says, she's mentally ill. She threw science out the window to make her theory fit, which it doesn't. Like one of our theories was wrong. The nothofagus isn't poisonous, as such. It becomes so through a chemical reaction when it

425

absorbs the discharge – the excreta, if you like, although it's not quite that – of the blood-sucking, infection-bearing ticks that colonized it. The worms we recovered from the Antarctic and Arctic waters – the ticks' parent pupae – expel the same discharge under stimulation, as getting into the digestive enzymes of a predator's gut would stimulate them.'

'Like a skunk?' suggested Stoddart.

'Good analogy,' accepted Geraldine. 'Skunks stink but don't kill. Our mites and pupae do. Next step, our falling-apart chromosomes in the dividing cells. Telomeres, which are supposed to hold chromosomes together, contain a catalyst called telomerase reverse transcriptase. That catalyst is mutated in all our victims, prehistoric and new. And there are RNA in telomeres.'

'So your new guy could be invading, causing the telomeres to shorten and finally give way?'

'Maybe,' conceded Geraldine, cautiously. 'Maybe it's not a direct invasion but a roll-on: there's a lot of cells being hit far too quickly. There's a group of gene-produced proteins called cytokines, which are important components of the human body's immunology. There's a group of non-coding DNA which activate these genes. In all our victims – except the cave children – those genes have been skewed into a mutation: sometimes knocked out . . .'

'You're beginning to lose me,' warned Stoddart.

'The scientific thinking is that cytokine genes evolved to protect children – and from childhood into adulthood – from intestinal parasites when there wasn't such a thing as hygiene . . .'

'Something else thousands of years old?' connected Stoddart.

'Right!' agreed Geraldine. 'And it's in the gut that we're finding the enzyme from our untraced RNA. Which throws up another commonality. Virtually all the new victims suffer respiratory problems: colds, influenza, even pneumonia. All those conditions produce mucus and cytokines are rather like an inoculated antibody. They "give" the victim a mucus to encourage the victim to cough and expel the virus or the parasites.'

'I'm seeing another chain,' encouraged Stoddart.

'So are we,' said Geraldine. 'We have to assume the Antarctic and Arctic victims were classically and directly infected by tick bites. But that the more widespread pandemic is coming through the food chain and bird droppings . . .'

'Wait a minute,' stopped Stoddart, remembering his Fort Detrick isolation and the revolving, paperless toilet. 'Detrick was analyzing from the beginning and there's nothing in anything I've read – and I've read everything – of anything being found in the faeces or urine of the people I brought back. How come we're only finding it in birds and animals?'

'I don't know. I don't fully understand *why* some of the things I'm describing are happening,' admitted Geraldine. 'It's only in the faeces of *some* birds and *some* animals. You want a hopeful question – how about it not transmitting through human body waste because there's some residual immunity that other animals and birds don't have: resistance that causes it to die, with its victims?'

'I've a better question,' challenged Stoddart. 'How are you going to send your RNA back to sleep again?'

'I don't know that, either,' confessed Geraldine. 'We might be able to, if we found the host cell, but we're a long way from that at the moment. All I'm talking about – *hopefully* talking about – is something like the zidovudine treatment that prevents the human immunodefiency virus, HIV, developing into full-blown acquired immune deficiency, AIDS.'

'You've got a cocktail already?'

'We're experimenting with synthesized cytokine and glutathione. And synthesizing a pseudo dyskerin and trying protein inhibitors,' said Geraldine. 'The aim is to stimulate the natural immunity: redefine the body's cytokine to revert to its original, necessary function and bring all the other antibodies along with it. If it – or a variation – works it'll hold the disease, like AZT holds AIDS. Give us the breathing space to find the host cells and reprogramme or destroy the rogue ribonucleic acid.'

'It could take a long time, moving on from laboratory animals to humans, couldn't it?' demanded Stoddart, objectively.

Geraldine hesitated. 'Everything has been passed on to the Moscow institute where Raisa Orlov is dying. They are doing whatever they can to save her.'

'Let's hope they do,' said Stoddart. Politicospeak was so easy.

'We all hope that,' said Geraldine.

'How long?'

'Just days, for an indication.'

'That would be something to celebrate,' said Stoddart, topping up her champagne.

'At the moment it's premature. So here's to your new job.'

'That's not what the champagne's to celebrate.'

'What then?'

'I've missed you like hell.'

Geraldine hesitated. 'I've missed you like hell, too.'

'I've decided it's love.'

'I thought we were going to give ourselves some living together time to make our minds up about that?'

'I don't need a trial. I'm asking you to marry me.'

Geraldine gazed into her glass. 'Want to hear a secret?'

It wouldn't affect how he felt, whatever it was. 'If you want to tell me.'

'No one's ever asked me before. Didn't seem to occur to anyone.' Did he love her enough to know about the abortion? Not yet. Not now.

'What's the answer, now someone has?'

'Yes,' she said, coming up from her glass. 'I want very much to marry you. And I'm glad it was you who finally asked. But there are things to do first.'

That night Stoddart finally called Patricia's brother, John, in San Antonio. Stoddart told him that his sister had been incredibly brave and wanted him to know she loved him. He'd been with her when she'd died and there hadn't been any pain. He left the Fort Detrick number for the man to call, if he thought there was anything he could do.

The president staged Stoddart's televised acceptance ceremony in the Rose Garden, with Amanda O'Connell in obvious attendance and Paul Spencer visibly more in the forefront than Richard Morgan. This creation of an entirely new department of government was, Partington insisted, unquestionably the most important of his administration, which was why Stoddart's official title would be that of Secretary. In advance of congressional approval there was to be interim executive funding for the emergency measures proposed in New York to be immediately implemented. The United States' navy and coastguard were being mobilised for initial clear-up operations and the ultimate budget to be presented to Congress would provide for whatever other precautions were adopted. A federal reserve fund was also being created upon which individual states could call. In Secretary Stoddart the United States of America, indeed the world, had a man of unparalleled commitment and integrity – one of the first men to warn of the catastrophe that had occurred – which was shortly to be proved by the environmental conference under his chairmanship.

To a nervous shifting from the man and those around him Stoddart repeated his Lincoln Room promises. He found no personal satisfaction in the vindication of his predictions. Instead he looked to the future and to proving wrong those different sceptics, those who believed it was already too late to reverse global warming.

Partington led the way back into the Oval Office, hurrying to the barricades of his special desk. It was a dangerous strategy, doing it here, but the integrity hypocrisy had to be put on record. Once it was, Stoddart would be bound in, knowing why he had to conform like everyone else. And it would be Spencer's voice, not his, Partington reassured himself: he could always claim he'd had no foreknowledge.

The rehearsal before the ceremony had been for the anguished Richard Morgan to escort everyone directly away, leaving only Stoddart and Spencer with the president.

Partington said: 'Quite a speech out there, Jack. You're turning out to be a natural born politician.'

'I guess I'm going to have to be, from now on.'

'From now on you've got to be a member of a team.

You're not going to have any difficulty with that, are you, Jack?'

Patiently awaiting his cue, Spencer heard, *You're under my control now, you son of a bitch, and you better realize it.*

Message time, Stoddart recognized. 'I hope not, Mr President.'

'It's got to go beyond hope,' said Partington. 'You talked a lot out there about commitment. That's what I want, too. People committed to me get my commitment in return. Total loyalty, both ways.'

'I'm sure I'll learn,' said Stoddart, sure that he wouldn't because he never had. How long would it take to get to the real point?

'You started the right way,' said Spencer, responding at last. 'And we're in there for you, all the way.'

Stoddart looked blankly at the man. 'I'm sorry?'

'That business at the very beginning: things said against you. People losing their minds. Understandable in the circumstances. Maybe not to a lot of people, though. But like I said, we're in there for you. No need to worry.'

The dying James Olsen and the lawyer demands, identified Stoddart finally. His first test at politics, he supposed. 'I have been concerned about that.'

Spencer smiled, confidently. 'Don't be. You any idea how much paperwork's been generated by all this?'

'Some.'

'Easy for things to get mislaid among a mass of material like that.'

They thought he had an embarrassment he'd want buried! A test beyond politics, he accepted. And he'd passed it already by the precautions he'd taken. 'I read something in the *Post* a few days back about James Olsen's wife,' prompted Stoddart, aware of the immediate look between Spencer and the president.

'White House counsel . . .' started Spencer, but Partington hurriedly smothered him, furious at the need to speak.

'I'm not sure what we're talking about here. Maybe you and Paul need to discuss it somewhere else. Over-running

430

my diary, as usual. Just wanted to say welcome, that's all.'

Get out! understood Spencer, rising.

Stoddart made the same interpretation, remaining in his seat. 'There's no problem, if what Olsen wrote has gone missing. I took a copy the Olsen lawyers can have. Government counsel, too, of course.'

'What'll they do?' asked Geraldine, when they spoke later that evening.

'Settle out of court,' said Stoddart. 'No alternative. They destroyed it, I didn't.'

'Would a settlement include your personal liability?'

'If it's legally thought I have any. I'm officially part of the government now.'

'For how long, after this?'

'Until I decide, not them.'

At the end of that week the news from Moscow was that Raisa Orlov's condition had stabilized, the respiratory infection was lessening and the organ degeneration appeared to have been halted.

The World Health Organization recorded more than three million volunteers within the initial two days of the halting drugs cocktail being announced.

Thirty-Eight

A lthough it was convened under the auspices of the
United Nations, Henry Partington officially opened
the environmental conference but left New York directly
afterwards, refusing to be overshadowed by Stoddart's presence as chairman. Every country, with the exception of
China and the Arab block of the southern and eastern
Mediterranean, accepted in advance and without argument
the emission reduction targets proposed by the conference
executive, which gave Stoddart twenty-three per cent more
than he'd expected to achieve initially, and China's internationally pressured compliance during the debate, along
with that of Algeria and Egypt, brought the figure up to
twenty-nine, with the pledge from every country to ratify
the agreement nationally within three months. Despite the
equally unanimous agreement of a permanent UN monitoring
group, Stoddart pragmatically assessed the global avoidance
or failure at twenty-five per cent, which still put him ahead
of what he'd hoped to have had agreed. Just as pragmatically
he knew that couldn't be met within the first year, but
it would provide the base figure from which to negotiate
further reductions at the second – again internationally
agreed – global gathering at the end of that first twelve
months. Other internationally concluded charters included
a total ban on ice-bore sampling at both Poles, including
Greenland, Siberia and Canada's North-West Territory, and
total co-operation in pesticide treatment of newly exposed
tundra in all those areas. With the recognition of the scale
– and possibly continuing need – of such undertakings,
it was agreed that as well as national and international

432

environmental agencies, designated divisions of all three military branches of each participating country should be mobilized.

Geraldine Rothman authored the scientific paper on the blocking cocktail and a separate, detailed account of the continuing search for the causative gene to stimulate the genome research globally, but at the first approach from Nobel committee emissaries from Stockholm made it clear she would not consider and certainly would not accept any individual recognition. She later regretted giving in to Peter Reynell's insistence that she be in the public gallery at the House of Commons for his inaugural premiership appearance, not aware when she did so that he would publicly identify her there and talk as if she had been the scientist solely responsible for the limited but seemingly effective breakthrough. Later, in Downing Street, Reynell offered her the choice of three safe parliamentary seats and the immediate appointment as science minister and dismissed as an obstacle the fact that she'd never voted for his party in her life. He left the offer open even though she said she didn't plan to remain in England, without explaining why. At that time she'd already refused professorial chairs of genetics at universities in Cambridge, Tokyo, Montreal and Sydney but asked two – one in New York, the other in Baltimore – for time to consider while she and Stoddart finalized their plans. She spent a lot of time personally at Cambridge with the group with whom she'd liaised from Washington, reviewing the scientific search for the mutated RNA gene.

Lord Ranleigh correctly predicted that the first challenge to Peter Reynell's overwhelming mandate would be to the policy reversal on genetically modified crops – which met with similar opposition throughout most of the European Union – and urged Reynell to limit the change until other countries, particularly America, established that one danger wasn't being exchanged for another. Reynell instead held a yes-or-no referendum and got a 78 per cent approval vote, which he personally flew to New York to announce at one of the final sessions of the environmental conference. He

433

went from there to Washington for Amanda O'Connell's induction as Secretary of State. They agreed that personally everything had ended very well. Neither suggested luck had been involved, because neither considered it had. Nor was there any mawkishness about things abruptly seeming different and it didn't occur to either to talk about missing one another, because neither expected to. She said she looked forward to seeing him when he was in Washington and he said he looked forward to seeing her when she was in London. They didn't exchange parting gifts or momentoes, although he did, as promised, give her all his direct line numbers.

Raisa Ivanova Orlov's mental condition was diagnosed as senile dementia, which it strictly wasn't, and although the self-induced ageing was arrested, the osteoporosis and arthritis was severe enough to cripple her permanently and she needed twice-daily treatment for glaucoma. She didn't for a long time recognize Gregori Lyalin, who sat alone by the institute bedside, praying silently for her. He did so with his eyes closed, his head bent, and so her sudden awareness startled him.

'I was right, wasn't I? Cured myself!'

'You're alive,' said Lyalin. 'That's good.'

'I'm being nominated, you know. For the Nobel.'

'I hadn't heard.'

'Couldn't cheat me this time.'

'No.'

'I'm going . . .' she started, but the curtain began to descend. '. . . I want . . .' she tried again but disappeared into her mental blackness and Lyalin quietly got up and left. He decided against visiting her again. He didn't need to be in her presence to pray for her.

Geraldine had been irregular since the abortion but she'd never missed an entire month before, and it was five weeks before she counted to be sure and even then she wasn't certain, because so much had been happening – the weekend commuting to Washington after a seventy-hour, so far fruit-less, week in genetics laboratories – to account for the miss.

434

She finally did her own urine test and spent a night of mixed thoughts before deciding it was wonderful and convincing herself that Stoddart would think so too. They'd used his Fairfax apartment to house hunt at their leisure and narrowed the selection to three, her favourite at Rockville because she'd decided upon the Baltimore offer. The vendors had children, the youngest a girl of three, and there was already a nursery. They looked at it for a second time the weekend of her confirming pregnancy test and on their way back to Washington she asked if he didn't think it was too far out of DC for his job and Stoddart said he didn't mind which of the three they took, as long as she was happy.

Geraldine said: 'It's convenient, there already being a nursery although I'd want to do it differently.'

Stoddart drove unspeaking for several minutes. 'Are we talking hopeful or are you trying to tell me something?'

'I'm telling you something.'

Stoddart pulled over to the hard shoulder and twisted in his seat to look at her. 'We got another first. No one ever asked you to marry them before and no one ever told me before that I was going to be a father.'

'What are you going to tell me?'

'I can't imagine anything better to complete our perfect picture.'

He turned at the next exit and agreed the asking price of the Rockville house. The sellers said they hoped they'd be very happy and Stoddart told them they already were. The following week Geraldine put her London flat on the market and asked for her resignation as chief scientific officer to be immediately effective, which it was. Peter Reynell hosted a farewell lunch at which he repeated the safe seat offer. She didn't tell him of the pregnancy or of the intended wedding.

She liked the interior designer to whom she was introduced in Rockville and agreed a yellow and grey colour scheme for the nursery. The commute was easy to Baltimore and because it was the city in which she would be spending most of her working time, she registered with a gynaecologist there

435

instead of the woman she'd consulted in Washington after the abortion. The Baltimore specialist, also a woman, said she didn't want to X-ray or scan so early but from the initial physical examination and the Washington case notes there weren't going to be any problems. Geraldine said she felt lucky not to be suffering morning sickness: any pregnancy discomfort at all.

Geraldine accepted that as with all the approaches she'd been offered the Baltimore Chair – and a salary four times higher than what she'd earned in England – because of her public exposure and philosophically endured the publicity of her arrival. She agreed her concentration would obviously be the continuing research for the age-triggering gene and insisted in every interview that its eventual location would not be an individual discovery but the result of a combined scientific effort. On her first working day the chancellor promised to provide any scientific facility, including additional staff, she considered lacking.

Geraldine and Stoddart amused themselves compiling a list of wedding guests they could have invited ('for so many cameras Partington would probably stage the reception in the Rose Garden') and settled for an unannounced registry office ceremony, with Walter Pelham and Amanda O'Connell as witnesses.

Stoddart went with Geraldine for the first X-ray and scan, announcing on the way that he wanted to be present at the birth. Geraldine said it would probably be possible that day to get an indication of the sex but wasn't sure if she wanted to know. Stoddart said he wasn't sure he did, either. When they got there the gynaecologist thought it was probably too early to tell so it wasn't a decision they had to reach for another month. They had coffee between waiting for the X-ray to be developed and the scan, which was the way the gynaecologist liked to examine. She wasn't carrying the plates when she came into the office and said they were ready for the scan and that Stoddart should come too. There were two nurses already in the consulting room.

Geraldine said: 'Were the X-rays OK?'

436

'Let's look at these pictures,' said the gynaecologist, starting to move the scan over Geraldine's abdomen but abruptly stopping.

It was one of the nurses who gasped, before the doctor, and then Geraldine cried out: 'No!'

The clear image was of a perfectly and completely formed, although minute, human being – a boy – already with a substantial growth of hair. The heart was beating.

Jagged-voiced, disbelieving, the physician said: 'It's not a three-month foetus. It's the growth of a two-year-old . . .'

But Geraldine didn't hear anything more because she'd lapsed into fainted unconsciousness.

Geraldine was kept heavily sedated that first day and during the one that followed, when with Stoddard beside her she was taken by ambulance back to the isolation unit at Fort Detrick. On the fourth day the scientists began carrying out preliminary but by now well practised tests, all of which were repeated on Stoddart in an adjoining chamber in an unsuccessful attempt to discover if he were a carrier. Everyone with whom Geraldine had been associated or with whom she had worked were put into quarantine, for matching investigation. Reynall insisted photographs of him taken through the separating glass of the English isolation unit be issued to the media.

Over the days Geraldine's sedation was gradually reduced. Stoddart demanded to be at her bedside when she properly awoke, which she did with an instant recollection of what she had seen on the gynaecologist's scan and for a long time sobbed in his arms. Even when she stopped crying, dry sobs shook through her. Stoddart respected Geraldine's intelligence too much to meaninglessly offer consoling words he couldn't think of anyway, so he just continued to hold her.

When Geraldine finally spoke her voice was jagged, uneven. 'Are we at Fort Detrick?'

'Yes.'

'Have you been tested?'

'Yes. Nothing registered.'

437

'Everyone else?'

'Everyone.'

'Is the sound on, to record everything?'

'Yes.'

'It's in the human egg,' said Geraldine. 'It's hosting in the ovum ova.'

'How . . . I don't . . .' tried Stoddart.

'I made a scientific mistake . . . a terrible mistake,' said Geraldine. 'I even warned about it during the investigation and then forgot to take it into account myself. DNA corrects itself, if it starts to mutate. But RNA – ribonucleic acid – doesn't. If it starts to mutate while it's replicating in a host cell it creates an entirely new strain of its parent. It's even done that to destroy the natural immunity that the cave children developed. It's exploding through the cells. Sometimes – confusing me – it's been blocked by latent, residual immunity. But sometimes – too often – it hasn't been stopped. And it's mutated too fast for us to find it . . . put up a chemically blocking fire wall . . .'

Stoddart made a helpless, lost gesture.

'We could have contracted it, you and I, in so many different ways,' monotoned Geraldine. '. . . Still be carriers without it being possible to detect, in the normal ways we tried . . . It could be sexually transmitted after all, like AIDS. And if it is, it will have been passed on a million – a trillion – times, everywhere there's been an outbreak . . . and that transmission is just one of the mutations . . .'

'But you . . . us . . . our baby . . .' tried Stoddart, in reality-losing desperation.

'I'm sharing his blood, he's sharing mine,' said Geraldine, voice flat in resignation. 'One of us will kill the other.'

'That can't happen!'

'I know. Like I know I've only got six months to find the way for one of us at least to stay alive.'

'It has to be *you*!'

Geraldine tried to find the words but couldn't. Instead she said: 'We've got to start all over again. *Now*!'

438